FORBIDDEN MONASTERY

SAM C. LEONHARD

DSP PUBLICATIONS

Published by
DSP Publications

5032 Capital Circle SW, Suite 2, PMB# 279, Tallahassee, FL 32305-7886 USA
http://www.dsppublications.com/

Forbidden Monastery
© 2015 Sam C. Leonhard.

Cover Art
© 2015 Aaron Anderson.
aaronbydesign55@gmail.com
Cover content is for illustrative purposes only and any person depicted on the cover is a model.

ISBN: 978-1-63216-799-6
Digital ISBN: 978-1-63216-800-9
Library of Congress Control Number: 2014953890
First Edition May 2015

Printed in the United States of America
∞
This paper meets the requirements of
ANSI/NISO Z39.48-1992 (Permanence of Paper).

Acknowledgments

Many, many thanks to my wonderful betas Mary M. Ardagna, Theresa, and Farzana Khan. Without you I wouldn't be able to write: you correct my flimsy grammar, kill my faulty gerunds, move the commas where they belong, and most of all, comment on the story, thus making it better. *hugs to all of you*

In addition, I would like to thank my editors at DSP, Rose and Yv. They gave invaluable input, thus making the story better, more logical, and a certain female character much less bitchy. Thank you!

PROLOGUE

OVERNIGHT, FOG had ascended from the valley, but now, just after sunrise, the world was ghostlike, cold and wet and beautiful. Tiny drops clung to the grass, to the trees, to every surface. Even the windows of the huge old mansion, just visible through the fog, were covered in silver pearls. So far, it was more a shadow than an actual house, but then, as soon as the sun had chased the two moons out of the sky, the fog would vanish along with Arwen and Galadriel, and the house would be there, dominating the landscape.

At the moment, however, the sun was low over the horizon, weak and pale and with no warmth to spare for the earth.

It was just as well for the man who was sitting on a branch of one of the big, old oak trees that surrounded the house. Preferring darkness, he needed neither warmth nor light.

He had been waiting for hours. He'd seen the fog rise and the sun too. He'd witnessed the first hesitant chirps of the birds waking up on the branches above him. His clothes, black as midnight, matched his black, spiky hair and his black, cold eyes. Only his skin was white, mainly because of the cold that seeped through the soft leather of his trousers and shirt.

This customer had asked to be killed around sunrise.

Dangling his legs, the assassin found a branch with his soft-shoed foot, turned, and jumped to the ground. He walked toward the back door, unconcerned that he might be seen—his customer had told him that he would be alone at home today and that the servants weren't up that early. He'd checked on that—never trust anyone who paid an assassin to commit murder—so he was sure his customer had told the truth.

The dogs hadn't been set free last night.

The footprints he left on the grass didn't bother him. After his job was done, he would open the dogs' cages, and their paws and curious noses would erase the only sign he'd been here.

The chill bit into his skin as he walked across the grass, and white clouds wafted from his mouth. Silently, he opened the back door with the keys the customer had given him. The kitchen behind it was empty, the hearth cold. In another half hour, the maid would be lighting the fire.

He'd be gone by then, of course.

It was a big house, old and filled with history and memories of past centuries. The old man living here, head of the house and about as old as the trees outside, was rich. He owned half the town and had interest in the other half. Magic was strong in his blood, and not only his. It was said that the old man's nephew was able to become invisible.

Without making any noise, the assassin went upstairs, following the map the customer had drawn for him.

Hiding in the shadows, the assassin cast a glance out the window. Still foggy—nothing more than a pale, golden, alien light.

Suddenly, he longed to be elsewhere. Outside on the streets, running off the tension in his muscles from the long night spent sitting in the tree. His back ached, and his neck was stiff. Lucky for him, this would be an easy kill. No need to hurry and no need to be overly cautious.

He touched one of the tapestries decorating the wall. It showed the empress as a young woman, strikingly beautiful. The scene showed her being crowned, sword in hand, with the severed heads of her enemies lying at her feet.

Shrugging and wondering why he had stopped to look at the tapestry at all, the assassin moved on. His victim was waiting behind the next door, and outside, the sun had edged a bit higher. It was time to finish this.

The door didn't even creak when he pushed it open.

Warmth embraced him. Flames were blazing in the fireplace, their heat caressing his cheeks almost painfully.

"Good morning." The voice that greeted him sounded as old as the hands resting on the small table.

The assassin bowed his head but did not say a word.

"I was expecting you sooner, but I am glad you were delayed. Watching the sunrise through the fog was a marvelous sight. Thank you."

The assassin approached and faced his victim. It was rare that he was asked to kill the one who paid him, but then he had very few rules, and this situation didn't fall foul of them. If the old man wanted to die, so be it.

"Please, take a seat," the old man said. "My valet told you what is expected of you?"

"You wish for me to kill you." The assassin's voice was soft, barely audible over the crackling logs. It was a warm voice, slightly hoarse, as if he knew smoke as well as drink.

The old man showed a toothless gum when he smiled. "Exactly. As you can see, I am not even able to move my fingers anymore. I am doomed to sit in this chair all day, propped up with cushions. My valet has to put me to bed, wipe my ass, blow my nose… feed me. It's time to move on, if you understand what I mean."

The assassin nodded. "You're tired of living. That's why I took the job. It's a nice change to be asked to kill a willing victim instead of a hated competitor or a cheating wife."

"Victim." The old man in the chair chuckled. He was as bald as an egg, and although the room was warm, he shivered under his big, fluffy blanket. He couldn't weigh more than a child. "Yes, you might as well call me that. So how will you do it?"

The assassin leaned back in his chair. "Your valet has paid me generously. I will kill you quickly and painlessly, if that is what you wish. I could make a mess too, of course, scare your family and all. Your choice."

A flicker of sadness crossed the old man's watery eyes. "No family to scare," he mused. "My wife died ages ago. My daughter was killed by a wild horse she insisted on riding at the age of twelve. The only relative I have is my nephew, who I managed to convince to be away today—it was, I assure you, not easy to arrange. No one will miss me. No one will be overly upset when I'm gone. No need to scare the chambermaid, though. Do it fast and without soiling the carpet with blood, if you please."

The assassin got up and stretched his legs. He took in the room, the untouched food on the table, the bed no one had slept in.

"You've been sitting up, waiting for me?" he asked, moving behind the old man. Almost gently, he put his hands on his victim's shoulders.

"I told my valet not to bother putting me to bed." The glasses on the old man's crooked nose were slightly askew. The assassin carefully took them off and put them on the table.

"Thank you," the old man said, his voice maybe a tad hoarse. "I'm George. Did I tell you my name is George?"

"No need to be scared," the assassin murmured into his ear and moved his hands so his fingertips connected with the main vein in his victim's throat. The pulse was surprisingly strong for a man his age. Without help, he may have lived for many more years. But it wasn't the assassin's style to question a job once he'd decided to take it.

Increasing the pressure ever so slightly, the assassin cut off the blood flow between brain and heart. Blood wasn't getting through the veins anymore, but as he didn't touch the windpipe, breathing was still easy for the old man.

"Not unpleasant," George whispered. There was a slur in his voice as though he were drunk. His head would have lolled forward had the assassin not caught it between his thumbs, supporting the old man's chin.

"I know," he replied softly, and then George's eyes fell closed. Keeping up the pressure with one hand, he placed his other on the old man's heart, sliding underneath the blanket and the dressing gown he was wearing. George's skin was clammy. Living must have been sheer torture, always being cold no matter how blazing the fire or how warm and heavy the blankets around him.

George's heart stuttered, stopped, and beat again. The assassin's hand was steady on his throat. Then the heart stopped for good. The silence in the overheated room increased so subtly that the assassin felt the small hairs at the back of his neck rise. Suppressing a shudder, he waited for a full two minutes to ensure the old man was dead.

"Safe journey, George," he said, then left the room, the house, and the garden in search of silence and peace.

SWEAT POURED down his face. The assassin leaned against a house wall, wiping his arm across it. The sun had killed the fog just like he had killed George—quick, silent, and painless—and her harsh beams burned the ground dry. A shower became more appealing by the minute.

But there was another need to fill first, and this street was just the place to look for it. What he wanted wasn't offered on a regular basis or in very many places. This town was considerably large, however, and if he was lucky, he would find the company he was looking for.

Groans emanated from a doorway, and he turned, watching for a moment. A bear of a man with his head pressed against the brick wall was pressing his groin into the face of a podgy young woman who seemed no older than fifteen but was, in reality, nearly thirty, her appearance being maintained with a bit of magic.

Disgusted, the assassin turned away and looked for someone more to his liking. A glamour, like the one that whore was using, was the perfect way to make his erection fade. Preferring a more natural look on the ones he paid for a fuck, he knew just where to go—to the dirtier parts of the street, the ones with the darkest corners, the ones with a smell of despair and loss. Usually, whores that did not use magic simply weren't able to do so, meaning they were either mentally or physically disabled. As a result, they charged less, which was just as well for him.

The girl that smiled at him from her bedroom window had only a stump and three fingers for a right hand. He smiled back, but went on—girls weren't his taste, although that one had been pleasant looking and not too dirty.

Twins approached him, one male, one female. "Not in the mood for a threesome," the assassin said and moved on. Both had distinctly childish grins on their faces, indicating that they were about as smart as a brush.

Over there, that one was better. Young, no older than twenty. Shaved head, earrings, a missing tooth. His left eye was missing too; the remaining one was a deep, striking blue.

"Hi there," the whore said, swinging his hips. "Want some company?"

"Depends on the price," the assassin replied, stepping closer.

He looked the whore up and down methodically, scanning for open wounds, a rash, or signs of drug abuse. Over the years, he'd gained some experience assessing his fuck toys. This one seemed surprisingly healthy given how he earned his money. Broad shoulders indicated he worked out, at least when he had enough to eat.

"How much do you charge?" he asked

"Seven."

"Forget it. You might be worth two Talents, but I doubt it. If you were that good, you'd be working the front half of the street, regardless of your eye." The assassin took a step back. "I'll give you one and a half if you make me hard in less than a minute."

For a brief moment, they looked at each other. Black eyes met a single blue one. The wind wafted through the street, rustling up some lonely leaves, chasing shadows, and causing goose bumps to appear on the whore's bare arms.

"Not enough," the young man whispered, stroking his hand on the assassin's thigh. "I'm good. I would work up front were it not for the eye. People get scared when they see me. You aren't scared. You aren't an old fart, either. I'd like you to fuck me, man. For *two* Talents. Have to live, you know."

His hand swiftly slipped higher, cupped the assassin's balls, and squeezed them. Skilled fingers made their way upward along the leather, sending heat and longing through the assassin's body.

The man in black smiled thinly at the whore, then whirled him around, pushing his face against the wall. It didn't bother him that the bricks were scratching the young man's face; all he cared about was his need. He opened his belt and undid his trousers as he pushed the whore's threadbare shorts down his bony ass. The thin bracelet braided around the assassin's left wrist got caught on a button. It might have broken had the assassin not twisted his wrist and freed it, his gaze lingering only briefly on the black strings the bracelet was made of.

More quickly now. The assassin craved his release, and so he spat into his palm for a bit of lubrication, placed his hands on the whore's skinny hips, and mercilessly pushed his cock in, not giving a damn about the strangled grunt his actions caused. He wanted to fuck, he wanted it now, and he wanted this to be over as fast as possible so he could go home and shower.

Briefly, the assassin shut his eyes in pleasure. He dug his fingers deep into the young man's flesh. There'd be bruises, but what the hell.

One last push, and he came, gritting his teeth to prevent a sigh of relief and keeping his balance by pressing one hand against the wall. Fast and dirty, just as he liked it.

The assassin already had his trousers up by the time the whore turned around. Business as usual. He buttoned his shirt and pulled up his shorts, not even bothering to wipe off the seed running down his legs. He hadn't even become hard. The young man kept his eyes downcast, seeming to have found something interesting in the mud at his feet, probably knowing from hard experience that if he was too demanding, he'd get beaten up, deprived of his work's due.

"Two Talents," he said without emotion. "Please."

Smoothly, the assassin pulled his knife. With his other hand, he grabbed the whore and pushed him back, knocking loose some glass shards from a broken window. "Look at me," he ordered, pressing the knife to an exposed throat.

One blue eye stared at him, wide and frightened.

"I always pay my debts. Two Talents. And one extra for being quiet and not pretending you enjoyed it." A flick of his wrist, and the knife was gone. Three silver coins landed on the ground.

As quickly as possible, the young man picked them up and stored them under his torn shirt. A hesitant smile flickered over his face. "Thanks," he said, but the assassin had already turned his back on him, leaving the street and the whore behind.

"What's your name? Come back any time, if you like!"

Stopping dead in his tracks, the assassin lowered his head. "I'm Rage. I'll be gone by tomorrow, and I never use the same whore twice."

CHAPTER
One

"EXCUSE ME," a thin voice said from behind Rage. "Am I correct that I should buy you a drink before talking about business? That is, of course, if you are indeed Master Rage?"

The assassin turned his head slowly. The tavern was empty except for him, a few boys trying their first beer, and the man in front of him. The barkeeper had vanished the moment Rage entered through the slightly creaky door, as if he knew his newest customer could only mean trouble. Which was true, but it was no reason to ignore someone who would at least pay for what he consumed. Rage had decided to wait another minute before going to search for the man—he could tolerate fear, but he couldn't tolerate not being served.

One look at the man who'd addressed him as "master" told him that he was a valet or butler, at most. Definitely a servant of some sort, and from his sallow skin, it was obvious he worked indoors. He was well dressed, around fifty years old, with a shock of white hair that made him look like a sad dandelion. Slightly smaller than average, not thin and not fat, but with an exceptionally large nose and surprisingly yellow eyes.

Rage took in the man's shaking hands and sweaty forehead and knew he wanted someone killed. It was about time. His last job had been months ago, and his pockets were nearly empty.

"Who wants to know?" Rage asked.

The man gulped and placed a hand on the greasy bar. Spilled beer, peanut crumbs, a bit of blood—it clearly hadn't been cleaned in weeks, if not months.

"Master Rage, my name is Jeeve. I have been trying to get in contact with you ever since I heard word you were in town. It is rare to find an assassin in this part of the world, so far away from the city." Maybe there was a slight hint of an accusation in his words; maybe he was just nervous at the proposal he was about to make. "So if I may buy you a drink, please? I am to make you an offer—a generous one. If you are Master Rage, of course. Otherwise, I apologize for my presumptuousness."

A sly grin appeared on his face; it was obvious he knew very well who Rage was. Wiping the sweat off his brow, he finally decided to sit on one of the bar stools.

"Cider."

Rage had spotted the bartender, who rushed to get him his drink. A slosh of the bittersweet liquid landed on the counter, adding to the already visible stains. The boys had moved to one of the tables, hiding their faces and the one glass of beer they shared from anyone who might know them by sitting as close together as possible. Rage dismissed them as unimportant but kept half an eye on them. One never knew, and he hadn't survived in his job this long by being careless.

He took a sip of his drink, then placed a large hand on Jeeve's shoulder. "Let's find us a more private seat," he said and pulled the surprised man from his stool. "The corner table should do. And be quick with your offer. I don't have all day."

Rage didn't like the man, but then he might be his ticket to a decent meal tonight.

Jeeve's nostrils flared as he sat down. Outside, opposite the window, a butcher tended to his business. The stink of blood, and more, wafted inside.

"Master—"

"Just Rage."

"Right. Erm. Now…."

"Spit it out. Who is it your master wants dead?" Best to be blunt, or the man would end up babbling for hours before coming to the point.

It was always surprising to Rage how hesitant people became when it came down to bare facts. Jeeve's master had probably made up his mind weeks, even months ago. There was a relative, a former friend, a spouse, an enemy he wanted dead. But as soon as it came down to saying it aloud—"I want you to kill…."—there was nothing but stammering, and it was just as valid for the servant proposing the offer.

Jeeve paled, then vigorously shook his head. "I—that is, my master—we don't want anyone dead! We would—*he* would—like you to arrange an accident involving Miss Lucinda of Babylon Manor. An accident that wouldn't kill her. Is that…. Do you think that is possible?"

Rage leaned against the flimsy back of his chair. Jeeve's breath was coming in fast, nervous gulps. He kneaded his knees as if trying to break them, and his eyes darted about the dimly lit room like crazy flies. He looked as if he didn't want to be there, like he was scared, and Rage guessed he would be dead by evening, killed by his master for fulfilling the given errand. No master liked witnesses to their crimes, even if they didn't involve death.

"Tell me about the girl." A bit of background, some information about the accident and the damage it should do, was necessary if he was to do his job properly. Usually, Rage dealt only in death, but he didn't mind an easier job on occasion.

Jeeve sighed deeply. "She is the young mistress of the house. My master's daughter, and he needs her—"

"How old is she?"

The bartender took a few steps in their direction but happily turned away when Rage waved him off. Only then did Jeeve lean forward a bit and whisper, "She is sixteen. Her birthday was on Midsummer."

"Hmm. Three months ago. Not a child anymore. She should be married already. Old enough in any case to be killed."

"She hasn't been a child since she scared the life out of the stable boy by chasing the dogs after him, and back then she was three," Jeeve snarled, not caring to keep the disgust out of his words. "She is a pleasant-looking girl, but she is evil. Nasty manners, horrible behavior, and totally uncontrollable. The master suffers because of her. She insults him, his friends, simply everyone. She refuses to obey his orders, especially when it comes to marriage, she—"

Rage smiled. "And that is why he wants to teach her a lesson?" It was a cold smile; he would take the job, but still, a father paying an assassin to harm his daughter was not to his liking.

Jeeve raised his head and sat up a bit straighter. "She is after the gardener's son! My master chose the perfect spouse for her, but she refused to even be in the same room with him, and now he's backed out of the arrangement. Instead, she messes with that boy. His name is Keiran, and she dares to call him her friend! Talks to him like no lady should talk to a servant. Spends afternoons with him and maybe, she's already…. But no, she wouldn't be that stupid. Of course, this is unacceptable. But, you know… if her spirit was broken, it would be possible for my master to persuade her to do the right thing."

One last sip of the cider. A familiar feeling spread through the assassin: relief at having a new job and thus enough money to survive another few weeks. Excitement about the details, the planning, working out the perfect timing. But also something akin to the disgust that had registered on the servant's face, though for different reasons: disgust at the people who thought murder, pain, and blood were good ways to solve their problems.

"What sort of accident does your master have in mind? That she should not die, I get. What else? Broken limbs? Concussion? Just a few scratches? My charge is fifty-five Talents."

All of a sudden, the servant's nervousness dissipated. Patting his pockets, he pulled out a small pouch and placed it carefully on the table. "I've got the money here," Jeeve whispered. "If you agree to take the job, it is yours. My master wants a specific kind of accident to occur, one that would prevent Lucinda from marrying at all. If she were damaged enough, she would have to stay at home, in her room, her face hidden behind a veil. If she didn't have a voice anymore, no one would have to obey her ever again. She wouldn't be allowed to leave the manor…. You get the picture!" Excited, he took Rage's glass, apparently forgetting for the moment that it wasn't his. With three long gulps, he emptied it, then beamed at the assassin as if they'd been talking about a pleasant trip to the brothel and not about destroying a young girl's life.

"On the Lady's day, Lucinda will go to church," he continued. "Not that she cares about our good Lady—she only wants to show off her new dress and hat. Anyway, on the way back, I want you to steal the chariot, take her somewhere quiet, rape her, beat her pretty face to a pulp, and then send her back. Not too much work for fifty-five Talents, eh?"

Rage wished he could break the man's neck right there. He could see in the servant's face that he would love to watch the rape of the girl, which made the cider in his stomach turn to ice. His job wasn't nice, but in his opinion, necessary. He was good at it. Apart from that, it kept him alive and fed, and it kept the past at bay. But seeing someone else nearly jerking off at the mere thought of him raping and destroying a young girl made him sick.

He nodded thoughtfully. "If done properly, not only her spirit will be broken. She'll be barren afterwards," he said, watching the man's reaction.

The servant grinned. "Precisely. No way *anyone* would ever so much as look at her again, not even the stable boy!"

With a smooth gesture, Rage took the pouch and threw it back into the servant's lap. "I'll kill the gardener's son for half the price, but I don't rape. Find someone else." And with that, he left the bar, leaving the speechless man behind.

THE SUN was low over the horizon; another half an hour, and it would be dark. Just the right time to head back for the barn where he was staying. It was a few miles' walk, but stretching his legs would take his mind off the man he'd left behind and maybe even erase the sour taste on his tongue.

It was time to leave this town. Coming to Windbrook had been a waste of time. Only one small job—breaking into one of the high, narrow townhouses and relieving the widow living there of her jewels—and nothing new in sight apart from the offer he'd just declined. This place was too small. More a village than a town, most streets not even paved. People obviously didn't need a professional assassin and, apart from that, seemed to like wading in mud each time it rained.

Above him, a window opened. A bucket filled with rotten lettuce emptied into the street, and he had to jump back so it wouldn't hit him. The bigger towns had cleaners who walked the streets with their carts and made sure the richer folks could get out of their carriages without treading in a pile of shit, but Windbrook was too small and too poor to afford that kind of service.

A mother carrying her child on her hip shot him a suspicious glance; an old man stepped aside when he went past. People knew he was a stranger, and they saw he could be dangerous. He preferred it that way. The people, unless they needed a job done, would leave him alone, and no one would dare to follow him into the night, fearing to meet a sudden and unpleasant death.

Rage left the dirty streets and narrow houses behind, each step taking him farther into the fields surrounding the village. A fresh breeze blew the smell of old beer, cold smoke, and unwashed bodies out of his nose, and he allowed himself to relax a bit, just enough to forget the servant with his offensive offer.

Raping a rich girl, most likely blessed with an abundance of magic. Impossible.

Rage forced the thought of rape out of his mind. The sound of his feet hitting the soft ground brought him peace; the sound of his breath in his ears erased every thought from his mind.

It was warm, and sweat made his shirt cling to his haggard frame. He was close to the river. The sun was gone; gray clouds gathered and swam in front of the twin moons, one partially and one nearly full. It would rain soon.

Unexpectedly, Rage tripped over a root hidden under a pile of last year's leaves and would have crashed to the ground had he not managed to snatch a low-hanging branch. His heart hammered. He'd been walking fast and would have fallen hard. A broken ankle would put him out of commission for weeks.

After a few moments, he caught his breath, the wind cooling his face. Stretching, he made sure he was unharmed. A quick check proved his knives to be where they should, and the few coins he'd dropped were quickly picked up from where they'd fallen. All was well, and he figured it was probably the perfect time to go back to the hay barn where he slept and kept his few belongings hidden.

Just as he bent to pick up the last coin, he heard the sound of a crossbow being discharged, and he dove headfirst into the bushes.

His left hand landed in holly, and twigs scratched across his cheeks, making blood well to the surface. The bolt had missed him and sank into the tree's bark about two spans above his head. Absently, he licked away some blood before getting his knife out, the one he could throw as well as use in close proximity. It had served him well since he'd stolen it from his sister's lover, many, many years ago and well before he'd killed both of them.

There. Someone to his left, trying to move quietly. He wasn't doing it well, though. A twig broke under his feet and leaves rustled under his shoes. Clearly an amateur yet clearly still dangerous.

Rage silently moved away from the tree. His hand stung from where the holly had pierced his skin, his fingers slippery from the blood that ran into his palm. He wiped it clean on his trousers. The red stain wouldn't be seen on the black leather.

Another twig broke. His attacker was to his right and getting closer.

Time to end this. Before Rage had walked into town, he'd made sure no other assassin was in the vicinity. A bit of competition wasn't the worst thing, but the few individuals who were accomplished in this trade not only stayed out of each other's way, they also did not kill each other. So this guy could only be someone who knew how to handle a crossbow for hunting purposes. He'd certainly be unable to deal with an assassin who knew ten different ways to break a neck.

Quickly, Rage leapt up and circled the place where the twigs had been broken. In the dim evening light, he caught a glimpse of blond hair, a dark tunic, and a reddened, sweaty face. The attacker was young, his hands shook, and he was looking in the wrong direction. Easy for Rage to come up behind him—easy to kick the crossbow out of his hands. Rage threw the man around and pushed him against a tree, knife at his throat, before he could comprehend that he had been caught.

When the thin, sharp blade cut into the soft skin of his neck, the man squeaked like a guinea pig, "Don't kill me!" But as the knife bit deeper into his throat, he said no more.

"Who are you?" Rage's hand was buried in the man's thick hair, keeping him under control.

"No one, I'm no one. It was a mistake. I thought you were a… a bunny?" Hope rang in the man's voice like a church bell, pleading and heartbreaking.

Rage didn't have a heart, though. Not in his business. With a smooth movement, he cut off the tip of his captive's nose.

The screams scared the birds out of the surrounding trees, and a squirrel dropped a nut and hurried irritatedly up the same tree the attacker's bolt had impaled moments before.

"Now who are you, boy? I want your name, and I want to know why you tried to kill me." Calmly, Rage cleaned his knife by wiping it across the shaking man's shirt.

"Pietar, my name's Pietar," he grunted, "and I was told to have you dead by moonrise. It wasn't my idea! This man, he said he wants you dead, and that's it, really, and please don't kill me!"

"Pietar," Rage said and put his knife back into its sheath. "Does the man who hired you have a name?" Both his hands rested on the young man's shoulders. It was nearly a friendly gesture, if only his thumbs hadn't put pressure on Pietar's Adam's apple.

Pietar nodded eagerly. "It's the lord of Babylon Manor." He was babbling now. "Lucius of Babylon. Blond, not massively tall. Met him outside the tavern in town. You know, the shabby one near the butcher? He paid me and sent me here. He said I should wait for you. Please have mercy on me. I needed the money!"

Rage sighed. Apparently, declining to rape Lucinda of Babylon had put him in a difficult position. Apparently the girl's father didn't like to get no for an answer.

"You should have stayed at home today," Rage said and broke Pietar's neck.

The corpse fell into the leaves face down, one arm buried under the body, the other one outstretched as if waving for help, even in death.

"Fuck." Rage spat, then searched the man's pockets for money. He only had a few coins, and the assassin took them as well as the crossbow. It was a decent weapon, not expensive, but he wouldn't leave it there to rot.

It was fully dark now. No use staying outside any longer. He was hungry and cold. He was longing for food and his bed.

Tomorrow, he would take a look at Babylon Manor and the girl living there, terrorizing the servants as well as annoying her father enough to want her broken and him dead. *Interesting family*, Rage thought, then put all thoughts of them out of his mind until he was in his makeshift bed, his stomach filled with bread and cheese, covered by a blanket, and drifting into dreamland.

CHAPTER
Two

COLD WOKE him. The barn's solitary window wasn't protected by glass, only by shutters, which he hadn't bothered to close. The morning chill, as well as the ever-present fog, had crept through the chinks in the thin wooden wall. It was late autumn, and in another few weeks, there would be ice on the water buckets.

Hay tickled and pricked him, telling him he'd need to get himself a better, thicker blanket soon. The straw he'd slept upon was dry and hard. Still, right now he was more or less comfortable but not entirely awake. He would have to go for a piss soon, but that could wait another few minutes. Maybe he could manage to think of something nice before starting his day.

The sun wasn't up yet. As often happened in the morning, he'd woken up half-hard. No use wasting the opportunity. It had been two months since he'd been with the whore. Sleepily, Rage reached under the blanket and undid his trousers. Never one to go to bed naked, he'd only shed his shirt the night before.

Fingertips touched wiry, black hair. Heat and a sudden rush of lust washed through him. Sighing contentedly, he began stroking himself, vaguely thinking of the whore he'd fucked in that dirty back alley. His mind drifted, and he thought of soft skin under his fingers, of warm, welcoming kisses, an eager tongue sucking him off. A hint of a gasp escaped his mouth as he sped up his fist's movement and banished every thought of the neck he'd broken yesterday evening from his burning mind. Maybe there was a name on his lips when he came; maybe it was only the sound of his lust being released.

Fully awake now, Rage sat on the side of his bed. He wanted to take a look at the master of Babylon Manor, the man who wanted his daughter destroyed, not only out of curiosity but out of self-protection as well.

"Lucius," Rage said aloud. "Best to find out what you are capable of."

But first, he would shower.

He took a small, black stone out of his bag and then kicked off his trousers. The stone was just big enough to fit into his palm. It shimmered as though it had been picked up from the dewy grass a moment ago.

The previous night, he hadn't had the mind to shower. Now, with his legs and groin as sticky as his hand, and his skin sweaty as well as bloody from the scratches he'd suffered, he was due for some cleaning. Naked, he walked to the window, where he placed the small, strange stone on the wooden frame. Closing his eyes, he concentrated and blew across its smooth surface.

Fog rushed into the room, gathering around the stone. The air chilled further, and then finally, from out of the fog, first one, then more drops of water fell to the ground.

Not enough. Rage blew at the stone again, urging its magic to do a proper job. He'd paid a fortune for the stone; unless it was a very dry summer, it never failed to work.

Heavy drops hit him when he stepped through the barrier the stone had created to prevent the room from becoming flooded. Cold drops—winter wasn't too far away, and he hadn't had the money to buy a stone that heated the water too. Besides, the cold woke him up completely, washing away the nightmares together with yesterday's sweat, blood, and sorrows.

A small piece of soap lay on the windowsill. He had placed it there when he'd moved in, and now he took it and brought it to his face. It smelled of lavender and honey, fresh and innocent. The scents never failed to make him smile, and he languidly dragged it across his skin, letting the rain rinse a mix of foam and dirt onto the planks before the magic vanished it.

When he was clean, Rage put a wet hand over the stone, and instantly the rain ceased. Lazily, the fog wafted out of the window, leaving nothing behind but a slightly shaking, naked man and an innocent-looking little stone.

The first birds had begun chirping their morning serenades. A squirrel was watching him drying and getting dressed, and because he was hungry, he killed it with a quickly thrown knife, pinning it to the rough bark of the tree outside the window. He had to stretch to reach it, but eventually pulled the knife out of the tree and caught the squirrel before it fell to the ground. It was still warm, hanging limply between his fingers, and when it twitched, not quite dead, he broke its neck, then skinned and disemboweled it with practiced hands. The tiny heart he devoured with one bite; the rest he wouldn't eat raw.

Minutes later, a small fire was burning outside the barn with the squirrel roasting over the flames. It would be a meager breakfast but better than nothing in any case. A long day awaited him, and Rage had no idea whether he would find anything else to eat.

As soon as the meat was done—and slightly burnt on top—he sat with his back against the wooden wall and ate his catch, washing it down with lukewarm water from his bottle, letting the food warm his chilled bones. Eventually, he covered the fire, gathered his things, and went to find Babylon Manor, its owner, and the girl.

THE HUGE stone wall was old and covered with moss. A grass snake peeked out from one of the holes, and a few mice scurried back into their small caverns as Rage set his foot upon the wall, his fingers searching for a hold. It was not long after sunrise, early enough to enter Babylon Manor unseen. Only the dogs would be guarding the place at this time of day. He'd deal with them once he was on the other side.

Searching for magic by placing his palms against the rocks, Rage was glad he found none. The stone wall was just that: a barrier made out of ancient rock. Although most people were able to do magic, it was mainly used for small tasks in the daily routine. Only a few were really powerful, and paying to protect a house with magic cost a fortune. Lucius of Babylon's magic was clearly not exceptional. If it were, he wouldn't live in the countryside, miles and days away from the city.

Rage silently climbed atop the wall. He had chosen a spot where he could sit for a while, hidden behind a bush, so he could observe the main house. The sun was strong this morning, but the stones were cold, and he shivered, wishing he could have stayed in bed instead of spying on the man who had tried to have him killed and would probably try it again.

Horses neighed, cows mooed, and there, faintly at first, was the excited sound of barking dogs.

"Picked up my scent quickly," Rage murmured and jumped to the ground, for the moment ignoring the manor in the distance and the smoking chimney, which indicated a maid had already lit a fire to prepare breakfast. What mattered at the moment were the dogs, large, wild wolfhounds, which were thundering toward him and, judging by their bared fangs, already anticipating the taste of the intruder's flesh and blood.

Calmly, Rage went down to one knee and waited for them. There were five dogs, their eyes half-mad with hunger. Their fur was rough and dirty, their fangs dripping with saliva—an impressive bunch, he had to admit.

When they were about two feet away from him, he closed his eyes and reached out his hands. "Hi, doggies," he said quietly, his voice a bit softer and deeper than usual. "I was awaiting you. Greetings, and don't tear me apart, or I'll have to kill you all in a quite messy way."

Head down, Rage listened to his heartbeat, the whispering of the nearby river, the mice coming out of their holes to watch what was happening. He listened as the barking and growling ceased and was replaced by a low whining. He felt curious noses and tongues rasp across his outstretched hands and then, after a moment's hesitation, across his face as well. He even thought he could hear the wolfhounds waggle their tails, but he couldn't be sure as their yapping was too loud.

He smiled. His fingers touched furry muzzles, noses, and silken ears. "Good doggies," he whispered, still kneeling. "Now let me get up and have a look around, will you? I'll say good-bye before I leave, and if I can, I'll bring you some meat. Agreed?"

The wolfhounds tread on each other in their haste to lick him with their hot, wet tongues. Rage slowly got up, each hand on a dog, trying not to fall over the warm, lean bodies. "Get lost now," he said, a low growl accompanying the words. "Find some other intruders."

Like ghosts, the dogs vanished between the trees, noses to the ground and tails high in the air. They wouldn't bother him anymore until he left, and they might even warn him if someone came too close to where he was hiding.

Good thing, having a link with animals, Rage thought, and made his way toward the main house.

THE FIRST servant he saw was the milk girl on her way to the cowshed. Looking barely older than ten, she swayed under the weight of the bucket, and Rage wondered how she would manage to carry it back to the kitchen once it was full. He followed her, watching her awhile before moving on to the barn and then to the backdoor, which led into the servants' quarters. Babylon Manor was big, but not huge. Lucius of Babylon was clearly rich, but not filthily so. Providing a bride price and taking care of his daughter's expenses might very well ruin him should she decide to marry below her status.

People were up now. The house and the yard were alive, and it wasn't as easy to hide anymore. Rage turned his back to the house, slipped into the woods near the river, chose a nice old oak to climb, and vanished behind the rustling leaves. As the dogs weren't on his track anymore, no one would find him up here.

Stretching out his legs, he leaned against the heavy trunk and breathed in the rich scent of autumn. Only moments later, he caught a glimpse of blond hair. The oak stood opposite the carriage and horse barn, and as expected, the master of the house was in the mood for hunting—a well-liked pastime for rich people to prove their bravery by killing small, furry animals.

"Keiran! The new stallion, and hurry. I don't have time to wait all day."

Lucius of Babylon Manor stomped into the yard, well fed, bathed, perfumed, and ready for some action. Rage leaned forward a bit, making sure to keep his balance on the branch. Less than twenty yards away, he could see the master of the house, hands on his hips, foot tapping impatiently. His boots were shiny despite the dirt kicked up by carriage wheels and horse hooves, his deep green trousers impeccably clean, and his coat freshly brushed by his valet. A thin whip was in his hand. The horse being led toward him seemed nervous.

It was a beautiful horse, no use denying it. Tall and lean, its luxuriously deep brown coat shone in the morning light like dark copper, and its golden mane was made to dig one's hands in during a long, wonderful ride.

The stallion was an expensive horse; pity it was so very shy. Right now, it was close to a panic, rolling its eyes so the whites could be seen.

Lucius wouldn't look good on it. He was, despite his expensive clothes, an ugly man, short and too fat with his stomach threatening to pop the buttons of his waistcoat. Were it not for his red face, his angry eyes, and his obviously choleric temper, he might have looked comical.

"Help me up," he snapped at the boy who held the horse, and he obediently folded his hands and lowered them so his master could place his booted foot into them. With a grunt, Lucius managed to mount the horse, holding the reins too tight so the stallion whinnied in pain.

No surprise the horse was so nervous.

"If he throws me off, I'll have him skinned alive," Lucius said to the boy, more than loud enough for Rage to hear clearly over the distance. The man was a shouter; he doubted Lucius could utter a single word without putting force and volume behind it.

Movement caught his attention, and Rage looked at the stable boy. And just in time—if he hadn't been watching so closely and intently, he wouldn't have seen Keiran slip something between the horse's lips. A sugar lump, by the looks of it.

A moment later, the scared horse calmed, and its shivering stopped. When Keiran let go of the harness, it lowered its beautiful head and awaited orders.

"You gave him a drug," Rage murmured, impressed. It took guts to do something like that, and right under his master's nose.

The boy obviously liked the horse. Or maybe he simply didn't want to see it slaughtered.

"Hmm. Better than last time." Lucius sounded somewhat disappointed. "Ron, Vic, come with me. I want twenty foxes dead by tonight. Keiran, clean the stables and then do as your father tells you."

The boy nodded, and Lucius smiled cruelly. "At least one of my servants knows how to keep his mouth shut." With that, he spurred his horse and galloped out of the yard.

Rage watched as Keiran looked after his master. The boy was gorgeous. Curly brown hair and amber eyes, long legs and narrow hips, strong arms and a perfect ass. Plus a lovely smile, Rage observed as the boy's lips twitched at the sight of the slowly trotting horse.

It was no surprise Lucius of Babylon's daughter fancied him.

Silently, Rage slipped off the tree and found a wolfhound waiting for him. The animal wagged its tail, obviously happy to see him. "Later, I said," Rage murmured. "Go and chase some cats. Cause a distraction so I can slip inside the main house."

Happily, the big wolfhound did as ordered.

Rage looked after him for a moment and pondered whether or not he should kill Lucius before leaving the manor. The man had the means to hire a killer, even if it was just a pitiful, useless example as Pietar had been. He might try it again, and the last thing Rage needed was someone hounding him. With Lucius dead, there wouldn't be any more attempts on his life.

Well, first he'd take a look inside the house.

A sound distracted him just as he was about to sneak across the lawn. Turning, he tried to determine where it had come from. Behind him was the brook he'd heard whispering over mossy stones earlier on. The riverbed curled between the rocks and trees' roots and fed the well in the center of the yard. Leaves danced on the spray. There was that sound again, small and pitiful.

"What the...?" he murmured, his eyes coming to rest on a gunnysack caught under a low branch. It moved.

Of course it moved. The water was playing with it. But the sound—something was inside, something alive enough to fight against certain death.

A few long strides and Rage had the sack in his hands. With his knife, he cut it open, already knowing what was inside—the meowing had given it away. When three wet furballs slipped out and into his hands, he couldn't suppress a low, frustrated growl.

He liked cats. He deeply disliked the custom of drowning the first litter, whether the kittens were healthy or not. The first litter was bad luck, people believed, so they were killed, always.

One kitten, a little tiger, was already dead. They were a couple of weeks old, judging by their size. Obviously, the mother had hid them well; obviously, someone had found them regardless.

The second kitten, gray like fog, was dying. Eyes closed, it didn't even shiver anymore, lying nearly unconscious on his palm, dripping, limp, and resembling a slimy frog more than a cat. He killed it gently, its neck breaking like a twig under his fingertips.

Carefully, he put the two dead kittens on the ground and focused on the last one, a little black one with white whiskers, white paws, and a tiny white patch at the end of its even tinier tail. Its eyes were open, and it watched him, pinning his skin with tiny, sharp claws. Wet as his siblings, he was nowhere near dying, so Rage knelt down, opened his shirt, and put the kitten inside so his body heat could warm and dry the little thing. Soft meows indicated the kitten was scared, cold, and lonely. A rough tongue on his skin indicated that it was hungry too.

"Damn."

He stroked the wet fur gently and rubbed the kitten dry with his shirt only to hear it purr and feel it snuggle closer. The kitten clearly enjoyed being close to him. Problem was, he had other things to do.

Delaying a decision, Rage took his knife and dug a hole in the muddy ground, burying the two dead kittens and covering the tiny grave with a stone he fished out of the brook—otherwise, the foxes might find and devour them.

When he was done, the kitten in his shirt was asleep, instinctively stomping at his stomach with tiny paws.

"Damn," he said again with a sigh and took the kitten out, holding it in the hollow of his hand. Yawning, it looked at him, then rasped a dry, rough tongue across his wrist and the black bracelet braided around it.

It stole his heart, but he put the kitten on the ground anyway. "You're on your own, little one," he told it sternly. "Can't take you with me, especially not with the hounds waiting for me. They'll eat you and me on top of it for hiding you. Go find the kitchen. Go get yourself some milk."

"Meow!"

"No," Rage answered and left the brook, the oak, and the kitten behind. There was no time and no room in his life for kittens.

Though he really liked them. Especially the black ones.

HOUNDS BARKED like crazy in the distance—they must have found a cat, after all. When Rage emerged from the tree line, the yard was empty, so he took the opportunity and entered the house through a stained glass window, carelessly left open by a lazy maid.

The air was cool inside, and the house felt strange, unwelcoming and unhappy, as if the people here didn't care for it even though it was a lovely place.

Rage found a half-eaten chicken and a big ham on one of the windowsills, probably left there by the same maid who'd forgotten to close the window. He took both and stored the meat away in his bag. The hounds would be glad for something to eat, and so would he, once he was out of here.

It took him another ten minutes before he found a corridor that looked at least vaguely inhabited. Seconds later he heard a voice, young and angry, ring through the silence.

He'd found the girl.

Fine. After all, he had come into the house to see her as well as make up his mind about Lucius, so he might as well take a look at her and find out whether she was really that awful.

"What exactly do you mean by 'The kittens are dead'?" Pure venom dripped from every word Rage could hear through the half-closed door. "I think I made it perfectly clear that the kittens were to survive. Which part of that order didn't you understand, Milly?"

Rage swiftly climbed onto a huge, old wardrobe so he could watch without being seen. The voice came from a room, the door of which stood ajar. He could see the plain skirt and naked feet of the maid, the corner of a bed, and a bright, colorful carpet.

He couldn't see the girl, though.

Milly, the maid, mumbled something Rage couldn't understand.

"My father told you to kill them," the angry voice said, and now Rage wondered whether it was such a surprise that Lucius of Babylon wanted his daughter's spirit broken. If she acted like this so early in the morning, he didn't want to know about her behavior when she was fully awake.

"The lord said the kittens must be killed to avoid bad luck," Milly whispered, audibly horrified by her mistress's temper. "He said I either drown them or have to find a new position. I'm already seventeen, mistress. No one would take me on!"

"The kittens were mine," Lucinda said. "Kittens can't bring bad luck over a house, no matter what people say. I gave you the order to keep them safe. You disobeyed me. I want you to pack your stuff and leave this day. If I see you again, I will have the dogs tear you apart."

Rage heard Milly cry, and he didn't know whether to grin or frown. The girl had quite an attitude. She was harsh and unfair, but still—she'd wanted to save the kittens, and he couldn't help but like her for it.

The door opened and Milly came out, head low, tears pouring down her face. She was a plump girl, not ugly, but certainly miles away from being attractive. Mousy hair braided in two boring plaits, spotty skin marked by pocks, and slightly bulgy eyes added up to the general impression of her having trouble finding a husband.

It would also be hard for her to find a new job.

"And take the tray with you, stupid!" Lucinda called and threw it after the maid. The cutlery clattered to the ground, butter and honey soiling the walls, tea sloshing over the clean-scrubbed floor.

Milly didn't wait for whatever else her former mistress might decide to throw. She broke into a run and thundered down the corridor, never noticing that there had been a witness.

Atop the wardrobe, Rage leaned forward and tried to get a glimpse of the girl. He could see her shadow on the walls, an arm, a leg when she passed the door, but nothing else. *Come on, girl, get out of there,* he thought. *Let's have a look at you.*

Suddenly, the door banged against the wall, kicked wide open by a frustrated teenager. For a moment only, Rage wished he could tell her that one of the kittens had survived and was waiting for someone to rescue it from the manor's ever-hungry wolfhounds. "Go down to the brook," he wanted to call out. An idle wish, of course. The kitten wouldn't be rescued. It wouldn't survive the night, the girl would grieve, and the maid would suffer from unemployment. Life was dreadful more often than not.

Then Lucinda stepped out of the room, and Rage's eyebrows shot up in surprise. He'd expected the average country beauty, well fed, not overly bright due to decades of inbreeding, with heavy bones, large breasts, and even larger, childbearing hips. Like the maid, she'd be all right to look at, but surely nothing special.

He was wrong.

The girl who stormed out of the room was slender, tall and graceful like a willow. Her hair was a pale golden blonde and reached down her back to her waist. Unlike the hair of every rich girl Rage had ever seen, it wasn't braided, just pulled out of her face with a plain ribbon, which was just another sign of her stubbornness—only poor girls and whores wore their hair loose. That she didn't care made it clear that her father had next to no influence over her anymore. If he ever had.

Simply put, she was the most beautiful girl he'd ever seen in his life, and she was surely turning heads whenever she chose to leave her rooms.

Rage briefly wondered where her mother was, and as she stormed down the corridor, he decided to follow her. She'd piqued his interest, but not because of her looks. He wanted to watch her a little longer, observe what she would do, where she went, with whom she would speak.

I like her, he thought. *Strange.*

The girl was heading for the stables, and Rage quickly went outside and climbed up to the roof. The slates were slippery from the morning dew, mossy due to lack of care, and some were even broken. Apparently, Lucius wasn't as rich as he pretended to be, or he didn't care about his mansion in general. *The latter*, Rage thought and stepped over an abandoned nest. *He wants more than this average house. He doesn't want to rot here in the countryside.*

"Keiran!" The girl's voice was deeper now, richer, and a tad seductive. The boy—hadn't Jeeve mentioned he was the gardener's son?—turned, pitchfork in hand, and when she walked toward him with outstretched hands, he bent so she could kiss him lightly on the cheek. Rage was right above them, watching every detail even though he was hiding behind the chimney, which was warm and dark with grime.

Black against black. Even if someone were to look upward, he was close to being invisible.

A smile tugged at the corners of Keiran's mouth, and after a heartbeat's hesitation, he wrapped his arms around the girl's slender waist and swung her around as if she were his sweetheart.

Her laughter spoke of pure delight, and when she hugged him, it was obvious that she was in love with the boy. At least enough not to scold him for his boldness—as a servant, he should have kept his distance, not looking at her, not touching her, and definitely not grinning at her with a sparkle in his eyes.

"I want Flash today," Lucinda said. "And you," she pointed at the stable master, "don't look at me as if I were dung under the sole of your shoe. This is *my* house, these are *my* horses, and Keiran is *my* friend. Get out of here before I dismiss you. I'm in the mood for dismissing people today. Milly is already on her way back to her mommy's cottage."

The stable master mumbled something into his beard, then turned away, but not without shooting her a pitiful glance.

"Flash, please, Keiran?" Lucinda pleaded. "I haven't ridden him for weeks. Lucius always gets him, although he cannot control him and doesn't care about him at all."

Keiran shook his head and nodded toward the woods. Somehow, he managed to tell her everything she needed to know with the nod, the gesture, and the sadness in his eyes.

"Damn." Rage had to read it from her lips as she didn't say it aloud. "Bastard. If he hits him again… if there is a single wound on Flash…."

Keiran put his hand on her arm and smiled.

Lucinda understood. Her face lit up, and she hugged the boy again. "Thank you," she said, and only because Rage knew the boy had slipped the horse a calming drug, he knew what she was talking about.

"Princess, then." Lucinda bit out the words rather than spoke them, and again, Rage had to smile at her fury.

"I need to find him. Milly killed the kittens, on his order, and I want him to know how very angry I am. Is he after the foxes again?"

Keiran nodded. A sunbeam got caught in his hair, a stray light having found its way through the clouds. Suddenly, his skin and eyes turned to liquid gold.

Rage's throat became dry, his trousers tight. Damn the Lady, but the boy was gorgeous!

He was about to take a better look at the gardener's son when the sound of hooves and a high, terrified scream destroyed the mood. Rage moved so he could look around the other side of the chimney and saw Lucius on the drugged horse coming toward the stables. A dead fox lay across the saddle, his trousers were smeared with blood, his face was dark red with fury—and his fist held two mousy plaits, knuckles white from the effort it took not to let go of the girl attached to them.

Milly. Screaming, crying, her bare feet bloody—she had been doing her best to run alongside the horse—and had Keiran not drugged it, slowing it down, she would have been half-dead or at least scalped by now.

"You damn little monster!" Lucius screamed when he reached the yard. Behind him, his servant tried to melt into his horse's rear end, clearly very unhappy at the scene about to unfold. "You dismissed Milly? I found her with her belongings on the wrong side of the gate. She said you sent her away for obeying my orders! You have no right to as much as order breakfast in this house, Lucinda!" Furious, Lucius of Babylon kicked Milly and threw her to the ground, where she remained motionless, her tears dropping into the dust.

Lucinda raised her chin just a bit. She seemed taller, older, and far more powerful than the sixteen-year-old girl she was.

"Magic must be strong in her," Rage murmured as he pressed his body flat against the roof.

"This is my house, Lucius," Lucinda said coldly and gave a small sign. Keiran picked up the crying girl and led her to the trough, where he poured fresh water for her.

And Rage noticed with interest that she didn't call Lucius "father."

Lucinda took a step toward Lucius. "She's killed my kittens. And she's one of my servants. *Was*, that is. Anyway, I was disgusted by the fact that you take her to bed and beat her bloody on a regular basis. She's better off away from you."

Milly, her now wet hair clinging to her swollen face and her dirty dress turned to rags by the journey from the gate back to the yard, cried a little bit louder.

Lucius jumped off his horse. Flash, not that drugged anymore after a morning of chasing after foxes, shied and might have run had Keiran not caught his lead.

"I take to bed who I want and do there what I please, and if you ever dare to talk to me like that again, I'll break your useless little neck," Lucius bit out through gritted teeth. His riding crop tapped an impatient, excited rhythm against his high leather boot.

Lucinda didn't budge. "No, you won't. You might be my legal guardian until I marry, you might administer my money and my land, but you know as well as I do that the manor belonged to my mother, that she gave it to me when she died, and that it will go to the Lady should anything happen to me. You will behave, Lucius, or you will end up on the streets, selling your sorry behind. Not that anyone would want to buy it. Still, in *my* house I do what I want, I dismiss whom I want, and I keep all the cats I want alive. Are we clear?"

Lucius flinched, looking as if he'd have a stroke any moment, but eventually, he backed off. Taking Milly's arm, he dragged the crying girl toward the main house.

"And if you ever as much as *look* at Flash, never mind ride him, I'll have you castrated!" Lucinda shouted after him. "A mule would be the better choice for you to ride! Or a pig!"

Rage shook his head at the scene below him, for the first time in years glad that none of his relatives were alive anymore.

At least now he understood the reason for Lucius's anger and the dirty little job Jeeve had offered. It must have been dangerous enough for Lucius to even consider such a plot. The girl owned the manor, the horses, the servants, and the land. Her father was no more than a barely tolerated member of the household. Undoubtedly, he would have loved to hire an assassin to actually kill the girl, but accepting this was impossible; given house and grounds would go to the sisters of the Lady, he'd gone for the next best thing.

There wasn't anything left to do here, and out of instinct, he decided against killing Lucius. The man was busy enough with his daughter; hopefully, he wouldn't bother to hire another amateur killer. Besides, Rage planned to be out of town by nightfall.

Silently, Rage slipped down the roof, landing behind the stables. A foal and its mother looked up at him. Other than that, the area was deserted, so he moved along the stable wall toward the main house, taking care not to be seen. From there, he would find his way back to the outer wall and then back to his barn. An upcoming thunderstorm was darkening the sky, it was nearly lunchtime, and he had some ham in his bag. Time to get out of here.

Upon stealing some carrots for his dinner from the vegetable garden, Rage heard someone cry out from a room above. *Milly*, he thought and spat on the ground. *I doubt she's in her master's bed willingly.*

Couldn't be helped. If only the girl had been smart enough to hide upon Lucius's arrival, she might be safely on her way to her mother's house. Stuffing the carrots, including earth and half a worm, into his bag, Rage went on until he was underneath Lucinda's room.

As the first thunder roared and the first heavy raindrops hit the earth, he saw a shadow moving under the same trees he'd been intending to use to seek shelter from curious eyes.

Question was, who was hiding under the trees, and what was his intention?

Hoping the shadow hadn't noticed him, Rage took a few steps backward, opened a tool shed, and went inside. Through a gap in the door, he tried to get a clearer image of the person, but the rain was now pouring down heavily. Unless whoever he had seen marched right up to him, it was highly unlikely he would see anything at all.

There—another movement. Rage pulled his knife and pushed open the shed door. The sudden chill brought on by the storm made his breath emerge in white clouds, so he fished out a black scarf from his bag and wrapped it around his face. Now only his hands and eyes could be seen in the near darkness of the storm and shed.

Unlike the one outside. Whoever he was, he wore a light gray shirt and dark blue trousers. Not dark enough. Rage saw him coming out from under the trees, taking one last look, and then running toward the house.

Toward the girl's room.

Now this was odd. A day ago, the agenda had been rape. Today, it seemed to be death. Lucius must be desperate to move ahead so quickly.

It could only mean he'd found out how to keep the manor even if his daughter died.

Why should I care?

The thought was strong, insisting to be heard. Momentarily torn between his wish to get out of there and a strange feeling of sympathy for the girl, Rage hesitated. His fingers played with the knife, and his eyes were focused on an old flowerpot where a forgotten sunflower seed was trying to push its way out of a few equally forgotten crumbs of earth.

"Fuck," he finally said and went out into the rain. According to his rules, she wasn't too young to be killed, but she liked kittens, and Lucius was too much of a bastard to get what he wanted. It was too late to walk away.

And anyway, if anyone was going to be doing the killing, it was going to be him.

The shadow hadn't seen him. He was heading straight for the girl's room, looking neither left nor right as though he were the only one in the world. Another amateur, which was just as odd as the rest of it. Lucius might not be the richest man in the world, but he surely had enough money to hire better killers than Pietar and this stupid idiot.

Silently, Rage left the shed and followed the man, who was at least older than Pietar had been but who stank of beer and seemed slightly unsteady on his feet.

Lucius of Babylon had hired a drunkard to kill his daughter?

Frowning, Rage watched as the man approached the house. He might be wrong here—the man might be a harmless servant, trying to get back into his rooms before anyone found out he'd been drinking. Not that he looked like the village idiot, but surely he wasn't suited for any task more complicated than lifting barrels.

Just when Rage began to believe he'd misjudged the man, he saw the knife. A moment later, he was climbing up the ivy without as much as checking whether he was being observed or not.

Thunder rumbled. The windows rattled in the wind, and the rain washed away any sound the intruder might have made.

It took Rage no longer than a heartbeat to decide what to do. He'd come here to learn about Lucius and the girl. He'd learned more than he'd expected, and now, somehow, he'd become involved. The cat-loving, snappy girl had become his responsibility, and he would be damned if he'd allow a drunkard to kill her.

Silently, Rage followed the man, who still hadn't bothered to look behind him even though he was inside the house now.

Rage was behind him the moment he touched the girl's door.

His arm locked around the man's throat. When he gurgled and struggled, he knocked him out with a quick blow to the temple, dragged him through the corridor, and threw him out the window, unconcerned with breaking bones. Rage quickly jumped after him, glad there were no servants around. He hated to be interrupted while interrogating someone.

Dragging the man through the wet, muddy grass was harder than he'd anticipated because he was heavier than he looked. Rage was glad when he was finally inside the shed with the door closed behind them. Binding him took only a few moments, and putting an old chair underneath the handle was done in a heartbeat.

Just as he finished, the man woke up and stared bleary-eyed at Rage.

"Who're you?"

The man hadn't yet noticed there was a rope around his throat. Only when Rage pulled on it did he become fully aware of his predicament, and he rose from his kneeling position, cursing, so the rope wouldn't strangle him.

Methodically, Rage tied the end of the rope to a beam, stepped around the bound man, and gently put his knife to the man's throat.

"You wanted to kill the girl. Who sent you?"

The man's eyes roamed over Rage's black clothes and got stuck at the small tattoo on his neck. It was a bird, black and no larger than half a man's thumb. Drawn directly above the pulse, it seemed to be slowly beating its wings.

The man's breath hitched when he made the connection between the black clothes, knife, and tattoo. "Fuck, you're an assassin! Oh, shit. Look, I dunno the man's name," he stuttered. "Blond. Fat. Said he'd pay off my debts in the bar." Struggling, he tried to ease his head out of the sling. He really wasn't smart at all.

So Rage had been right. Lucius had swapped raping for killing. He must have found a way to get around the girl's will.

Which didn't really matter.

Suddenly, the man grinned, revealing rotten teeth and a rash on his lips. "He said he'd hired someone else. Thought you were younger. Hey, can't we do this together? What d'you say? You can fuck her first before I have a go, and then we smash her head in. Deal?"

Rage tilted his head, then stepped backward so he wouldn't have to breathe in the air his victim breathed out. He stank, and not only of beer. He stank of unwashed clothes and illness. He stank of poorness and hate.

He stank of murder.

Rage put his hand on the rope and pulled.

At first, his victim didn't realize the rope was tightening around his throat. He continued to grin—until he couldn't breathe any longer.

Only then did he try to scream.

Too late. There wasn't any more air for screams.

A little higher off the ground. It wasn't easy given the man's weight.

His feet kicked helplessly, and his face turned blue. Frantically, the man tried to stretch so his feet would touch the ground. Frantically, he tried to free his hands so he might be able to shove his fingers between the rope and his throat.

All in vain.

Rage watched him fight, glad that the man wouldn't be able to put his dirty fingers around the girl's neck and seriously surprised at his strong reaction to the idea of her getting killed.

Bulging eyes; desperate gasps for air that wouldn't go down his throat.

When he was dead, Rage let go of the rope. With a heavy thump, the man fell to the ground. He'd leave him in the garden shed; sooner or later, someone would find him and maybe even bother to bury him.

For the third time today, Rage went in through the open window. Only this time, he didn't stop in front of the girl's door. This time, he opened it and stepped inside.

Tears were drying on her cheeks when she turned to him. Her sea green eyes were dark with suppressed emotions. "Who are…." she began, but Rage, truly sick by now at the day's outcome, crossed the room before she could finish her sentence and knocked her out. Unceremoniously, he pulled a pillowcase over her head, threw her over his shoulder, checked the corridor for stray servants, and exited the house, his burden not moving but at least breathing evenly.

"Why am I doing this?" Rage asked himself, contemplating the differences between a live body and a dead one. "I could be home by now, eating ham and carrots. Instead, I'm kidnapping a spoiled little brat so she doesn't get killed. I must be going soft."

But he hated to see children getting killed, and she was, though legally not a child anymore, still too young to end up in a grave.

The rain covered the sound of his steps—there was no time to be subtle anymore—and erased his tracks. Amongst the trees, he felt safer. There was the brook, swollen with rain, and there was the wall. Luckily, the girl weighed next to nothing, or it would have been hard to climb over with his burden.

When the hounds thundered through the bushes, he fished the chicken out of his bag and handed it over. "Good boys. I did tell you I'd bring food, didn't I? It's not much," he said, cutting off most of the ham as well and only keeping a small piece for himself. "Now let us leave."

With waggling dogs watching him, Rage climbed to the top of the wall and was about to jump down the other side when something caught him by the shoulder, sharp claws piercing into his flesh. A surprised sound escaped his lips, and he very nearly killed whatever had attacked him.

A soft, desperate "Meow" in his ear, however, convinced him otherwise. He dropped the girl on top of the wall, not caring that her head hit the stones, hard. She was unconscious and would remain like that for a little bit longer, which was just what he wanted.

Carefully, he plucked the little cat from his shoulder, the black one he had saved hours ago. It must have climbed up a tree, out of the dogs' reach. "I can't believe you waited for me, thinking I would take you along," he said, holding it by the scruff of its neck. "You seem to be as stubborn as your mistress."

"Meow," the kitten said and began to purr.

He looked at the pitiful creature, wet again because of the rain and hanging between his fingers, weakly trying to get a grip on his wrist. Tiny claws, dirty with mud, peeked through the fur of paws too small to carry their hungry owner.

"Fuck," Rage swore and sighed. Stuffing the black-and-white kitten into his shirt and throwing the girl's limp body over his shoulder, he headed home.

CHAPTER
Three

CARRYING THE girl back to the barn was more difficult than he'd expected once she had woken up. Pity she couldn't be persuaded to remain still.

And pity he couldn't bring himself to knock her out again. He didn't want to risk giving the girl a concussion. She was struggling, weakly so far, but struggling nonetheless.

"I'll break your neck if you try to bite me once more," Rage said through gritted teeth, but he might as well have been talking to a tree for all the good it did—instead of biting, the girl tried to kick him in the ribcage with her knee.

Finally Rage dropped her, ignoring her muffled cry when she hit the ground. Blood appeared on her elbows and knees, torn up by the stony ground.

Impatiently, Rage wiped the still-pouring rain out of his eyes. There wasn't a dry stitch left on him. He was cold, hungry, and more than just a little bit annoyed with himself for kidnapping the girl rather than killing Lucius and being done with the whole problem. This girl meant trouble, which was the last thing any assassin needed.

Using her teeth, Lucinda tried to get the pillowcase off her head, but failed. Clearly frustrated, she then tried to get up only to have her feet swept out from underneath her.

Rage looked down at her. "I told you to lie still, and I told you to stop behaving like a spoiled little brat. I mean you no harm, but I can guarantee you broken bones if you kick me once more. Are we clear?"

Lucinda tried to wriggle away from him, but Rage put his foot on her neck and pressed her face into the mud. Kneeling next to her, he took off the pillowcase.

"That's enough," he said and pulled her face up roughly by her hair, making her cry out. "We'll be home soon. I can drag you along, or you can come voluntarily. Which shall it be?"

Wide-eyed, she stared at him. Rain dropped from the tip of her nose into the mud that was only inches away. Finally, and only when he yanked harder, she nodded.

As soon as Rage let go of her hair, she shrugged and tried to get him off-balance by pushing her head against his legs.

"Stubborn, stupid little bitch." Rage sighed, moved out of the way, and watched her slip into a puddle. Then he dug his hand into her hair again and began pulling her along.

The kitten, at least, had decided to remain silent, or he would have lost his temper and killed either one or both of them.

IT TOOK him ages to reach the barn, but only because Lucinda had continued to fight against him even though every time he tightened his grip it must have nearly ripped off her scalp. Every now and then she tried to kick him, and every now and then she tried to break free.

At least she didn't talk to him. He hoped she thought it was below her dignity to do so, but then, Rage doubted it. Much more likely, she was collecting all the curse words she knew so she could throw them at him as soon as she was back on her feet.

"I should knock you out again," Rage said to her.

Lucinda growled.

"I could also kill you," Rage continued, trying not to fall on the slippery ground. "It would be easier. Already killed one man yesterday and another one today, and without pay on top of it. One more wouldn't really matter."

Lucinda fought against his grip. She might have managed to knock him over now that they were going downhill, so instead of keeping hold of her, Rage let go of her hair and watched as she slipped, rolling to the bottom of the hill. The rain running down her face might have been mingled with tears.

He didn't care.

"Home, sweet home," he murmured and opened the gate to the barn. He pulled her inside and then up the stairs. The girl seemed tired, and he knew she must be even colder than he was, being covered with mud and grass, her clothes thin and not suitable for the weather. She wasn't fighting anymore, and when they reached the top of the stairs, Rage let go of her. She dropped to the floor and didn't move when he went to nail a piece of leather to the window frame, creating some shelter from the wind and rain.

"No attempt to flee?" Sarcasm dripped from his words. Apparently, the day had been a bit too long, otherwise he would have had his voice under control. Swiftly, he took the rope and bound her to a big, old beam. Tired or not, the girl had too much stamina for her own good.

Rage was hungry and tired. Outside, night had fallen, and as he knew there would be only a few hours of sleep for him, he devoured the slim slice of ham he hadn't fed the dogs, and the carrots.

The girl watched him, her sea green eyes dark with hate, fear, and disbelief at him not sharing his meager meal. Her hair clung to her face, her clothes were plastered against her body, and she shivered.

She wouldn't be able to get free.

Being cold himself, Rage opened his shirt and dropped it to the dusty floor, quickly followed by his soft-leathered boots and trousers. It didn't bother him that the girl saw him naked—she wasn't the first and wouldn't be the last—and there wasn't much to see anyway. He wasn't ugly, but not good-looking, either. Too many scars for the latter, and he was too old and too wiry to make an impression on a sixteen-year-old girl who was in love with a gorgeous, broad-shouldered boy. Still, he could feel her eyes on his skin, and maybe it made him hurry a bit more than usual to get into dry clothes.

The only problem was how to keep her quiet while he took a nap. The day had been long, and he hadn't slept well the previous night. He couldn't afford her calling out, and he couldn't afford her trying to break free. He would probably wake up at her attempts to get out of the rope, but he couldn't be sure.

Thoughtfully, Rage looked at the girl, who stared back at him with loathing. He was just about to knock her unconscious again, hoping it would last a bit longer than last time, when a small sound caught his attention.

Purring.

Surprised, he knelt and poked through the wet shirt lying in a crumpled heap on the ground. He'd completely forgotten about the kitten; now he looked at the little furball, covered by the dripping fabric and nearly asleep already.

He took the kitten and placed it on his palm. Keeping his distance from the girl, he showed her what he'd found and saw with satisfaction how her eyes widened in recognition.

"You know this cat. You tried to save this one and its siblings too. Except Milly killed them anyway."

Lucinda nodded, her lips pursed into a ruler-thin line. It was the first sign that she actually understood what he said.

"And you know what I am?" With his free hand, Rage pulled his knife and made sure the girl saw how sharp the blade was.

She nodded again, slower this time.

"I'm an assassin," Rage said to make sure they were talking about the same thing. "I kill for money. I have no intention of killing you, but if you try to break free while I am asleep, I will kill the cat. He likes me and will sleep next to me tonight. Consider that before you do anything stupid."

Slowly, he got up and went to his bed. The kitten hopped onto the bag he used for a pillow and sniffed it. The tiny body radiated fatigue, and it looked positively delighted at the prospect of warmth and sleep. Rage sheathed his knife, took his wet shirt, and gagged the girl before she realized what was happening.

"Can't have you calling for help." Then he stretched out on the hay. The kitten moved closer; a moment later, it found a nice, comfortable spot on his chest.

Exhausted, Rage closed his eyes. The tiny weight was reassuringly warm, and he was certain the girl wouldn't risk the kitten being killed by trying to get free. She might try to wriggle out of the rope, but it wouldn't work. She might try to find something to cut the rope with, but that was just as impossible.

A few deep breaths and Rage was asleep, along with the kitten, which obviously had no intention of moving so much as an inch away from him.

A LOW rumble woke him. The kitten was lying on his face, purring like mad.

"Damn you," Rage murmured and pushed it off. Unimpressed, the kitten crawled under the blanket, seeking warmth.

One look assured him the girl was still there. Fast asleep, she'd sunk to the side, her head resting on the dusty planks. Her clothes were still damp; she'd need dry ones soon or she'd catch a cold.

Stretching, Rage got up and searched for his rainstone. He was useless without a shower in the morning. At least there would be no lack of water after yesterday's thunderstorm. Wishing he could stay in bed a little while longer, he dropped his clothes and stepped under the icy spray.

With blue lips, but clean and fully awake, he stowed the rainstone away only minutes later—it was too cold today for a long shower. Anyway, he wanted to get some information out of the girl and then find something to eat. It was unlikely he'd kill another squirrel with the first one's blood on the tree, so he would have to spend some of his last coins on breakfast and, maybe, a hot cup of coffee.

Rubbing his hair dry, he suddenly realized the girl was watching him, neither concealing her curiosity nor her disgust at the sight of him. When her lips quirked into a dismissive grin, it was also clear she had managed to get rid of the gag.

"You are old," Lucinda said and coughed. "I'm thirsty. Any chance for water?"

Fine. She'd found her voice, just as expected.

"And you're ugly," she continued, looking him up and down as if he were a horse on the market. "Too many scars. Where do they come from? Lost some fights? Beaten up by your opponents? Don't tell me you've got a girlfriend. I wouldn't believe it for a moment. No decent woman would ever touch you. I bet you have to pay if you want intimacy. How much do they charge you, ten Talents? Fifteen? You couldn't pay me enough to so much as look at you, never mind actually touch you." Wrinkling her nose, she didn't stop staring at him.

Rage took a step toward her. "You're already looking without me paying you a penny."

Her glance didn't even waver. "Sheer curiosity," she said airily. "You know, the same reason we can't look away when someone is hanged."

He closed the distance between them, and when he saw the look of fear deep in her eyes, he said, "You're stupid, girl, even for a rich brat. Insulting the one who kidnapped you while being bound and helpless is not a wise thing to do. Questioning the manhood of your kidnapper is even worse. I am not that surprised that your father wants you dead. I would have ended your life years ago were I related to you and your dirty mouth."

Casually, he turned away from her, found his clothes, and got dressed.

"What do you mean, my father wants me dead? He can't do that. It is my house and my land, and he… he wouldn't dare!"

The kitten on the bed stretched, yawned, and made its way across the crumpled bedcover. Rage picked it up and held it in his palm once more. "You would do for breakfast," he said thoughtfully, stroking it underneath its chin until it was helplessly purring with delight. "I don't like to eat cats, but I am hungry. On the other hand, there is barely more on you than a mouthful. Too much effort to skin you." He dropped the kitten onto the floor, where it began playing with some dust bunnies.

"If you kill the kitten…." Lucinda said, but Rage interrupted her.

"You will—what? Dismiss me like Milly? Don't be ridiculous. And don't look so shocked. I watched you for the better part of yesterday. I know what you are capable of. If I want to kill the cat, I will do it. I killed a man yesterday, one who was on his way to end your life. Your father's servant tried to hire me beforehand. Back then, he wanted you just raped and broken. I declined the job. He first tried to kill me, then hired someone else to kill you. Did you even know your father hates you that much?"

The girl raised her chin and pursed her lips. She was shivering. A moment later, she sneezed, which ruined her haughty composure.

Rage barely managed to suppress a grin. If he wasn't careful, he'd begin treating her more decently, given he already liked her enough to have saved her life.

He cut the rope that bound her to the beam, and with more force than necessary, he pulled her up and held her between strong hands as if she were a rag doll. Methodically, he ripped her light silk shirt off her body, not caring that now she was kicking and screaming as if he were about to rape her.

That was probably exactly what she was thinking.

"Hold still," Rage said and undid the laces on her bodice. It dropped to the floor, accompanied by the stockings she'd worn and a pair of light, silk slippers not at all suited for walking more than a few steps.

When she was wearing nothing but her underwear, he let go of her. She fell against the wall, and Rage expected her to crawl away from him and seek out her clothes or maybe the blanket from his bed. Rich brats were useless once they were naked, as if their clothes served as armor no matter how thin the fabric was.

Lucinda, though, surprised him. Instead of crying and begging for mercy, she screamed and attacked him. Head pulled low between her shoulders, she went for his stomach. If he hadn't been watching her so closely, she might have managed to knock him down.

Damn, but he should have known she'd try something stupid.

As it was, he caught her by the shoulders and threw her into the next corner. A heartbeat later, he was on her, his knife cutting into the soft flesh of her throat. "You're annoying. And brave. Stupid, too, but well, you are young."

"My father will skin you alive for as much as touching me," she hissed and tried to bite him.

Rage hit her across the mouth. A thin line of blood ran down her chin, and tears welled up in her eyes.

He would have bet they were born out of hate and maybe pain, but not fear.

"Will you listen to me, girl?" He sighed, let go of her, and pulled out some dry clothes from his bag. He threw them at her—an old pair of trousers he only wore when there was no other choice, his second best shirt, a pair of nearly clean socks—and stuffed the blanket into the worn leather bag instead.

"Lucius tried to hire me. Yesterday, his servant offered me a generous amount of money for kidnapping and raping you. That makes me think your father has no intention of skinning me for merely touching you. I didn't take the job, though. Instead, I saved your life by kidnapping you. Don't ask me why—I must have been mad. Now get dressed. I'm hungry. I don't want to eat the cat, which means you need to come to the village with me. Where we also might find some proper boots for you. You'll come with me until we find a place where you're safe and where you can think of a way to deal with your father's wish of getting rid of you."

Her eyes narrowed as she picked up the shirt he'd given her. "It is old and ugly, just like you," she said and dropped it. Her little pink tongue dashed out between her lips and licked off the drop of blood drying on her chin.

"You've got a point." Rage took the rainstone out of his pocket. "My clothes are old, but they are clean. You are not, and you stink. Take a shower before you get dressed." With satisfaction, he saw that her eyes widened in surprise at the suggestion.

"Don't worry," he said with a cold grin. "I've got no interest in you. Too young, too blonde. Why do you think I refused to take the job?"

"You continue babbling about that as if mentioning it as often as possible will make it true," Lucinda snapped, snatching the stone out of Rage's hand. Examining it closely, she said, "I've heard of these, but never seen one. This is a rainstone, yes? It's for people who don't have any magic of their own. What—are you telling me you are crippled? Are you telling me," she lowered her voice conspiratorially, "that you can't do magic?"

"I'm not telling you anything other than to get clean," Rage replied and handed her the soap.

"Moron." Raising her chin, she activated the stone by blowing onto its surface, but instead of just taking the water from the surrounding air, she twisted the magic the stone contained and made it dry her underwear as well. Grinning widely, she then made the stone hover in front of her, held her hands underneath, and caught the drops. Like that, she managed to clean her hands and arms, her face, and her feet without getting any wetter than necessary. Mud, grass, and leaves landed on the planks, having been stuck to her skin from the previous day.

Briefly, Rage watched her, satisfied he'd been right about her magic. She was good. She wouldn't have needed the rainstone to conjure water, but he suspected hunger and a restless night had taken its toll.

"Towel," Lucinda said and snapped her fingers.

Rage considered strangling her, but instead, he threw a towel in her direction. She wasn't worth getting angry over.

"Are you expecting visitors?" Lucinda asked. "By the way, the towel is awfully rough. There's someone out there, watching this place. Someone I don't know. Someone—" She took a step toward the window, the towel wrapped around her shoulders. "Someone with a weapon."

She frowned. "You know, I was thinking about getting home. Not that I'm afraid of you, but at least I'd have a proper breakfast. And I could do with a good shouting at my wonderful father. But with that guy outside… I don't know. On the other hand, with you claiming to be an assassin, you should be capable of getting rid of him, shouldn't you?"

Rage would have thought she was trying to play tricks on him had he not seen her face: it was open and unguarded, with true puzzlement written all over it. "The one out there—is it one of your colleagues?" she asked. "How sick is that? First, I get kidnapped. Second, I have to use bought magic because I'm too hungry to do it all myself. And third, a stalker's out there, trying to kill me." She frowned. "At least, that's what it looks like…. Yes. The guy out there has murder in mind." She turned to Rage and poked a finger into his chest. "This is your fault. Had you left me in my room, I would—"

"You'd be dead already," Rage interrupted her. Carefully, he stepped to the window, loosened one end of the leather, and glanced outside. "How do you know someone's out there? I can't see anyone. And you get dressed, girl. Seeing you running around half-naked will give me nightmares for at least a month."

Just as he was about to replace the leather over the window, an arrow shot through the opening and missed his right eye by mere inches. A second one soared through the leather as if it were warm butter and buried itself in the opposite wall.

Lucinda, for once having obeyed an order, was fighting with the trousers, trying to get them over her damp legs. Staring at the arrow, she dropped to the ground immediately.

"At least you've got some brains," Rage stated. "Hurry. We need to get out of here before the someone outside decides to come inside. If there are more than three, it could be a problem."

"It's just one," Lucinda said in a low voice, buttoning the shirt and then taking out one of the leather strings that usually held it closed. With the string, she bound her hair back. Suddenly, she didn't look like a rich, spoiled brat anymore but like an angry cat, small, thin, and aggressive.

She came over to him, crawling across the floor and only getting up when she was right next to him. "I can feel him," she whispered. "I can sense if someone is around who wants to harm me. I had the same feeling yesterday, and then you stormed into my room. My father would love to have these skills himself, but I got the magic from my mum. Lucius is an idiot, nearly blind when it comes to even the most basic skills. Can't do Tracking magic, can't do Curses, fails half the time at Fire magic. I mean, come on, *everyone* can do Fire magic!"

"You're talking too much," Rage murmured and reached out for the crossbow. "Now shut up and catch the cat. Stuff him into the bag. I don't want to leave him here now that he insists on staying alive."

He peeked out the window again. Why did those amateurs always make more noise than a sounder of wild boars? It was practically an insult, the poor job the one outside was doing. True, he'd nearly caught him with the arrow, but nearly had not been good enough so far.

There he was, hiding behind the bushes. Not a bright thing to do, wearing a blue shirt, not in a wood made of green and brown. Rage drew the crossbow's string back. A second later, a muffled cry indicated he'd hit his target.

"Come along," Rage said and reached for the girl's hand.

She held the little cat tightly in her arms. "Where are we going?" she asked, sounding awfully young. "And when will you find something to eat? I'm hungry, the cat is hungry, and anyway, this couldn't be my father's doing. From what I understood, there are several killers out there. Lucius loves to spend his money on wine, clothes, and food. I doubt he would hire a killer, not to mention more than one."

The cat meowed, and it sounded weak. Rage, already on the ladder, looked at the girl. "Are you coming or not? Make up your mind. Stay with me for a while and live. Stay here and die. Your decision."

Lucinda bit her lip. "I don't know what's going on here and who's outside," she finally said, "but I will accompany you until I know who is behind this."

"Whatever," Rage replied. "The one out there might not be dead, so we need to hurry. I'll arrange for some horses. Once we get some miles between him and us, we will talk."

"A MULE? You stole a horse for yourself and a mule for me?"

Getting into the saddle, Rage looked down at her. "It's the mule, or it's walking in boots that are too big for you. Or you could go back to the barn and ask the man with the arrows what precisely he had in mind for you."

"I am the owner of Babylon Manor. I have the finest horses. I have more servants—"

"If you don't get up on that mule now, I will go on without you." Nudging the horse on, Rage made sure his bag was safely attached to the saddle and headed for the woods. It was unlikely the horse and mule would be missed in the next few hours, but then, the devil was a clever bastard, and the farmer might check on them earlier than usual.

Fighting with her disgust at the sight of the rather ugly mule and the dangers awaiting her if she went back home, Lucinda finally swung herself onto the back of her animal and went after Rage. "Only because I don't have anything better to do today," she shouted at his back. "You're amusing, and this is the most interesting thing that's happened to me in years. The boots really are too big, though. Couldn't you have stolen a pair that fits my feet?"

Glaring at Rage's back, she stroked the cat. The assassin had stolen milk and dried meat along with the horse, the mule, and the boots. At least she as well as the cat, which she had decided to call Sammy, had a full stomach.

"And you're pathetic. Can't even do magic. In case you wondered why I'm not afraid of you—that's why."

Rage turned in his saddle. His black eyes seemed to drill holes right into her soul. "You don't want to find out what exactly I am capable of, Lucinda," he said softly. "Pray to the Lady you will never find out."

She opened her mouth for a snappy reply, but no words came out. Suddenly, Rage looked different—dangerous and deadly and more bitter than old Ma Shell, who'd lost her husband and child on the same day and hour.

Suddenly, she truly believed he would kill her should she provoke him too much.

"Don't call me that," she finally managed to say. "I hate that name. Call me Luca."

Rage's horse disappeared into the trees. He didn't answer, and it was unclear whether he had heard her at all.

"I hate riding a mule. I wish I had Flash. He'd be perfect to show that idiot who I am." Sulking, she kicked the mule, and it tried to bite her. When Rage gave a low whistle, it flapped its ears and broke into a slow canter, willingly following after the one who had pardoned it from turning the millstone all day long. If mules were able to feel something like gratitude, this mule certainly showed it.

Hours passed, during which neither Rage nor Luca said a word. He didn't follow a street or a path, just made his way carefully through the woods. The lower branches of the trees reached out for their hair and clothes, the animals' tails got repeatedly caught in bushes, and occasionally, a fox would pass by. Her mule was nervous; Sammy was nervous. She was nervous, too, and only Rage didn't show a single sign that he was bothered.

Not much light made its way through the trees, and it didn't help Luca feel any less uncomfortable than she already was. A cold breeze made her shiver. The shirt she wore wasn't made to be worn in autumn, and the threadbare fabric made it even worse. These clothes had seen much better days, and that was probably years ago.

"I'm cold," she told the mule and felt, to her shock, tears prickle in her eyes. Annoyed with herself, she bit her lips, but that didn't help at all. She felt lost and scared, abandoned and wishing someone would come and rescue her.

Rescue her. How ridiculous. No one cared enough about her to so much as worry about her absence, let alone bother to find her now that she was missing.

Well, Keiran, maybe. If he even realized she was gone.

Wiping a hand across her eyes, Luca rubbed her arms to bring some warmth back into them. "How about a break?" she called, hoping the man riding in front of her would hear her and answer. The hours-long silence was unnerving. Nothing but birds singing and squirrels rustling through the leaves and that ever-blowing wind, which was turning her ears and nose into icicles. "Listen, I'm about to fall off my damn mule from hunger," she continued and reined in the animal in question. "And I bet Sammy won't survive for much longer if I don't feed him soon."

The assassin abruptly halted his horse, and the mule nearly bumped into it. For the first time in hours, they stopped moving. Rage's head was low as if he were thinking about his next move. After a moment, he glanced over his shoulder as if he weren't sure whether or not he'd heard correctly.

"Sammy?" he asked, and Luca hated him because he neither looked nor sounded even a third as tired as she felt.

"He needed a name," she snapped. "So can we have a break? Pretty please?"

Rage sighed. "There's a river not too far away. We'll reach it just after sunset. Can you wait that long, or will you drop dead off your mule right this very moment?"

Luca took in his hunched shoulders, the whiteness of his hands on the reins, and she heard—now that she was looking for it— fatigue in his voice. "I can wait," she said. "If you promise me something to eat, I can take care of the fire and make sure no one will be able to find us."

"Bread, some dried meat, fruit. Hopefully enough to restore your energy, girl."

"It's Luca. In case you didn't hear me earlier."

"The last one who told me his name, I killed a couple of minutes later. Not that I need a name to do my job. I kill whenever I have to, and that includes little girls who can't keep their mouths shut." Rage slipped off his horse and stretched. Luca suspected from the shadow of pain flickering across his face that he was unaccustomed to spending a whole day in the saddle. Taking the horse's reins, he began walking down a hill covered with nettles. The ground was tricky, and had he stayed in the saddle, the horse might have lost its footing.

Luca could hear water in the distance. The mule, unimpressed by the rocks under its hooves, followed the horse without any problems. For the first time, Luca was glad she was riding it. Walking through nettles wouldn't have been at all to her liking, especially not with loose-fitting boots. She'd have blisters in no time.

"Doesn't it sting?" she asked Rage, swaying in her saddle as the mule made its way downhill.

"Like hell, even through the trousers," Rage replied. "I'll gladly take the seat on the back of your mule if you lead my horse downhill."

"By the Lady, are you always such an asshole?" Annoyed with him, the mule, her empty stomach, and the much too quiet kitten in the bag hanging from the saddle horn, Luca urged the mule on until it was in front of Rage and his horse.

"See?" she said, "Like that, the mule tramples down the nettles, you don't have to suffer and moan, and your horse gets down to the river safely at the same time. Is there a brain hidden somewhere in your skull, or were you born as daft as you look?"

"I thought I just looked old and ugly." To her surprise, a smile tugged at his lips.

"Well," she began, but didn't know how to continue. She finally decided to shut up as well as ignore the burning sensation creeping across her cheeks. He *was* old and ugly. No need to be ashamed of telling the truth.

The sound of water became louder by the minute. Between the leaves, she could see the river, and in the distance there was a waterfall.

"Is there a reason why we are going where we are going?" Luca asked.

"I've been hiding in these woods ever since a particularly nasty and difficult job. It's a good place to hide, far away from the main street. There are provisions and blankets in a cave near the river."

The sun was already going down behind the trees, and the wind, tired of having blown all day, calmed down. Some stray beams danced on the surface of the river, sending golden stars all over the place. Grass, soft and green, grew along the bank. It was beautiful.

"You couldn't have found us a roadhouse, could you?" Luca grumbled.

Rage laughed, and with a practiced hand he took the saddle off the horse and dropped it in the grass. Then he loosely bound the horse's legs so it could walk and find itself some grass to eat but not run away. "You'll have to do without bed and servants, girl. But first, we'll eat. I need you alive and more or less well if you are to do the Protection magic."

Carefully, Luca took the kitten out of the bag and walked down to the river. It was more of a brook, to be honest, and the waterfall, though gushing down wildly, wasn't that large either. Ignoring Rage, she knelt at the bank, quenched her own thirst, then scooped up some water in the hollow of her hand and held it out to the kitten.

"Drink," she said quietly. "I don't have any milk, but you look old enough to survive on water. That nasty man said he has some dried meat. If you drink the water, I'll make a fire and then cook the meat so it is soft enough for you to eat. But first, you drink, do you hear me?"

Rage, having come up close without Luca noticing, made her jump when he knelt down next to her. "You drink, cat, or we'll have you for dinner," he said and put one finger onto the kitten's tiny, furry head. When it meowed and tried to scratch him, he smiled. "He'll live," he said, and as if to prove him right, the kitten licked the remaining water out of Luca's palm.

"Now do as promised. The meat is in my bag. Eat as much as you need to get some strength back. Then the fire and the Protection magic. I want to know half an hour beforehand if anything bigger than a badger gets close to us. In the meantime, I'll find the blanket I promised you. Come on, girl, move." Taking the cat out of her hand, he put it into his shirt, where it promptly began to purr. It was strong, this little one. Much stronger than it looked, or it would have died hours ago.

"I gather you'll break his neck if I try to run away?" Luca got up slowly.

Rage just looked at her.

"Right," Luca said. "Food first. Protection magic will take its time, though. An hour, at least. Sammy can't wait for another hour. Feed him, and I'll swear an oath that I will do nothing to harm you or run away."

Rage had put a stack of wood on the ground. Raising her hands, she observed that they were slightly shaky from hunger and fatigue. Ignoring it, she closed her eyes, concentrated on the logs and the smell of fire, its fragrance, and the bright, beautiful colors. Instantly, she felt its heat on her skin and heard the soft sound of burning wood.

"There," she said and opened her eyes. "Fire. Happy?"

Oh, dear, the world was swaying. Or maybe she was.

Rage took her arm, preventing her from falling. "You look exhausted. Sit. I'll get your blanket and some bread and meat. Eat first, then take care of the Protection magic. No use trying it now, you'll only collapse."

Grateful, Luca sank to the ground. Usually magic came to her as naturally as breathing. Persuading wood to burn wasn't any more strenuous than brushing her teeth, but then, she hadn't eaten since the few bites they had for breakfast. Her stomach felt like a small, hard stone sitting hot and burning inside her.

Rage handed her a strip of meat. Chewing it felt like chewing cotton, but after a few minutes, the meat became softer and even developed somewhat of a taste. Oblivious to her surroundings, Luca ate, wrapped up in the blanket the assassin had finally put around her shoulders. Vaguely, she was aware of him doing things—taking care of the horse and mule, putting a kettle on the fire, getting some more blankets, adding herbs to the boiling water—but it was as though she were watching him though a veil.

When the smell of boiled meat first hit her nose and then made it up to her brain, her mouth began watering, and she opened her eyes wide, seeing clearly for the first time in an hour. It was completely dark now. Up in the sky, a thin scythe of a moon could be seen. It was green; Galadriel, then, the smaller moon. Arwen should follow quickly.

Sammy sat on Rage's lap and fished for the meat the assassin handed him. One tiny bit after the other—the kitten devoured whatever was given to him. One bite for the man, one for the cat, on and on. Luca had to smile at the sight.

Her stomach growled. Rage looked up and nodded at the plate next to her. Meat and wild potatoes, a cup of coffee—she had no idea when he'd done it, when he'd prepared dinner, when he'd been close enough to put the plate next to her.

"I didn't notice you packing any pots when we left the barn," she said, picking up the cup and drinking deeply. The coffee was good, hot and black and bitter. Then she began eating greedily, for once glad she didn't have to bother with a fork and knife—they would have only slowed her down.

In the darkness, she could barely see Rage.

Apart from his skin, everything else was black. Only the flames shed some light, just enough to see that he was shivering with cold and that he was stroking the cat's full little belly. His jacket, she only now noticed, was around her shoulders and the second blanket wrapped around her legs. He sat on the bare ground, cross-legged and patiently waiting for her to come back to her senses.

"The pot was in the stash I hid here some months back." He sounded hoarse; she could hear in his voice that he needed sleep. "It's a shame I didn't think of leaving some clothes as well. I could have done with a warmer shirt." His long, pale fingers constantly stroked the cat, and it purred sleepily.

Luca shook the blanket off her shoulders, along with the jacket. "I didn't mean to… pass out, sort of," she said. Putting both her hands on the ground, she chased the coldness away, telling the fire to spread its warmth not only to the air, but to the earth as well.

Her backside became warm and then her feet, which had still felt like icicles despite the closeness of the flames. Then Sammy stretched, climbed down from Rage's lap, and curled up on the grass instead.

Curious, Rage placed a palm on the ground. "It's warm. Good. Now how about performing some Protection magic and then going to sleep? I want to get another thirty miles between us and this place by tomorrow evening, and for that, I need you in good shape."

Luca picked up the jacket and threw it at him. "How about saying thanks?" she snapped. "Anyway, it's you who looks like a frozen fish. Care to tell me why you can't perform the Protection magic yourself? In which way exactly are you crippled?"

Rage caught his jacket and pulled it on in one smooth movement. "None of your business," he said and got up. All of a sudden, a mean-looking knife was in his hand. "But I tell you what—if you weren't such a lazy, spoiled little princess, you would have performed the Protection magic the moment you'd got off your beautiful mule. And I wouldn't need to kill yet another man." He threw a blanket over the fire, extinguishing it, then vanished into the darkness, melting into the night like a bodiless shadow.

"What?" Jumping up herself, Luca whirled around, expecting arrows to hit her, expecting strangling hands around her throat, expecting everything but what she saw once her eyes adjusted to the darkness and the pale, silver-green light the two moons cast.

Someone was standing between the trees. Someone tall. Someone with empty hands.

Someone she knew.

Her heart began to race.

"Don't kill him!" she called, desperate to prevent a catastrophe. Magic sprang from her hands as she jumped forward, wild and barely controlled magic, and it seeped into the trees and the air and the ground, even into the river. This hadn't happened to her since she'd been a little girl, wild magic causing damage to her surroundings. She'd long since learned to control it. Apparently, she was still too tired, too hungry, and too scared to keep it in check.

The wild magic caused blossoms to bloom and grass to grow, and it heated the brook's water before it dissipated. At the last moment, Luca managed to twist her magic so it wouldn't hurt anyone. She only hoped the magic hadn't hit Rage, but then, if it had, she would have heard him scream. Wild magic, no matter which twist she gave it, always caused pain when hitting a living thing.

There was no sound apart from her own voice. "Keiran, it's Keiran," she yelled, "and if you touch a single hair on his head, I'll… I don't know what I will do, but you won't like it!"

CHAPTER
Four

MAYBE, JUST maybe, she heard a knife drop to the ground, but perhaps she only imagined it given there were more important things in her head than the surrounding sounds. The only thing that counted was her friend who'd come to rescue her, standing tall and strong and beautiful under the trees, accompanied only by a horse.

"Keiran," she cried once more and threw herself into his arms. She usually wasn't the emotional type and ordered people around rather than embraced them, but this was the first time she'd been kidnapped, not to mention he'd been close to getting killed by that nasty assassin.

Keiran dropped the horse's lead and was about to hug her back when a shadow stepped out of the darkness right behind them. Rage's fingers closed around Keiran's throat with an iron grip.

"You better tell me how you found us," Luca heard him hiss into Keiran's ear. "And if you can't keep your magic under control, girl"—the glance he shot at Luca could have shriveled plants to dust—"you better get lost. People die from wild magic. I don't need any of this shit around me."

Luca grabbed hold of the hand around Keiran's throat and bit deep into the assassin's pale flesh. Blood welled up in her mouth, and she gagged and spat and hit the assassin with small, hard fists until he let go of Keiran. Stepping back and cursing nastily, he held his bleeding wrist.

"Don't touch him," she panted, wiping some loose strands of hair out of her face. "He's my friend. He's here to save me—from *you*, assassin! Hopefully, you've got no horrible diseases, now that

I've bitten you. This is the first time since I was a little girl that my magic has got out of control, and only because you couldn't manage to provide me with something decent to eat. It's your fault. Anyway, it won't happen again."

Keiran slipped an arm around her, calming her. It worked, like it always did. She sighed deeply and forced the tension out of her muscles. Briefly, she pressed her face to Keiran's shoulder, inhaling his scent. He smelled of horses, earth, and home; she very nearly became homesick.

"Children," Rage sighed. "What if he's been sent by your father? What if he's been followed? What if—"

"There is no one else around, at least no one who means us harm," Luca interrupted. "I would know. And I'll do the Protection magic now, all right? Just calm down a bit."

She slowly went to the fire and picked up the blanket. Smoke welled up. At first, it was only red, but a heartbeat later, newly awoken flames licked at the logs. Luca shook out the blanket. Embers dropped to the ground, and for a moment, the night was illuminated by tiny glowing sparks.

"Here," she said as she handed Rage the blanket. "As good as new. I might not have caught all the burn holes, but at least the stink of smoke is gone. Take it. Unlike me, it won't bite you." She tried a smile, hoping the assassin wouldn't rip her head off. In the light of the flames, he looked like a panther ready to devour his prey. *Stupid idea, annoying a wild animal,* she thought and added, "Don't expect me to say sorry for having bitten you. Keiran was trying to rescue me. You had no right to hurt him."

"As if he could." Rage took the blanket and examined it carefully. "No holes, no smell. Good. Now move your ass and work on the Protection magic. I don't want any other surprises tonight." He pulled the blanket around his shoulders. "You," he snapped. "Boy. Tell me how you found us."

Keiran smiled, a wide, happy grin that lit his whole face. The fire cast a golden glow on his skin, and even the freckles on his perfect nose could be seen. He picked up the horse's lead and wrapped it carefully around a young tree. The horse, faceless in the darkness, bent its huge head and began to graze while the boy, with a somewhat embarrassed gesture, rubbed his hand through his unruly locks, then stretched out his hand invitingly.

Rage raised an eyebrow. Looking the boy up and down, he saw he wore far from the best shoes, trousers with holes, and a shirt too thin for this time of year. "Lucius didn't send you, did he?"

The boy just stood there, still holding out his hand. Then he put his left hand to his heart and slightly bowed his head. His smile was easy, as though he neither knew nor cared how the man in front of him earned his living.

Somewhat embarrassed, the assassin took the boy's hand and shook it. "Rage," he said. "And you're Keiran, according to the girl's screams. Now, will you tell me how you found us, or do I have to beat it out of you?"

Keiran shrugged. He pressed his lips shut, then smiled again.

"He's mute," Luca called from somewhere near the river. "Can't speak a word. He's got no magic either, of course, so he's really no threat. Give him the rest of the meat and some coffee. And some water for the horse while you're at it. We've been friends since we were children, you know? For some reason, he can always find me, no matter where I am. When I was six and he was nine, I ran away and broke my leg, and he found me. He just followed his instincts, and now here he is."

Yawning widely, Luca came back to the fire and sat down, pressing her hands to the warm ground. "Done," she said. "Not even a mouse can get through the magic now."

Keiran sat next to her, accepting the mug she poured him. He didn't seem concerned that he was miles and hours away from the manor he'd grown up in, his father's hut, a warm bed, and a set-up table. As if he'd spent his whole life in the wilderness, he sat cross-legged on the ground, mug warming up his fingers, with Luca's hand on his thigh.

Rage sat down too, and Luca saw he was moving carefully. "Did my wild magic hit you?" she asked, snuggling up a bit closer to Keiran. "If yes, then I guess you must be feeling awful. You know, if you aren't careful, you might lose your mind and begin to kill squirrels, mistaking them for enemies, or shout at your own shadow."

She grinned smugly.

Keiran put his arms around her shoulders, and she relaxed. Someone had once called them a beautiful couple and said that their children would be a pleasure to look at. At the time, she had blushed with delight at the comment. But when Rage looked at her and then at Keiran and smiled in a knowing way, it drove her crazy, and she snapped, "I know what you think, and you are wrong. I am not in love with Keiran."

Rage took out a small leather pouch from his bag. His hands trembled, and Luca knew she'd guessed correctly: wild magic wasn't to be underestimated. He should consider himself lucky he wasn't harmed worse. Nervousness was one of the side effects, cramping muscles another, and she knew he wouldn't be able to sleep much tonight, nor would he feel particularly well in the morning. He looked as if he wanted to jump up and search for attackers who weren't there.

She had to admire his self-control when he remained seated and rolled himself a cigarette instead.

Only—she could smell it wasn't just tobacco he was using.

Fine. The weed would be like a soft breeze on his burning nerves and howling muscles. Hopefully, it would also mellow his dark mood so he would behave during the night and not run around chasing ghosts.

"The Protection magic is working perfectly," Luca said carefully. "If you don't mind, I'll try to get some sleep now." Pulling the blanket over herself, she stretched out, her head on Keiran's leg. *Let those two continue to stare at each other*, she thought. She was looking forward to a nice, quiet night. When Sammy came to join her, she couldn't have been happier.

THE HERBS kicked in and played tricks with his mind. Rage thought the boy was watching him. He saw him smile, he saw the freckles, and he wondered how it would feel to kiss those perfect lips. Rage hadn't kissed anyone in a very long time. He never kissed the whores he chose for a quick fuck, and he hadn't met anyone who looked this gorgeous in years.

Only now did he remember why he usually never smoked in company. Too dangerous—he risked doing or saying something stupid. But there hadn't been a choice. Had he not used herbs to calm down, he might have been accompanied by two corpses in the morning.

There it was again, that half-cute, half-mischievous smile. The boy knew how to catch someone's attention. The girl's head was on his lap, her arm draped sleepily over his leg, but nevertheless he flirted with Rage.

Or at least, Rage thought so. Before he knew it, he smiled back, nothing more than a quick flash across the flames. He felt stupid about the smile, knowing all too well that the boy was interested in no one but the girl at his side. And who could blame him? She was, despite her sharp tongue and her annoying habit of arguing with him and not obeying his orders, exceptionally beautiful, a fairy turned into human form. Even the borrowed, oversized clothes and unwashed hair couldn't change that.

The weed called for him. Rage held the smoke long in his lungs, feeling his head become as light as a cloud. Good feeling, especially after the many unplanned killings of the past few days. Even better as it mellowed the burning pain in his bones caused by the girl's wild magic.

A warm hand on his arm made him open his eyes, which must have dropped closed, somehow. The herbs were strong; he was already far more affected than he'd expected to be after one small cigarette.

Amber eyes not too far away from his face. Dark brown locks, screaming to be curled around his fingers. Skin as soft as a peach. And that smile, that damn smile, which pierced the assassin's heart even though many, many people would have sworn he didn't possess a heart at all.

Keiran nodded at the small butt in Rage's hand. His eyes seemed to ask a question—*May I?*—which was, of course, impossible. Eyes couldn't speak.

When Rage didn't react, Keiran tentatively reached out and took the butt out of his fingers. With nothing more than a slightly tilted head, he asked for permission, and when Rage nodded, he nodded back in silent agreement and thanks. The toke he took was short, and he didn't keep the smoke in his lungs for long. But he didn't cough, nor did his eyes begin to water.

"Smoked before?" Rage asked, and the boy nodded, holding up three fingers.

Keiran sighed contently, took a sip of coffee, but didn't hand back the butt. Instead, he shifted his position until Luca's head was on the blanket rather than his lap. When tiny claws emerged from under the blanket, he briefly stroked the kitten's paw until it yawned and went back to sleep.

Keiran smiled at Rage. His arm touched the assassin's ankle, and the warmth his body radiated went right to Rage's groin.

Fuck, he thought, *that's not good. He's too young, and anyway, I'm stoned. Forget about him!*

"Go to sleep," he said aloud. "I'll keep watch."

Keiran looked at him, another question in his eyes.

Strange, how easy it was to understand the boy. "I'll wake you in a few hours, if you want to take your turn. Until then, I'll stretch my legs a bit. I'm not much more used to spending the day in the saddle than you are."

Without awaiting an answer—and without taking the cigarette back from the boy—Rage turned and went toward the river, his eyes adjusting slowly to the darkness. The night's chill caressed his flesh, and he shivered. He would have preferred to take a nap himself rather than stroll aimlessly through the night. But apart from the restlessness caused by his humming nerves, it would have meant staying close to the boy. Not an option. Another few minutes near Keiran, another toke from the cigarette, and he would have done something stupid, like leaning closer maybe, or inhaling the boy's unique fragrance a bit deeper than necessary.

Stars danced in front of his eyes. Bright little specks, cast by the herbs, danced through his brain. Rage felt taller than he was, and thinner too, as if the wind could blow him away at any moment. Usually when he had a smoke, he stayed inside, and ideally in bed. Walking felt strange; his feet seemed miles away.

It was no surprise he lost his footing and slipped on the muddy bank of the river.

Had he not been stoned and had his muscles not insisted on cramping despite the herbs he'd smoked, Rage would have never lost his balance. The riverbank wasn't that steep, and now that his eyes had adjusted to the darkness, he was able to see the ground as well as the surface of the water. But as he was wobbly on his legs and dizzy in his head, he struggled for only a heartbeat before he fell, twisting his ankle on the way down.

Expecting the coldness of the water to embrace him, Rage held his breath—he was cold already and didn't look forward to the impact.

Rage hit the surface with his back first, and he gasped out of instinct only to realize the water wasn't cold at all. He tumbled. His head went under the water, and he stirred up the sand of the riverbed. When he tried to get his legs underneath him, his feet slipped again on the mossy stones. Water was closing in above him. Stones scratched his legs, and he got water in his lungs as they hadn't yet understood that he was under water. Coughing, he reached out and touched a crawfish scurrying away hurriedly under his searching grip.

Warm, his mind told him. *The water is warm!*

Rage finally got his knees underneath him. Head first, he broke the surface, staggered once more, and stood, dripping and shaking with suppressed anger. It cost him a lot not to curse, to shout out his frustration at his own stupidity, but he kept control and silently got his balance back, which wasn't easy given his head was spinning even worse than before.

Suddenly, part of the bank broke loose and a large stone rolled into the water. It would have hit Rage's still hurting foot squarely had he not jumped out of the way just in time. Of course, jumping around in a river in the middle of the night wasn't a good idea. Waving his arms wildly so he wouldn't fall again, the assassin bit his lip so as not to shout an outraged "Fuck" into the night air. When an arm wrapped around his waist, steadying him, he knew he had been about to land in the water once more. Warm breath brushed along his neck, and the body pressing against his was reassuringly strong and welcomingly male.

Yes. Definitely male. And very definitely aroused.

Turning, Rage dug his fingers in Keiran's shoulders to steady himself. He was wet from head to toe. Behind him, the waterfall cascaded over the rocks, spraying him with warm drops.

"The girl's wild magic caused some unexpected results." Rage spat out a mouthful of water.

Keiran grinned. His arm was still around Rage's waist. They stood as close as lovers. Had Rage been sober, he would have pushed the boy away.

He wasn't, so he didn't.

Keiran's trousers were wet up to his thighs, but his shirt was dry. So was the cigarette he held in his free hand. Unruly brown locks fell into his face, and his eyes sparkled in the light of the twin moons.

Rage moved his hips. Tentatively, and not entirely sure this was a good idea, he let his hand wander from the boy's shoulder down his back.

"You were following me? Although I had told you to go to sleep?"

Keiran nodded.

"Why?"

A smile. Keiran took a deep toke from the cigarette he'd hidden between his fingers, bent over, and pressed his lips to the assassin's.

At first, Rage was too surprised to react. Then Keiran's strong, callused hand found its way between Rage's legs, found the assassin's cock, and squeezed.

Rage gasped when his cock reacted instantly to the caress. His lips parted, and Keiran breathed out, pushing the weed-laced smoke he had been holding in his mouth deep into the assassin's lungs. It burned all the way down, but nevertheless, it was the most intense kiss he'd received in a very long time. It brought up old memories, which made Rage's knees weak with longing and fear at the same time.

Because of the rush of adrenaline his fall had caused, Rage had sobered somewhat, but the weed kicked in quickly again. Rage's legs turned to jelly, and he embraced the boy, melting in his arms. Every muscle went limp, every joint lost its hold, his body lost contact with his mind, and slowly, like a drop of water sliding down a chilled glass, he staggered backward, bumping into the rocks behind him.

Keiran let go of him, watching him, seeming to be waiting for something. Then he dropped the butt, and with an inaudible sound, it died in the churning water at his feet. He reached out, touched Rage's cheek, and with the side of his thumb stroked his thin, cold lips. Slowly, he opened the top button of Rage's wet, black shirt, then a second one before he stopped, a question written all over his face.

Rage could have stopped him. He wasn't so far gone that he was unable to make decisions. So the question was—did he want this?

Hell yes!

Moonlight made the water look like liquid silver—Arwen needed maybe another week to be full—and because of the girl's uncontrolled outburst of magic, it was wonderfully warm. In the morning, it would be as cold as ever, but right now, shedding his clothes seemed like an exceptionally good idea.

On the other hand, he didn't know much more about the boy than his name and the fact that he was mute. He was nineteen. He was a gardener's son, and he liked Luca enough to steal a horse and follow her into the night. Rage didn't know how the boy had grown up, what he liked and disliked, or even whether he had a knife hidden under his shirt, ready to stab him once Rage gave in to his desire.

Not knowing a thing about the ones he fucked had never bothered Rage in the past. He took them and dismissed them afterward. He never sought out the same whore twice. He could search the boy, take him, and be done with him in a few minutes, and it would be impossible for Keiran to attempt to harm him with his face pressed against the soft, slippery, strangely oily moss that covered the rocks.

The thought alone made Rage hard.

Keiran, having watched him closely, perhaps even having read the assassin's thoughts from his unguarded expression, opened his shirt and threw it onto the riverbank. Threadbare trousers slipped down over narrow hips. The boy stood naked and hard in front of him, his nipples kissed erect by the breeze rustling though the leaves.

No hidden knives to be seen.

And the unspoken question was still standing between them.

Do you want this?

"A kiss, then," Rage said casually and opened the rest of his shirt buttons himself. Lanky and wet, it hung off his haggard frame, revealing his chest and the scars cast by a long forgotten catastrophe. "And more too." His eyes roamed over the boy's naked body, the long, slender legs, the broad shoulders, the flat, muscular abdomen, and, of course, they lingered for a long moment on Keiran's cock. "But I thought you were with the girl."

Keiran shook his head and placed both his hands on Rage's hips, letting his cock touch the front of the soft leather trousers the assassin was wearing. Then he leaned in and brushed his lips across Rage's throat, added gentle pressure, and sucked once.

Rage groaned. "You're more into men, it seems," he managed and felt the boy's smile on his skin and his hands high on his legs. The laces of his trousers pulled open, and although the leather was soaked, Keiran pulled them down easily. Kicking them off, Rage vaguely thought about throwing them ashore but forgot about it entirely when the boy dropped to his knees and took his now fully hard cock into his mouth.

There was one thing to do before this went on any further, beyond the point where he could still end it. Rage forced his eyes open and brought his left wrist up where he could see it. It was dark, but not too dark. In the moonlight, he looked for the bracelet.

It was black against his pale skin.

Perfect.

Thrusting his cock into the boy's mouth, Rage gave in to pleasure, not thinking anymore, just enjoying Keiran's undivided attention. His hands rested lightly on the boy's head, his back was protected by the rocks behind him, and the waterfall's warm spray left a million tiny, sparkling pearls on their skin.

Sharp teeth in combination with an eager tongue—he would come soon if Keiran continued like that.

Somehow, Rage regretted that this would be over in another few seconds. He was enjoying the boy's attention, even more so since Keiran had sought and found him of his own accord and not because he expected payment. This was not the mechanical ministrations of a whore, of someone who could barely hide his disgust at his customer's lust. The boy was hard too. Rage could feel his cock at his leg, large and beautifully shaped.

Hands on his ass, kneading. Lips on the tip of his cock, then near his belly button, then higher, crossing his ribcage until Keiran found one of his nipples, nibbling and licking it until it was hard as a cherry stone. They stood face to face now, black eyes staring into amber ones. Skin to skin. Heart to heart.

Keiran's fingertips brushed over the black bird on Rage's throat. He smiled.

Rage couldn't suppress a shudder. Apparently, the boy knew exactly what he was. Apparently, Keiran wasn't as innocent as he'd thought.

Another kiss, soft and tender. Rage wasn't used to tenderness, as much as he wasn't used to kisses. A whore didn't kiss, nor did Rage wish to kiss someone he had no feelings for.

Keiran's lips touched Rage's shoulder, his neck, the spot right underneath his ear—very personal, very lovely, and Rage thought about stopping him when the boy turned him around and pressed him against the slippery rocks, spreading his legs with one hand whilst the other captured his wrists.

Didn't see that coming, Rage thought dreamily and rested his forehead on their entwined hands. Distantly, he wondered if it bothered him not to be the one in control.

When Keiran touched his entrance with wet, oily fingers, Rage smiled. So what if he preferred to be in charge whenever he bought himself a whore? Keiran wasn't one, and this wasn't some dirty back alley. Rage couldn't even remember the last time he'd been totally naked during sex. At the moment, those fingers teasing his hole were all he could think about anyway. One slipped inside him, quickly followed by a second.

He groaned. Not being in control definitely wasn't bothering him at all right now.

Rage spread his legs a bit wider, and his hands searched for cracks in the rocks beneath the waterfall to hold on to. Keiran's breath kissed his back as he finger-fucked him, slowly, carefully. Anticipation shot through Rage when he thought of the boy's cock pushing inside him, and he believed he hadn't been this hard in ages.

Their bodies were slippery from the moss. So easy to lean against the boy positioned behind him. Easier still to be penetrated, stretched, filled by the boy's beautiful cock. It would only take a single, smooth push. Rage slapped his right hand on his buttock to encourage him and spread himself, awaiting Keiran.

"Yes!" he hissed when the boy removed his fingers and entered him, nibbling on his exposed neck as he pushed inside.

Warm rain on their skin—no, the waterfall's spray, but it felt like rain streaming out of a dark, star-filled sky. Rocks under his fingertips, cold compared to the water.

The boy went slowly and thrust carefully. Soft moans indicated Keiran was enjoying himself. No doubt his grip would leave dark bruises on the assassin's pale hips.

"Harder," Rage rasped and sank his strong fingers into the flesh of Keiran's ass, urging him on. "I'm not made of glass. You won't break me, Keiran. So fuck me. Fuck me deep!"

It was the first time he'd ever uttered the name of one of his casual partners during sex.

Keiran thrust harder and deeper. Rage listened for groans but heard none. Only the labored breathing in his ears indicated that Keiran was enjoying this too. They moved as one, together, their heartbeats and souls in perfect sync.

By the Lady, that's good. Blindly, the assassin reached behind him, burying his fingers in the boy's unruly locks as the water sloshed around their shins. Keiran put his hand on the assassin's cock, stroking him as he fucked him.

Rage's body acted of its own accord without awaiting orders from his brain. It pushed backward, meeting the boy's thrusts. It pushed forward into the boy's stroking hand. Heavy was his heartbeat, fast, almost racing. His chest moved as if he were running, had been for hours. Joined with Keiran at that single point, Rage's head fell back and rested against the boy's forehead. Black, wet hair brushed across golden skin. The boy licked the water off his throat, kissed his cheek, and a strand of brown hair slid between his lips. It tasted sweet, bitter, and salty.

Perfect.

"Make me come," Rage breathed.

How could it be possible that he saw the boy smile behind him? How could it be possible he saw the desire and the joy in Keiran's eyes when there was nothing but rocks in front of him?

One last stroke. One last, deep thrust. Water spilled into Rage's mouth when he threw his head back in orgasm.

The boy shuddered too and embraced him, remaining inside him for a few moments before going soft. Gently, reluctantly, Keiran loosened his grip and stepped back, giving Rage some room and time to catch his breath.

Rage sank to his knees. Water dripped from his hair into the river. Seed ran down his legs and was washed away. Shaking, he pressed both his hands into the river's dark, sandy ground. Water, still warm, landed on his back, laved down his sides, arms, and legs. It took him a minute or more to recover enough to turn around and lean against the rocks.

"Damn it, boy," Rage rasped, exhausted as well as surprised. "No one has fucked me like that in a long time. Usually, I wouldn't have allowed you to take me and use me for your own pleasure."

Keiran flashed him a wide smile, dropped to his knees and knelt between Rage's legs. Clear admiration shining in his eyes, he stroked Rage's legs until he thought he'd melt under those hands.

"Stop it," he said, but instead of getting up, Keiran leaned in and kissed him, slowly and thoroughly.

Maybe if the water hadn't gone cold at that very moment, there would have been a second round, but as it was, the cold hit them, and Rage gasped, jumping up and shaking himself like a wet cat. Together, they leaped onto the bank, crashing to the ground with the boy landing on top. Rage grinned, then laughed openly. Quickly, he got to his feet and offered his hand, pulling Keiran up.

"Another half an hour of warm water would have been welcome," he said and saw the boy grin in agreement.

You enjoyed it, Keiran's eyes said. It wasn't a question.

"I did," Rage replied, picking up his shirt and looking for his trousers. They had floated to the bank and were stuck in the low branches of a bush, just touching the surface of the river. When he pulled them free, he knew the leather would still be wet in the morning. Getting into them wasn't easy. In fact, it was a nasty feeling, putting on wet clothes, but he refused to stay naked another moment.

When Rage looked up again, he saw the boy's eyes following his every movement.

"This stays between us," Rage said, forcing a bit of coldness into his voice. It made Keiran frown in puzzlement, but Rage couldn't afford to care about that. His own interests counted first and alone. Whether or not the boy expected a friendly word was none of his concern.

Picking up his shirt, Rage wrung it out, shivering in the cold breeze. "Understood? Don't let her know. She thinks you belong to her, and as long as I am stuck with the both of you, I want her to continue believing that illusion. Another day, maybe two, and this will be over anyway, once she's thought of a safe place I can take her."

Keiran looked at him for a very long moment. He was still naked, his shirt and trousers hanging forgotten in his hand. Finally, he nodded. A few heartbeats later, he had vanished into the darkness.

For some reason, Rage would have preferred a bit more resistance to his orders. And another kiss.

CHAPTER
Five

BY THE time Rage returned to the fire, the flames had burned low and were barely casting any light. Silently, he put a few more logs on and sat, watching the flames lick at the wood. Warmth reached him as he fished for the one spare blanket and wrapped it around his shoulders.

He'd laid his shirt next to the boy's wet clothes, which were draped across the ground near the fire. *Keiran is naked underneath his blanket*, he thought and briefly wished he could stretch out next to the boy, embrace him, press his cold, scarred body against the warm, soft skin.

Bullshit.

"Get a grip," he murmured to himself and lit a cigarette, this time without herbal lacing. "He was just curious. I might be able to seduce him once more before he turns his attention back to the girl."

Pulling the blanket tighter around his shoulders didn't really help. His trousers were wet, and the coldness seeped into his body, claiming him.

When the cat appeared at his feet and climbed onto his lap only a moment later, he didn't object. It was some warmth, at least.

The soft, content purring helped make him sleepy. With heavy eyelids, Rage edged a bit closer to the fire, always listening to the night and its various sounds. Occasionally, he stole a glance at the sleeping boy, his face, part of a naked shoulder. Those shoulders rose evenly with steady breaths, as silent as the boy himself.

Kisses on his neck. Hands on his hips. Lust rushing through his veins like a drug. A cock moving inside him, making him beg for more.

Rage tore his eyes open, chasing away the unbidden memories. He couldn't afford to remember. He couldn't afford to get distracted. They were in the middle of nowhere, and as much as he would like to believe that Lucius of Babylon didn't have the patience, money, or stamina to follow them here, he hadn't survived this long by relying on what he wanted to believe.

Besides, his nerve ends had begun to hum with pain again, chasing away the feeling of contentment left by the fuck. Rage felt like ants were hurrying over his skin, ants with burning feet. The prospect of sleep, tantalizing as it was, vanished with every breath he took.

Waiting for sunrise, waiting for his trousers to dry, waiting for Keiran and the girl to wake so he could figure out how to be rid of them—it turned out to be a very long night, and one where he didn't wake the boy as promised so he could have a turn at keeping watch.

When Galadriel and Arwen finally set, Rage's mood had dropped below the freezing point. In the pale light of the morning, the leather of his trousers was still as damp as expected, especially around his backside and along the legs. To make things worse, his muscles were hard and aching, partly because of the day spent in the saddle but mostly because of the girl's wild magic.

And his head hurt.

Gritting his teeth against the millions of hooves that thundered through his skull, he got up to put on his shirt and kicked the boy awake.

"Get dressed," he hissed when Keiran opened his eyes. "At least your clothes are nicely warm and dry now, so don't look at me like that. I want to be on our way in an hour."

Sleepily, Keiran stretched and yawned. The girl had snuggled up to him during the night, and he tenderly brushed a long strand of blonde hair out of her face as he smiled and pulled the blanket a bit higher so she was covered up to her chin. He got up and stretched once more. That he was half-hard and in clear view of Rage's angry eyes didn't seem to bother him at all.

"If she wakes now, she'll wonder why you've slept naked. You don't want to make me lose my patience by parading naked in front of me," Rage bit out and nearly slapped the boy when he just grinned. At least he took his clothes and got dressed. Had he waited any longer, Rage wasn't sure if he would've been able to hold his temper.

It was a cool morning, so when Keiran handed him a cup of hot coffee, Rage gratefully wrapped his hands around the mug. The first sip was pure bliss, and he stepped closer to the fire. Maybe his trousers would finally dry. Riding with wet leather between his ass and his horse was definitely something he didn't crave.

Birds began to sing their lonely autumn songs, and fog waved along the river. Soon, the sun would be up. It was time to find a place to hide the girl. Jobs awaited him, new towns, new customers, and new deaths.

A warm hand on his shoulder distracted him from his gloomy thoughts.

Keiran.

"What?"

A nod in the direction of the mug; a raised eyebrow.

"One is enough. Keep the rest for the girl. The cat ate the last strip of meat around midnight. We will have to steal something to eat once we are out of the woods."

Keiran looked slightly surprised, then slapped a palm hand against his forehead. With a few, long strides he was at his horse, which was still grazing quietly where he had bound it. He rummaged through the saddlebag neither Rage nor Luca had seen in the darkness the previous evening. Grinning widely, he then produced a loaf of bread and a big chunk of cheese, holding both out to Rage like a present. He seemed embarrassed, as if he should have thought about the food before, and the assassin couldn't help his lips twitching at the sight.

Taking the bread, he broke it into three parts. Then he cut the cheese, kept one piece for himself, and handed Keiran the other two shares. "Wake her," he said. "There's a town not too far away, a few hours at the most. We should be there long before nightfall."

Keiran, mouth full, looked at him. *What happens when we reach the town?* Rage didn't consider it odd anymore that he could understand the boy so easily even though not a single word was spoken.

"You two cannot stay with me." With two long gulps, Rage emptied his mug. The last bits of cheese and bread vanished into his mouth. "It is up to her to find a place she can stay until the business with her father is sorted."

Keiran didn't look happy about that.

"You like her," Rage stated.

Keiran nodded.

"She's good-looking, I give you that. Are you after her inheritance? If she marries you, you'll be the Lord of Babylon Manor. A big step up for a servant."

This time, Keiran laughed. It was an odd sight, seeing him so deeply amused without hearing a single sound, but then, the boy couldn't even groan and gasp while fucking.

Silently, Keiran made it clear that he wasn't after marriage and that Luca's snappiness didn't bother him, either. *We're friends,* his eyes said, and he knelt next to her and shook her awake. When she managed to sit up, her tousled hair looking like mice had used it for a nest during the night, he handed her the last mug filled with coffee.

"It's too early to get up." Luca yawned. She was clearly not a morning person.

"Move, girl," Rage said harshly. Anger laced his words, though he didn't know why. Maybe it was because the boy had just pecked a kiss on the girl's cheek or because the cat had jumped onto her lap, purring again. "I'll take you to the next town. From there, you'll be on your own. Get back to Babylon Manor or find a priest who's willing to marry you two. At least you'll be able to take over once you are a married woman. Get rid of Lucius as your legal guardian. Do whatever you want, but move your ass."

Indignant, Luca threw off the blanket and got up. Her hair was wild and unkempt, with leaves stuck in it, badly in need of a wash. Her clothes—Rage's clothes, actually—were crumpled, and her cheek had impressions where she'd lain on the seams of the bag Keiran had given her for a pillow.

"Good morning to you too," she hissed, snatched her share of the bread and cheese from Keiran's hand, and began to eat. "And by the way, you look awful. Haven't you slept?"

A burning, lustful memory flashed through Rage's mind. "I've kept watch," he answered, a cold calmness in every word. "Protection magic is nice to have, but I don't trust you."

"Idiot!" Her eyes were already blazing. She was easy to annoy and went off like fireworks once there.

"Get moving, or I will drag you along by your hair again. Keiran, put out the fire. We are leaving." Without waiting for an answer, he pulled on his jacket.

His headache increased with every step he took, every word he spoke. *The morning better improve soon*, he thought wearily, *or I don't know how I am going to get through the next few hours.*

"WHY COULDN'T you steal Flash?" the girl moaned for about the tenth time since she was in the saddle.

Keiran, who was leading the mule, dropped his head in despair. Luca had insisted on riding the stallion he had taken from the stables of Babylon Manor, a tall, lean animal with stamina and strength. It was a decent horse, fast as well as frugal in his needs, and the sole reason he had been able to catch up with them. But he wasn't young anymore, and he wasn't a beauty. He wasn't Flash.

"Had he taken the best horse in your father's stables—"

"My stables!"

"—your father would have chased him down and hung him before yesterday lunchtime," Rage continued, unimpressed by her interruption. "So shut up. For a little while at least?"

His head was in agony.

Halfheartedly, and not entirely sure why he didn't just do it, he wished he could tie her up and throw her over the horse's saddle. Ah, yes. Lack of energy. It took all the strength he had to keep himself in the saddle. He feared if he tried to overpower her, she would end up winning.

Luca reined her horse in. "I will be quiet when all I have to say is said," she snapped. "First, your manners are disgusting. Second, your clothes are unworthy to serve as rugs, let alone touch my skin. Third… I'll think of a third once we're out of these woods. If we ever get out of here. Do you even know where we are going?"

From the corner of his eye, Rage saw Keiran trying to suppress a grin.

Rage nudged his horse on. The sunlight was playing tricks with his mind. He was having trouble seeing the path ahead, but he guessed they would soon cross the line where the Protection magic stopped working. Inside the magical ring, they were safe. Outside, anything could happen, which was a problem since he wasn't as alert as he should be due to his aching head.

The woods were thick and surprisingly dark. Anyone and anything could be hiding behind the huge trees or in the undergrowth, going unseen until it was too late. The girl was too upset to concentrate on anything except her own thoughts, trusting too much in the magic she had woven and ignoring the fact that sooner or later, her magic wouldn't be protecting them anymore.

Sighing, Rage rubbed a hand across his face, trying to get rid of the headache as well as his fatigue. Didn't work, of course. He was sick of arguing with her. All he wanted was for her to be quiet so he could listen to the sounds of the woods. He was also sick of his headache, which was making it hard to concentrate and harder to listen. As it stood, it was too easy to overlook an important clue or neglect to hear a sound that didn't belong in the woods.

The prospect of several more hours in her company—and the chirping birds and the sunlight and his empty stomach and, actually, everything—made his skull explode in raw, fresh pain.

Something hit him in the back. Rage had his knife out before he realized the girl had thrown a fir cone. "I'll kill you myself if you don't behave," he growled. He had a fleeting thought of his hands around her throat, strangling her until she ceased kicking.

Her green eyes were sparkling, and in her hand was a second cone. "You didn't answer my question concerning the direction. Do you know where this path will lead us? I really don't like my questions remaining unanswered. Besides, I've noticed you are practically ignoring Keiran. I don't like that either. You'd best behave yourself in his company."

A few deep breaths to calm himself down, and he bit out, "We're heading south. Remember to tell me when we are outside the Protection magic."

He knew he'd told her that before; he also suspected she tended to forget whatever she considered of no concern to her. Dropping the cone, Luca raised her chin and pulled herself up, spurring the horse on as if she were the empress herself.

"I will tell you the moment we cross the line, just as promised." When she was alongside Rage, she leaned closer and added, "You know, I think I know why you dislike Keiran. I think you've realized he prefers men and now you are disgusted."

Rage blinked.

"Ah. I can see the shock in your eyes. So I am right. Not only ugly and old, but small-minded too." She sadly shook her head. "Should have expected it. Truly, it is high time we went our separate ways. Riding with you is the worst experience I ever had in my life."

Rage was just about to slap her across her mouth when suddenly, a hard realization made it through the haze around his brain: he didn't hear the birds anymore. Out of the corner of his eye, he saw the boy nearly explode with suppressed laughter and the girl grin, and then the wind picked up and a branch broke just ahead of them, crashing to the ground and making the horses shy.

Knife in hand, Rage jumped off his mare and caught the harness of Luca's horse. "Quiet," he said, which earned him a kick in the head.

It was a strong blow, probably harder than she had intended. Rage crashed to the ground, blinded, the combined pain of his headache and the kick holding his brain tightly in its grip.

"Don't touch my horse, he's edgy enough without you scaring him. And it was just the wind." Luca took up the reins. "Come on, Keiran. He's an idiot, and—"

"Did we cross the line yet?" Rage managed to croak over the pain. He staggered back to his feet, swearing a silent oath to beat some manners into her once they were out of the woods.

"Actually, yes," she repeated. "We did so about three steps ago. I would have told you, but you insisted on scaring my horse instead. By the Lady, you're impatient!"

A second branch fell, and the mule kicked in panic. In a matter of seconds, the wind became a storm. Hailstones as big as eggs fell from a perfectly blue sky. One glanced off Luca's head, and she yelled, half in anger and surprise, half in pain. A moment later, another branch fell, hitting her just above the right ear. Like a rag doll, she dropped off her saddle, blood running down the side of her face. Unconscious, she didn't move, didn't cry, didn't even moan anymore.

"One down!" The words came from a cheerful voice, clearly audible above the storm.

"Hide!" Rage shouted, cursing the fact that someone had been waiting for them and that he'd missed it because of his fucking headache, his crippled magic, and the constantly babbling girl.

Too late to be sorry now. Rage rushed to Luca's side, Keiran jumped off his horse, and together, they dragged her behind a fallen log. Roots and broken branches reached out for him, scratching over his skin—he looked at the sky, watching as huge storm clouds gathered in seconds. The birds had gone dead quiet, and frozen leaves were drifting toward the equally frozen ground.

Whoever was behind this was used to wielding magic. A magician, most likely, and a strong one.

Fuck.

Keiran wrapped his hand around Rage's wrist, nodding toward the woods. *They're out there. More than one.* Rage had no reason to doubt him.

"Stay with her," he whispered into Keiran's ear. "And keep low."

Just as he was about to get up, a burning piece of wood flew through the storm and hit the mule straight in the throat. It gurgled, stumbled. Then it fell, legs kicking, braying loudly and annoyingly, screaming for help. Wide-eyed, foam dripping from its muzzle, it tried to get up as the flames began to eat away at its fur. It would burn to death, and they would be witness to it were they to live that long themselves.

The horses fled, saddles, bags, and all.

"Fuck," Rage muttered and threw his knife. It sank in the mule's left eye, killing it instantly.

Eerie laughter could be heard from the woods.

The hail ceased as quickly as it had started. Instead, a shower of stars rained down upon them from empty air. As soon as they made contact with a surface, they exploded. Several trees erupted into flames.

"More of those, Emmett," a voice called through the noise. "Burn them! Kill them!"

"There's two. One to the left and one straight ahead behind the bushes." Rage handed Keiran his second knife. "I'll try to get the one on the left. If they attack you, try and kill them."

New stars exploded, burning holes into the log they were hiding behind. Rage jumped up and ran, looking for another place to seek shelter. On the way, he snatched up his bag, which he must have dropped when the girl kicked him. He also still had the crossbow. Together with the bolts in his bag, he might be able to disable the attackers.

"Now, Emmett!" The voice was excited and definitely female. Her voice came from his left, so Rage changed direction just as an arrow caught him high in his leg. He struggled and cursed, but made it behind a bush before one of the exploding stars could hit and kill him.

"Two down, Mel!" another voice shouted, and that was the moment Rage saw movement to his left.

His target was behind the oak—"Emmett" according to the woman.

Blood ran down his leg, soaking the leather. The muscle trembled. Biting his lips and bracing himself against the pain, Rage broke off the shaft—there might be hooks on the arrowhead, and he couldn't risk just pulling it out. Next, he took out his belt and fastened it tightly just above the wound. It hurt, and he knew he would need to tend to it soon or he would lose too much blood.

Barely lunchtime, and I am totally sick of this day.

Dropping on all fours, he crawled along until his leg gave way. Rolling to his side, he clamped his hands around his thigh, sweating and trembling and, for a long while, blind to his surroundings.

Neither Mel nor Emmett came to finish him off. Keiran and Luca were silent, still behind the log.

Prying his fingers off his leg, Rage managed to roll onto his stomach and crawl on toward the bushes where he suspected

Emmett to be. Then right in front of him, he saw a patch of brown that didn't quite match the brown of the trees.

A coat.

Silently, he put a bolt into the crossbow, all the while feeling his injured leg going colder and number with every beat of his heart.

It dawned on him that the arrowhead had probably been poisoned.

Emmett's head emerged, looking toward the place Rage assumed Mel was, and in his hand was a bag full of exploding stars. Just as he was about to free them, Rage lifted his crossbow and pulled the trigger.

"Mel, I'll light the re—" Emmett began, and then Rage's bolt connected with the base of his neck. The bag dropped to the ground. The stars spilled over the ground, unlit, harmless.

Another few feet, just a few more, and Rage was next to the man, putting a bloodied hand on his pulse. There was none. Rage sighed with relief. Only one more to deal with.

They must have followed the boy after all, Rage thought, gritting his teeth as the broken shaft sticking out of his leg scratched along the ground with every move he made.

"Emmett?" the woman called.

The storm receded. Apparently, the two of them were a pair, their magic strong only if they were both alive and feeding it. Now that the man was dead, it should be easier to take out the woman too.

Rage turned the dead man onto his back. He looked around seventy judging by the wrinkles on his dirty face. The man's mouth hung agape in deathly agony, and strangely enough, he looked like a kind grandfather—except that his hands were covered in magical tattoos so he could handle the power he launched with his tools.

"Emmett! What's up, you old fool? We need to finish this, or they'll get away!"

The woman became careless. Her high-pitched voice indicated that she didn't like Emmett not answering. When Rage peeked through the bushes, he could see the log behind which Keiran and the girl were hiding. It was burning, but not badly enough to force them to leave their shelter No more stars were to be seen. Emmett must have been the only one able to throw them.

Vaguely, Rage wondered what the woman's specialty was. His leg was trembling badly now. There was no time for idle pondering. Determined, he put the second bolt into the crossbow and pulled himself up into a sitting position. He wasn't able to crawl much farther. Before he could reach her, blood loss and the arrow's poison would get the better of him. And the woman was already suspicious because of her partner's silence.

Maybe he could use that.

"Mel?" Rage called. His hands were sweaty. His head, only minutes before throbbing badly, felt light and cotton filled. "I suggest you surrender. I've got your pal here. Doesn't look well. Let's see who you are, and I might consider not killing you too slowly."

Nothing but silence answered him.

Rage picked up one of the dead stars and threw it into the clearing. It landed with a soft thump between the hailstones.

"Emmett!" The shrill shriek indicated that Mel now believed something had indeed happened to her partner. "If you hurt him, if you so much as pull out a single hair from his head—"

"You'll do what?" Rage said, more to himself than to her. "You'll kill us? You've already tried that."

"You'll all die!" the woman screamed. Like a jack-in-the-box, she jumped up, hair flying, wide, gray clothes flapping like the wings of a huge, clumsy bird. Unintelligible words pierced the too cold air. Rage tried to shoot her but missed—she was too fast, running toward Keiran's hiding place, arms raised and eyes burning with hate. "Die, all of you! Die a nasty death, just *die!*"

She jumped, and Rage was too far away to do anything about it. Keiran and the girl would be dead within seconds.

And all he could do was watch because his damn leg wouldn't carry him and because there was zero chance he could take her out with the crossbow at this distance.

The boy caught her in midair. His hands wrapped around her twig-like arms and threw her away as if she didn't weigh more than a bird.

Mel cackled. By rights, she should have had broken bones, at the very least have been unconscious. But she wasn't. With a wave, she tried to call back the fading storm, but somehow, the wind wouldn't obey her orders. Outraged and worried, with a well-trained gesture, she pulled something out of her clothes and threw it at Keiran.

"Fuck," Rage muttered, fighting to get up. He leaned heavily against a tree and saw that the boy went down with a silent scream.

If she's smart, she'll pull a knife and cut his throat.

But she didn't. Instead, she turned and headed carelessly in his direction, toward her dead partner. She didn't even bother to seek cover behind bushes or trees. She didn't look left or right, and she didn't see him hiding, crossbow cocked.

Patiently, not once taking his eyes off the running woman, Rage waited until she was close enough. With considerable effort, he kept his shaking hands under control and then plunged the last bolt into her heart. She fell not ten feet from her partner.

The last bit of the storm dissipated for good at the same time her heart stopped beating.

The pain in Rage's leg doubled when he tried to take a step, but he forced it into service nevertheless. He tossed the crossbow to the ground in order to steady himself on every tree in his reach, but he was still exceptionally and frustratingly slow.

"Keiran!"

Damn, his voice wasn't usually that weak. The boy couldn't answer anyway, regardless of whether he was alive or not. Rage scanned the area, but the boy was nowhere to be seen, leading him to the conclusion that he was flat on his back, injured or dead.

Cursing, Rage fought the dizziness trying to claim his too sluggish brain. He couldn't feel his leg anymore, which made the pain more bearable. On the other hand, walking with seemingly only one leg was quite difficult, and by the Lady, how far away was that fucking log?

A hand suddenly appeared on the bark of the log, fingers outstretched as if seeking help. Keiran's head followed. He was pale, his eyes wide with pain. His other hand was clutched around his upper left arm. Smoke emerged from between his fingers.

Rage crossed the remaining distance with a few strides, ignoring his leg as much as he could. The ground had turned slippery now that the witch and the wizard were dead. Melting ice soaked the earth, and even if Rage hadn't been wounded, it wouldn't have been easy to walk across it. When he passed the dead mule, he bent and pulled his knife out of the beast's skull, wiping it clean on his shirt.

Finally, he reached the fallen tree and sat down heavily, Keiran kneeling in front of him. The boy's knuckles were white, he clutched his arm so hard.

"Let me see," Rage said much more calmly than he felt. "If it had been one of the stars, it would have exploded already, and you'd be dead. So she must have used something else."

It felt like ages before Keiran loosened his grip.

Using his knife, Rage cut open the shirtsleeve from wrist to shoulder. Goosebumps appeared on the boy's skin, and he inhaled sharply when Rage touched him, wrapping his fingers tightly right above the elbow.

There was a hole in Keiran's arm roughly as big as a copper coin. Deep and black. No blood, only a clear liquid oozing out of the wound.

Rage was about to say "not too bad," when he saw something moving away from the hole toward the boy's shoulder. It was small, a lump no bigger than a sparrow's egg. It moved slowly but steadily.

Keiran's eyes were focused on the lump, his lips pressed tightly together. His injured arm hung limply at his side, and his forehead was covered with a thin film of sweat.

Rage knew exactly how he felt.

"I don't know what this is, but I will cut it out," he said and added, "You'll be fine. Those who attacked us are dead, and we'll be out of here in no time. Think of the nice meal and warm bed that awaits us once I manage to get the horses back."

For the first time since the attack, Keiran smiled. It was a shaky, slightly lopsided smile, but it gave Rage some hope they might all survive their encounter with the magicians.

Circling his fingers tightly just above the lump, Rage lifted his knife, aimed, and stabbed it deeply into Keiran's flesh.

A scream, high-pitched and unearthly, nearly made him drop the knife. But it wasn't the boy who'd made the noise. Keiran looked paler than ever, watching the blood running down his elbow.

The scream had come from the thing underneath his skin. It fought against the knife, but Rage had no intention of letting it live. He pulled the knife out and stabbed it again before cutting it out completely.

Luckily, the thing didn't resist anymore. When Rage dug the blade underneath it, the two halves of the lump slipped out and landed in the mud between the two men. It looked like a broken shell. Here and there, a soft shimmer like mother-of-pearl could be seen.

Rage was just about to step on it when it exploded. It didn't make a big sound, but it stank, and the flames licked at their shoes and clothes. Rage suspected that had the shell still been in one piece, it might have killed both of them.

With sudden force, the pain from his own wound returned, pounding through Rage's leg and sending waves of agony through his spine up to the base of his neck where it woke his headache. Squeezing his eyes shut, Rage winced, but they couldn't linger here any longer. They needed to get out of these woods as fast as possible and find shelter, given all three of them were injured.

Great. Less than ten minutes ago, he'd been arguing with the girl, cursing his decision to take her along. Now, he wondered if she'd still be alive by nightfall. He didn't want the girl to die, today even less than when he'd kidnapped her. Now she was his responsibility.

Swiftly, he undid the buttons of the too big shirt she was wearing, revealing her throat, shoulders, and the top of her small breasts, so he might figure out what was wrong with her before he lifted her up.

Keiran caught Rage's attention by snapping his fingers. The dry little sound said, *She's broken a bone*, so the assassin checked her jaw, neck, and shoulder joints.

Then he saw it. The left collarbone was not as straight as it should be, and when he traced it, the girl moaned with pain.

There wasn't much he could do but steady the broken joint, so he ripped off the sleeve of her shirt and bound her arm tightly to her body. Eventually, she'd need a proper healer. For now, it had to do.

Had he really thought the day couldn't get worse?

A shrill sound made him jump. Keiran, two fingers in his mouth, was calling the horses. If they were really lucky, they hadn't run too far and would still able to hear the boy's whistle.

Standing wasn't easy, but Rage had no choice. "Help me with the girl," he said to Keiran, who was swaying gently himself. "I can't lift her onto the horse on my own, should the damn beasts turn up at all. Which of the horses is stronger? Mine?"

The boy frowned and shook his head.

"Yours, then. Can you ride? Because I will ride with her, keeping her upright. We'll take your horse, and you mine."

The sound of hooves, hesitantly getting closer, magicked a smile on Keiran's winter-pale lips. Like Rage, he was bleeding, though not as heavily.

The assassin tightened the belt around his leg with gritted teeth. Impossible to cut out the arrowhead himself with his shaking hands and his hazy head. And impossible to do anything about the poison since neither he nor Keiran could wield magic. He knew that if a healer didn't take care of the wound soon, he might lose his leg or even die. Right now, all he could do was prevent the loss of more blood.

A soft neigh in his ear and warm breath on his cheek. Apparently the horses weren't bothered by the coppery smell of blood. Together, Rage and Keiran lifted the girl into the saddle.

Keiran made sure she didn't slip to the ground until Rage had wrapped one arm around the girl's waist. Her head lolled helplessly.

"A meal and a warm bed. I promise," Rage managed to say, picking up the reins. "Follow me. Coldwell can't be that far away." He didn't want to die in these woods, nor did he want to leave the kids behind in order to more quickly get to safety himself.

Had he bothered to think about it, he might have realized how much his priorities had changed in the past few days.

CHAPTER
Six

GETTING OUT of the woods took hours, during which the girl stayed mostly unconscious. If Rage hadn't kept an arm wrapped tightly around her waist, they would have both slipped off the horse.

At regular intervals, he loosened the belt around his leg to prevent the muscles and nerves from dying. He didn't want to lose his leg if he could help it—it would put him out of business. Without the possibility of earning his living, he might as well lie down and die here and now.

Each time he opened the belt to allow the blood to reach his toes, he feared it was one time too many. He did it nevertheless. And he hoped by losing blood, the poison he could feel creeping through his veins would lose its strength as well.

It was late afternoon, and Coldwell was another hour away, or more likely two given the horses' slow trot. Not even the sun bothered to come out, hiding behind clouds that hadn't been there in the morning. It was colder than last night, and when Rage rubbed his palm across the bloody, slippery leather of his trousers, he could feel the frost creeping into his bones.

Fuck.

Keiran wasn't faring much better. His hand was clutched tightly around his arm, his teeth pressed together, and he was sweating with pain.

When they finally emerged from the woods, Rage thought for a moment that night had fallen before he realized he was close to unconsciousness.

He needed help if they were to actually reach the town. "Take the reins of my horse," he told the boy, who looked at him in surprise. "Make sure we reach Coldwell. It's behind that hill, no more than two miles. Can you do that?"

Keiran took the reins out of Rage's numb fingers and briefly brushed the palm of his hand over the assassin's dirty, stubbly face as if to reassure him that yes, he could do it and yes, they would survive.

Rage sighed and relaxed. He wasn't responsible anymore. Keeping his eyes open was hard enough. Leading the way had become impossible. Luckily, the boy seemed more awake than he looked.

The soft trot of his horse made him sleepy, and he shivered with cold and probably an oncoming fever. His head hurt, still or again, he couldn't even tell. With each step the horse took, the movement went up his spine and exploded behind his closed eyes. In a way, it was reassuring—as long as he was in pain, at least he wasn't dead.

Smoke in his nose; the smell of burned food. Noise faint in the distance. The eerie feeling of being watched.

More attackers? Danger? Death?

No, just some children playing on a dirty road, screaming and yelling like children do when adults aren't around.

The sight of houses and people and the smell of food, burned or not, sent some strength into his body, and Rage took the reins back from Keiran. In a town like this, it wouldn't be good to show weakness, no matter how lousy he felt.

"Coldwell," he croaked. "Haven't been here in ages. Would have headed for Carrock had I had the choice, but this town was closer. And it's bigger. Now all we have to do is find a harborage."

He headed for the part of Coldwell called the Shadows. Thieves lived there and beggars, the poor folk, and the whores. They would be safe, at least for today.

"See the river? That's where we are going. Stay close to me, and don't look up even when you are addressed. The people living in the Shadows don't like strangers."

Keiran nodded. He didn't look happy, though.

Rage managed to curve his lips into a humorless grin. It felt like someone else was doing it. He'd lost contact with his own body, maneuvering his limbs as if he were a puppet master and his body a stubborn, disobeying doll.

"The people living in the Shadows will know what I am, Keiran. They won't dare to turn us down, no matter how bad we look."

Once more, Keiran nodded. When Rage nudged his horse on, he followed.

There weren't as many taverns that offered beds as he would have hoped. Two landlords shook their heads when he asked for a bed for the night, explaining they only sold beer, not shelter.

"Damn," Rage muttered and only vaguely felt Keiran next to him, steadying him on the horse's back by putting a hand on his shoulder when he swayed.

At the third tavern they approached, Rage didn't take chances. He was beyond tired, and his leg hurt badly enough for him to wish someone would just cut it off. All he wanted was a bed so he could lie down and pass out.

"Stay with the girl," he said, or at least hoped he said it— somehow, he couldn't hear his own voice anymore. He slipped off the horse and promptly fell.

Great.

The girl slumped forward, and only because of Keiran, she didn't hit the ground as well.

No way to take care of her now. First the landlord, then rest.

Scrambling back onto his feet, Rage limped around the building. The tavern was small and askew, with shingles missing from the roof and a broken window, and it would surely have a back door. His injured leg didn't want to support his weight, but he forced it into service and prayed to the Lady he wouldn't fall again. The back door stood ajar, and a look inside confirmed that he'd found the kitchen and with it the woman who ran the tavern. It was most unlikely she had beds to rent. The way he felt, he would sleep in hers if he had to.

The woman stood bent over a pot, stirring and cursing at the same time. Her hair, neglectfully wound into a bun and pinned to the back of her head, was a dirty brown. Loose strands hung dangerously close to the soup she was cooking.

To Rage, whatever was in the pot smelled delightful.

Ignoring his growling stomach, he pushed the door open and stepped into the kitchen, leaving bloody footprints on the already dirty floor. The hand that held his knife shook, but even half-unconscious she didn't stand a chance against him. The knife was at the woman's throat before she knew anyone was there, the blade cutting her skin. Rage wasn't in the mood for a lengthy discussion.

"You own this place?" he croaked into her ear, pressing against her back with one hand on her shoulder so he wouldn't collapse before he finished his business.

Her body stiffened. She smelled of beer and fish. "What do you want?"

This one wasn't easy to scare.

"A room for the night and food for me and my friends."

"You could have asked nicely. I don't have beds to rent, and even if I did, I wouldn't rent to people with knives. Not to people who put their knives to my throat, anyway."

Rage knew she was thinking about fighting him, so he cut her deeper—not much, just enough to keep her still. Had she fought him, she would have won. As it was, she froze midmotion, snarling like an angry old cat.

"I need a bed," he bit out. "Now."

Slowly, the landlady began stirring her soup again. Had someone been watching them from outside, he might have mistaken them for a couple, as close as they stood.

"Can you pay?" she asked. "Ten pennies, food extra."

Her spoon banged against the sides of the pot; the sound caused stars to explode in front of his eyes, making him lose hold of the woman's shoulder.

Quick as the wind, she spun around and pushed him away, sending him flying halfway through the kitchen. Unable to keep his balance, his injured leg gave way, and he crashed hard onto the dirty floor.

The woman grabbed a bread knife and came closer, towering above him. "You look like shit," she stated. "The blood on your clothes—is it yours?" Swiftly, she bent and snatched the purse from his fingers. He couldn't even remember taking it out of his bag.

"You're dead if you try to betray me, woman," Rage managed to say, once more fighting to get back on his feet. It wasn't easy. It took him a moment to realize the floor was slippery, not only from dirt and some fish guts but also from his own blood.

She snorted. "The name is Lindsay," she said, opening his purse and rummaging through its contents. "Yeah, definitely your blood. And you have money enough for food and a bed. That's all that counts for me, assassin. You are an assassin, yes? I mean, I haven't seen many of you around, but the clothes and the tattoo sort of give you away."

"Of course," Rage bit out. Pressing one hand to the ground and one to the wall, he wondered if he would ever manage to get back on his feet when Lindsay hauled him up and placed him on a stool.

"Are you alone?" Lindsay asked. "More importantly, is the one who hurt you still alive and on your trail?"

Tiny stars in front of his eyes; a whooshing noise in his ears. Not much longer and sitting wouldn't be an option for him anymore. "Two more up front." He wondered whether he had said it aloud. "All injured. You sell Healing magic?"

Wiping her hands clean—or as clean as possible given that her apron was as dirty as the floor—she counted out thirty pennies and five extra for the food. "Healing magic? Nah, pal, not me. But down the road you can find Teddy, the thief. He's good. But why not do it yourself? The money in your purse doesn't cover for no magic."

Rage shot her a look. "Does it look like I'm able to do anything but breathe, woman?" he hissed, not wanting to admit that he was unable to perform even the most basic magic.

"Sure, you look more dead than alive to me," Lindsay mused and put the coins into one of the inner pockets of her many skirts. "Three, then. There's the attic. Not big, and as I said, I usually don't rent out, but in your case…. Ben! Mike! Come here, you useless lads!"

Alarmed, Rage tried to get up, but Lindsay put a hand on his shoulder, holding him down as easily as if he were a three-year-old child. "My sons. They will help you upstairs, and your friends too. I took your money. You are my guest. I will make sure you get the bed you paid for and the food too. Though you don't look as if you need any food. You look as if you could do with an undertaker instead."

Rage bared his teeth in an attempt to give a scary grin. "I'm not dead yet," he rasped and finally managed to get back onto his feet. His knife dropped from his shaking hands. "Can one of your boys cut out an arrow?"

Lindsay nodded knowingly. "So that's where all the blood's coming from. Sure, Mike is good with knives. He'll have the thing out of your leg in no time."

Rage closed his eyes in despair at the thought of some brute getting close to his leg. "Lovely," he said as the boys stormed into the kitchen, all noise and light and unpleasant smells. One caught him, preventing him from falling for the third time in ten minutes. Rage watched as the other one went over to his mother, towering above her. She was small despite her strong hands and wide hips. She gave him orders. Rage could hear her talking but couldn't make out any words.

What the hell. The boy to his side was tall too, and strong on top of it. Strong enough to help him upstairs, strong enough not to stumble when Rage nearly fell backward down the steps.

"You Mike?" Rage asked, not really remembering why he wanted to know. Only that... someone... was supposed to do something for him.

"Mike's my little brother. I'm Ben," the man said in a low voice. He pushed open a door, keeping his grip on Rage's arm easily. "Mike is getting your pals. One's slipped off the horse. She sick or what? And in one of the bags is a cat. Too small to be eaten."

"She'll rip your heads off if you touch the cat," Rage mumbled and struggled against the younger man's grip.

A bed. Sunlight. Warmth. Rage didn't care about anyone else but himself anymore, just stumbled forward and fell, face first, onto a surprisingly soft mattress. It didn't smell bad, either, which was good, or he would have thrown up. Or tried to—his stomach was far too empty for his liking.

Sound drifted away and came back, at least gradually. It was noise, really—people trampling around, voices giving orders—and Rage wanted to shout at them, tell them to be quiet, only to find that nothing but a soft moan emerged from his lips.

"Turn him onto his side, Ben," Rage heard someone say and felt hands on his shoulders, rolling him around. Hands on his chest, opening buttons, undressing him. Weakly, he tried to kick them away, but someone laughed and held him down, easily, carefully.

"Shit, that's a nasty wound. Got the knife, Mom?"

What do you need a knife for? Rage wanted to ask, and *Why am I naked?* But then the pain increased, shooting up his spine and down to his ankle, radiating from one small, burning point high on his leg. He heard someone scream, deep and harsh, and wondered if it was him.

"It's poisoned, Mom. That arrow, it's out now, but he'll die anyway. He needs more than the bit of magic I can do."

Knew it.

"You did a good job on him. Ben, get me some soup. What about the girl and the boy?"

Whispers. Quiet discussions. Rage wished he could understand more, but for that, he would need to wake up fully, and he really, really didn't want to do that. Half-unconscious was, in his opinion, not a bad state at all.

His leg felt as if they'd cut it off after all, not merely taken out a rather small arrowhead. How would he be able to climb walls with only one leg?

But he wasn't alone. He had taken on a responsibility when he kidnapped the girl, and he had promised them both a warm bed and food for the night. Drifting off to dreamland only because he'd been shot wasn't an option. They were injured; they needed Healing magic.

And anyway, hadn't someone said he'd been poisoned?

His eyelids were heavy as lead, but Rage managed to force them open anyway. The sunlight was red and golden, which meant that night wasn't too far away.

Where had the day gone? And the afternoon?

His throat was dry like the desert; apparently, he had been unconscious for a while. "Water," he croaked.

"We awake, then?" Lindsay asked, helping him into a half-sitting position. "Fine, that means you can drink some soup. Will get you back on your feet, at least for a little while. Bit of magic in it. And Ben, get some of your trousers until I've washed and mended his. Don't want to have him sitting around naked with those kids in the same room and all."

A large mug was pressed into his hands. It was warm, and the smell of its contents was not unpleasant. Rage took a sip, only to feel as though he had drunk liquid fire. He coughed, and Lindsay took the mug back so he wouldn't spill the soup all over the bed. With watering eyes, he asked, "What the hell is that?"

"Lindsay's Best Health Soup," the landlady replied proudly, patting his back. "Drink it all. Will take care of the blood loss and some of the pain too."

"It will burn my insides to ashes," Rage wheezed, and Lindsay laughed before urging him on to empty the mug in one go.

When he'd stopped coughing and cursing, he actually felt better. The dizziness was mostly gone, and he could move the toes of his injured leg without yelling in pain. Finally, he was able to examine his surroundings.

He was in a small room in the attic of Lindsay's tavern. The walls and roof were made of wood, there was only one window, and the door led to a narrow, steep staircase. One big bed was in the middle of the room and a small one was pushed against the wall.

Keiran sat on the only chair, looking like a three-day-old corpse. His eyes weren't able to focus anymore, and his mouth stood slightly agape, as if he was having trouble breathing. His shirt hung over the back of the chair, and the wound on his arm was covered by a bandage.

"Keiran," Rage said, trying to get his attention, but he didn't react.

Damn.

The girl lay on the smaller bed, still unconscious. "Concussion, that one," Mike said, his hand on her throat to check her pulse. "I mended the broken collarbone. That's about all I can do for her. She'll come round, I guess. But your friend"—he nodded toward Keiran—"is beyond my skills. Was it a beetle that caused his wound?"

Sitting wasn't that bad, Rage decided and held out his hand. It was shaking only slightly. "Beetle?" he asked, looking at Mike with a frown. "No, it was something magical. Small, shaped like a shell.

It moved underneath his skin. Cut it to pieces. Exploded once it was out. Purple flames, and it stank."

Mike nodded. "A beetle. They crawl towards the heart of their victims. Nasty death, I say. Good you got the thing out, but he still needs Healing magic. The wound won't close on its own. He'll bleed to death without help. And you, you're as good as dead too. The arrow's poisoned." Sympathetically, he patted Rage's shoulder, eyed the assassin's knife that lay on the windowsill with one last, longing glance, and left the room, pulling his brother with him.

"And I thought nothing could be worse than being stuck with a spoiled little brat like her." Rage's head hurt still—no surprise there—and his stomach clenched at the prospect of another sip of soup, so he put the mug aside, pulled the bedsheet around his waist, and got up. Lindsay was watching him, her arms crossed over her chest.

"What you think you're doing?" she asked as he fished around for the rough linen trousers Ben had found for him. There was no other choice but to drop the bedsheet in order to get his legs inside, but then, it was unlikely that the landlady would be dreadfully shocked by the sight of his naked ass.

"Getting dressed."

"I can see that," Lindsay snapped, reaching out to steady the assassin when he swayed. "What for?"

"Teddy, the thief." It was hard to talk and fasten the buttons of the trousers at the same time. They were far too big for him. His belt was somewhere on the floor, so the rope Ben had left together with the trousers would have to do. At least all his knives were in perfect condition, so he stored them in their usual place and headed for the door.

Which was blocked by Lindsay. "You're not going anywhere. You paid me for a bed and food, not for letting you kill yourself."

"I'll die in your bed if I can't persuade Teddy to sell me some Healing magic. So will the boy." Grabbing Keiran by the shoulders, Rage hauled him up and pushed him toward the big bed, coming to the conclusion that the boy would be better off lying down. It was frighteningly easy—Keiran was a grown man, and it shouldn't be that easy to get him in the bed, especially when the one putting him there was anything but healthy and strong and was balancing on one leg.

As soon as Keiran hit the pillow, his eyes dropped closed and his muscles went limp. The hand that had been clutching the wounded arm dropped to the mattress.

At least the girl didn't look like she would die anytime soon. She was fast asleep, obviously already profiting from Mike's sparse abilities in healing.

"You won't even make it down the street," Lindsay said but stepped aside to let him past.

"Don't underestimate me." With gritted teeth, Rage got downstairs, putting as little weight on his injured leg as possible. "Although I wish you could get what I need."

Lindsay snorted, having followed him down the stairs. "As if I run errands for my guests. Anyway, you don't have enough money to buy Healing magic. You'll need to make a deal with Teddy. That's something I can't do for you." She sighed, watching with her arms crossed over her bosom as Rage swayed past her. "Take this at least, stupid," she called after him, rummaging in her apron. "Here. One at a time. Suck them slowly. They will take the pain away." Taking the small bag, Rage saw what looked like three tiny, brownish pieces of candy inside.

He raised an eyebrow. "You think drugging me is a good idea?"

Lindsay grinned, showing the gaps in her teeth. "Not just drugs, assassin. Medicine. It'll keep your head clear and the pain at bay. Won't work forever, though. Be back here by midnight if you plan on sleeping in your own bed instead of the gutter."

For the first time since they'd been attacked, Rage checked the color of the bracelet he wore around his wrist. Usually, it was as black as his eyes, giving visible proof that he was neither injured nor ill, but the color had changed. Instead of black, it was a sickly yellow-green—the color of poisoning.

Fuck.

Not having a choice, Rage took one of the small candies and put it on his tongue. It had a bitter, almost burning taste, but it numbed his tongue instantly and the pain in his leg lost most of its bite. Tentatively, he put some weight on it and carefully took a step.

It worked.

"Thanks," Rage said and made his way down the street to find Teddy the thief.

COLDWELL WAS, though not a small town, nothing compared to the empress's city. The houses were mostly made of wood, not stone. The stables were small, and the beasts stocky and strong rather than tall and beautiful. It was a farmers' town, the river running through it separating it into a rich half and a poor half. The town was surrounded by endless acres of fields. The streets weren't too muddy, considering that not many chariots came to Coldwell for business. The people here were happy if no one bothered them, especially the empress's soldiers. A stranger was easily spotted.

Rage knew he was being watched, and he could feel his presence was unwelcome. An assassin was rarely needed in a town like Coldwell, the people tending to kill in passion rather than cold-blooded calculation. Rage might have managed to get some jobs, but they'd be small ones, consisting of threats and torture rather than a clean murder.

He hated torturing his victims, which was why he usually avoided towns like Coldwell.

Teddy the thief lived about ten houses down from Lindsay's tavern, and had the landlady not described his hut in detail, Rage would have overlooked it. It was small and resembled a shed more than a house. The shutters were already closed, as if to keep the night away together with unwanted visitors, and there was no answer when Rage knocked.

"I'll set fire to the whole damn city if you don't let me in," Rage barked. "My week started bad, my day was a nightmare, I've been shot and had to drink some awful soup, and I am truly in no mood for this shit. Open up, Teddy. Last warning."

A creak, and a bright blue eye peeked through the gap. "It's Theodore. And I don't do business with assassins."

Before the man could close the door again, Rage shoved his foot in the gap and pushed hard. The door flew open, the sound of crashing pots indicating the man had landed hard among his belongings.

"You will make an exception today," he growled as, from out of nowhere, pain shot up his leg, making him stumble into the thief's hut. Rage quickly put a second pill into his mouth. This time, however, it didn't work as fast or as thoroughly. "I need Healing magic. For myself and a friend of mine who's been hit by a beetle. Can you do it, and how much do you charge?"

The small, slender man got up from the floor, brushing off shards of broken pottery. His sandy brown hair fell into his face, covering slightly protruding eyes that made him look like an overgrown frog. Every now and then, he rubbed his palm across his nose—a tick he couldn't control and which made Rage wish he could bind the man to a chair only to keep his hands still.

"I don't do Healing magic," the thief said.

"Lindsay says otherwise. I'll pay whatever you charge, but I need it now."

Instantly, the man's behavior changed. He became all businesslike, whipped some books off a chair, and told Rage to take a seat. "Lindsay sent you? Why didn't you say so! You have money?" he asked eagerly. "Good woman, Lindsay. Always thinks of me, she does. Times have been bad, recently. Not much business going on. What sort of Healing magic are we talking about? I can give you something that heals wounds cast by a beetle, but only if the one injured is still alive. Takes a better magician than me to bring people back from the dead. And what about you? I mean, you are still alive, yes? It's hard to tell, pardon my frankness. What's wrong with you?"

A small glass appeared in his hand, a bottle in the other. He filled the glass up to the rim and offered it to the assassin. "Homemade," he said proudly. "Apart from organizing whatever is needed, this is the other part of my business. The empress's soldiers don't approve of it, of course. Drink it. Will warm you up, I promise."

Overwhelmed by the sudden outburst, Rage accepted the offered glass and sniffed. His eyes immediately began to water, and he put it down onto the table, amidst coins, parchment, quills, inkpots, and dead snakes. "I am grateful for the offer," he said, "but I don't dare drink it. I was shot. Poisoned arrow. Lindsay's boy cut it out but said I'll die if the wound isn't healed properly. Can't do magic myself. Here—" He found the arrowhead in his trouser pocket and threw it onto the table. "That's the thing that hit me."

The thief narrowed his eyes, then put on some gloves and picked up the small piece of metal. With a magnifying glass, he examined it, his eyes huge behind the lens. For a while not a sound was heard in the small, cluttered hut but the breathing of the two men.

Finally, Theodore lifted his head. "Nasty magic, this is," he said. "I can give you something that will cure you, though. Will cost you seven and a half Talents. The Healing magic for your friend is included. Beetle wounds, phew, a baby could heal them. Will take a day at the most before he's as good as new." Wiping his hair out of his face, he handed the arrowhead back to Rage.

"I don't have seven and a half Talents. Actually, I have no more than thirty-four pennies left."

Magnifying glass still in hand, the thief stared at him, disbelief and disappointment written all over his face. "How much did you say you have?"

"Thirty-four pennies," Rage repeated tiredly. The second pill had already lost its effect. He'd need the third pill soon, and he didn't dare think what would happen if he wasn't in bed when the last one stopped working too.

Actually, he should get up and shake some sense into the small man. Except he knew he couldn't. Even crushing a grape would be asking too much of him.

Rage pinched the top of his nose. He was about to do something he rarely did, and he hated having to do it now. But if he didn't, he was dead. Not much of a choice.

"If you sell me the Healing magic, I will owe you a favor," he bit out. "I'll give you the money I have, and I'll do whatever you ask of me once I'm better. You have my word on it." Opening the leather pouch he kept his money in, he let the contents fall onto Theodore's table. One coin spun and rolled toward the edge, landing on the floor after a slight hesitation. Rage didn't bother to pick it up.

Theodore's eyes widened, and his mouth sagged open. "I could ask you to kill the empress, and you would have to do it now that you have given your word."

"I know."

"A favor?" the thief repeated, trying to clarify the matter. "As in… a favor?"

"I would appreciate if you could tell me beforehand what sort of favor you want in exchange for the magic, but yes. A favor as in a favor."

Was it dark outside already? The sun had been up when he'd left Lindsay's tavern. There should be daylight, not darkness, in front of the window. When he put his hand on his leg, his fingers turned red from fresh blood welling from the wound.

"Make your decision, thief," Rage managed to say. He was—though slowly—on the way to the door, popping the third pill into his mouth. When had he gotten up? How did he manage to walk? His leg burned, pain shooting down to his ankle as well as up to his neck. He would be lucky to make his way back to the tavern. Apparently, Lindsay's warning about falling unconscious in the gutter hadn't been an understatement.

"A goat!" the thief called after him. "Can you steal a goat for me once you are well again? Not any goat, of course. I can steal goats myself whenever I like. I want a prize goat from our beloved empress! Can you do it? I know it's nothing special, and you wouldn't have to do any killing, but—can you do it? My little girl would get a chance to become something other than a whore were I to have a prize goat that I could use to raise prize lambs which would get my little girl a decent bit of cash!" Eagerly, he followed after the assassin, tugging at his sleeve. "Here. Take this. In the phial, there's a potion. It'll fight the poison in your system. And the salve is for your friend's injury. I take your word and the coins on the table. I take your favor instead of the seven and a half Talents. Deal?"

A goat. Rage frowned, momentarily wondering what a goat actually looked like.

There was no choice anymore; there was no time left. "Deal." Not caring anymore whether he was supposed to steal a stupid animal or murder the empress herself, Rage held out his hand. It was, like the rest of him, shaking, but Teddy grabbed it and shook it enthusiastically.

Theodore had put the salve and phial into a little bag, which Rage nearly dropped. If the thief hadn't caught it and thrust it—more firmly this time—at him, it would have landed on the floor.

"You ought to take the medicine soon," Teddy said, worry clearly showing in his voice. "You cannot steal goats if you are dead."

The thief opened the door. Cool night air embraced him. A few stars sparkled, but neither Arwen nor Galadriel were to be seen in the night sky. It was earlier than he'd thought—midnight was hours away.

Good news, for a change.

Good news also that two men were waiting for him outside Teddy's hut, two men who seemed vaguely familiar, though Rage couldn't quite place their faces. They were both tall, they both stank of fish, and the smaller one had no front teeth.

"Mike," the taller one said. "Remember me? Mom said to get you home."

Right, Mike....

Who was Mike?

"Take his feet, Ben." Mike sighed when Rage collapsed into his arms. "We'll have to carry him. Mom will break our necks if we come back home without him."

No one carries me, Rage thought, and then, *Seems midnight was a bit of an exaggerated guess,* before the night became even darker and he didn't think anymore.

CHAPTER
Seven

LATE AT night or early in the morning? Rage didn't know and didn't care. Pale green moonlight shone through the window next to the bed, making shadows dance through the small attic room, hiding under beds and behind curtains and playing tricks on one's mind.

Rage was awake, but just barely. It was a state between sleep and wakefulness, and he was too exhausted to so much as think about it. He didn't ache anymore, which was good, but he was very thirsty, which was bad. His tongue was sticking to the roof of his mouth, and after a while it bothered him enough to make him wake up fully and open his eyes to the darkness.

For a long time, he watched the dancing shadows and tried to figure out where, exactly, he was and what had happened for him to end up in a bed.

Ah, yes. The arrow. The magicians. Teddy, the thief.

Goats.

Carefully, Rage tried to wiggle his toes.

Bearable. Just.

A single candle stood on the windowsill, flickering in a breeze that had made its way through a gap in the wall. It looked like he'd been asleep for only a few hours, given that it was still night. As little sleep as he'd had, he felt surprisingly well. Apparently, the little thief's magic had been worth the price.

Pondering on it for a while, Rage tried to remember what exactly they had agreed upon as his eyes roamed the dimly lit room.

Eventually, he sat up just enough to be able to see out of the small window.

Shouldn't it be another few days until the full moon?

Rage rubbed the sleep out of his eyes and as he did so, checked the bracelet on his wrist. It was as black as it should be, thanks to the Lady and a very effective antidote to the arrow's poison.

His stomach growled furiously. Trying to think when last he ate, he failed to recall anything but a bit of bread and cheese and Lindsay's horrible soup. Given how very hungry he was—and thirsty—it was unlikely that he'd been asleep for just a few hours.

Where was everyone else anyway?

Checking the bed, just in case he'd overlooked a full-grown man lying next to him, Rage finally had no choice but to accept one of two conclusions: either Keiran wasn't resting next to him because he was dead and buried, or he was up and about, which meant Rage had slept far longer than he'd first believed.

Will take a day at the most before he's as good as new, Rage heard the thief's voice say in his head, and refused to believe Keiran had died.

Footsteps on the stairs—they creaked horribly, and Rage couldn't believe he'd slept through that noise until now. When the door opened, he prepared to see Lindsay or one of her sons. He forced the frown off his face and swore a silent oath to keep his tongue in check for them having undressed him once more and not woken him sooner. After all, they had brought him back here instead of dumping him in the gutter, which was more than he'd expected from people who didn't even know him.

Swinging his legs out of the bed, Rage was about to get up when Keiran came in, tray in hand as well as another candle. When he saw Rage was awake, his face lit up with joy as well as relief. Nearly tipping the tray, he quickly put it on a small table next to Rage's bed.

"Looks like you survived," Rage said and reached for the water Keiran had brought. Greedily, he emptied the glass and held it out to the boy for a refill. He refused to focus on anything else until his thirst had been quenched.

The floor was cold, so Rage decided to stay in bed until he'd eaten. Keiran had brought meat and warm bread, generously spread with butter.

"How long have I been asleep?"

Keiran sat down next to him on the bed and held up four fingers.

Mouth full, Rage nodded. "No wonder I'm starving. Tell me what happened. Can't remember a thing from the moment I left Teddy's hut."

It took Keiran a while, using his hands and his strange ability to accurately mimic, to tell Rage what he wanted to know. Rage occasionally asked some questions, but all in all, he had no problems at all following Keiran's silent story.

Most importantly, no one had attacked them again, and Luca was well too. Keiran had needed no more than a day to recover and had since looked after Rage, who'd been in a critical state until the day before. Mike and Ben had carried him home—a fact that made Rage cringe—put him to bed and, with Lindsay's help, had also washed him.

"Lovely. Just what I dream of on quiet nights—an old, graying matron and her two overgrown sons taking care of me."

He stretched out his legs comfortably, for the moment content with his situation. Lucius must have given up after losing the magicians he'd hired. Hopefully the hunt was over and he could finally find somewhere to leave Keiran and the girl. He was down and out, not a single coin left in his purse, the last ones having been handed over to Teddy.

"I owe Lindsay the rent," he realized with a sigh. "She only took enough for one night, not four. Maybe I'll just steal two goats instead of one so she'll get her payment."

The puzzled look on Keiran's face nearly made him laugh. "Teddy wants a goat for his help," he explained. "Fair price, given that we all survived. That is… give me your hand."

Without hesitation, Keiran held out his hand, palm upward. Rage placed his left hand on the boy's warm skin, not letting his bracelet out of sight.

It stayed black. Good.

"Yep, you're fine," he said and, upon seeing the questioning look on Keiran's face, felt an unbidden need to explain himself. He had never done so before—he was a secretive man with a dangerous job, and he couldn't afford to share his secrets.

Still, the boy was different.

Rage touched the bracelet around his wrist. "Cost me a fortune, this one," he said. "Apart from the rainstone, it is the only thing I own that contains magic. As you can see, it is black. If I fall ill or I touch someone who's ill, the color will change. Very handy when getting poisoned or fucking someone you don't know."

Keiran grinned.

"It also shows me if someone is wearing a glamour. I loathe glamours, and the bracelet prevents me from getting too close to someone who uses them."

Suddenly, Rage became aware of how close the boy was and remembered that beneath the rough woolen blanket, he was naked. He also noticed that he was half-hard, longed for a kiss, and would have liked Keiran next to him, skin to skin, instead of sitting at arm's length.

The realization came as a surprise. He had expected he'd lose interest in the boy after their encounter in the river.

Keiran, though, was different in that respect too.

And he was still holding Rage's hand.

Rage cleared his throat and stared at their entwined hands and the midnight-black bracelet telling him that Keiran was as healthy as a man could be, not using a glamour, and completely without magic.

The boy was also quite bold, as Rage found out when he felt Keiran's lips on his open palm, breathing a kiss on his skin.

"What you think you're doing there?" Rage asked.

Keiran looked up at him. *Seducing you,* his smile said. *Again.*

"Ah. And you think that's a good idea?"

Keiran's eyes answered, *Oh, yes. Excellent idea.* His fingers danced along Rage's forearm and up to his shoulders, resting on the pulse in his throat before he finally pulled the assassin's head in for a tentative kiss.

Their tongues touched; it was as tender as the first kiss they had shared but sweeter as well, because Rage knew it was an honest kiss and that there were more where this one came from.

He had two choices: he could give in, or he could stop the boy and throw him out of the bed and out of the room. Really, that would be the logical choice. Whatever was happening between them, it would complicate his life in a most unnecessary way, and if Rage loathed anything, it was complications.

The hand on his cock, though, made it hard to argue. Keiran kissed him, pulling the blanket away, which soon lay on the floor along with shirt and trousers.

"Not so fast," Rage managed to say, taking the boy's shoulders and putting some distance between them.

In the candlelight, he looked as gorgeous as he had in the moonlight some nights ago. The golden shimmer of the flames added to the natural colors of his skin and hair, making Keiran seem to glow. Rage admiringly ran a hand across Keiran's chest, along his ribcage down to the dark brown patch of pubic hair. Cupping the boy's balls, he forgot about logic and choices and what he would have done under normal circumstances. Nothing here was normal. He never traveled in company, he didn't care about others, and no one had ever carried him to bed. Before he had kidnapped Lucinda, the last time he had spoken to a girl had been in a bar, ordering her to clean the table.

"What the hell," Rage said and pulled Keiran onto the pillows next to him.

Willingly, Keiran spread his legs and shifted his pelvis. His cock, large and fully erect, lay snug against his flat, muscular belly. Arms above his head, he looked like a living invitation to sin, and Rage grinned—sin had never been a problem for him. So he captured the boy's wrists and pressed them to the mattress, spread the boy's legs with his knee, and slipped on top of him. He kissed those lips, and then he fucked the boy, slowly and thoroughly, until they both came, Keiran as silent as ever and Rage with an unexpected harsh, dry sob.

"WILL YOU be getting up sometime today, or do you plan on spending another lazy day in bed?"

Satisfied, Luca watched her words cause Rage's eyes to rip open. He stared sleepily at the face looming above him, her pursed lips, angry eyes, and long blonde strands of hair—as she intended—all radiating disagreement.

"Because if you stay in bed, I will have to get your breakfast, as Keiran is obviously just as lazy as you are. And I dislike serving you, especially since you are naked under that blanket. I bet if Lindsay knew you and Keiran had some fun last night, she would skin you alive."

Tucking her hair behind her ears, Luca could barely suppress a grin at the thunderstruck expression on the assassin's face. She was pretty sure that under normal circumstances, he would have been up long before her and would have never been caught with his lover sleeping in his arms. Of course, he'd been dreadfully ill and simply wasn't in any condition to get up before sunrise. Still, it was amusing to see the disbelieving look on his face as he sat up, looking down at Keiran as if he were a ghost.

"It seems you are not as narrow-minded as I thought, at least not when it comes to men preferring other men as bed partners. You do remember last night, don't you?" Luca asked lightly. "I bet the whole house heard. Actually, I am surprised Lindsay didn't storm upstairs to beat some manners into you—seducing an innocent boy! Or, hang on, maybe you didn't seduce him. Maybe you raped him! Truly, the more I think about it, the more I wonder if perhaps I should call the guards. A few years in prison would do you a world of good."

Luca watched him closely, trying to estimate his reaction. She expected him to make a few sarcastic comments or insult her. After all, he was naked. What harm could a naked man do? Everyone knew a man was only powerful when wearing his clothes, feeling vulnerable and weak when his private parts were dangling around. She had learned that much before she'd turned ten years old, having been a curious child with her eyes everywhere and her ears open to every piece of gossip she could gather by eavesdropping.

Lifting her chin to make it clear she was honestly considering calling the empress's soldiers should Rage do something stupid, she saw his eyes narrow and braced herself for whatever harsh words he had in store for her. He reached over and touched Keiran's cheek with gentle fingertips, but then he jumped out of bed within the blink of an eye, fast as a striking snake. His hand was around her neck before she could so much as cry out in surprise, and he pushed her hard against the wall next to the window. He was sleep warm, and there was an air of tightly suppressed anger, which scared her tremendously.

Somehow, he had managed to capture her wrists above her head with one hand. She was unable to move with his body pressing against hers and his other arm across her throat. He felt like stone, hard and unyielding.

Luca opened her mouth to say something, but he shut her up effectively by adding more pressure to her throat.

"I'm quite sick of you, missy," he whispered. "Of you and your nasty mouth and your accusations. One more word about me and the boy, one more word about rape, and I will forget that not too long ago I actually felt a small bit of sympathy for you. One more word, and I will make sure your father finds you. Next time he hires a killer to track you, I won't protect you. Next time you do something stupid like carelessly running headfirst into a trap, dragging me and the boy along, I will turn my horse and leave you to die. Do I make myself clear?"

Stars danced in front of Luca's eyes due to lack of air and— she had to admit—fear. For the first time, she truly understood he wasn't an idiot, a brute, or merely an ill-tempered man who barely could tell left from right.

He was an assassin. And he was smart.

With his hand nearly strangling her, with his body so dangerously close, with him not giving a damn about his nakedness or the fact that someone could enter the room at any moment, she realized he was much older and stronger than she and that he possessed a power she could only dream of. He would kill her should he decide to do so. Assassin—why had it taken her so long to understand what that meant? Rage killed people for a living, and she had treated him like a peasant, unworthy of her attention and her time.

"Please," she rasped, probably the first honest plea in her entire life.

"Please what? Please don't kill me? Please don't hurt me? Please forget what I've said and be nice again?"

"All of it," Luca wheezed.

As unexpectedly as he had caught her, Rage let go of her and stepped back. "What I do and with whom is none of your business. But if you accuse me again of rape, you'll have to deal with more than just a few bruises around your neck."

"Right," she agreed and sat abruptly on the floor.

It seemed he had a soft spot where Keiran was concerned.

Luca stayed on the floor and out of his way, only watching him when he splashed water on his face. Finally, Rage knelt on the bed and put his hand on Keiran's shoulder, shaking him.

"Wake up," he said. "We need to move on before someone finds us here."

Keiran yawned. As Luca expected, a pang of jealousy rushed through her heart, though it wasn't really that strong. After all, she'd always known he preferred men. She'd always known he'd never touch her.

But still—Rage? She sighed and shook her head, making sure neither man saw it.

Rage quickly checked on their few belongings and was about to head down the stairs when sharp claws drilled into his calf, right through the leather of his trousers.

"Sammy!"

Before Luca could reach him, Rage plucked the cat from his leg, holding it at arm's length. It meowed, then licked his hand and tried to climb up his arm with needle-sharp claws.

"I thought I had eaten you," Rage said. Then he took a closer look. "He's grown. Considerably. Not yet an adult, but not a kitten anymore, either. A youth, insufferable and annoying. Just like his owner." With a flick of his wrist, he threw the cat into Luca's arms. "What did you feed him? Magical rats?"

Sammy swiftly climbed onto Luca's shoulder and began cleaning his face.

"Meat and milk," she answered. "But that's not the reason why Sammy has grown. It's because of the wild magic that hit him the night before we were attacked. Remember?"

Hah! The snappish tone that had taken her ages to cultivate was back, laced with a bit of arrogance. For a moment, she'd feared Rage had scared it out of her.

"The night your magic went wild," Rage said thoughtfully. "How could I forget?"

A smile lit up Keiran's face.

Hmmm. She'd heard them making love last night and had thought it had been the first time. Maybe she'd been wrong.

"Well, it means he can survive without you feeding him, catching mice on his own. It also means his flesh's too tough to be eaten. Pity, I like cats."

Luca stuck her tongue out at him, nearly making the assassin smile.

"What did you mean, we need to move before someone finds us?" she asked. "There have been no further attacks. We can stay here as long as we want."

Before Rage could answer, there were shouts from below. Loud, filled with panic.

"Fire!"

Luca paled, forgetting their quarrels and the problem of whether to stay or to leave. A fire was one of the biggest, most dangerous catastrophes possible in a town built of wood. Nothing else counted in the face of flames.

"Fire! You, up there, get your asses down here and help carry water!" Lindsay's voice, hard and commanding.

"Lucinda, you carry the cat," Rage ordered, taking care of his weapons. "Keiran, take my bag. We're heading for the kitchen. From there, it's just a few steps to the stable and to the horses. The quicker we are out of here, the better. We'll use the distraction and vanish in the crowd."

"Coward."

Luca blushed furiously when Rage turned toward her, but she held his gaze. "The town might burn down, and all you care about is your own life? Fine, cut my throat for my words, but well, it doesn't change the fact that only a coward runs away in such a situation."

"Better a coward than dead," Rage retorted, equally furious. "Your life cannot mean much to you if you are considering staying anywhere near a burning town."

A distinct smell of smoke hung in the air—this wasn't a small fire, and it wouldn't be easy to extinguish.

"My father wants to kill me, I'm miles away from home, I'm in the company of an assassin, I've been attacked. A burning town is nothing compared to my other problems. Besides, I might be of help." Resolutely, she stomped downstairs, right into the chaos.

Rage and Keiran had no choice but to follow her.

Lindsay shouted orders to her sons for making the house safe, blocking the windows and splashing as much water on the wooden walls as possible. Small children were all over the floor, brought inside for their own safety, along with the smaller cattle, the chicken, and the pigeons.

"You!" The moment Lindsay saw them, she pointed at Rage. "Are you fit enough to help in fighting the fire? Keiran, grab a bucket and get outside. The fire's down the street. Teddy's house. Might be he's still alive. Doubt it, though. Probably smoking in bed or done something equally stupid." She picked up a small boy who had both his index fingers up his nose, gave him half a bun, and placed him on the kitchen table so she wouldn't tread on him. "Stay out of the way," she scolded him, then bumped headlong into Rage.

The assassin had stopped dead in his tracks the moment Lindsay had mentioned whose house was burning. "Teddy? The one who sold me the Healing magic?"

"Yep, that's the one. Dangerous bastard, smoking his filthy cigars indoors with his hut packed up to the roof with parchment and herbs and the Lady knows what. Now will you—"

Rage wasn't listening anymore. He pushed the landlady out of his way and went outside, right into the chaos.

So much for him being a coward, Luca thought, somewhat proudly, and wondered if she could do some useful magic to keep the fire in check.

BLACK, STICKY smoke filled the air, combined with screams, shouted orders, and cries for help. The flames had set three more houses afire already. Men and women alike were trying to crash down the burning houses in order to extinguish the fire more easily or were splashing water on the walls and roofs of the houses nearby. Some had formed a human chain down to the river, passing buckets from one to the other, but it was a losing battle. There was no one coordinating the action, no one telling them what to do and where to do it first—and another house, and yet another, caught fire.

"By the good Lady," Lindsay breathed, standing behind Rage and staring at the catastrophe. "We must leave while we still can."

"And lose everything? Don't be ridiculous." Luca shook her head in disbelief at the scene in front of her. "Why don't you use magic to put out the fire? It might take a while, but it would be a lot easier than water. And it would work."

Lindsay laughed bitterly. "Magic? You joking, girl? We don't use magic that often in the Shadows. A bit here and there, nothing big. We might have been able to extinguish the fire at the very beginning, when only a wall was burning. But not this many houses. We're not good enough for that. No one here knows how to use magic that way." She wiped her nose on a dirty sleeve, the ash clinging to the fabric smearing over her sad face, and a moment later her sleeve was wiped across her eyes too.

"But she's skilled enough." Rage put his hand to her shoulder. "Lucinda, do what you can to stop the fire. Keiran and Lindsay will make sure no one disturbs you, and I will check whether Teddy was really that stupid or if someone helped with the initial spark."

"That would be *Luca*, you idiot," the girl snapped and crossed her arms over her chest. "Only my father calls me that other name. I hate it, and if you call me Lucinda once more, I'll kick you."

Lindsay's eyes became big and round, darting from one to the other and back. "You… you can do magic that big?" she finally asked and then snatched Rage's hand just before he could vanish in the crowd. "Are you saying that someone did this on purpose?"

Rage freed his hand. "I'll give you an answer once I know more."

Quickly, he made his way through the crowd toward Theodore's hut, the one he had visited only a few short days ago. After all, he owed the owner a favor, and although Theodore had wanted a prize goat, Rage saw more sense in trying to find and ideally rescue the little thief rather than letting him burn to death.

It wasn't easy to get through to Theodore's hut, partly because it was where the fire had started and partly because too many panicked people were on the streets, blocking his way and trying to survive the tragedy. Mothers carrying their children, men dragging women away from their houses, children crying for their parents, animals getting stolen and old folks getting trampled—it would have been easier to cross the river and approach the Shadows from the other side, but for that, it was too late. Rage was in the center of it all, and it seemed to take him hours to reach his destination.

When he finally saw Teddy's hut, he knew he was too late.

Despite what most people thought, Teddy had been a good thief, and he had invested a good deal of his income in his home. The hut might have looked shabby from the outside, but it had been built with stones rather than wood, but covered with some rotten planks so his neighbors wouldn't get suspicious. Now, the wood had burned away, along with the window frames, the stairs, and the straw roof. Only the skeleton of a hut was left, the beams still burning as well as everything that was inside. Not really a blazing inferno anymore, but not a safe place to be, either.

Rage didn't think twice before snatching a bucket of water from a passing woman and pouring it over his head. A second bucket followed, and a third, until he was as wet as he could possibly be—not a single dry thread was left on his body, and he shivered in the wind that was spreading the fire quickly from house to house.

A hand whirled him around, and he stood face-to-face with Keiran. The boy shook him, his whole face asking one question: *What the hell are you doing?*

"I'm going inside, and you should look after the girl."

Keiran shook his head and pointed toward the burning hut. *You're crazy, going in there!*

There was no time for lengthy discussions. "Do you really think the thief died because he was too daft to put out his candle?" he hissed into the boy's ear, one arm around his shoulder. "I was here a few days ago. He saved my life, yours too, and now he's dead. I need to know if someone helped him along, and for that, I need to find his corpse."

Stubbornly, Keiran shook his head again. *You can't go in there,* his eyes said and, *Come back with me!*

Feeling the fire at his back, feeling part of his clothes freeze in the wind and part of them dry from the heat, Rage did something he hadn't done since he was a boy himself: he pulled Keiran closer and kissed him, capturing the boy's face between both his hands. Deliberately, he put a lot of emotion into the kiss so the boy would hopefully think he cared about him, would come back for him, wouldn't ever lie to him, and all the other nonsense Rage wanted him to believe.

"I'll be quick," Rage promised with a perfectly hoarse whisper. "I swear I'll be back to kiss you again, but you need to let me go. We barely escaped death the last time Lucius tried to kill us. If he is behind this, I need to know."

For a heartbeat, Keiran stared at him, narrow-eyed and suspicious, but then he relaxed and nodded. He let go of Rage and walked away without another look back, using his elbows to get through the crowd.

He believed me, Rage thought with a somewhat bitter feeling deep inside him. *Luckily, I'm a good liar, and luckily, the boy is so fucking naïve.*

Cracking beams and burning wood, bursting stones and the sizzling sound of water being splashed against hot walls—Teddy's hut seemed to call for Rage, so he didn't linger any longer and kicked in the remains of the door, hoping against all odds that the little house would fight against its downfall for another ten minutes.

Smoke in his lungs, the same thick, black smoke he'd seen outside, billowing toward the sky. Rage coughed, then put an arm across his nose and mouth, breathing through the wet sleeve of his shirt. It didn't make much of a difference.

Smoke in his eyes too. If the roof hadn't burned down already, it would have been impossible to see a thing. As it was, daylight and the remaining flames made it easy to maneuver without bumping into doorframes or the few still standing walls. The flames licked at his boots and legs, the heat kissed his neck and his hands. Had it been a house with several rooms and a second floor, or had Rage not decided to go inside immediately—had he given Keiran one more kiss—the corpse on the floor would have been buried by the table, which was just about to collapse under the weight of ash, burning parchment, and crumbling brick stones. But it was just a hut—one room, and a small one at that.

The corpse was lying halfway underneath the table. It was badly burned. Clothes and boots and hair were gone, nails and even fingers were missing, Black teeth grinned at Rage from a skull with one missing eye and another staring lidless into the next world.

The assassin had seen a lot of dead people in his life, most of whom he had killed himself or at least had been responsible for their death in one way or another. But he had never seen a body as destroyed as Teddy's corpse. Had the thief not been such a small man—distinctly smaller than average and even smaller than most women—Rage wouldn't have even been remotely sure he'd found the right man.

Under the circumstances, he decided that unless Theodore walked up to him safe and sound, he'd call the corpse Teddy and carry it outside for further examination.

The body was sickeningly light, stank beastly, and threatened to fall apart when Rage carefully lifted it up. Step by step, with the noise of the fire and the screaming people outside constantly in his ears, he made his way out again, stepping over shattered phials, leaking bottles, and tons of ash.

The air outside, although anything but fresh, was like cold water for his lungs. Dropping to his knees, Rage lowered his burden to the ground, ignoring the people around him. He looked just like them, black and dirty and covered with ash and grime. His skin was prickling from the sudden absence of heat. Then three things happened at once: Rage realized that most of the fires were under control, he heard a thin, wailing cry from inside the ruined hut, and he saw people building a circle around him and the corpse.

He hated to be the center of attention.

And the wailing continued.

The problem was there was nothing but an empty, gutted room behind the blackened walls, and the last few beams would crash down any minute now. How could there be wailing when everything in there should be burned or dead?

"'s that Teddy?"

"Did he kill him?

"Who is it?"

"Didn't Lins take him in few days ago?"

"I thought he was dead, looked dreadful last time I saw him."

Questions and comments whispered from man to woman to child. Questions, like wind rustling leaves. Each question was about Rage, and everyone was looking at him, and the wailing became louder, and eventually, he couldn't stand it any longer.

He shouldn't be here. He should have left, with or without his companions—without, rather than with them, if he were to be honest with himself. An assassin being watched by every adult and child within a mile radius was a really bad thing.

Slowly, he got up, ash blowing to the ground as he stretched his legs. Looking for an escape route, he considered taking one of the smaller children hostage until he was safe and Coldwell was well behind him. Until the wailing became a scream.

"Who the fuck is still in that hut?" Rage exploded and forgot about the corpse. People took a step back—he was furious, and it must have shown on his face. Rage pointed at the dead man at his feet. "He lived alone, didn't he?"

People exchanged looks. Water buckets still in hand, children still crying, and the last flames still eating away a few remaining wooden walls, they were unsure what to do. With the catastrophe over nearly as quickly as it had started, and with a dead man in their midst being protected by an assassin, some might have thought about attacking the stranger. Some, maybe even most, were intent on getting back to their homes and rebuilding what had been taken away by the flames.

Finally, a woman raised a hand. "Teddy had a daughter," she said and swallowed when Rage focused on her. "Came to pay a visit every now and then." Quickly, she hid behind her husband, who looked like a blacksmith, his balled fists ready, probably to protect his wife should Rage decide to come another step closer.

"Mommy!"

The cry came from inside the hut.

The small hairs on the back of Rage's neck stood up. It was an awful sound, lost and forlorn and scared, and it was even worse because there was no answer to the call, no mother anywhere nearby to pick up the child, to soothe her, to dry her tears.

"Fucking shitty day," Rage sighed, poured another bucket of water over his head, and went back inside the hut.

CHAPTER
Eight

NO ONE could have survived inside Theodore's place. There was only one room, and it had burned down. The flames had destroyed every sign of life. There simply couldn't be a child crying; the sound must be coming from somewhere outside, above, underneath—

Underneath. The helpless cries for some unknown, cruelly absent "Mommy" were coming from beneath the floor.

Sweat ran down Rage's dirty face. The fire had claimed the furniture and most of the floorboards, and although the roof beams weren't burning anymore, it was still as hot as hell in the hut and sheer suicide to have entered it a second time. But the child's screams went straight to Rage's heart. He had a soft spot where children were concerned, and there was no way he could turn away without having found the thief's daughter.

If she was even here. If what he heard wasn't a hallucination, a result of breathing in too much smoke, the lack of food, and his recent poisoning.

Another sound began to accompany the cries: small hands banging against wood.

"Where are you?" Dropping to his knees, Rage knocked on the remaining floorboards, trying to find the one place where it had to be hollow.

There wasn't that much floor that hadn't been covered with furniture. Coughing, his eyes burning and irritated, Rage swore under his breath, listening for any sound, anything, that might indicate the child's location.

Silence answered him. Outside the hut, he knew the crowed waited with bated breath for the roof to finally come down and bury him. Even he waited for it. Occasionally, through the still burning window frames, he noticed someone trying to see what was happening inside.

Nothing was happening inside. Rage was banging, calling, shouting, and cursing, but the child, wherever she was, had stopped crying.

"I'll leave you here to die," Rage managed to say between coughs.

Silence.

"You'll burn to death like your daddy, and believe me, it's not a nice thing to experience. It hurts. Do you want to burn?"

He'd have to get out of here in another minute. The beams were cracking dangerously, and not even for the sake of this child would Rage die in this hut.

"Mommy."

Barely a whisper. To his left, underneath the table, a trap door opened.

Wide, brown eyes peeked out, set in a ghost-white face. "Papa's dead."

It wasn't a question.

On all fours, Rage crawled under the table, hoping it would hold the roof beams' weight should they come down. The fire crackled gently as the wind blew up ash and half-burned parchment.

"Come out of there," Rage whispered, partly because he was hoarse from all the smoke and partly because he didn't want to scare the child even further.

"I want Mommy." The trap door began to close, the child retreating back into the hole under the floor like a little mouse.

Rage held out his hand. "She's outside, waiting for you," he lied. "She sent me in here to get you."

They both jumped as a window burst, sending glass shards raining to the floor, and Rage banged his head on the underside of the table. Cursing, he pushed the table aside—if the kid didn't come out of the hole soon, he would have to grab her, no matter how loud she screamed.

Slowly, the trap door opened a bit wider. The child couldn't be older than four or five. Her pale, chubby cheeks were streaked with tears, her hair was peppered with straw, and the thumb of her left hand was safely located in her mouth.

"You didn't kill my papa," she mumbled, climbing onto Rage's lap and putting her free hand around his neck.

Thunderstruck, he held the child in his arms. In general, he had no contact with people younger than teenagers, and those only if they served him his cider. He didn't kill children, he didn't fuck them, he had no reason to talk to them, and that this one was now close enough for him to feel her heart beating against his chest, wild and fast like that of a caged bird, made him as speechless as her words.

"Did you see who killed Te—your papa?" he asked as he stood up. A glance at the roof told him that they had just enough time to get outside. The child was warm, but she was shaking too. To Rage, it was obvious she had seen much more than any child should ever be forced to witness.

The door had burned down, so it was easy to get outside, back into the crowd, right in the midst of the dozens of people waiting for them.

The whispering began the moment the assassin stepped onto the street.

"Found her…."

"Did he kill Teddy?"

"Is that Teddy's girl?"

"Is she dead?"

"Who is he…?" Endless murmuring. If Rage had had the choice, he would have gone out the back way.

When he went to put the girl down, she clung to him, taking her thumb out of her mouth so she could wrap both her arms around his neck.

"Let go of me," he told her.

"Want Mommy," she replied stubbornly and tightened her grip.

The circle of people around them became tighter, men and women getting closer and angrier.

They've just survived a fire that nearly destroyed their homes, killed their cattle, and turned their kids into beggars, Rage thought. It seems they had found someone to blame.

Me. Shit.

"Let go of the kid," someone yelled, immediately followed by others ordering him to do the same.

But the child in Rage's arms made no attempt to get away from him. In fact, she clung to him more tightly, especially when the shouts became louder and fists were balled in the air. Teddy's daughter squeezed her eyes shut and pressed her face against his shoulder.

At least like that, she wouldn't have to look at her father's corpse, lying less than ten feet away from them.

The situation could have turned ugly. Burdened with the child, Rage couldn't get to his knives, and because he was surrounded by angry, scared people, he couldn't run, either. Already, he was looking out for stones being thrown in his direction, for clubs swung by fire-blistered hands, for secretly drawn blades. With the mood as heated as it was, anything could happen. Worst-case scenario, the crowd would kill him as well as the child.

He took a step back, toward the ruins of the hut. It would probably be less dangerous inside than out here.

A man raised a hand, wielding an ax.

A woman pushed the man aside, kicked him, and then slapped the back of his head. "Rory! What do you think you are doing, you old fool, threatening one of my guests?"

It was Lindsay, who now scowled at the man called Rory and then stared down most of the men who had just been about to join their friend in committing murder.

"He killed Teddy," Rory growled as he lowered his ax. "See? That's him there on the ground. Burned, but I recognize him anyway. Been no one else living round here who's that small, and the buckle, that's his all right. And that one"—he pointed at Rage—"he was in Teddy's house a few days ago. Seen him with my own eyes."

Lindsay snatched the ax from his hand, swung it, and drove it deep into the ground. "His name is Rage, and he's been in bed until about an hour ago. He wasn't even awake when the fire started, and if you don't believe me, ask my sons. They've both been regularly checking on him."

"He's visited Teddy," Rory replied stubbornly.

"So have you when in need of Healing magic," Lindsay snapped.

Rory rubbed a hand over his dirty face, eying his ax, Lindsay, the assassin, and finally the woman—probably his wife—who stood at his side with equal uncertainty. "But he won't let go of the kid," he said. "Might kill her and all, you know."

"Sure," Lindsay said sarcastically. "That's why Debbie is clinging to him as if he were a lifeline. He got Teddy out, didn't he? Why would he do that if he'd killed him in the first place? If I were a killer, I would make sure my victim burned to ash, not drag him outside for everyone to see what I've done. And I wouldn't risk my life to save my victim's kid, either. You got a brain in your head, Rory Blacksmith, or a dried plum?"

People looked at each other, some even blushing. The circle broke up. Some stepped back, some formed new, smaller circles to talk amongst themselves. Rory took his wife's hand.

Rage made a mental note not to get on Lindsay's wrong side. Making Lindsay angry didn't seem to be a good idea.

"Sorry, Lins," Rory mumbled. "Sorry, erm, Master Assassin. No offense meant. 'S just that the kid… I know her mom. She's a whore, and Debbie was with Teddy most times she had to work." His voice trailed off, and he stared at his feet as if he didn't know what else to say.

"Can you take the girl to her mom?" As if the man hadn't threatened to behead him only minutes ago, Rage stepped next to the blacksmith so he could whisper in his ear. "I don't want her to see her father's corpse. So if you can persuade her to let go of me, I swear I won't come after you some quiet night to carve some manners into your flesh."

Rory paled, nearly crushing his wife's hand in his. Only when the woman stroked Debbie's back, murmuring soothing words, did he gather himself and say, "Come to Uncle Rory, Debs. I know where your mommy is. Hop onto my shoulders. I'll take you to her."

Rage's shirt was wet from the kid's tears. She wouldn't allow Rory to take her from his arms.

She looked at Rage intently. "Papa played with me," she said, not knowing that everyone nearby was perking up their ears to catch every single word she said. "Hide 'n' seek. I always hide under the floor, but he never finds me there. I have to call and he pulls me out and we giggle and then he makes me hot milk."

Carefully, Rage shifted her weight until she sat on his hip before wiping the tears from her cheeks. "What happened this time?" he asked. "Did Papa make you hot milk today?"

The little girl shook her head. "'Twas a knock on the door. Papa said he wouldn't open, but the man outside said bad words, and Papa said I should go under the floor. Said it was a game and I should be quiet like a mousy."

More tears ran down her face. She made no attempt to wipe them away, as if she weren't even aware of them. Hastily, as if scared of the words she was about to say, she continued, "The bad man shouted at Papa and then he put something around his neck and then Papa stumbled, and the man pushed the candle over although Papa always said how dangerous that is, and then the bad man left, and Papa didn't get up even when I called for him, and I was scared and stayed hidden, just like Papa told me."

Debbie reached out and put her fingertip on Rage's nose, which was about level with her face. "The bad man didn't have black hair. It was all white, like an old man's hair, and his nose was as big as a carrot."

Rory's wife pulled at her husband's sleeve. "Let's take Debbie to her mom," she said, clearly feeling uneasy in the assassin's presence. She managed a half-curt nod, and this time, Debbie didn't resist Rory taking her.

Rage was already kneeling next to the burned corpse. Methodically, he searched through the remains of burned trousers, pockets falling apart, shirt crumbling beneath his fingertips. He found nothing apart from a silver coin, old and black but shiny underneath. Questioningly, he looked at Lindsay.

"Was his," she confirmed. "Showed it around whenever he was drunk enough."

Had there not been people still standing around, talking and gossiping, had there not been a few remaining flames still crackling and burned wood crashing down, Rage might not only have heard the sound of hooves in the distance but drawn some conclusions as well. But there was too much noise, and he was still slightly dizzy from the smoke and the fact that he'd saved a life instead of taken one, so he didn't find it odd to hear galloping horses in the Shadows, where horses were a rare thing. He concentrated fully on the task at hand.

Rage had reached the corpse's neck. Touching the burned flesh was unpleasant, but when he found the belt, he knew it had been worth it. Peeling the leather off Teddy's throat, he held the belt up, showing it to everyone who was still there.

"The kid was right," Rage said as he got up. "Someone strangled her father. And it wasn't me. The fire was no coincidence either."

Brushing off grime and dust and ash and getting even dirtier by doing so, Rage dropped the belt next to the dead thief. "Bury him," he said to no one in particular. "It wasn't his fault that the fire started. He neither fell asleep in bed smoking, nor was he careless with his candles." A slight threat was heard in his voice and noticed by the ones who were about to cover the corpse with a blanket.

"We'll bury him properly," a man said. "Teddy was one of us. No need for threats."

SIDE BY side, Rage and Lindsay walked back to the tavern. The wind had blown most of the smoke toward the river. It was cold, and in his still mostly wet clothes, Rage shivered.

"Are the boy and the girl all right?" he asked, wrapping his arms around his body. "I didn't expect her magic to be that good. The fire was out much faster than I could have hoped for."

"And lucky you are she's good," Lindsay said, "or you'd have burned in Teddy's house. You owe her a big thanks for that. We all do."

Suddenly, the sound of hooves was very near. Six or seven horses at least, fast, strong, and well fed, nothing like the sorry nags to be found in the Shadows.

"Guards," Lindsay said casually, as if she weren't walking with an assassin, as if she didn't buy and sell stolen goods like everyone around here. "They always turn up too late. Could they have been here an hour ago, helping with the fire? No, of course not. Bastards."

Rage finally caught up with events. He should have vanished the moment he'd gotten rid of the child. He wasn't fond of guards, and he currently had too many other problems to waste a single moment with them. But it was too late. And he had been careless enough to be walking in the middle of the street to avoid getting his head smashed in by falling roofs.

Stupid.

A new circle formed around Rage, this time guards on horses. Each guard had a lance, and each lance pointed at his heart.

"And I thought the day started off bad enough with the fire," the landlady said dryly.

"Since I began traveling with Lucinda, I have found that even the worst day can be topped by something even more horrible," Rage said with a deep sigh.

The guards' leader leaned over on his horse. He was a tall man with bright red hair and a bald patch on his crown. His moustache nearly reached down to his belt. Swiftly, he grabbed Rage's wet shirt and forced him to look up.

"We don't like your kind here in Coldwell," the guard said. "And then a man came to us, a guy called Jeeve, said you kidnapped Lord Babylon's daughter and that you could be found here. For that, we will disembowel you. If you tell me where she is—and if she is alive and unharmed—I might consider cutting your throat not too long afterwards. I am a friendly man, if treated nicely." Grinning, he let go of Rage and then spat a thick blotch of tobacco-laced saliva into his face.

Lindsay impatiently batted away one of the lances pointed in her face. "There's for sure a girl traveling with him," she said loudly, "but she's not been kidnapped, or she would have run by now. This man is a guest in my house, and he's been ill for the past few days. The girl's looked after him, wiped his head when he had the fever, washed and sewed his clothes. Hang him for something he didn't do, and you'll be a murderer." She defiantly balled her fists, which caused waves of laughter to erupt from the guards.

"You better shut up if you want to survive the day," Rage murmured. There were too many soldiers with too many weapons to do anything but behave.

The guards' leader dismounted his horse and, with a bowlegged gait, crossed the distance between his horse and Lindsay. "Your guest, he is, eh?" he asked, kicking Rage's legs out from underneath him so he landed face-first in the dust. "Then I will take you to prison, too. It's not particularly illegal to help scum like him, but I don't care. The girl, I've heard, is not yet of age."

Lindsay frowned and looked as though she wanted to give a sharp and detailed reply concerning the guard's quality as a human being when two of the horses neighed in irritation and kicked, threatening to throw off their riders. Rage, raising his head just enough to see a bit more than boots and hooves and dirt, saw slender legs walking toward the guard.

Damn the girl, he couldn't help thinking, *and damn my stupidity for not getting out of here in time.*

Too late for that. Luca, looking tired but very pleased with herself for having managed to get the fire under control, was now the center of attention. Her long, blonde hair flowed down her back, unbraided. The tight trousers she wore showed off her legs much more than was appropriate, and the shirt—well, the shirt she had borrowed from Lindsay only this morning was the shirt of a poor woman, bright and colorful and nothing a lady would dare touch.

"Whoever says I'm not of age is a liar," Luca said. "I turned sixteen this Midsummer, which can be proved by my entire household. With whom I ride and where I stay is my decision. What is your name, Corporal? I intend to inform the empress about your insolent behavior. And you." She pointed her finger at a guard who was pressing the point of his lance against Rage's throat. "Step back and let the man get up. He just saved a child, and he certainly didn't kidnap me. Anyway, who sent you?" She waited for an answer, tapping her foot impatiently.

The corporal looked her up and down calculatingly, taking in her dirty face, her second-hand clothes, and her loosely flowing hair.

Slowly, he began to grin. "You're Lucinda of Babylon, eh? Since when do good girls wear trousers instead of silk and velvet? Since when do good girls wear their hair like a common slut?"

Luca narrowed her eyes. They became darker when she was angry, resembling a stormy ocean. Something must have shown in them—magic, maybe hate, or both—because the corporal involuntarily stepped back.

"I just got the fire under control, which very well might have destroyed this whole town had it not been for me. Do you think I care about proper clothes or hair fashion when there are lives to be saved?"

With a finger snap, the corporal ordered his man to step away from Rage. "I'm Hunter," he said with a brief nod. "If you are truly Lucinda of Babylon, we have orders from your father to bring you back home. He is very worried about you."

"He is full of bullshit," Luca said, and the corporal's mouth sagged open in surprise at her words.

"He wants me back because he thinks he'll be able to kill me easier when I'm locked up in my room. Why do you think I left home? I have been attacked several times in the past few days. My friends and I were injured, and now this fire... I'm sure my father is behind all of it. Jeeve, the man who sent you here, is his servant. Obviously, I will not go anywhere near him before the question of his involvement has been answered."

Uneasily, Corporal Hunter twirled his moustache between his fingers. "Lady Lucinda—"

"That would be Lady of Babylon to you."

Rage shot her a glance and couldn't help but grin at the girl's words—she was as snappy and snarky as always, and right now, she had the upper hand in the situation. Which wasn't a bad thing at all given that he was of no help whatsoever. Carefully, so he wouldn't provoke more lance stabbing, Rage got up.

Hunter bared his teeth at Luca. "Well, whatever. It seems you are who you claim to be, and as you are obviously fine with being amongst thieves and don't want to come with us, we'll leave you alone. None of my business who you have quarrels with. Charlie,

Bill, I want the assassin bound and on a horse in less than thirty seconds. Let's move, boys!"

Luca was after him in a heartbeat, catching his horse's harness before he was back in the saddle.

"What do you mean, bound and on a horse? I told you he hasn't kidnapped me!"

Hunter swung his leg over the horse's back. "He's an assassin. We don't like his kind here in town, and I prefer to be on the safe side and lock him up before he kills someone. It's not what the law says, but it's what I will do. So unless someone vouches for him— someone who has the right to vouch for him, that is, a relative or a spouse—I will be taking him with me."

Rage heard a roof collapse somewhere behind him. He smelled the smoke and wondered how it would feel to be hanged, or disemboweled for that matter—so far, no guard had ever laid a hand on him, as he had always been very careful to stay away from them and left any town where he'd completed a job long before his victim was found.

The guard named Bill pulled Rage's hands behind his back and bound them with a rope. The skin on his wrists cracked as the guard tightened the loops. He knew his fingers would turn black within hours were the rope not loosened but knew as well that the guards didn't give a damn about the well-being of an assassin's hands. His mouth was filled with sand and ash, and he was thirsty as well as hungry. Pity he would get neither food nor drink in prison.

He would be dead by tomorrow evening.

Luca sighed. "As he's my husband, I guess I have the right to vouch for him. He is mine. Untie him."

What?

Luca let go of the horse's harness. Gracefully, she brushed her hair behind her ears, making more than one man gape with desire. She was clearly so very different from any girl the guards—young or old—had ever met that there was no doubt she was truly the Lady of Babylon Manor, that she had the right to order them around, and that it would be much better to obey her orders than argue with her.

Once more, Rage had a hard time suppressing a grin.

Corporal Hunter stared at her as if she'd grown two heads.

"You—what? Him? I mean, he is your… you truly married *him*?"

Rage very nearly told him the girl was talking nonsense. Almost belatedly did he realize that the wrong word—any word, actually—would land him in prison.

Losing her patience, Luca crossed the distance to Rage and slipped her hand into his, bound as they were. With cold fingers, she searched for the knife in his belt, found it, and cut the rope without even bothering to wait and see if the guard believed her words. She nicked his skin, but then the rope fell to the ground, and he was free.

Before he could do or say anything, before he could even appreciate the feeling of freedom, the girl raised up on her tiptoes and lightly kissed him on the lips.

"Let's get you inside, husband," she said tenderly and once more took his hand. "It's been a long day, and you belong in bed."

Tingling lips; sweaty hands. Rage managed to keep himself upright, but that was about it—the events since he'd awoken had become overwhelming. His wet clothes were slowly turning his bones to ice, and all he could think of was how on earth he was going to make it back to Lindsay's attic room without support.

A crowd had gathered by then, too large to be controlled by only a few guards. Rage knew that if the guard insisted on taking him prisoner, if he so much as asked for proof of their marriage, this might very well turn into a fight.

Silently, the corporal stared at both him and Luca for a long moment. Then he turned his horse and signaled his men to follow.

"Let's get inside," Luca said again. This time, her voice trembled.

LATER THAT night, Luca lay awake on her bed in the attic and thought about the day while Rage and Keiran ate and drank downstairs, celebrating that they were alive and free. They weren't the only ones. The whole street had found their way into Lindsay's tavern, and everyone had brought something to eat or drink or stories to tell.

No one considered it odd an assassin was sitting amongst them. He'd saved a child, who clearly stated he hadn't been the one to kill her father. Lindsay had stood up to the guards, telling them to get lost. The people living in the Shadows were proud of her, and they were proud, as well, that an assassin could be bothered to eat and drink and laugh with them.

Luca had gone to bed early that night. Partly because she was tired. Using her magic to get the fire under control had been thrilling but a lot more strenuous than she'd thought possible.

In the quiet darkness of the attic room, it felt even stranger now that the people seemed to accept her. No one but Keiran had ever considered her anything but a nuisance.

The other reason for avoiding the crowd downstairs was what she'd witnessed after she'd announced to the whole world she was married to an assassin. She hadn't seen any other way to save Rage, and as saving him had been the right thing to do, she'd done it.

Tsk.

Then she thought of Keiran. *Her* Keiran. *Her* best friend, who was so hopelessly in love with that damn assassin. How he'd smiled at Rage.

Keiran had never smiled at her that way.

Restlessly, Luca paced the small attic room, trying to get the images out of her mind. Very bright and intense images. Their existence, of course, was her fault. Had she stayed in the kitchen instead of following Rage and Keiran, she wouldn't have seen anything.

But no, she had been too curious for her own good. She never could resist a riddle, and when she saw Keiran get up and leave the crowded kitchen, she had wondered what he was up to.

Only moments later Rage had followed him.

Closing her eyes didn't make the images go away, so Luca sat on her narrow bed and pondered what she'd seen.

"They went to the stables," she said aloud to Sammy, who was idly chasing some dust kitties, "the small one behind the tavern where they keep the cows and our horses. There's a hayloft too. You need to climb a ladder to get up there, and I tell you, it wasn't easy to follow them without being seen."

She'd been curious, so she'd used a little magic, hid behind the barrels of oil and wine, and then saw them kiss.

She'd seen Keiran's perfect body, his long, strong legs, the muscles in his back and shoulders. She'd seen light and shadow playing across Rage's face, contrasting with his midnight-black hair and pale skin. His eyes were soft for once with heavy long-lashed lids, and there were barely audible sighs whenever Keiran trailed kisses down his chest.

Keiran, her lifelong friend, sinking into the hay with spread legs, hands outstretched, smiling again. Rage at his lover's neck, kissing his throat, ass moving, thrusting into Keiran, her friend's legs slung around his hips.

So... gentle, Luca thought in the darkness of her room, clutching the pillow to her chest for comfort.

She definitely was very, very jealous.

Her eyes refused to close. Her mind refused to forget the sight of the two lovers.

She eventually came to a decision before finally falling asleep.

CHAPTER
Nine

RAGE WOKE often during the nights that followed, and always, he had to fight the urge to flee, to hide. He would struggle against Keiran's embrace, never for long, and not hard enough to disturb the boy's deep, peaceful sleep, but struggle he did. Only when he remembered where he was—in Lindsay's tavern in the large bed in the attic—did he relax and, listening to the boy's steady breathing, drift back to sleep.

Whenever he thought about moving on, his body protested very loudly that it had had enough. He needed the break, badly. Going back on the road would have been irresponsible in his condition. He was too tired, and his leg still hurt. He knew when to listen to his body's needs and when it was okay to neglect them.

At first, he had tried to argue the point with himself, only to realize there really was nowhere else they could go—at least nowhere safer than the Shadows. So far, Lucius's minions had found them wherever they'd gone. They might as well stay where they were until they were well again. Not even a stray dog could approach Lindsay's tavern unnoticed, much less a man, woman, or anyone who hadn't grown up here. Teddy had been murdered, a fire had been set, and everyone was alert, angry, and more than willing to protect the people amongst them who had fought the flames.

In his half-sleep, half-awake state, Rage smiled at the irony of the situation. Had they not come here, there wouldn't have been a fire in the first place, Teddy would still be alive, and the guards would never have set foot in the Shadows.

Keiran sighed in his sleep, and Rage opened his eyes in the darkness.

The girl had saved his life. Bold and brave and arrogant as hell, she had vouched for him, tricking the guard with a blatant lie. She had cut the ropes around his wrists and led him away as if she actually cared for him.

Yet he'd been sure she hated him.

Covered by blankets and embraced by the boy, Rage shouldn't have been cold, but he was. Longing for the morning, for sunlight, for the opportunity to get up, he felt caged in this bed, in this room, although he knew it was the only place right now where sleep was actually not a death trap.

Married. Him.

Never.

Sleep wasn't going to come anytime soon, it seemed. So instead of persisting in keeping his eyes shut, Rage carefully turned in Keiran's arms so he could face the boy, put one arm under his head, and just watched his lover dream. The girl had moved into another room. The attic was all theirs now, and Rage found that fucking the boy was the best way he could think of to relax and heal.

Only a few hours ago, he'd taken Keiran up to the hayloft again. The hay's sweet fragrance still clung to his shirt and hair, and when he brushed his hand over Keiran's head, there were some stalks in the brown curls.

Of course, the boy was still nothing but a pastime. As soon as—

The thought made Rage frown. *As soon as what?* he asked himself.

Until today, he'd always known his path and had followed it. He never had any doubts about the life he'd chosen. Now, he was stuck with two companions and a cat in a town he barely knew, with guards on his heels and a murderer who obviously didn't shy away from extreme actions. Teddy the thief hadn't died from a heart attack, and the hut hadn't caught fire because of a forgotten candle.

WHEN RAGE awoke, sunlight was streaming brightly into the attic room. The big bed was empty. Keiran had gotten up early without waking him.

"Fine with me," Rage said to the beams above him.

He'd burned his fingers while rescuing the child from Teddy's hut. They still hurt when he moved them, so he decided against taking off the bandages Lucinda had wrapped around his palms and wrists. It would mean he couldn't take a shower, but then, he needed his hands to be in perfect condition. The shower could wait.

In another day or two, they should all have recovered perfectly. There would be no reason to stay in Coldwell any longer.

He realized it would be harder than he thought to leave this town. It had been years since he'd slept in a real bed without having to worry about someone breaking in the door and demanding answers. Maybe it was a good time to enjoy this—the bed, the roof above his head, his extraordinary landlady, as well as his unlikely traveling companions. Both the girl and the boy had proven worthy to travel with, and even the cat—purring nuisance that he was— made him feel comfortable.

On the other hand, a comfortable assassin was usually a dead assassin.

"To hell with worrying," Rage said aloud and turned over for another half hour of sleep. He'd been shot, poisoned, cut open, burned, and captured. He'd been kissed and stroked, and he'd fucked more often this past week than he had the previous year. He had earned a bit more sleep, especially since he'd been awake again half the night.

He would have preferred not to be alone in bed, though. Memories of the hayloft teased him, and he got hard quickly when his nose caught the boy's scent on the pillows and even on his own skin. Hopefully, Keiran was just finding breakfast, a task that shouldn't take too long and would lead him back to the attic eventually.

Footsteps on the staircase, light and fast. Rage's eyes snapped open, and he stopped stroking himself. Getting caught with his hands around his cock by Lindsay wasn't something he wished to happen.

The door opened. Keiran came in, carrying a tray laden with fresh bread and butter, a small jar of honey, and a steaming pot of coffee.

The boy smiled, hesitant and shy.

"Morning," Rage said. "Put the tray down and come back to bed, or did Lindsay give you some errands to run?"

Keiran just shrugged.

"Perfect. Shove the chair under the door handle. I don't want anyone walking in on us for another hour. Lindsay isn't a woman who knocks before entering, should she change her mind concerning you and her errands."

Keiran blushed at his words. He put the tray swiftly on the bed and poured a mug of coffee. His hands were slightly shaky, Rage observed, but the coffee was good.

Just as the boy was about to step out of reach, Rage set the mug aside, caught Keiran's hand and pulled him down. Sudden desire squeezed his heart and his cock, strong enough to make him dizzy and careless. In a matter of seconds, he had forgotten about breakfast.

"Come to bed," Rage demanded, knowing only too well the boy was always as eager as he was for a fuck.

Out of habit, he glanced at the bracelet around his wrist, remembering only then that it was hidden under the bandage. He briefly considered undoing the long, white cloth strip. He should check the bracelet's color before becoming intimate. He shouldn't neglect it just because he'd had the boy before.

Then Keiran put a hand on his cock, and Rage arched his back into the touch while inwardly shaking his head about his own suspiciousness. This was Keiran, not some unknown whore. He was neither ill nor capable of doing magic, and he'd known that from the first day.

Keiran grinned, obviously pleased at the hardness beneath his palm. His lips were parted, his eyes wide and curious, and Rage grinned back as he reached for him. He pulled the boy lower, kissed his neck, then murmured, "Get undressed and into bed so I can touch you and taste you and fuck you," only to groan with desire as Keiran's grip through the fabric of the blanket tightened.

Struggling to get the blanket out of the way, Rage watched Keiran get up and shed his clothes. In the morning light, the boy looked more like a dream, slightly blurry at the edges, unreal in his beauty. The shirt dropped to the ground, the trousers followed, and the tray rattled as the boy fell back onto the bed. Rage quickly took the tray and placed it on the floor so the mugs wouldn't break.

Keiran's amber eyes roamed over Rage's body, over the scars, which didn't end at the waist but went lower, crisscrossing over thighs, calves, and ankles. As if he hadn't seen them before, Keiran knelt on the bed, touching Rage's pale skin with only his fingertips, leaving goose bumps in their wake.

"Old and ugly," Rage said flatly, somewhat uneasy at the boy's intent gaze, and Keiran's head snapped up, shocked.

"'Tis what the girl called me." Dismissively, Rage took Keiran's hand and pressed his lips to the warm palm.

Keiran shook his head—it wasn't possible for Rage to understand what he meant, but as he was really hard now, he didn't think about it any longer.

"Come on top of me," he murmured, placing his bandaged hands on the boy's hips. "You're as hard as I am. Let's fuck."

Not more than a heartbeat—but Keiran hesitated, long enough for Rage to raise a questioning eyebrow at him. Only when Rage moved his hands, trying to pull the boy down for a kiss or at least brush over his cock, Keiran blinked and slipped smoothly atop of him. Before Rage could say a word, he leaned forward, captured Rage's hands, and pinned them to the mattress.

Something's different, Rage thought, watching the boy's face. But it was a strangely arousing thing, being held like this. And he liked Keiran to be in control every now and then, so Rage sunk into the pillows, closed his eyes, and enjoyed the boy's attention.

Only moments later, Keiran spread his legs and lowered himself—slowly, perfectly slowly—onto Rage's painfully hard cock.

A low groan emerged from Rage's lips, and when the boy moved as Rage's cock drove deeper into the boy's hot, tight ass, for the first time he wondered whether he should truly leave him behind.

Keiran's jaw was set, and sweat had broken out on his brow. He didn't move, only sat and breathed deeply with his hands still grasping Rage's wrists tightly.

What's wrong with you? Rage wanted to ask just when Keiran leaned forward and swirled his hips.

Wrong, wrong, wrong, Rage's mind sang, and then he saw the pain in the boy's eyes and the fear.

Rage broke free from Keiran's grip, wrapped his arms around the boy and sat up. The movement drove his cock deeper into the boy's body. Usually, Keiran would have kissed him now, sharing, heightening their combined lust.

Instead, Keiran moved, but awkwardly, arrhythmically.

As if he's doing this for the first time, Rage thought distractedly. *How did he—*

Keiran embraced him, pressing his face at his shoulder. After a hesitant moment, they began to rock gently. It was a very different way of lovemaking compared to the various times before. But strangely intimate and tender.

Strangely wonderful.

As often, Rage thought he could hear the small gasps of pleasure Keiran made, soft sighs indicating he was enjoying this as much as himself. If there really had been pain, it was gone now, and Rage smiled, moved, and got on top of the boy.

Wide eyes looked at him, so full of surprise it made Rage laugh.

He fucked the boy until he came, too impatient to wait for Keiran to spill his seed too. He would take care of his lover's cock once he had gotten his breath back. For now—

A flash of pain shot from his left wrist to his shoulder.

Wrong, his mind screamed with agonizing force.

Vertigo claimed him. Rage pushed himself off the boy, struggling to remember where up was and where down. Collapsing onto the bed, the unpleasant sensation of falling while lying flat on his back made him sick, and his stomach cramped.

Keiran, leaning over him. A strand of hair brushed his face.

But Keiran's hair was too short to reach that low.

Blood began seeping anew through his bandages.

Rage's stomach heaved. He pushed Keiran out of the way, turned on his side and retched, eyes watering, feeling as though he wanted to throw up everything he had ever eaten in his whole life.

More pain, blinding, heartbreaking. Not knowing where he was, or who, Rage fell. He crossed miles and eternities before he hit the floor, then crawled away from the bed.

Magic, strong magic was all around him, killing him.

"What's wrong with you?" a voice asked with irritation.

There shouldn't be a voice, not one his ears could hear, anyway. Keiran was mute even at the height of passion, and besides, he wouldn't have asked such a stupid question.

Everything was wrong.

Frantically, Rage tried to get the bandages off his left arm but failed because his fingers were too weak and feeble, so he used his teeth instead. Tasting the blood and the salve that had seeped into the fabric, the bandage was gone, finally allowing him to see the bracelet.

It wasn't black anymore. It glowed a bright red, as red as the blood that was dripping onto the wooden planks.

Red. The color of magic.

"No!" On all fours like a dog, Rage crawled toward the outer wall, his hands leaving dark prints on the floor.

Panic gripped him. Red was the worst color, worse than the color of poisoning, worse even than the pale gray the bracelet took on when he was close to death.

"Who are you?" he croaked. He was trying to reach the window. If he managed to jump, if he broke his neck in the next few seconds, he might be able to prevent the otherwise inevitable catastrophe.

Words fell into his brain. They did not make sense as his brain was burning, just like Teddy's hut.

"I am sorry for having tricked you," a voice said, a hand touching him, cool, distant. Not Keiran's hand. Smaller and a lot less calloused. "But I saw no other way. You're a married man now. You are safe. And I am safe too."

No sense at all. Nothing made sense anymore. Rage tried to get up but couldn't because his hands were once more slippery from blood. Cheek against wood, Rage lay there, naked and bleeding and filled with pain and realization.

There was a leg in front of him. Small ankle, pale skin, short blonde hairs.

A girl's leg.

"But," Rage croaked, staring incomprehensibly at the leg and then the bracelet around his wrist. "But you've got magic."

"Of course I do," Luca said, confusion showing in her voice. "So what? What's important is you're bleeding all over the place. Tell me what's wrong with you!" She knelt beside him, a thin sheet wrapped around her body, and almost gently touched his shoulder. "I didn't want to hurt you. I don't know how this happened. I'll get Lindsay."

Faintly, Rage heard himself laugh. He sounded raw and bitter. "Too late," he whispered. "She's dead. You're all dead."

More blood and more pain—his flesh was being flogged off his bones, and he began to scream, just like the last time this had happened, when he'd killed his love, his friends, his family, his entire village.

Hopefully, this time he would die too.

CHAPTER
Ten

No! LUCA thought when Rage came deep inside her. *Just when it begins to get good, he is done!*

Biting her lips so as to not say a word, she sat on the edge of the bed and tried to get her breathing under control. A moment ago, the assassin had been on top of her, inside her, pinning her down with his weight and his lust and that crooked little smile that made him look almost nice. True, when she'd taken him in—with her eyes squeezed shut and her mind protesting and telling her that this was a really, really bad idea—it had hurt. Stunned and sweating with the pain, all she'd been able to do was sit on him, wondering how to go on from here and whether she wanted to go on at all.

He'd frowned; he'd seen the pain in her face.

This was *not* a bad idea!

So she had moved, and after a moment, he had moved with her. And she had hugged him. And he had hugged her back, and then he had been on top, and had it been her choice, he wouldn't have stopped quite so soon.

He had enjoyed it. He had spilled his seed inside her, which was nearly the most important thing, but he had also enjoyed it, and for some reason, this was even more important in her eyes.

Luca pulled a sheet around her shoulders, and with a quick word, she dropped the glamour that had made her look like Keiran.

The insides of her legs were sensitive to the touch. Luca wondered if she could bear to put her trousers back on and, for the first time since Rage had kidnapped her, wished she had a skirt instead. A shower would be good too. Maybe, if she asked nicely,

Rage would allow her to use his rainstone because, frankly, she was too tired to use magic.

Her legs were sticky, and she was disappointed. She'd hoped to lie in his arms for just a few moments, bathing in his body heat. She had wanted to tell him why she had done what she had done and apologize properly for it, but he had thrown up, and now he was on the floor, crawling away from her, bleeding, scaring her to death.

Across his naked back, a long wound ripped open as if he'd been whipped. His scream made it shockingly clear that he wasn't all right at all and that he wasn't just sick, either.

Instantly, she knelt beside him only to see him crawl away from her.

"I'll get Lindsay," Luca said, a shiver of fear running through her. Surely the landlady would know what to do with him. She'd saved his life before. She'd—

"You're all dead," Rage rasped, a statement said so flatly, so bitterly that the small hairs on Luca's neck stood up. She forgot all about her plan to shower, about breakfast, about what she needed to do next to get rid of her father. And she forgot about Lindsay.

With trembling hands she pulled the sheet tighter around her, went after Rage, and hesitantly placed her palm on his shoulder.

He was hot, burning under her touch. More wounds appeared out of nowhere, and he screamed again, cradling his head in his arms. His whole body shook as one slash after another appeared on his skin.

Biting her lips to keep her fear under control, Luca sealed the attic room. The magic obeyed hesitantly for she was too tired to have much strength left, but she did it anyway.

No sound could get out now. No one would hear Rage scream. She was the one with the best knowledge of magic. If she couldn't deal with this, no one could.

"Tell me what's wrong with you," she urged as she shook him. By the looks of it, he at least would be dead soon.

His screams dwindled into low, weak moans, and a pool of blood was forming around him. He wasn't moving anymore, though he still seemed conscious. He'd balled his fists, eyes wide open and full of fear and staring right through her.

The sheet had long slipped off her, and she was as naked as he, stroking his sweaty face. The ends of her hair were bloodied from where they had brushed against his body.

He grabbed her, found her hand on his chest, and pulled her closer.

"Tell me what to do," she whispered. "Tell me what's wrong with you!"

His words were just a hiss. "Nothing, you can do… nothing. Run. Save yourself. Take the horse… and the boy. Run!"

"You're trying to keep control, aren't you?" Fervently, she thought of everything she'd ever learned about magic, remembered the long, slow afternoons she'd spent in her mother's library, hidden behind the sofa with piles of books around her. Her father had never thought of looking in that place. She'd been safe there.

Some of the books had been centuries old, and it had been hard to read them given that the letters looked like they'd been written by a drunken spider. Magic was for the poor as well as the rich, but only the rich had books they could learn from.

But not even in her books had Luca read of someone like Rage, who was obviously neither physically nor mentally disabled but still claimed not to be able to do magic. She had never seen him perform even the easiest bit of Fire magic, but then she hadn't been with him all the time. Maybe he'd lied to her. Maybe he could do magic and just didn't want her to know.

But—there was no reason for him to lie about his magical abilities, if he had any. Not doing magic was what caused suspicions and questions. Not doing magic was also a sign of weakness. As an assassin, he surely wouldn't want people considering him weak?

His hand was still locked around her wrist—running was impossible even if she had wanted to. Which wasn't the case. She was curious about Rage, about his magic, about the reason he wore the bracelet, and most of all about his secrets.

A wave of wild magic so bright it nearly blinded her shot through the room. It was so much stronger than the wild magic that had escaped her the night Keiran had found her that for a moment she refused to believe it had happened at all.

No one was that strong!

"Can't keep control. Get out!" Rage's back arched, his muscles tightening, his joints creaking under the pressure caused by an onslaught of magic.

The wild magic rattled the windows and pushed the bed against the wall. On the roof, the shingles came loose and fell to the ground.

"Is it because I'm female?" Luca asked, frantically trying to find a reason for this madness. "Is it because of something I did or didn't do? By the Lady, Rage, I am sorry for this, but you need to tell me why this is happening!"

"'Cause there's magic in you," Rage rasped as bloody tears ran down his cheeks. He looked horrible, and it was obvious that he was desperately trying to hold back the waves of magic that emanated from him. "Can't be with anyone with magic. Sets something in motion.... You... need...."

More wild magic, strong enough to make the people in the house and the ones passing by scream with pain.

His magic would kill her, and given the strength of the waves, it would kill the people downstairs too—Lindsay and her sons, the horses in the stables, everyone who was near.

Keiran too.

She couldn't let that happen.

When she looked at Rage, she saw that he wasn't with her anymore, lost in his own world filled with pain. He murmured something, unintelligible words....

She bent, her ear close to his lips. Listened. It was a nursery rhyme, and word by word, Rage bit it out, concentrating on the syllables, the simple rhythm. It was obviously helping him not to lose the last strands of control. Luca guessed the moment he passed out, the magic inside him would erupt like a volcano, taking down everything and everyone that was too close.

There were scars on him underneath the blood. She had seen them when she'd been in bed with him and had wondered what had caused them.

"This is not the first time this has happened to you," she murmured as Rage's grip became weak. His eyes rolled back.

And then she had an idea. Just a small one, just the scrap of a thought. She broke free of his grip and lunged for his belongings, which were lying in a heap next to the bed.

"Where is it?" she growled, anger streaming through her and washing away the fear. "Come on, I know you are in here, stupid little thing!"

By the Lady, how many things did this man carry in his bag?

There it was, the little black rainstone. Once, she had discarded it as useless, had considered it a pitiful tool for the helpless, those poor fools who had to walk through life without magic. She had even playfully twisted the magic stored inside so it would provide warm water.

Now it might save her life.

Rage lay motionless on the floor, magic seeping out of him like yolk out of a cracked egg. Slamming the rainstone onto his chest and trying her best to ignore that she was now covered in his blood, she concentrated on the magic stored in the stone. Praying to the Lady she would have strength enough to pull this off, she began to wield her own magic.

Praying the next wave of wild magic wouldn't kill her.

Underneath her hand, Luca felt Rage struggle. She could smell the blood on the floor and the sweat on her own skin. She heard him scream. It didn't matter. She was very calm now as she strengthened the stone's magic, bit by bit, adding her own magic until she'd built an impenetrable wall around Rage. It was so easy she nearly laughed—except she cried instead as she pressed her hands onto the rainstone and onto his chest as well, weaving her magic into her tears, which were mingling with his blood.

Maybe it would even work.

THE STREET was covered with ash, and the air still smelled of smoke as Keiran walked through the Shadows in search of the little girl Rage had rescued. Luca had sent him, had asked him to find out where she was and if she was well. She'd wanted him gone for a few hours. No reason not to do as she had asked—if a friend asked for a favor, you did it no matter what.

Although Keiran would have preferred to stay in bed with Rage.

He grinned at the thought. Being in bed with Rage—or in the hay or the river or wherever, actually—was beyond good. It was perfect, and just thinking of it made him hard.

No time for that. He had an errand to run, and if he did it quickly enough, there might be time for lunch with Rage. In bed.

Vaguely, he wondered what Luca was up to. Something she shouldn't do, surely. Bending the rules to her will was her way of coping with the world. Occasionally, she bit off more than she could chew, like the time she'd broken her leg when she ran away because her father had the first litter of her favorite cat killed and made her watch. Since then, she'd hated him even more than before.

People on the street greeted him with grumbling nods, acknowledging that he'd been there during the fire and that he'd helped to keep it at bay. With a nod, they said, "We know you," and, "You are no stranger to us." It was a good feeling, being seen that way, not as an intruder, not as a danger to their lives and families. Keiran didn't like being hated and feared.

This part of the Shadows was darker and shabbier than the area around the tavern. The fire hadn't reached these streets, which was good, as the houses were even closer together here. The flames would have destroyed many lives.

A woman directed him to a small house at the end of the street, and Keiran nodded his thanks. She returned a toothless smile— although barely older than twenty, syphilis had turned her into an old wretch long before her time.

"The kid's with her mommy right now," the woman said, eying him greedily. "Bella doesn't have to work until midday. You should find them at home."

Keiran saw in her face and in her shiny, drugged-up eyes that she wanted to touch him. She wanted to drag him inside her hut and push him onto her bed and ride him until she fainted—her wishes were as clear to him as if she'd said them aloud.

Swiftly, he bent and kissed her cheek, making her blush with the simple, friendly gesture. Then he turned and walked away. He wouldn't have gone with her. As it was, the kiss would hopefully prevent her from lashing out at him for turning her down.

Sometimes his ability to manipulate people scared him.

Yes, another hour in bed with Rage would have started off the day for the better. His lover responded to touch like no one Keiran had had before, and he liked to be seduced into lovemaking. At first, he had thought Rage might be too dominant to surrender to his kisses, only to find out he was wrong. Rage radiated aggressiveness combined with a tightly controlled power Keiran found oddly intriguing, but he was just as willing to bottom, which was even more intriguing.

From the moment he'd set eyes on him, Keiran had been lost.

The last house on the street was shabby, the roof rotten, some of the windows broken. The sight took Keiran's thoughts off Rage and their bed in the attic. After a short knock, he went inside without waiting for an answer. He didn't want to linger on the street. Somehow, he had a vague feeling of being watched.

"What d'you want?"

The woman's voice was sharp, and underneath was a layer of fear easy to detect for Keiran. He never had trouble hearing what people were really saying despite the words they used. One look and he saw their hearts and minds, like flames in the darkness. Luca's flame was bright and orange, the wizard and the witch who'd attacked them both had sickly green ones, Lindsay's was a steady purple, and Rage's was, what else, clear and black.

Keiran often thought of people by thinking of their color. It helped tell them apart, and it made it a lot easier to tell who wanted to do him harm and who was good. This woman, for example, didn't know whether to attack or flee. She was scared as well as aggressive, and it showed in the color Keiran saw in her: red mixed with a pale yellow. To put her at ease, he showed her his empty hands, and he smiled. On her arm was the girl Rage had saved from the fire, Debbie.

"Hi," the little girl piped up.

Keiran's smile widened. In her face he could see she could hear him. Apart from Rage, and sometimes Luca, adults weren't able to catch his thoughts unless he used his hands to explain himself, but often, there was an instant link with a child. Debbie seemed to be one of them.

"Mommy, he says hi too," the child told her mother. "He says he was sent to see if I'm well."

"Didn't hear him speak," her mother snapped. "Is he mute?"

Keiran nodded and held out his hand. The woman looked at it as if she'd never seen a hand before, thought about it, and finally shook it.

"Who are you, then?" she asked, clutching her daughter.

She was a tall woman, haggard and looking older than she really was. Greasy black hair fell down to her shoulders, and under her eyes were shadows suggesting she hadn't slept well in a long time.

Keiran bowed his head, then focused on the child. She was young enough not to question his way of communication. He gently touched her cheek.

"His friend got me out yesterday, Mommy," the child said. "The black man."

The woman's eyes widened. "That man—Rage? You know him? Can you tell him how grateful I am for what he did? Teddy was a good father, under the circumstances. With us not being married and my job and him being a thief and all. If you see this man Rage, I want him to know we'll be always in his debt."

"Says it's not necessary, Mommy." Debbie beamed at Keiran and wriggled in her mother's arms until she put her down.

Keiran pulled out the letter he'd written earlier and handed it to her. What needed to be said was too complicated for a child to repeat, and he wanted the mother to know what had happened prior to Teddy's death. Rage had told him—sometimes, he could be talkative after lovemaking—and Keiran knew Rage didn't like to owe a debt, so he'd decided to write a few things down.

The child took the letter, trying to open it with chubby little hands. When her mother scolded her and snatched at the letter, the girl pulled a face and tried to hide behind a table, letter in hand, grinning from ear to ear.

"Give me the letter, little frog," her mother said, her eyes darting to Keiran. When she dared to smile at him, he smiled back. Inclining his head, he left, leaving mother and daughter to their friendly quarrel as well as their grief. His task was done. He could tell Luca the child was fine, and Rage would know the favor he owed Teddy now belonged to Teddy's wife and kid.

Walking through the streets and back toward the tavern, Keiran found his thoughts drifting back to Rage. He couldn't suppress a lopsided grin. *I've fallen for him*, he thought, not knowing whether it was a good thing or a bad thing to be in love with an assassin. Rage certainly thought of him as nothing more than a pastime, using him for pleasure whenever he felt like it. He knew that for sure; being mute didn't mean he was dumb, although many people believed just that.

Not Rage, though.

There was something hidden inside the assassin, something Keiran believed Rage wasn't aware of. Nothing as simple as a wish for a companion, for sex, or a different life. More like a part of him was hollow, longing for light and color. Keiran had no idea if that place could be filled, or even if the assassin wanted it filled at all. It seemed to define him, and to Keiran, it was absolutely clear Rage wouldn't allow anyone to get close or even admit he was fond of someone he'd met only recently.

Rage's black flame was bright even now although Keiran had left his bed a while ago and was still at least a mile away from the tavern.

Suddenly, Keiran felt cold. He absently rubbed his arms, then looked at the sky to check if the sun was hiding behind the clouds.

The sun was high in the sky.

Frowning, Keiran came to a halt. Being born without magic, he was used to paying more attention to his surroundings and the people he was dealing with. If he wasn't careful, he sometimes even scared people with his ability to read them. Empathic, Luca had once called him, and back then, he'd laughed. As time went on, he knew she was right.

The air grew colder, and Keiran gasped, then staggered. A shadow touched him, a shadow that had emerged from his lover, dark and red at the same time.

Luca.

She'd planned something, and she'd carried it out, but whatever she was doing to Rage was wrong.

Dangerous.

She was killing him.

Breaking into a run, Keiran didn't care about anything but getting back to the tavern. Not bothering to watch out for people crossing his path, he pushed them out of the way rather than going around them. And he totally forgot about the odd feeling he'd had earlier on, the feeling of being watched.

The assassin's flame turned from black to blood red.

Keiran thought he could hear him scream.

He ran faster, fear of what Luca might have done gripping him. She was stubborn, and when she got an idea in her head, she often forgot to ask herself whether she was endangering others to achieve her goal.

Had he bothered to give a nearby back alley a cursory glance, he might have seen the man hiding behind the barrels. He might have sensed the danger, might have seen the bitter flame of yellow hate burning inside the man's chest and in his eyes, the feeling of betrayal and loss.

But Keiran didn't see the man, and he didn't see the bat.

The power of the swing threw him off his feet, backward into the dust. The wind had been knocked out of his lungs. His nose broken, his cheekbone cracked, his face covered in blood.

The sky above him was blue; it would have been the perfect morning for a long walk along the river. As Keiran lost consciousness, his last thought was of Rage, and the last thing he heard were his lover's screams and someone cursing nastily.

HANDS WERE on his face, his shoulders, moving down to his belly and upward to his shoulders.

No pain; no fear.

Not bad, he thought.

Hands on his legs, turning him over. Hands on his back, his ass, then moving back up again.

Strange. There was nothing arousing in this touch, only a certain coolness combined with determination.

Murmured words. He knew that voice. An annoying voice, for the most part. What were the words? Nothing sweet. Nothing dirty, either.

Hard wood underneath him. He wasn't in bed.

I should be dead.

At that thought, Rage opened his eyes. He struggled to roll on his side before flopping onto his back. Sunlight made him turn his head toward the window, and he saw the bed towering above, blue sky, and his outstretched, naked arm. Tentatively, he moved his fingers.

A slender foot came into view, tapping impatiently.

The foot touched his arm, prodding it as if checking if he were still alive.

"Stop 't," Rage mumbled, his tongue sticking to the roof of his mouth. "W' happ'd?"

"Guess you need some water so you can talk properly," the voice said.

Rage heard liquid being poured into a glass, then felt a hand slip under his neck, lifting his head. Cool, wonderful water flooded his mouth and washed away the taste of blood and bile he only became aware of now that it was gone. He coughed, his muscles cramping with the attempt to breathe, expelling stray drops of water. Then his stomach heaved, and he spat out most of it again. Like a half-dead fish, he lay on the floor, struggling and trying in vain to remember what the hell had happened.

"You're not dead, in case you were wondering," the voice said, surprisingly gentle and with a touch of remorse woven into the words.

Gathering what was left of his strength, Rage sat up. Leaning against the bed, shaking and shivering, he observed he was in the attic room.

The girl was watching him.

"You're naked," Rage said, wracking his brain for at least a small hint of past events.

"So are you," Luca replied, but without her usual snap. "Just for the record, I just saved your life. You were about to destroy yourself and everyone around you, so I performed a bit of ingenious magic and prevented a catastrophe. I truly had no time to get dressed amidst my various tasks."

What she said didn't make any sense to him.

"You look totally dumbstruck." Luca sighed. "Look, this is my fault. And I am sorry for the pain I caused. I seduced you, remember? Looking like Keiran? I didn't see another way out of our dilemma, and I feared that if I asked you, you would have said no. And a no was not an option, not with the soldiers out there and my father and Jeeve. Of course, I didn't know you have a problem with magic, but well, I took care of it, didn't I? You didn't die. Actually, a thank you would be nice."

Seduced me, Rage thought weakly. "How—" And then he did remember her coming into his bed, looking like the boy. He remembered making love to her. He remembered the fear and the pain in her eyes and how she had clung to him, how they had rocked together.

How he had, even back then, wondered about the tenderness in their lovemaking and how much he had liked it.

He also remembered what had happened afterward. And the loss of all the lives, unexpectedly, made his throat dry with sorrow.

Rage froze as he realized that, outside of these four walls, there must be heaps and heaps of corpses, killed by him and his awful, unpredictable magic.

Just like last time.

"Don't you think it's time to get up?" the girl asked, clearly not knowing why he was so quiet. Shocked. "You're filthy. I healed the wounds your magic caused, but you've got to wash off the blood yourself."

Rage looked at the girl, really looked at her for probably the first time since they'd met. Her long, blonde hair was sticking to her small breasts, her skin glowed in the sunlight, and her eyes were bright and clear like an enchanted lake. She was beautiful, sitting on the side of the bed like she was, never mind that there were splashes of his blood on her.

"You should have let me die." There were other things he wanted to say. *Why did you seduce me?* for example. *Why are you still alive?* But thinking didn't come as easily as he'd wished for.

"My, are we dramatic this morning. It's just a shower."

Somehow he wasn't getting through to the girl. Somehow, she did not understand that healing his wounds, saving his life, was unimportant compared to what horrors had happened outside the room.

Slowly, Rage got to his feet. He didn't have the strength to get to the window. "I cannot be with someone who is magical," he said softly. "For reasons no one has ever been able to explain to me, the magic I was born with is too strong to be controlled. I burned down my father's house when I was three because I wanted to light a candle. I killed my dog simply by touching her. I wanted to heal her nose, which had been pierced by a porcupine. My magic slashed her to pieces."

Luca's eyes widened. "I—"

"When I was eight, having accidentally conjured a river to flood my village, I was forbidden to use magic. When I nearly burned down the whole village at eleven, I finally stuck to it. I've learned how to keep it hidden inside me. Not the smallest Fire magic, no Healing magic no matter how dire the circumstances, not even the words for mending a torn shirt. Nothing. And I was fine with it. There were other things I could do, and in the countryside, magic isn't that important anyway."

Luca took his hand and pulled him onto the bed next to her. He sat down heavily.

"You scared me, assassin. The blood and your screams and then your magic began slashing at you. Has something like that happened before?"

Rage nodded, his eyes closed in despair.

"Like—how? Did you use your magic although it was forbidden?"

"No. I fell in love."

Luca waited for him to continue. She sat on the bed with him, the perfect image of a good girl had it not been for the total lack of clothes and the blood soiling them both. "That's not such a bad thing," she said quietly when the silence went on for too long.

Rage laughed, a bitter sound that hurt his ears. "It was an awful thing, in my case. I slept with him was what happened. I was fourteen years old. I adored the earth he walked upon, and when he chose me, I couldn't believe my luck. He was two years older than me and barely able to do basic magic himself. Nothing compared to my own buried abilities. He was blond, like you. A farmer's son, hardworking, hands callused and skin burned dark from spending his days in the fields. He was my sunshine, my reason to be."

He didn't have a clue why he was telling her all of this. He only knew that if he didn't speak, the words would choke him.

"He took me to the woods one evening. There was a small lake amongst the trees. We swam and laughed, we ate together, and eventually, he pulled me close and pressed his lips to mine. They were warm, *he* was warm, although the lake's water had been cold. He was so damn beautiful, and when he pressed me to the ground, I surrendered without doubt. That my magic was stirring inside me I didn't even notice. When he fucked me, I was too far lost in pleasure to realize something was wrong. Wild magic erupted from me. When it couldn't get out fast enough through my mouth and eyes, the magic slashed me, cutting me open like my father used to cut open swine. I survived. He did not."

"That's where the scars come from." Luca swallowed hard.

"It—I—killed everybody. My lover, my family, my friends— the whole village was dead when I came back to my senses. I never understood why the magic didn't kill me as well, but then, I didn't really care anymore. I buried my love, my parents, and my older sister. I changed my name and ran away. I got myself a charm that told me if someone is magical, and ever since, I've not touched anyone who possesses magic."

Absentmindedly, Rage hugged himself, shivering with cold and exhaustion. On his skin, there were new scars.

He should have died.

"I didn't sleep with you to hurt you." Luca sighed deeply. "I willingly gave you my virginity. You willingly caressed me, kissed me, and came inside me. We are married, Rage. It had to be done because of that stupid soldier asking too many questions. I found a solution for a problem that, unsolved, could have landed both of us in prison. I knew about the bracelet, so I covered it with the bandage. I sent Keiran off on an errand and put on a glamour. I tricked you, but I did not force you, and frankly, I would have chosen a bit more romance for my wedding night had I had the choice."

She still did not understand. "Was solving a problem, as you put it, worth the death of dozens of people?" he asked, looking at her and realizing that there were unshed tears burning behind his lids.

Luca rolled her eyes. "No one's dead, idiot. And I thought my reasons were clear even to someone as thick as you." Taking Rage's wrist, she pulled him to the window. "I told that guard we were married, if you remember. Which was, at the time, a lie. He was angry when he left, humiliated. I feared he would come back and demand proof of my statement. Hadn't I seduced you, hadn't I made true what had been a lie, he could have hanged you on the spot and brought me back to my father. Who wants to kill me? Honestly, Rage, I am sorry for this whole mess, but what would you have done in my place? Sit around and start believing in a fairy godmother solving my problems?"

Rage was slow on his legs, and his brain was slow to understand her words.

Impatiently, she pushed him forward. "I said I saved your life, didn't I? Do you think I wouldn't have mentioned corpses in the street? Don't you ever listen to me? Look out the window, assassin, and tell me what you see!"

Disbelievingly, Rage did as ordered. He looked out of the window.

Lindsay was talking to the neighbor's wife. They were both quite serious until Lindsay made a joke, and they both burst out laughing. Ben was grooming one of the horses at the stables. The man was whistling with the steady rhythm of his arm, up and down across the horse's coat. He saw the burned houses, smelled the smoke still hanging in the air, and heard voices from the kitchen.

He didn't see any corpses.

Impossible.

Luca's hand slipped into his. Had someone seen them, standing naked and hand in hand, he might have thought them lovers. "No one died," she reassured him gently. "When I saw you collapse, I realized things had gone terribly wrong. Then I remembered the rainstone magic and thought I could try to keep your magic inside the shield instead of the water. It worked perfectly, and by using your magic to feed the shield, I accomplished two tasks at once. You were drained, the shield became stronger, and everyone else was safe." Raising her chin, she looked him up and down. "You *could* say you're proud of your wife."

Rage frowned. "I don't do marriage," he said, and then he laughed at the absurdity of the situation, and then he picked up that insufferable girl and swung her around until they both crashed to the floor, a heap of naked, happy, dirty limbs.

Not entirely trusting his voice, Rage took Luca's face in his hands. "I am not entirely sure yet about my feelings concerning this marrying nonsense, but in any case, I am deeply in your debt, Lucinda of Babylon."

"And that would be Luca to you," she replied with a sweet smile.

CHAPTER
Eleven

"You're filthy." Holding the rainstone in her hand, Luca looked him up and down, making Rage feel, quite unexpectedly, uncomfortably vulnerable.

He was filthy. He was naked and three times as old as this girl he'd just been in bed with.

She had tricked him in a way he didn't want to think about right now.

She had saved his life.

And apart from one other person, she was the only one who knew about his past.

He sighed.

"Shower?" she asked.

"Shower," he agreed.

"I can twist the magic again so we can have warm water." Luca put the rainstone on the windowsill, blew at it, and watched the first drops gather in invisible clouds directly beneath the ceiling. It looked as though the beams were crying.

"Come on." She tapped her foot again. "I'm tired and hungry. We need to shower together, unless you want to wait and put up with cold water."

It was an easy decision, given Rage was chilled to his bones. He took a tentative step toward the falling drops. They were indeed warm. The girl pulled him underneath the spray, apparently unconcerned about her nakedness.

"You're bold," Rage said, more to break the silence than to make conversation. This was an unusual situation, and he didn't quite know how to deal with it.

"We're married now. No need to be shy in front of one's husband." She raised her face into the water, grinning and flickering her eyes in his direction. "I didn't expect you to take it quite so well." She stretched as she rolled her shoulders.

Clumsily, because of his burned hands, Rage took the soap. Flakes of blood were washed away, dirt and foam, but it was taking him a while to get clean with his hands feeling so strangely numb and tingly.

Luca was watching him.

It was unnerving.

"Hand me the soap," Luca suddenly ordered. "I can see your hands hurt. Like this, we'll be here for another hour, and I don't have the strength to keep the water warm for that long."

When he hesitated, she just took the soap out of his hands. Roughly—now that she was this close to him, she was a little less bold, he realized—she dragged it over his head.

"Bend down a bit so I can wash your hair. Sorry, but I was focusing on healing the really bad wounds. I will try and take care of your hands later."

"You could have healed them right after the fire," he stated but then frowned. "No, you couldn't. You needed my hands burned so you could bandage them and my bracelet with them. How did you know about the bracelet's magic?"

"I kind of overheard your conversation with Keiran."

Once more, Rage sighed, then bent his head as ordered. Silently, with his eyes closed, he stood and endured her touch. She wasn't gentle, her fingers strong, but someone taking care of him was a surprisingly nice experience.

When he was clean, Luca washed her own hair. "Have you never slept with a woman?" she asked casually, as if she were talking about gardening. "I only ask because you don't seem the slightest bit interested in me even though I am standing naked right in front of you."

He turned to her and captured her hands in his. Her bones were fragile, her small fingers like a sparrow in his grip.

She froze.

"Rage—"

Intently, he gazed into her eyes. They became darker, just a tad, like the ocean closely before a storm.

"Coming into my bed scared you." His voice was dark and dangerous. "Sleeping with me caused you pain. You are barely more than a child, and still you deal with problems in a way a much older woman couldn't. You expect me to accept you as my wife. You expect me to forgive you for having tricked me into having sex with you. Had it been the other way round, would you not accuse me of rape?"

She held his gaze. The spray made it look as if she were crying, but she did hold his gaze.

Maybe she was crying.

"I did not see another way," she whispered.

He tightened his grip around her fingers. "You needed a husband. You love the boy. You could have taken him." Foam dripped from his hair onto their entwined hands. It was just a little bit pink.

She swallowed. Blinked. Took a breath. "You are strong. You kill people. The life you live—the way you are—it makes you see people in a different way. Do you believe in love, Rage? I mean, even if you are in love, do you admit it to yourself? I don't think so. Marriage means nothing to you. Sex with someone you don't know means nothing to you. You take whores, you said it yourself. And you enjoyed sleeping with me. I did not force you. I thought—I lay awake all night and thought about this! I couldn't take Keiran because he believes in love and marriage, and had I done this to him, he couldn't have dealt with it. Besides, marrying him would have saved only me. It would not have saved you, and no matter what you think, I like you, and I would have never *raped* you!"

Her voice had become louder, and her chest heaved from the words she had shouted at him. Her hands captured in his, reaching barely up to his shoulders, skin to skin she was not scared of him now.

Very slowly, he released her. Very gently, he took her face between his hands instead. His face was only inches away from hers.

He kissed her, a short brush across her lips, nothing more. He felt her surprise more than he saw it, and he couldn't help a smile.

"I like you too," he said. "And I did enjoy being with you. I will not accuse you of rape again." Brushing her hair behind her ears, he plucked out a few strands, then did the same with his.

"Marrying the old way requires a ring made in the old way. Do you have enough magic left to do it?"

She took the strands, blonde and black, and tilted her head. She looked as if the impact of her actions became clear to her only now. "Keiran will kill me," she said helplessly. "How shall I explain this to him?"

Then she twisted the strands and murmured some words, and then she held two rings made of hair and magic on her open palm. Swiftly, she took his hand and put the larger ring on his finger.

He did the same with hers, and when he was done, she placed her hand on his chest. "You are not that ugly, really, nor that old," she said with a hesitant smile.

Rage felt an urge to laugh bubble up inside him. "You're crazy," he said. "Completely nuts. Keiran knows that."

"But he loves you. He will think I tried to steal you away from him."

Suddenly, the water turned cold, preventing him from having to comment on what she had said.

That he did not belong to the boy and that it was unimportant to him what Keiran felt. That he would leave both of them behind and forget about them within a few days.

That as an assassin, his job was to kill, not to care.

Rage stopped the rainstone's magic, took the stone, and stored it in his bag. By the time he was done, Luca had already dressed.

She was wearing his old trousers again and the shirt she'd borrowed from Lindsay. Her hair was braided into a simple plait.

Rage got dressed before tentatively flexing his fingers. The skin on his palms was red and thin, cracked in places and unpleasantly sensitive to the touch. He wouldn't be able to use his hands properly for a while. He saw how pale the girl was and took fresh bandages from his bag. "Forget about healing my hands. You're done with magic for a few days. I can live with aching hands for a little while."

Luca dropped on the bed. "You don't have a choice anyway. Ask Lindsay for a salve."

She joined him on the way down the stairs, slipping her hand into his. "Will you tell Keiran about this? I mean, now? I would like to eat first before all hell breaks loose."

They stood in front of the kitchen door. Behind it, Lindsay was fussing about whatever she'd decided to fuss about today.

Rage lowered his face until he was eye to eye with the girl. "One of these days, I'll strangle you."

"Of course you will," Luca replied sweetly. "Once your hands are healed." Pecking a kiss onto his stubbly cheek, she pushed open the door to the kitchen.

Lindsay looked up from the table she'd been towering over when they entered, Luca first, Rage behind her. "About time you got downstairs," she said. "I would have sent Ben to get you, but I needed him here. They've found your friend on the streets. They just brought him back here. I don't know how bad it is, but he doesn't look well."

Keiran was lying stretched out on the table, one hand hanging limply over the side. He was paler than usual, and his face and hair were matted with blood. Obviously, his nose was broken. It made a hissing sound whenever he took a breath.

The cat, white paws neatly together, sat next to Keiran's head, his green eyes staring intently at the silent body as though trying to read the boy's thoughts.

Rage was at Keiran's side in an instant. Taking the boy's hand in his, he bent low, brushing some bloodied strands of hair out of Keiran's face.

"He's unconscious," Rage stated flatly. "How did this happen?"

"Found him near the place where Teddy's woman lives," Ben said from the other side of the table. "Mom said to keep an eye on all of you. Followed him when he left this morning. I saw the guy who hit him but thought you'd rather have him back alive than me chasing down the one who did it."

Rage wasn't really listening. The pale face in front of him was all he saw, and the harsh, slightly ragged breathing all he heard.

"I did some Healing magic on him," Mike said. "Gonna do his nose in a minute. Patched up his skull so far. Guess it's sheer luck the guy didn't kill him."

"You saw the man who hit him?" Rage asked absently, fingertips resting lightly on Keiran's neck.

"Old guy. White hair, decent clothes. Didn't belong here. He must have found a really good hiding place."

White hair. "Did he have a big nose?" Rage asked.

"Yep. Why?"

"Debbie said the man who killed her father had a nose as large as a carrot."

Luca, having stepped next to him, gently stroked Keiran's limp hand. "It's Jeeve. It seems my father has found us."

Keiran's eyes snapped open, his heartbeat quickening under Rage's palm. *You're safe*, said Keiran's eyes and his smile. *I heard you screaming. I ran to get back to you when—*

"I know," Rage said. "Ben brought you back here. You're injured. Broken nose, broken cheekbone. You look horrible."

A crooked grin flashed over the boy's face. *And you look furious.*

Sadness claimed Rage's heart. Without hiding it behind schooled features, without calculation or falseness, Keiran had just admitted he'd go to hell and back for the assassin. The boy had fallen in love with him, and he was neither able nor willing to return his love.

Rage couldn't deal with this right now. Stepping back from the table, he ignored the hurt, confused look that shadowed the boy's beaten face. He didn't want the boy's love. He hadn't the time for it, either.

"I will put an end to this," he said to Luca. "I'll find your father and talk him out of his desire to kill us."

"We can go to the guards," Luca objected. "And you"—she shot a look at Keiran, who was trying to get off the table—"will stay where you are. No getting up for you, is that clear? I've seen enough blood for one day."

Rage was already out the back door and on his way to the stables, suppressing a sudden and irrational urge to kiss the boy good-bye. "Talking to the guards might land me in prison." Halting, he turned to the girl and Lindsay, who'd been watching and listening in stunned silence. "Promise me you'll stay in the house," he said to Luca.

"But—"

"Promise me!"

"All right, we'll stay inside until you're back. But as soon as Keiran is able to ride, we'll come looking for you."

Ben had saddled the assassin's horse in wise comprehension of events. He even held it by its harness until Rage had mounted, then stepped back and put an arm around his mother's shoulders.

"Lindsay, you are responsible for their safety. Swear you won't let them out of the house for a week at least. Can you do that?"

Lindsay's eyebrows shot up. "I knew there was something between you and the boy, but that you care about Luca as well—you surprise me, assassin, you really do."

Slapping the reins across the horse's neck, Rage galloped down the road and out of town without looking back.

RIDING FELT good. It was a simple joy, though it was combined with a strange pang of remorse over having left the boy behind.

The horse had been inside the stables for days now without the chance to stretch its limbs. It had been well fed and was well rested, so they were approaching Babylon Manor quicker than Rage had anticipated. If he carried on like this, he would be there by the next day.

Not that he was looking forward to it. The prospect of getting back to where it had all started held no appeal for him. Had he had the choice, he'd have gone north, where he knew of a safe place to stay. A bit of rest, with no killers on his heel and no one bothering him with their wishes and problems, would be nice.

But he had no choice. Maybe he could have escaped Lucius's wrath, but the girl and Keiran wouldn't have had a chance. If he wanted them to be safe, a word with Lucius was inevitable.

"I hate having to care for people," he muttered. "Damn the day I decided to take a closer look at Babylon Manor!"

It was going on evening when Rage finally slowed the horse down, allowing it to have some grass and water and continuing in a slow trot until nightfall. He was tired, hungry, and dreading the next day.

Lucius had to answer some questions. Rage was quite sure force would be needed to learn the truth as well as to persuade the man to stop the attacks.

Rage frowned. Damn torturing. Last time he had to break bones before his target admitted to having raped and killed a child. The confession had been part of his job, and his target's crime had been the sole reason for him taking on the job in the first place.

Arwen, the larger of the two moons, was rising, closely followed by Galadriel. They cast an eerie, unreal light, flooding the world with pale green and silver beams. It was a beautiful sight if one had an eye for it.

Rage, forcing his mind away from images of torture, thought of Keiran instead, the softness of the boy's lips, his tender, skillful hands, but most of all, his smile.

That smile....

"Enough of this." Thinking about Keiran distracted him from the task ahead, and it made him wish he hadn't left the tavern.

But that smile was worthy of remembering.

In that moment Rage decided not to go back to the tavern, no matter what happened at Babylon Manor. He'd been with the boy long enough, and that marriage nonsense would make his life unbearably complicated.

To hell with the girl. She'd be better off without him and would probably persuade the boy to warm her bed before long. Lucinda of Babylon always got what she wanted.

He did not slip the ring off his finger, though. And somewhat reluctantly, he remembered how strangely wonderful her tenderness had been.

When the horse tired, Rage dismounted and walked for the rest of the night. Feeling the earth under his feet was a good thing, but after an hour, his injured leg began to ache. After two, he was limping, but not enough to slow him down considerably.

Rage left the main road about a mile before Windbrook, the village belonging to Babylon Manor. The horse followed him willingly, sensing that the end of their journey was near and smelling there was water not too far ahead. Finally, they reached the hay barn Rage had used as shelter last time.

Slowly, the sky turned from black to pale gray. It was close to sunrise, and Rage was beyond fatigued by now. Nearly twenty-four hours had passed since he'd left Lindsay's tavern. He guessed he'd need another three before he was done with Lucius.

After that, he would head north.

As Rage wanted to tie his horse to a tree, it shied and hopped back several feet. Its ears lay flat against its skull, nostrils flaring—it was scared, and when Rage got close enough to take hold of the harness, he knew why.

The smell was incredible. Foul, rotten, disgusting. Only a corpse owned that particular smell, especially one that had been dead for a while.

Behind some bushes, he found the body of a young man of average height, average build, and a badly carved longbow crushed underneath him. When Rage knelt next to him, he found a wound a bolt had caused.

Most likely the man who'd attacked him and the girl.

At first, Rage assumed his bolt had been the cause of this man's death, but he soon discovered he was wrong. He'd hit the man all right, but only between the ribs. Not a nice wound, but usually not fatal.

What had killed him was a clean cut across the throat. The head was nearly severed from the shoulders, the gaping wound smiling a cruel, deathly grin. The corpse's eyes were wide open. Flies were feasting on the flesh, and worms had found a home in the mouth's cavern.

Rage got up. "You were too young and a lousy shot. Just like the last two who tried to kill me. I wonder if Lucius is daft or just too miserly to pay for a decent killer."

THE DOGS were awaiting him, their tails wagging with excitement. Rage patted their heads, stroked them, and gave them some dried meat from his bag—they'd earned it as they hadn't barked even once as he was climbing over the mossy wall.

"Good boys," he murmured, always keeping an eye on the main house. "Keep an eye out for me. I'll have some more meat for you once I'm back."

All was quiet so far. Good.

Rage sent the dogs away and made his way to the wing where Lucius had his private rooms. From Luca, Rage had learned the location of the wine cellar and that only Lucius had a key. It would be the perfect place for a few questions.

Finding the right window and getting inside the house was as easy as last time. If Rage lived here, he'd do something about the servants keeping an eye on his property, but as this wasn't his house, he was glad for their lack of attention.

The corridors were empty, and as expected, the big oak door to Lucius's rooms was closed, so Rage slipped into the smaller room next to it and from there onto the balcony. From there, it was just a few steps until he could see into Lucius's bedroom.

When he saw the girl standing in front of the big bed, Rage thought for a confusing moment that it was Luca. The same long, blonde hair flowed openly down her back. The same long, straight limbs, the slender waist, the triangular, cat-shaped face.

Only this girl was a bit shorter, her face was tanned from the sun, and her hands and feet rough from working in the fields. Her breasts larger than Lucinda's. Her posture did not speak of arrogance but fear. Rage guessed she was a farmer's daughter, and he also guessed she had taken Milly's place in Lucius's bed.

Tears were pouring down her face, and Rage could see beat marks on her body. Her hands were bound behind her back, and the left side of her face was bruised and swollen.

And she was scared. Trembling, she stood and waited, staring at the bed, which was hidden mostly behind thick, velvet curtains.

She flinched when there was movement behind the curtains.

Involuntarily, Rage balled his fists. The girl was younger than Luca, thirteen, fourteen at the most. Nothing more than a child, and when children were affected, his crude morals jumped into action. If at all possible, he would not only get his answers from Lucius, but also get this girl out of the house.

A hand came into view, pulling the curtain away. Plump and short-fingered, it was the hand of a middle-aged man who ate too much, drank too much, and was entirely too fond of young girls. The arm attached to the hand was hairless, the belly coming into view round like a barrel. He was naked.

Lucius of Babylon's eyes were focused on the girl. In his hand, he held a whip Rage had seen before. Back then, however, Lucius had been about to hit a horse. Now, he was about to hit the girl.

Rage's stomach clenched at the sight. To him, it was obvious this was nothing more than foreplay. Luckily, the girl was still on her legs and not yet in bed.

Lucius breathed in heavy gulps, his cheeks red with excitement.

Both hands clenching the window frame, Rage wasn't surprised the man hadn't yet seen him. He was fully focused on the girl, not once checking if he had an audience. When the girl took a step back in fear, Lucius leapt, reaching out with the whip. His erection bobbed as he jumped, the whip's thin leather slapping hard across the girl's shoulders. When he hit her again, he aimed for her flanks, her thighs, and her bottom.

Leather broke skin. The girl screamed, blood dripping onto the expensive carpet, mingled with tears.

Rage could see Lucius shout but couldn't hear a thing.

Sound magic, Rage thought and kicked in the glass.

The silence shattered into little pieces, leaving noise in its wake: the girl's strangled sobs, Lucius's shouting, and the whip clattering to the floor as Lucius realized someone had broken into his bedroom.

"What the hell?" Lucius screamed, dumbstruck at the sight of a stranger standing in his bedroom.

The girl hadn't even twitched at the sound of breaking glass. She just stood, naked and bound, and kept crying.

Rage crossed the distance between them and shoved the man backward onto the bed. He struggled and squealed when Rage pressed a pillow over his face, but he didn't stand a chance against the taller and stronger assassin.

Head down, the girl still didn't move.

"Fucking piece of shit," Rage hissed and pressed the pillow down harder until the struggling ceased and the man lay still, his arms and legs motionlessly draped across the bed.

When Lucius was unconscious, Rage turned him onto his belly, ripped off a cord from one of the curtains, and slung a hangman's noose over Lucius's head before binding his feet with the same length. Like that, feet and throat were connected, and Lucius would struggle less once he was awake again—any attempt to free himself would suffocate him. Lastly, Rage bent his victim's legs and used the now loose middle part of the rope to tie up the wrists.

It would be easy to get the answers he wanted.

Getting up from the bed, Rage turned to the girl. She shivered as he came closer. Her long hair was plastered against her skull, and when he touched her, he found her skin cold and clammy.

"How long have you been here?" he asked, using one of his knives to cut her free.

Arms hanging limply at her sides, she said in a flat, monotone voice, "Today? I don't know, not that long. He hasn't yet taken me."

"You've been with him before?"

The girl nodded. Tears dropped to the carpet, but she didn't move, and she didn't look up.

Rage pulled one of the curtains down, wrapped it around her, and forced her to sit down. "He won't hurt you again," he told her and inwardly cursed himself for having made yet another promise he might not be able to keep. Unless he killed the man, which he hadn't planned to do.

Taking a glass that stood on the bedside table, he wiped it clean on Lucius's shirt, which he found neatly folded on the dresser. When he was done with the glass, the creamy white silk had some ugly stains. Rage poured some wine, laced it with water, then held the glass out to the girl. She didn't touch it.

"Drink, or I will have to force you," Rage said. Only then did she take it, holding the glass between her shaky hands. She winced as the alcohol touched her cracked lips.

"What's your name?"

"Rebecca."

"Rebecca. Can you do magic?"

The girl nearly looked at him. At the last moment, she thought better of it and clenched her teeth instead. Her shoulders trembled beneath the curtain.

"Yes, sir," she whispered. "I can do magic. What would you like me to do for you? I am capable of… various… ways to pleasure you."

It was rare that Rage didn't know what to say. After a few moments of silence, he decided to light a fire in the grate so the girl could get warm.

"I'm not interested in you pleasuring me," he finally said. "I want you to seal the window. Sound will carry out through the hole in the glass, and I can't have that. Seal it for me. Please, Rebecca."

For a split second, she closed her eyes, obviously hoping he wouldn't harm her. It went straight to his heart.

"Will you let me go if I do what you want?" she whispered. "Can I go home… afterwards?"

Lucius stirred on the bed. Unintelligible words tumbled from his mouth into the pillow. Another few minutes, and he would be trying to get free.

"I have some business with him." Looking for a poker, he found one next to the fireplace and stuck it deep into the glowing coals. It would come in handy soon. "I can't let you go before I'm done with him. I'll have to knock you out, but I swear by the Lady that I won't touch you and that once this is over, you can go wherever you want to go."

Like a scared deer at the sound of a twig breaking under heavy boots, the girl jerked her head up. Not only was her mouth bloody, but the whip had slashed her already bruised cheek too. She bared her teeth and glanced quickly at the bed. "You're an assassin," she stated, taking Rage in from head to toes. "Are you going to hurt him?"

"Yes."

"Let me watch." It wasn't a plea. It was a demand.

Rage raised an eyebrow. "Why would I do that? This is no joke. I will hurt him badly, and I could just as easily hurt you. Be glad I haven't already killed you."

She grinned; with the blood smeared on her teeth and her face, it was an awful sight. "Last year, he had my little sister," she said, suddenly sounding like something old and rotten, something best hidden behind thick doors and in deep cellars. "Her name was Jennifer. Two nights and one day he had her in here, and when he sent her home, she wasn't herself anymore. This man"—she pointed a shaky finger at Lucius—"he broke her jaw when she dared to scream. She couldn't eat anymore, she only cried, and after a month, when our mommy was asleep, she sneaked out of the house and jumped into the river. Jenny was only nine, and when we buried her, I could still see the fear in her face. Let me watch."

It was the way she'd said "our mommy" that changed Rage's mind. Despite her looks, this girl wasn't a child anymore, hadn't been ever since Lucius had decided to use her as his toy. She had a right to see what he was about to do.

"Fine. Seal the window, then don't move and don't speak. I had planned to take him to the wine cellar, but this place will do as well."

Rebecca shuffled to the window, the curtain trailing across the floor like the train of a wedding dress. Kneeling, she put her hand to the glass and muttered a few words, not repairing the glass, just the Sound magic that protected the room.

"The cellar wouldn't have worked." Her eyes were dead when she turned toward him. "He's got some magic down there warning him if someone gets too close to his precious wine. Up here, you're safe. No one will hear him when he screams." She wiped the blood off her mouth. Then she went back to the armchair, pulled her legs up, dragged the curtain closer around her fragile, beaten body, and settled in to watch.

THUS FAR, Rage had never had an observer when doing his job. Her silent presence made his skin prickle. So when Lucius groaned, clearly not unconscious anymore and ready to be questioned, he was glad. He would concentrate on the task at hand and forget about the fact she was there and watching.

Lucius tried to stretch his legs. Rage knew his blood circulation had slowed by now, and his wrists, calves, and knees hurt. The rope was strangling him.

"Let's see if we need the poker after all," Rage said, loud enough for Lucius to hear him. "If you tell me what I want to know, there is no need for me to burn holes into your flesh."

"Wrrrrsss," Lucius grunted and, as predicted, tried to get his hands and legs free.

The rope around his neck tightened.

"You should stop fighting," Rage said, pressing Lucius's legs down just enough for the rope to loosen a bit.

Gasping and spitting, his victim gulped in air. "Who're you?" It was an outcry more than a question. Rage could hear the early signs of panic in the words.

"I'm the man who's torturing you." His hand was still on Lucius's feet. Blue veins were visible beneath the skin. "I want you to stop sending killers after me. I don't like being a target. The men you sent are dead. The wizard and witch are dead. Jeeve escaped, but setting fire to the Shadows went too far. So tell me, what do I have to do to make you stop?"

Lucius struggled so suddenly and viciously that Rage let go of him. The rope cut into his throat and he gurgled, but he seemed too determined to get away from Rage to care that he was about to fall to the floor.

Rage caught him just before he fell, pushing him harshly back into the middle of the bed. The veins on Lucius's forehead stood out from the effort of not stretching his cramping muscles, and he was hyperventilating. His eyes were big and round, dribble running down his chin and tears welling up in his eyes.

The girl on the chair watched in silence.

Sighing, Rage pressed the man's legs down once more until he'd caught his breath, then let go so suddenly that Lucius groaned with shock.

In panic, he croaked out the words, "Didn't send any killers. Don't know about any wizards or witches!"

"You're one stupid idiot." Rage got up and pulled the poker out of the fireplace. He brought the glowing end close to Lucius's face so he could see the red tip and smell the heated iron.

Lucius screamed even before Rage touched his toes with the poker. The instant his flesh began to stink, he began to howl.

"Wrong answer, Lucius." Damn, but he hated torture.

Lucius just screamed.

Eventually, Rage put the poker back into the fire. "You have no idea how many parents ask me to kill their offspring," he murmured, more to himself than the naked man on the bed. "But that is not the point. Tell me, Lucius, do I have to kill you to make you stop chasing us?"

For a moment, Lucius lay completely still on the bed. He didn't even seem to breathe. Then he pressed his sweaty face into the sheets and murmured something Rage couldn't understand.

"Say it again," he demanded harshly. "I have no problems putting the poker to your balls."

Without warning, Rage cut through the rope connecting Lucius's legs with his neck, threw him onto his back, and pressed his knife to his throat. "You decided to get rid of your daughter," he prompted, hoping in vain that this would end soon. "First, you offer the job to me, only to hire the dumbest killers in the village once I declined the offer. You decided to kill her so you could get the manor. It was a nice plan until I got in the way." The knife cut deeper, making blood seep into the sheets.

"W-wanted to fuck her, not kill her," Lucius whimpered, and his eyes darted to the silent girl in the armchair. "That's why I got that bitch there. I treat her the way I would have liked to treat Lucinda." He spat the last word out as if it was poisonous.

The knife wanted to cut deeper. Rage could feel its pull as well as the pressure of his own blood telling him to kill the bastard, the sooner the better.

Yet he refused.

"You wanted to lay with your own child? Well, that at least I can believe. What I don't believe is that you don't want to see her dead."

Casually, he reached for the poker. Equally as casually, he pressed the red tip deep into the soft flesh underneath Lucius's ribcage.

An ugly smell poisoned the already stale air, and even through Lucius's yells for mercy, Rage heard the girl cough. He couldn't blame her; he was glad his stomach was empty.

"Didn't... couldn't... kill her!" Lucius yelled, and then his legs cramped, and he threw up all at the same time. He made a mess of the bed and himself. Rage stepped away so he wouldn't get dirty as well.

Eventually, Lucius curled up in a fetal position. Tears were streaming down his fat cheeks, and he had pissed himself.

Poker in hand, Rage stepped around the bed so the man could see him. "I think you'd like to see her dead. I think you'd love to kill her yourself, preferably while you fuck her."

Calculatingly, he watched the man on the bed, saw his wide, panicked eyes, smelled his sour sweat and unwashed body, the fresh piss, and the vomit. He saw him trembling and shaking and knew he would tell the truth now.

"C... cannot kill her," he wheezed, his eyes darting to the poker. "Find... they'd find out!"

From the corner of his eye, Rage saw Rebecca lean forward, an unreadable expression on her face.

"Find out what?"

Lucius wet his lips. "Lucinda's not my child," he bit out. "Her mother was seven weeks pregnant when we married. The bitch told me after the marriage. I nearly killed her for lying to me, but she had all the money, and I had nothing. Got my revenge after her death. Treated the little bitch like a piece of shit." He coughed and spat out a mixture of phlegm and blood.

Rage frowned. "I don't get it. Explain yourself."

"It's the burial rite," Lucius stuttered. "Once she's dead, the priest would find out I wasn't her real father. Blood magic, man! No family connection between her and me. I'd get chased off the manor the moment they found out. I never tried to kill her!"

"Then who sent Jeeve?" Rage pulled a chair close to the bed and sat down, his legs lazily crossed at the ankles and not looking at all like a man who'd just inflicted pain on a defenseless victim.

The poker was back in the fire, though. Just in case.

Lucius stared at him blankly.

"Jeeve," Rage repeated patiently. "One of your servants. White hair, yellow eyes, large nose. Remember him?"

"Jeeve," Lucius rasped. "He's not with me anymore. Vanished some weeks back. Thought he'd finally managed to get his neck broken by an outraged husband. Was after married women, he was. Dirty little bastard."

Rage couldn't completely hide his surprise. He hadn't expected this—denial, of course, blatant lies, yes, but not such a simple fact. "You know I can easily find out whether or not you're telling the truth. If you've lied, I'll cut off the fingers of your left hand and make you eat them."

Lucius became paler than he already was, but he didn't say another word.

"He's right," Rebecca said quietly. "I know Jeeve. He used to pick me up from my mommy's house. He didn't this time. The cook said he's gone."

"What would Jeeve gain from killing Luca?"

"So you'd think I'm behind this, come to torture me, and kill me," Lucius spat out.

Good point. "And if you were dead, then what?"

"With me dead and the bitch dead, the manor wouldn't have anyone running it." Something like hope appeared in Lucius's watery blue eyes. He obviously believed Rage wouldn't kill him now that it was clear he wasn't behind this mess. "Jeeve would be the perfect candidate to step in. Knows everything and everyone. The manor would go to the nuns just as Lucinda stipulated in her will. They would probably consider him the right man to run the place. He'd pay them, they'd leave him alone, and he could live happily ever after without me kicking him around."

Fuck, Rage thought.

Lucius was right. He wasn't behind this, he had nothing to do with the attacks, and Rage had no reason to torture him any longer. This was over, and he'd achieved nothing. His only chance to stop the attacks had turned out to be a dead end.

Lucius watched him. Expectantly, he twisted his shoulders so Rage could cut his hands free.

Disgusted, Rage slammed his fist into the man's temple hard enough to make him slip off the bed. Unconscious, Lucius hit the floor.

He should kill him. Letting him live was a bad idea given how powerful Lucius was. He could, if he wanted, send an army after Rage.

He also would be after Rebecca again.

But Rage had done too many killings in the past weeks. He was sick of death. Sheathing his knife, he turned to the still silent and motionless girl. "I'll leave now. Come with me if you like, but I'm telling you, you and your mum should move to another village."

On the table were leftovers from Lucius's dinner. After wrapping them in a piece of paper, Rage stuffed them into his bag for the dogs.

Rebecca's voice was strangely flat when she said, "My mommy died this spring." She got up, a little girl wrapped in velvet curtains with a face straight out of a nightmare.

Rage saw her walking to the fireplace. He was a tad too late to prevent her from taking the poker.

Just a tad too late to reach her in time. As he leapt toward her, she gracefully bent and burned out Lucius's eyes.

Lucius was unconscious and didn't move but shat himself anyway.

The poker clattered to the floor. Rebecca, looking like someone who'd just woken from a really deep sleep, swayed. Rage caught her as her legs gave way. The smell of burned flesh and blood and shit was making him wish he had eaten enough to be able to throw up.

"We'll leave, Rebecca," he murmured into her ear.

Her head lolled forward. "Oh fuck," the assassin said wearily, threw her over his shoulder, and left the same way he'd arrived.

Twice, he had broken into this house. Twice, he had shed blood. And twice, he voluntarily had burdened himself with much more responsibility than he had believed himself capable of.

He would not come back here, for any reason in the world.

Just as he was about to climb the wall, he heard the dogs barking.

CHAPTER
Twelve

THE DOGS found them as Rage neared the wall, sniffing at his legs and wagging their tails.

"Easy, boys," he said as he took the meat out of his bag and gave each one a piece.

Rage left them to their meal and smiling their big, silly dog smiles. Last time he'd done that, he'd been carrying the manor's mistress over his shoulder. She'd been heavier than this one, not only because she was older but better fed as well. Rebecca's bones poked into Rage's flesh. She was skinny for her age. He guessed that her life hadn't been easy in general and that since her mother had died she had been living at Babylon Manor as a maid. And with Lucius's attention focused on her, she probably hadn't been that hungry lately, either.

The horse neighed softly when it heard Rage approaching through the woods. It had spent the time grazing and resting and now wanted to move along. The hounds' barking made it nervous, and its ears twitched suspiciously when it saw the burden over Rage's shoulder.

Staring blankly at the horse and the trees, the girl refused to stand although she wasn't unconscious. When he shook her, she felt like a rag doll in his hands. When he let go of her, she sank to her knees, her head bowed, dirty hair touching the leaves on the forest ground. She still wore nothing but the curtain.

He couldn't afford to travel with her. She would slow him down.

He could kill her. Her bones looked as fragile as a sparrow's. Breaking her neck wouldn't take more than a few seconds. She'd probably even welcome it, as it would mean no more memories, no more pain, and no more fear.

Rage looked at the girl at his feet, pondering the bruises on her skin and the wounds from Lucius's whip. Blood seeped through the curtain's fabric.

Killing her and leaving her beaten body behind as if she were nothing but garbage was something he couldn't bring himself to do.

Instead, he picked her up and put her on the horse. She nearly slipped out of the saddle, so he swung up behind her, wrapping one arm around her waist and taking up the reins with the other. It wasn't a comfortable way to ride, but at least they were on their way.

She didn't struggle. In fact, it seemed as if she didn't even notice he was there.

Nudging the horse into a fast gallop, Rage left the woods around Babylon Manor. He headed north, as planned—it was a scarcely inhabited area, but he hadn't been home in years. On the way there was a nunnery where he could leave the girl. North also would take him far away from Babylon Manor as well as Coldwell and the memories both places held.

Briefly, Rage considered the option of going back to Coldwell. Lindsay would take good care of Rebecca, and he could make sure Keiran was recovering. Forgetting about the day's events would be easy while resting next to the boy. Planning his next steps concerning the murderous Jeeve might actually be simpler with Luca's help.

But no. Going back would lead to nothing but pain. He'd grown fond of the girl, in a way he had not expected. He'd grown fond of the boy, way more than was good for him. And the boy thought himself to be in love. Going back….

Resolutely, Rage sped up his horse and headed north.

HALF A day's ride later, the girl still hadn't moved. Occasionally, Rage felt for her pulse. It was always there and always feeble and hesitant, as if her heart couldn't decide whether beating was worth the effort. Her face was sweaty, and her breath came in uneven gasps. Rage feared she'd die before nightfall but had no idea what to do about it. There had been a village about an hour back, but it had no more than fifteen, twenty houses, and none of the people living there had opened a welcoming door for them. Even if they had, he wouldn't have left Rebecca with them, as she needed more profound help than a warm meal and a roof over her head.

The sisters serving the Lady would help her, if only he could find their nunnery. He'd been in this area only once before, years ago. He'd passed the sisters' house, had glanced at it, and decided to get on instead of seeking shelter. They were known to ask too many questions, and back then, he had been too young and too scared to resist their curiosity.

Today, he longed for the sight of the big front door more with every passing moment the girl hung limply in his arms.

When the nunnery finally came into sight, it was close to sunset. Knocking on a door was a rare experience—Rage usually sneaked into houses silently and was out again before anyone but his victim noticed his presence. He slipped off his horse and caught the girl. It was nearly impossible to detect her pulse.

He banged his fist on the door, and finally, he heard the latch being undone. A wrinkled face looked at him, hidden behind a thin, blue veil.

"What do you wish of the sisters of the Lady, son?"

"We need help," he answered, nodding at the girl in his arms. "And I need to speak to the abbess."

Mild eyes took him in, calculating as well as careful. The sister's gaze rested on the girl wrapped in a stained curtain, and she opened the door wider. "Would you please carry the child to the infirmary? She looks as if she could do with some rest."

"She could do with a new life," Rage said. "She's seen too much and had to endure too much lately. I would be grateful if you could help her."

The sister smiled. "Certainly the first time we've earned an assassin's gratitude. To the right, if you please."

With small steps she led him to the infirmary, her blue robes swishing over the dusty ground of the yard. Trees cast shadows, a low sun shone through threadbare clouds, and suddenly, Rage became aware of the fact he hadn't slept or eaten in more than two days.

For a moment, all sound vanished; for a moment, all he could see was the sun's reflection on the tiny pond near the outer wall.

Then the sister put her hand on his arm and pointed out a low building with large windows. "Follow me, please. We do not have many guests at the moment. We will be able to take care of the child immediately."

Inside the infirmary were seven beds, each one separated from the others by screens. Three beds were occupied. On the fourth one, Rage placed the girl, relieved to let go of her.

"We'll take care of her," the sister repeated, sitting next to Rebecca and putting a hand on her forehead. "The abbess is down the hallway. If you could, please tell her what happened to this child and how we might be able to ease her pain beyond caring for her more obvious wounds." With that, she dismissed him, focusing her concentration and her protection on Rebecca.

As requested, Rage went down the hall, his legs feeling like lead.

He would tell the abbess what he knew and then leave.

THE ABBESS was a surprisingly young woman. Rage had expected someone much older, but she was in her early thirties, quite a bit younger than himself. There was an aura of power around her he instantly recognized. She was used to leading people, to giving orders and having them obeyed. Clearly, she hadn't been born in a poor man's hut, hadn't grown up earning her living in fields or in dirty back alleys. She had once been an heiress, daughter to a rich house, and she could easily have been one of his customers, asking him to kill a relative, a spouse, or a lover.

But unlike the ones who bought his services to have someone killed, this woman also possessed a friendly heart, easily seen by the way she smiled at him. There was no suspicion in her eyes when she reached out and took both his hands in hers, no disgust at what the color of his clothes must have told her, no anger at the blood on his hands.

"You look tired," she said. "Please, sit down. I saw you brought us a patient—I must admit, I was watching through the window as you walked through the door. I am too curious for my own good. Can I offer you a meal? Some wine? A bed?"

"Just some water. Please," Rage added belatedly.

The abbess smiled again. "My name is Laure. Abbess Laure, officially, but well, I prefer the first name only. Out here we are not as strict as we ought to be, I'm afraid."

She poured a glass of water and held it out to him. When he took it, he observed that his hand was as steady as ever although his shirt was soiled with Lucius's blood.

Here, in this quiet sanctuary, it seemed obscene to think about torture.

"Tell me what happened to your companion," Laure prompted the moment he put the glass to his lips. "Why did you beat her unconscious? Did she not comply with your wishes?"

The water went down the wrong pipe, and Rage coughed viciously, dropping the glass in the process. It shattered, the shards painting a beautiful pattern on the floor. Laure jumped up and helpfully slapped his back, then handed him a piece of cloth with which to wipe his face clean.

"I apologize for my rudeness," she said, and there was an edge to her voice.

Rage suspected she knew a lot more about beaten girls—and from firsthand experience no less—than she should have as the daughter of a rich man. As his encounter with Lucius of Babylon had proved, rich men were just as capable of beating up their daughters as poor ones.

"You see," the abbess continued as if she'd read his thoughts, "I have witnessed similar scenes far too often—fathers, brothers, husbands, boyfriends knock on our door and carry in a daughter, a sister, a loved one. Sometimes even an alley whore. Often, the girls are unconscious, and most times, the one who's responsible for the wounds cries bitter tears as they take them to our infirmary. The men behave as if they were the victims, not the one bleeding on our sheets. They expect us to comfort them and tell them it's a normal thing to lust after a child, to abuse a woman. I no longer care about the one who committed the crime. I only care about the victims. So tell me what you have done to her so we can help her."

Silently, she looked at him. Through the thin blue veil she wore, Rage could see her lips had gone white, and there was tightly controlled hate in her eyes.

It resembled his own feelings so perfectly, he nearly laughed. "I met the girl only this morning," he said, brushing some glass shards off his trousers. "It wasn't me who hurt her. Her name is Rebecca, and she's been raped repeatedly, beaten, and whipped. A few hours ago, she burned out the eyes of her tormentor. I had the choice of leaving her there to get hanged or bringing her to you. Choosing the latter doesn't seem such a good idea anymore, considering you are accusing me of a crime I didn't commit."

The abbess considered his words for several moments. "Why should I believe you?" she finally asked.

"So far, I've never taken anyone by force. If I do happen to use a whore too roughly, I pay generously afterwards—and I am willing to swear an oath to prove I am not lying on that matter." Palms up, Rage held out his hands.

They looked at each other. Frowning, the abbess put her own hands above his, closed her eyes, and muttered some words. Light began to glow between their palms, warm and gentle.

Eventually, Laure nodded. "The truth indeed," she said and went to the door where she spoke to the sister waiting outside. Rage couldn't make out the words, but it was obvious the abbess told the sister what he'd just said.

"No one has ever offered to undergo the Truth magic," Laure said thoughtfully once she'd closed the door again. "Is it true Rebecca injured the man who did this to her?" She poured another glass of water. "Peace?" she said, a small smile tugging on her lips. This time, there was no hate in her eyes when she looked at him.

Rage took the glass. "Peace," he said and was able to drink undisturbed.

"I shouldn't have allowed her to watch me questioning him," he said when he'd quenched his thirst.

"But you did?"

"Her sister had killed herself after an encounter with the same lord who's been raping her. She begged me to let her watch."

"I see. What do you expect of us? Should we send her back to her village once she's better, or should we keep her here?" Laure leaned back in her chair, a frown on her face.

A look out the window confirmed that it was already later than he'd expected. He needed to move on.

"She cannot go back," he said, searching for the heavy purse he'd stolen from Lucius. He took out some of the smaller coins, pocketing them, and dropped the leather pouch on Laure's worm-eaten desk. "Her family is dead, and she is too young to take care of a field on her own. Besides, the lord will have her hung once he's back on his feet. She was there when I questioned him. He cannot let her live and know about his humiliation."

The abbess took the pouch, peered inside, and whistled approvingly. "We will keep her here, then, at least as long as she is willing to stay with us. We do not imprison the ones in our care." Holding out the pouch, she added, "But we will look after her for free."

Rage got up. "Keep the money. Right now, all I need is a meal, a drink, and a bed I can collapse into once I am properly drunk. I took enough money to accomplish that task. The rest is for you. I've seen your infirmary needs a new roof."

Laure tilted her head. "My thanks, assassin," she said. "Will you tell me your name so I can include you in my prayers?"

"The name's Rage. And you don't need to pray for me. I'm in hell already."

THERE WASN'T even a village. Just the roadhouse, with miles and miles of road on either side of it and a few trees, low bushes, and a tired little brook near the stables. It was a shabby place but the only one Rage had been able to find before darkness fell.

At least it offered alcohol in abundance.

His body ached, and his legs were numb as he put his horse in the stable. His head pounded, light with fatigue, and his hands itched, but he didn't like to think of his hands. Or anything at all, for that matter.

The stink of burned flesh. The yelling, naked man. The boy's hurt look when he'd turned away from him.

Luca, slipping the ring of hair over his finger. The very ring he still hadn't thrown away.

Rage went into the roadhouse, chose a table close to the wall, ordered a bottle and a glass, and tried to forget the past few days.

Or weeks, rather. Too much had happened, too much he hadn't planned and had been unable to control. Too many deaths and way too many catastrophes.

Rage didn't order anything to eat. He concentrated only on the drink in front of him. Cider, according to the landlord, but it could as well have been horse piss as long as it contained alcohol and that alcohol went straight to his head.

He became drunk quickly.

"Staying in the nunnery's infirmary would have been the wiser idea," he mumbled, more or less still aware of the fact that he was anything but well.

Instead, he was here, neglecting his body's needs even further by downing one glass after the other.

Guests came and left. They kept their distance and so did the landlord. Once every couple of hours, he put a fresh bottle on Rage's table and took one of the coins stacked in front of him. Rage hadn't asked for a room. He had enough money to keep him drunk for another day and a half. Who needed a bed when one had alcohol?

He should have taken a shower. On his hands, there was Lucius's blood and probably some of Rebecca's too. When his stomach began to rumble, he kept it quiet with more cider.

The stack of coins melted with every passing hour. When he realized he had not enough money to stay drunk forever he found the tobacco in his rucksack and the herbs and kept himself outside of reality with smoke.

How long had he been here—a day? Two? All he knew was that by now, he was beyond sleep and that he was close to losing his own name in the next bottle.

His bones still ached and his head, his hands were so itchy he took off the bandages, he saw burned out eyes in the face of every customer in the roadhouse, and he was determined to get rid of the memories whatever it took.

He should eat and sleep. And since neither drink nor smoke could erase the memory of the boy's kisses, he should stop drinking and stop smoking and go home.

But Rage stayed at his table, drank and smoked, and only got up for the occasional piss.

He guessed the landlord was hopeful someone would come and take care of him before he decided he was in the mood for trouble. He guessed the other guests left him alone because they saw his clothes and the blood on his hands, deciding a fight with him would only end with their own death.

No one was going to come. And he would kill anyone should they dare so much as look in his direction too obviously.

Admittedly, Rage hadn't expected to fall in a hole this deep and black. Torture, though not a task he did willingly, wasn't new to him, and so far, he'd always been able to quickly get used to the memories, even forgetting them after a while. This time, he couldn't. Lucius's screams resounded in his head. The burned-out sockets of his empty eyes stared at him accusingly, and his arms still felt as if he were carrying Rebecca's unconscious body.

Lindsay would have sent him to bed after a giant helping of her horrible soup. She would have argued that being up and about so soon after nearly dying wasn't something a sensible man should do.

Rage grinned at the thought of her.

Then he took a deep swallow from the bottle.

The bottle was empty—again—and Rage's mind began playing tricks. He'd smoked more herbs in a day than he usually did in a year. The herbs in his pouch would, under normal circumstances, last for ages, but now, in this dirty little roadhouse, there was probably enough left for another two or three cigarettes at the most.

Rage touched his glass, realized it was empty as well. Again. The glass moved away from his hand as he tried to grab hold of it, hopping across the table like a pissed-off bunny. And the bottle felt strange—soft, furry even. When he grabbed it harder, his hand went right through it as if it were nothing but smoke.

Not good. He was drunker than he'd thought.

"Food," he mumbled, stunned at the croakiness of his voice. It seemed he hadn't spoken in a while.

And where was he? The room seemed unfamiliar. The faces of the people sitting at the next table were nothing but blurry blotches.

Sudden anger washed through him. His hands stuck to the table; he couldn't get them free no matter how hard he pulled. As if someone had nailed them to the wood. He hated this. He hated that he'd smoked enough to make his brain go soft.

Confused, Rage got up. His legs were somewhere else. Maybe he'd left them back with the sisters. Walking without legs wasn't easy, but it wasn't as bad as the sight of his arms stretching and stretching until they were thin and weak like blades of grass.

Didn't matter. He needed to get out. Out into the cool darkness. Hopefully, he wouldn't be able to see the boy's face anymore in the darkness. It was impossible to see in the dark, wasn't it? He wouldn't be haunted by those amber eyes or that beautiful smile.

By the Lady, alcohol wasn't worth the price if it couldn't manage to erase even such simple memories!

Staggering outside, he was greeted by the night, a cold wind slamming the door shut behind him. Noise, smoke, and the smell of beer and whiskey were gone in an instant. Clouds hung low in the sky, telling of the nearing thunderstorm.

There, near the barn, was the boy's shadow, waiting for him. He saw it clearly before the wind blew it away.

Out of his mind, Rage slammed his head against the roadhouse's outer wall, trying to force himself to think of something else.

Impossible.

His head hurt, and the first drops of rain hit his exposed neck. Cold drops, cooling his heated skin. He raised his face toward the clouds, catching the water and wondering why it didn't taste of alcohol.

Absently, he rubbed his hands together, feeling the dried blood and dirt form tiny little lumps before getting washed away by the rain. The skin was still tender from where he'd burned them.

Tender. Not raw anymore.

"Fucking hell, how long have I been here?"

No one answered him.

He even missed the girl. And the cat.

As usual, he only recognized happiness when it was too late.

Slowly, Rage's legs—which he still couldn't feel—gave way, and he sunk to the muddy ground, rain dripping from his hair and his nose. Had someone seen him, they might have thought he was crying.

"Pathetic," Rage murmured into the mud in front of his face. His clothes were soaked. He should go back inside.

"You'll catch a cold, you know," the girl's bodiless voice whispered in his ear.

Rage flinched. He'd hoped that in a thunderstorm, at least, she'd be quiet for a little while.

"Go away," he croaked, looking up.

Sure enough, he could see her standing right in front of him, the familiar arrogant gleam in her eyes. At least she seemed as wet as he was although he knew she was made of nothing but smoke and clouds erupted from his stupid, intoxicated mind. She wasn't real, and as much as he wished he could force his mind to end this hallucination, he knew his mind would disobey.

She sat next to him on the wet ground. Even more bizarre, the cat was with her, his black fur as wet as her long, blonde locks. Sammy didn't look happy about it, and he wasn't purring either.

"Care to tell me why you are outside?" she asked. "Because there is a roadhouse just behind you. A few steps and you could be warm and dry, and I am sure I could persuade them to offer you a bed no matter that you look like something better kept in a cage."

The girl looked surreal in the rain with the cat on her lap. He could see the stables behind her—actually, he could see the stables *through* her.

"You're a nightmare," he stated, getting up on wobbly legs.

"Heard that before," she said airily. "But your rude statement doesn't really answer my question about why you're out here. Unless, of course, you are trying to drown?"

"By the Lady, why couldn't I have imagined Keiran?" Rage was swaying. He needed food sometime soon, or he wouldn't get back on his feet at all. "He at least would have kissed me. You have nothing better to do than argue."

"I could kiss you too," the girl's ghost pointed out. "But I won't do it for two reasons. Want to know them?"

"No."

"Well, for one, you don't want to kiss me," she continued regardless—how typical of her to ignore his wishes although she wasn't even real! "And secondly, you stink of alcohol. Anyway, Keiran's taking care of the horses. He'll get you inside as soon as they are fed."

That made him ponder, and it felt like it took half an eternity to figure out what he was pondering about.

"I took one horse," he finally managed to come up with. "Left one horse for you and the boy. Where does the third come from?"

A mischievous grin appeared on her lips. "Did you think you are the only one who can steal horses? You have definitely been a bad influence on me, assassin."

Her image wavered before his eyes. For some reason, she'd slipped an arm around his waist. As if he needed help—ridiculous! He was taller than her, and stronger, and he certainly didn't need—

"Oops," the girl said, catching him before he could crash into the bushes. "Look, Rage, this is silly. You're as drunk as a banshee. Come inside, will you?"

With both his arms around her neck, he pulled her close, trying to focus on her, which wasn't as easy as it should have been. There was something he needed to tell her, something important, and it didn't matter at all that his hazy mind had created her.

"Your father," he began, not sure how to continue.

"Is he dead?"

"He's blind."

The girl's image sighed. "You're not making any sense at all. Truly, one cannot leave you alone for a couple of days without you getting into trouble."

He pushed her away and saw her stagger. *Serves her right.* "I'm not in trouble," he said with as much pride in his voice as he could muster. "Go back where you came from and leave me alone."

"It took us a while to find you," she objected. "Only because Keiran can sense you even better than he can sense me, we were able to find you at all. No way we're going back, especially not in this weather."

"I bet Lindsay wasn't unhappy to see you leave," Rage mumbled.

He was practically standing in the bushes, and it was raining—when had that started? Suddenly, he was very cold.

"I'm going to bed now," he told the hallucination, or whatever it was he was talking to. The girl smiled. "Finally, a good idea! Hopefully, they'll let you inside. There's mud all over you." Her hand slipped into his. It actually made the world less wobbly, so he accepted her touch.

"Mud and blood." He had nearly forgotten about the blood. "Your father," he said, his voice slurring. "It wasn't him. The servant… what's his name again…?"

"Jeeve?"

It was surprising how real a girl made out of booze and herbs could feel. Her fingers intertwined with his, her breath on his face—had he not known better, he would have sworn she was here, right in front of him, her teeth really chattering in the cold rain.

No matter. Time to go to bed. Abruptly, he let go of her, pushed open the door to the roadhouse, and made his way to the staircase, which led to the rooms. Surely, he'd been smart enough to pay for a room when he'd arrived?

There were whispered comments as he walked past, which he ignored. Someone cursed, probably because he'd left the door open, allowing the wind and rain inside. Or maybe it was because he left muddy tracks on the floor. He didn't care. Tomorrow, he would move on, leaving the roadhouse and hopefully his memories behind once and for all.

The room he found was dark and cold, and Rage hit his shins on the bed. Swearing, he reached out—and touched warm flesh.

Damn. Apparently his dreams, wishes, hopes—whatever was causing these hallucinations—had followed him upstairs.

"Told you to get lost, girl," he muttered. "I'm too tired to argue with you any longer."

I'm not here to argue. I'm here to make sure you sleep in the bed and not on the floor.

By the damn Lady, now the boy had managed to get into his thoughts too.

"You aren't really here," Rage said, a little shocked at how much longing there was in his voice. "You're just a meaningless hallucination my stupid brain created to make me forget how fucking lonely I am."

Keiran put a steadying hand on his shoulder and wiped the rain off of his face with the other. It felt so damn real that Rage, for a brief moment, believed the boy was actually there.

I'm not a dream, and I'm not a nightmare, either. I'll undress you now.

"Undressing's always good," Rage murmured to the darkness of his room and fell onto the bed. His boots were taken off his feet, and some logs were lit in the small fireplace—proof that he was already asleep and dreaming this was happening. After all, if Keiran was undressing him, who had created the flames?

The boy's fingers undid the buttons of his shirt. It felt good. More than good—it was just what Rage had hoped for, a nice erotic dream before passing out. Ideally, the dream would not be ending too soon. Ideally, he'd manage to pull himself off so he could find release and stop fantasizing about the boy's perfect ass.

Warmth spread through his body once the wet clothes were gone. What the hell—how had he managed to undress himself while lying flat on his back? Oh well, best thing to do was enjoy this dream as long as it lasted.

Maybe he could make it even better than it already was. This was his dream. The boy had already sneaked his way into his mind without permission, so he could make him do more than just unbutton his shirt.

Not as sleepy as he'd thought he was, Rage searched for the boy and found him sitting on the bed next to him. Wet clothes, wet hair… but the boy's skin was warm and welcoming, and he didn't turn his head away when Rage sat up and kissed him hungrily.

Their tongues touched; Rage's hand found the boy's neck and pulled him closer, feeling the coldness of the fabric as well as the heat of his skin. *I've missed you*, Rage thought, fascinated by the fact he hadn't spoken at all and knowing only too well that had the boy been anything other than a bodiless hope his mind had created, he'd never have dared to admit such a personal fact.

Missed you too.

Being completely drunk and stoned and half-starved on top of it didn't seem too bad at all. Plenty of things one could do in an empty room with nothing but one's mind as company.

"You don't plan on doing anything intimate here, do you?" a voice asked from a dark corner, and Rage flinched as though slapped.

"I told you to go away," he hissed.

His fingers were opening Keiran's shirt and trousers. Feeble work. Maybe he should rip them off. After all, the boy wasn't really here, so it didn't matter what happened to his clothes.

Soft footsteps. Warmth brushed over Rage's naked back.

"I'm locked in here with the both of you," the girl hissed into his ear. "I just wove a bit of Protection magic into the walls of this room, in case you were wondering. No one will be able to get in here while we're asleep, but it means I cannot leave without breaking the magic. However, it seems you two have no intention of sleeping. Pity. Seems I'll be having a restless night, too."

Rage saw the girl's image waver before his eyes. From her hair, raindrops the size of apples hit the floor, changing color as they fell, turning the wooden planks into an ocean.

Beautiful.

Rage slipped to the middle of the bed, pulling the boy with him and feeling more than glad when the ghost girl became pale and paler before eventually vanishing into the fireplace.

"Gone," he murmured. "About time."

The boy's hands returned, caressing him, stroking him—it felt exceptionally good given that he wasn't sober. Usually when he was drunk, he lost his sense of touch, all taste for sex, and only wanted to sleep. Tonight, he craved more than just touch. He wanted every bit of sex he could get. Luckily, the boy had the same in mind, which was no surprise as Keiran only existed in his dreams.

He felt real enough. And his clothes had vanished too.

Perfect.

Contentedly, Rage sunk back onto the mattress. His skin was burning, whereas a moment ago, he had been freezing. His heart directed his lips, and Keiran welcomed him, opening his mouth and returning his kisses as if he could read thoughts.

He probably could, at least tonight.

Rage's dizziness became less prominent the longer he kissed the boy. The crackling of the logs and Keiran breathing in his ear made his cock pulsate with need—he hadn't expected his body to scream for company quite so loudly. His legs spread of their own accord, and when Keiran's hand moved from his throat downward, across his belly to his inner thighs, he moaned deeply and harshly for more.

The boy's fingers were slick and warm, and he was traveling kisses across his skin, his cheek, his mouth. Keiran was in the mood to play. His fingertips danced across Rage's belly button, twisted his nipples just sharply enough to make them hard, brushed over his ribcage, and ended by painting wet circles on the inside of Rage's right thigh.

Rage groaned, spread his legs wider, and dug his hands deeply into the bedsheets, fearing he'd fly away if he didn't grab hold of something real.

Keiran's mouth closed around the tip of his cock, sucking gently, then suddenly hard enough to force a yell out of Rage's lungs. He was painfully hard—his hips bucked, pushing his length deep into the boy's hot mouth, eager to end the teasing, eager to come.

Dream, just a dream, Rage thought and laughed.

Keiran laughed with him, his silent, beautiful laugh. Then his mouth was gone and was replaced by his tongue dragging from base to tip in one long movement.

The sound of his rough voice was even more proof this was nothing but a drunkard's dream. He never laughed in bed. He never showed this clearly how much he loved this very special human game. In bed, he was fast and quiet. Occasionally, a moan escaped him, but nothing else. So who was this guy who'd just laughed like a much younger and more innocent man? Surely, it hadn't been him. Nor could it be he who was begging for more.

I never beg.

But he did.

Please, Rage heard himself say—wordless once more—and laughed when Keiran placed another kiss on the tip of his cock. *Please*, he thought again, knowing the boy would do whatever he wished. After all, Keiran was only in his head, so he ought to know what should happen next. He ought to know Rage wanted more, and he did know, and he let his mouth wander lower. Like a wet spear, Keiran's tongue slipped inside him, and by the Lady, Rage had never allowed anyone to do that to him.

Just when he felt like begging again, the tongue was gone, replaced by long, slender fingers. There it was, the second yell, and a third when the fingers touched that sweet spot deep inside him, the very place that made his brain melt and his senses explode.

"You know me too well," Rage rasped, reaching out blindly and locking his hands behind Keiran's neck.

But those fingers didn't vanish; they moved, slowly at first, slipping in and out easily, making him shiver and groan and beg. *Please*, he pleaded. *Please, please, please*, again and again and nothing else because coherent thought had fled several minutes ago.

There must be a way to find release, or was this torture after all and bitter payment for what he'd done to Lucinda's father?

Sudden fear washing through him, Rage ripped his eyes open and found the light cast by the flickering flames too bright to be endured. He blinked, and for a brief, endless moment, he couldn't see anything at all.

The girl's face swam into focus. Frowning, she was looking down at him, her sea green eyes unreadable, her head slightly tilted as if she was trying to figure out what he was doing lying in her lap.

"Hi," Rage said and might have questioned why she was still bothering him—why she was in bed with him, by the Lady!—had Keiran not chosen that exact moment to replace his fingers with his cock.

For a long moment, Rage looked into the girl's face, drowning in her eyes. With one hand, he touched her cheek; with the other, he caressed her and wiped the tears from her eyes.

Forcefully, impatiently, Keiran pushed inside him, spreading him, filling him, claiming him. No teasing anymore. No gentle intrusion. Unlike the last time the boy had taken him, there wasn't any questioning tenderness or any hesitation.

Rage forgot about the girl, dropping his hands to his sides. Arching his back, he met the boy's thrusts with equal impatience and strength. It was how he wanted it, how he needed it.

His fingers dug deep into the boy's flesh as they moved in unison, their faces close enough to share breath, the sweat on their bodies mingling. Hours passed, or maybe only seconds—to Rage, it didn't make any difference at all. He'd lost all sense of time, and he didn't want to have it back—at least not now. All that was important were their joined bodies, Keiran's lips and teeth on his neck, and his own orgasm drawing nearer with each ragged breath he forced out of his lungs. Maybe he rasped out the boy's name—he didn't know, and it was of no importance, anyway. Keiran was in charge. Keiran used him, fucked him, made him beg and whimper until he feared he'd break under the boy's continuous onslaught.

In his drug-induced heat, Rage thought he could feel Keiran's come deep inside him the moment he came himself. Washing through him like a tidal wave, he was helpless in their combined orgasm's claws, shuddering, gasping, screaming and not knowing whether it would end anytime soon or—for that matter—if he wanted it to end at all.

He lay exhausted on the damp sheets, damp because of the rain he'd brought in from the night and the sweat they'd shed during their passion. Finally, he was sleepy, the fire inside him reduced to a dim glow and the desire that had ruled his mind and his actions sated.

Finally, the herbs and the alcohol had done their job, giving him a wonderful dream and peace of mind.

The sheets turned from wet to soft and warm. The wooden bed frame was reassuringly solid. Eyes closed, Rage let his hands wander over his face and hair, brushing briefly over his softened cock and the stickiness on his belly. His breath seemed loud in his ears, his lips were dry, and briefly, he thought about getting up and searching for some water.

When his fingertips touched the boy's body, he decided against it. Not sure whether he was still dreaming or not, he pulled Keiran closer, glad he wasn't alone and equally glad it was Keiran in his arms and not some nameless, faceless whore.

For the first time in days, if not weeks, he didn't ache.

The logs in the fireplace crackled. The room was properly warm now, and in the morning, his clothes would surely be dry enough to wear.

Just when he was about to slip into deeper realms of sleep—deeper and dreamless—a thought began to nag at him, something Lucius had said. It made him open his eyes, but the thought had been too faint. It was gone before Rage could catch and examine it.

Had the thought not popped up, he wouldn't have noticed a thin body slip into bed with him, a body with cool arms, cold feet, and long, damp hair.

Rage sighed. Apparently, the dream wasn't over yet. "I thought you'd be gone for good," he told the girl's ghost.

"You were wrong there," she replied tightly, edging a bit closer, and stole part of the blanket Rage had pulled over himself. "I've put more logs onto the fire and dried the sheets. Now shut up, will you? Tomorrow, you'll go crazy realizing that you haven't been dreaming at all. You will shout and threaten to kill me only because I witnessed you getting fucked senseless. Before that happens, I want at least a few hours of sleep. And yes, I'm naked. My clothes are as wet as yours. I just want to sleep, and I don't want to do it on the floor."

Rage didn't know what to say, so he closed his eyes and was asleep a few heartbeats later. It didn't even bother him that she'd slipped one arm over his waist in an attempt to get as close as possible and steal some of his body heat along with the blanket.

CHAPTER
Thirteen

SUNRISE WAS still a few hours away when Keiran awoke to the soft light of the dying fire. The room was warm, and sometime in the past few hours, either he or Rage had pushed the cover to the floor.

Carefully, Keiran slipped out of bed, making sure he didn't wake up anyone. Rage had been exhausted even before they had made love, and afterward, he'd fallen asleep with alarming speed. Which hadn't come as a surprise for Keiran.

He found the small chamber where the pot was kept, a metal basin, and a jug of water. He poured the slightly stale water into the basin. The water was cold and refreshing when he washed his face, his hands, and finally his body.

That open, unguarded expression on Rage's face. His pleas, the genuinely happy smile on those thin, hard lips. Keiran hadn't expected that. Rage hadn't come back to Coldwell, had left him and Luca behind because neither of them meant anything to him.

He had no doubt about that fact.

Water dripped from his hair to the floor, and as Keiran went back to the bedroom, his naked feet leaving wet prints on the planks, he shivered.

Back in Coldwell, when he had woken on a table with his nose broken, Rage had been standing over him, and the look on his face had told him clearly that whatever they'd had was over.

And Luca had told him what she'd done.

He still didn't know how he felt about it. In any case, he had been that close to hitting her and only reined himself in at the last moment. He had refused to communicate with her ever since.

Despite Lindsay's explicit wishes, he had gotten onto a horse the next day, heading after Rage.

Ignoring Luca, who had come after him. Ignoring her frantic attempts to talk to him. Ignoring the fact that after a while, she had become as silent—and maybe even as sad—as himself.

Without making a noise, Keiran sat on the bedside, watching his lover and his friend sleeping together in one bed. Sammy, who was purring gently and twitching his ears, didn't even bother to open an eye.

It had been Luca who'd persuaded Rage to get back into the tavern. When he and Rage had started to kiss, she had made sure the room was warm and their clothes could dry. She had spoken to Rage, but not to him.

Rage had lain in her lap whilst Keiran had fucked him. He had caressed her face.

She had been crying.

Right now, Rage had his arms around Luca. They looked good together: blonde and black, male and female—the perfect opposites, the perfect match. Keiran felt a sudden stab of jealousy at the sight.

They're married.

The thought made him grit his teeth. Performing such an impetuous, stupid stunt was so much like her. Getting what she wanted no matter the cost, and cheating fate, her father, even the whole world, was what she did best. Now she was in bed with his lover—her husband—and he sat on the bed, cold, shivering, watching.

Tentatively, Keiran touched Rage's shoulder. It was as bony as the rest of the man, covered by hard flesh, muscles, and scars. The old ones were pale and barely visible. The new ones, vaguely red, spoke of the dangers of wild magic. On his upper leg was the still not completely healed wound cast by the arrow. His gaunt ribcage revealed he hadn't eaten properly in days. Keiran quickly took the blanket and covered them both so he didn't have to see their naked bodies any longer.

I love him, Keiran thought, surprised at the strength of this emotion, but not at the sadness it caused.

Realizing that Rage did not want him had hurt, but it hadn't been able to stop Keiran from going after him. There was a connection between them Rage might not be aware of, but it was there nevertheless. It pulled at Keiran, it dictated his actions, and when he'd sensed Rage's pain and despair, when he'd felt him drifting and drowning in alcohol, drugs, and loneliness, he forced his horse into a gallop.

Now he was here, looking down at his lover, and didn't know what to do. If he stayed, Rage would break his heart. If he left, it would break all the same.

Slowly, Keiran crawled back into bed and nudged Luca out of Rage's arms. It wasn't easy, but apart from craving Rage's touch for himself, Keiran could not stand the sight of them sleeping so closely together any longer.

Moaning in her sleep and murmuring unintelligible curses, Luca moved just enough for Keiran to slip between her and Rage. Where she had been, the sheets were warm, and Rage immediately pulled him into a tight embrace.

Keiran closed his eyes. He moved a bit closer to Rage's body and made sure he did not touch Luca.

KEIRAN WAS still awake as sunrise neared, filling the room with a pale, pearly light. As much as he had tried not to ponder, not to worry, he hadn't been able to accomplish the simple task of falling asleep despite his body as well as his mind longing for rest.

Rage would be waking up soon. In the past half hour, Keiran had felt him become restless. Occasionally, he had muttered a word or two, "Lucius" being one of them as well as "Rebecca." The muscles in his lover's arms and shoulders tensed at the mention of those names, and Keiran wondered whether Rage would tell him what he'd done or if he would be out of the bed and out of his life the moment he was fully awake.

Luca's hair was tickling his nose, and she had stolen most of the blanket. Her skin was cool despite it, and since she had edged closer during the night, her bum was pressing against his thighs.

He moved away from her as much as he could. As a result, he felt Rage's cock stir, and he got hard. He shifted his hips. Delighted, he felt Rage edge closer and the cock in his backside grow.

The onslaught of conflicting emotions made him flinch: his wish to have sex with Rage, his sadness resulting from the knowledge that his love wasn't to be returned. The anger he still harbored for Luca despite the more logical part of his brain telling him that what she had done made, at least from her point of view, a lot of sense. His urge to put his arms around her since in her sleep she was hugging herself, shivering.

Last night, Luca had been forced to watch them having sex.

That they had ended up in one room together had been inevitable. When Rage had stumbled upstairs, it had taken Luca her sweetest smiles and most of the coins they'd stolen on their way to organize one at all. She had protected it with magic, not knowing whether the killer was still at their heels. And since the bed was the only place to sit apart from the floor, she had found herself a spot and had taken Rage's head into her lap so he wouldn't try to get up whilst Keiran took off his wet clothes.

Keiran had completely ignored her presence, had kissed, seduced, fucked his lover, and maybe he had done it to hurt her.

She had still been in bed, holding Rage's head in her lap when he came.

Suddenly he felt horrible at having made love to Rage in her presence. Suddenly he saw her again as what she was: his childhood friend, the girl he had protected from the moment they'd met. What she had done to Rage had been unforgiveable only moments ago.

Now, it wasn't important anymore because Rage would stay with her no more than he would stay with Keiran.

Suddenly, he just had to give in to his urge to pull her closer.

And he wished it had been her he'd fallen in love with. She, at least, would love him back.

Rage's grip on his waist unexpectedly tightened, and a wet, sleepy kiss landed on his bare shoulder. The hand that had been limp a moment ago searched for his cock, found it, and began to stroke it lazily.

"You weren't a dream, then," Rage murmured in his ear. "Don't know if I should be glad or furious."

All thoughts of Luca vanished from his mind like mist in the morning sun when Rage continued kissing him and then entered him.

One last good-bye fuck was better than nothing.

Another kiss to his neck, a bite, a gentle sucking. Rage was deep inside him, rocking slowly and stroking and kissing him, and truly, Keiran wished he would never stop.

Rage laughed softly as Keiran put a hand on his hip, urging him on.

This was torture, sweet, desired torture. Keiran relaxed and forgot about his worries and fears. Rage would leave once this was over, but for now, he was his.

Keiran moved with the man behind him, and his hand, in its need to find something to hold on to, reached out.

His fingers found soft skin and a small, firm breast.

A gasp, small and shocked, cast neither by Rage nor him.

Keiran froze. He had touched Luca.

Keiran, getting fucked slowly by his oblivious lover, realized with embarrassment how pleasantly his hard cock was pressed against Luca's small, firm ass.

The cover rustled as Luca slipped out of bed. Pale as a ghost, she looked down at them. Eyes wide, she quickly turned away.

Keiran had been wrong. Rage wasn't oblivious to her presence. Fast as always, now that he wasn't drunk anymore, he reached out and caught her wrist.

Her head spun back. Her eyes, blazing with a mixture of mistrust, hope, and anger, were darker than usual. "Let go of me," she hissed.

"Come back to bed," Rage said calmly.

Luca's jaw dropped. When Rage pulled her onto the mattress, she didn't resist.

"You can't do that," Luca whispered, but her eyes continued to drift from Rage to Keiran.

"You were there last night." Letting go of Luca's wrist, he touched her cheek as he had done when he'd been lying in her lap. "You were crying."

"I didn't... I—" she stammered.

Rage put a finger on her lips. "You are welcome should you wish to stay." Then he dropped his hand, putting it back on Keiran's thigh. His fingers were warm and strong. Not breaking eye contact with Luca, he moved his hips, picking up his slow thrusts once more.

The emotions inside Keiran tumbled and fell. He wished Rage was concentrating on him and him alone. On the other hand, he saw his friend kneeling naked and vulnerable in front of him and wished he could wipe the sadness from her face. She seemed frozen, unable to think or move.

So he pulled her closer, gently cupping one of her small breasts and stroking her until she lay down next to him.

He kissed her neck, closing his eyes and opening his heart instead. This was not a competition between him and Luca. Rage didn't belong to either of them. Nor did he have any reason to be jealous simply because his lover now moved his hand from his hip to Luca's.

Her skin was cool, and she looked scared despite her obvious arousal. Hesitantly, she pressed her bum into Keiran's erection. He could feel her breathing a bit too fast, a bit too ragged. Clearly, she didn't know what do to or if she should do anything at all.

Scared he was doing the wrong thing, Keiran squeezed his fingers between his groin and Luca. It was a strange feeling. Then Luca spread her legs, just a bit and just wide enough for his cock to slip between her thighs.

She was wet and hot, and she moaned as Keiran's fingers touched her entrance. "Please," she whispered. "Please, Keiran?"

He slipped inside her easily. She was lonely, sad, and in need. How could he not offer her comfort and pleasure? How could he deny her the relief he was longing for himself?

The rhythm of their lovemaking was tender and complicated. Luca swirled her hips; Rage rocked into Keiran almost gently, careful not to disturb the delicate balance they'd accomplished. Keiran, being in the middle, didn't move at all. It was the strangest thing he'd ever experienced thus far in his life, but despite his initial hesitation, he somehow managed to enjoy it.

Rage's cock seemed to become larger the closer he got to his orgasm. When Keiran touched Luca's small breasts, he found her nipples hard, and harsh, short gasps escaped from her lips. She threw her head backward to rest on his shoulder.

"Keiran," she whispered as her fingers tightened on his leg. Her body seemed to cramp—it took him a moment to realize she was coming. It took him longer to realize he was coming too.

A groan in his ear, harsh and deep, and one long, last thrust—Rage also reached his climax. Together, limbs entangled, they lay on the bed, the cover long cast to the floor, and just breathed, hearing, feeling the others' heartbeats as sweat dried on their skin.

CHAPTER
Fourteen

"You look like you're freezing," Rage said.

Luca stood near the window, wrapped in nothing but a thin sheet. Keiran was downstairs, organizing breakfast.

He'd told the boy to leave so he could have a few minutes alone with the girl.

"I'm fine."

"No, you are not. You are cold, you are confused, and you don't know whether to run after Keiran or to stay and strangle me. Make up your mind, but while you do, come back to bed. We need to talk." Rage fished for his trousers and pulled them on.

Luca continued to stare out the window.

Then she turned. Her face was pale and her eyes such a dark green they were nearly black.

"Why'd you do it?" she asked, pulling the sheet tighter around her body, shivering.

"Do what?"

"Make Keiran… touch me. He didn't want to, you know. He wanted you, just like last night. I was in the way, and by the Lady, Rage, I do not like feeling like a substitute."

Rage sighed. Talking to the girl was hard enough under normal circumstances. Fresh out of his bed, it would be a lot harder than anticipated, even in his worst dreams.

"I didn't make him do anything," he finally said. "He did what he wanted to do, of his own accord and with his brain in perfect working condition. He touched you because he likes you."

"He likes me all right, but he wants you and you alone." It was barely a whisper.

Rage hadn't expected her to sound so beaten. He stepped next to her, put his hands on her shoulders, and led her back to the bed where he made her sit down.

"I will be out of both your lives by tonight. Sooner or later, he will realize that being with you is the best thing that could happen to him."

Luca shook her head. "How blind are you? The way he looks at you, the way you two can have a conversation without saying a word, the way he fucks you, for crying out loud—he loves you. He will never be with me, no matter what happens. And even if he'd agree to try, I wouldn't want him. Being with someone who doesn't love you breaks you. It is what happened to my mum. It won't happen to me."

STALE AIR greeted Keiran when he emerged downstairs. The windows hadn't been opened, and it stank of unwashed bodies, beer, and cold smoke.

Lovely.

The roadhouse was quiet. Apparently, no one was up yet although it was already way past sunrise. Maybe everyone who had stayed the night was still asleep; maybe everyone who'd been here had gone home during the storm instead of wasting money on a room.

Sammy rubbed his head against Keiran's legs. *Let's find some milk for you,* he thought, trying in vain to get the memories of their lovemaking out of his head.

Rage's kisses, tasting sweet and lonely and irresistible.

Sleeping with Luca…. It surely wouldn't make their friendship any easier.

Forcing his thoughts away from them, Keiran went behind the counter and found the small kitchen attached to the bar. It was barely bigger than a broom shed, but on one of the shelves, he spotted half a bottle of milk, butter, and some remnants of meat. Keiran poured a little milk onto a plate, brushed the bits of meat onto a second one, and put both plates on the floor.

A pot with coffee bubbled on the stove. Obviously, the landlord was up and had set about making breakfast for himself and the maid before being called out of the kitchen by a more pressing task. He would be back soon. Better to hurry and carry a tray with coffee, bread, and butter upstairs to avoid an early-morning discussion on whether or not customers were allowed to serve themselves.

Watching Sammy devour his breakfast, Keiran became aware of his own empty stomach. He found a pot with honey and put it on the tray as well as cups and plates—he wouldn't be hungry for much longer.

A sound on the other side of the door made him turn. It could be a customer, but more likely, it was the landlord. Keiran went to the counter with a friendly smile on his face and low hopes for the customer theory—it was simply too early for anyone wanting a beer. Any travelers would show up closer to evening, after a long day on the road.

Keiran tried to remember how the landlord looked. He'd seen him only briefly when he'd taken the horses to the stables.

Ah, yes. A bulky man with long, greasy hair, large hands, and a surprisingly high-pitched voice. There was a big possibility he'd be thrown out instantly once the landlord realized he'd been rummaging around in his kitchen without permission.

The door opened, and a stranger walked in, shoulders hunched up. It wasn't the landlord.

"Damn shitty weather out there," the newcomer said, his lips and hands pale with cold. His focus was on the loose catch of the door. When he turned to Keiran, his eyes narrowed. The expression of friendly curiosity was replaced by sudden and fierce hate.

"Fuck the damn Lady! I really hoped I'd killed you back in Coldwell!"

RAGE SAT next to Luca. "Jeeve is behind the attacks, not your father. It took me a while to get it out of him, but he had nothing to do with any of it."

Luca, still wrapped up in the bedsheet, wiped a bit of the fabric across her sea green eyes and shook her head. "Jeeve? My father's servant? Never. He's too dumb. It must be Lucius."

Seeing Lindsay's shirt hanging over the bed's headboard, he handed it to her. "There's no doubt Jeeve planned the attacks. Your father is—at least as far as attacking us or hiring me as your rapist—innocent."

Luca slowly took the shirt. Her hands trembled only slightly when she touched Rage's hand. "That cannot be true. Jeeve is a servant, not a killer. Simply put, he hasn't got the brains to plan something more complicated than dinner. And what for, anyway? Why would Jeeve want me dead?"

She had found her trousers, too, and both were now dressed. Nothing except crumpled sheets told of the night and how they had spent it.

Rage raked his hands through his hair. His stomach growled. Briefly, he wondered why Keiran was taking so long to find some coffee and bread.

"Well, it seems the man has hidden talents. Jeeve was pulling the strings the whole time. It was he who tried to hire me in the first place. Jeeve not only planned your death, he also wanted to put it on Lucius's shoulders so he could take over the manor once your father was out of the way. Simple, really."

But something was wrong with this scenario. If only he knew what.

Luca rubbed her hands over her arms and looked up at him. "Don't tell me you believed Lucius because you inflicted a bit of pain. I need more than that to believe it wasn't my lovely father."

Damn. Rage had nearly seen the flaw in his reasoning, but now it was gone again. "He isn't your father," he said absently. "Lucius married your mother when she was already pregnant. You are not his blood. He wouldn't have risked your death. Upon burying you, it would have been revealed. You cannot inherit anything from someone you are not related to."

Luca's mouth sagged open.

"I apologize." Rage mentally slapped his head for having told her so carelessly. "I'm not really good at this talking nonsense."

"Phew. Tell me about it." Suddenly, Luca's eyes widened. "Last night you said Lucius is blind," she stammered. "How…. Did you take his eyesight?"

"No. Rebecca did."

And then Rage told her everything in detail. He hadn't wanted to, but he figured the girl had a right to know exactly what had happened and what sort of man Lucius of Babylon was so she could deal with him once she was back home.

BY THE way the man held his knife, Keiran could tell he was an expert in throwing it—one wrong move, and the knife would be lodged in his heart or throat. As slowly as possible, he put the tray down.

"You," the man said, kicking the door behind him closed. "I had hoped I would find the damn assassin here, but no, it's you again, just like last time. I thought breaking your skull back in Coldwell would draw the bastard out, but those idiots carried you away. I would have followed you if I could. My bad luck, I guess. Should have swung the bat harder. Empty your pockets. Quickly, I don't have all day."

Keep him busy, Keiran thought and put a hand into the back pocket of his trousers. *As long as he doesn't go upstairs, Rage and Luca are safe.*

There wasn't much in his pockets. A coin, a bit of string, a piece of paper. In the other he found an acorn and a few sunflower seeds. Deliberately forgetting he had front pockets too, he showed the man his empty palms, making it clear there was nothing else to be found.

The man narrowed his eyes. "I said empty your pockets. All of them," he hissed. "What are you, dumb?"

Keiran offered his sunniest smile—if the guy wanted to believe him to be a dimwit, so be it. Patting his pockets as if trying to figure out if there was something in there, he shrugged and kept grinning.

"Fuck," the man growled, stepping closer. "An idiot. Just what I need."

Snorting—whether with disgust or disappointment, Keiran couldn't say—the man patted him down with his left hand, keeping the knife at his throat while doing it. When he was sure nothing remained hidden, he stepped back and singled out the coin lying on the table.

"A penny. A single fucking penny is all you have?" He squeezed the coin in his fist as though wanting to crumble it to pieces.

He's the killer. He will kill Rage and Luca. Gulping, Keiran felt his smile falter—not a good thing, he decided, forcing the corners of his mouth upward just like the idiot the killer believed him to be.

"Well, well, well." The man looked at him, yellow teeth showing when he grinned. "I put Tracking magic on the coins, hoping it would lead me straight to that damn, useless assassin, but no, you had to steal his money, and now I am stuck with you. Stupid asshole. And Rage," he practically spat out the name, "could be anywhere."

The man pushed Keiran against the counter and took a step back, kicking Sammy out of the way. The cat had been peacefully lapping his milk, not sparing the newcomer more than a disdainful glance. An older cat would have sensed the danger, but Sammy was young and had ignored any feeble warning he may have felt tickle along his spine in favor of filling his empty stomach.

When the man's boot hit him, Sammy didn't even have time to flick his tail. He hit the wall with a sickening thud, fell to the ground, and didn't move anymore.

Keiran clenched his fists, but didn't dare so much as turn his head, assuming—absolutely correctly—that moving would mean death.

"Damn cat," the killer muttered. His knife was dangerously close to Keiran's throat. "Did you steal the coin?" he asked. "And don't lie. I bet he kicked you out of the way as soon as possible, wanting the little bitch all for himself."

Keiran's heart skipped a beat. If the man knew he'd been traveling with Rage, if he knew about Luca, it could only mean he'd been on their trail for a while.

The stranger slapped him. "I asked if you stole the coin."

Managing a surprised look, Keiran shook his head eagerly and lifted his shoulders, trying to strengthen the man's impression of him being about as bright as a brush. Sheepishly he looked at the killer.

Before the fire, Lindsay had given him five pennies, back in Coldwell, and had told him to buy carrots. Which he had done. One carrot had been given to Blake, the horse he'd taken from the manor. The rest had landed in Lindsay's soup.

He'd gotten one penny back and hadn't returned it to Lindsay.

One could call it stealing.

One penny. And from what the killer had just said, it must have been one of the pennies from Rage's pouch, the money he'd used to pay for their beds.

One penny soiled with Tracking magic.

The man frowned. "You could be lying. But then—maybe the bastard gave you the coin to keep you happy. Or to have you out of the way while he fucked the girl?" He cackled, sounding like a happy chicken. His eyes, though, were mad. The hand that held the knife didn't shake.

Cold with fear, Keiran nodded.

The killer sat on one of the tables. The clothes he wore, though expensive, were dirty, his face pallid, his teeth yellow and uneven. Not precisely an ugly man, but a man who had neglected himself recently.

"I should have known it wouldn't be that easy to find him again," he grumbled. "Lost him before, haven't I?"

Keiran quickly risked a glance to where Sammy lay. He wasn't moving.

For the first time in many years, he wished he had a voice so he could warn Rage and Luca. This man was crazy. And he was obviously the very man who wanted them dead.

"I THINK you are crazy."

"I never said I am not. I've told you the truth nevertheless."

"But… how can you be sure?" Luca sounded small and young, and Rage felt a sudden, irrational urge to hug and protect her.

"I was there," he said simply.

Goose bumps showed on her neck. Rage couldn't blame her for shivering after what he'd told her.

Bright and warm, the memory of Luca's skin under his fingertips flared up in his mind. It made him wish they had stayed in bed together a little while longer, all three of them, enjoying each other's company.

Lost in thought, Luca sat on the bed, crumpling the sheet in her fists, head hanging, brows knitted. "I know Rebecca," she said. "A girl from the village. I... I never thought she looked like me."

"Lucius did."

"I think I have seen Jenny too. Once or twice, on Sundays when I went to church or visited my mum's grave."

Maybe he had been wrong. Maybe he should have spared telling her of Lucius's desires.

"So she poked his eyes out. I don't think I can blame her, given what he did to her. I always knew he was a bastard. I didn't know he was a monster."

She hung her head lower. "The problem is, now there is no chance of sending Lucius away. People won't understand since he is disabled, and I cannot tell them the truth without betraying Rebecca. They will want to ask her. She might even have to testify in court. I can't do that to her. This means I will have to feed and clothe Lucius for the rest of his life, giving him shelter and money...." Her voice trailed off.

Rage admired her strength. She was only sixteen, after all. She should be safely at home, not sitting in a dirty little roadhouse with him as company.

"Good thing is, you can go home now," he pointed out. "Lucius is no danger to you, and I am sure you can handle him. As for Jeeve, now that I know he is behind this, I will track him down and kill him. No more attacks on your life, Lucin—"

"Don't you dare," she hissed, her head whipping up. A long, hard finger poked into his chest. "If you *ever* call me Lucinda again, I swear I will do something highly unpleasant to you."

An amused smile quirked Rage's lips. "I can imagine. Luca, then. Better?"

She exhaled as if a huge weight had been taken from her shoulders. "Much better. I hate my name. I think I've mentioned that before. Anyway, how do you think you will find Jeeve?"

Rage was about to answer when he realized Keiran had been gone for far too long. "Something is wrong in this whole scenario with Jeeve and Lucius," he said slowly, "but I can't figure out what it is."

He found his bag lying abandoned in a corner of the room and checked the contents. Satisfied, he saw the landlord had been bright enough not to steal from a drunken assassin.

"Let's get downstairs. Keiran must have decided to have breakfast without us. Maybe I can figure out what isn't making sense once I've eaten."

"And after you've eaten, you'll be sending us on our way?"

"No reason why the two of you can't go back home now that it's clear it was Jeeve behind the attacks."

"Keiran would rather stay with you. So would I," Luca said.

"You have to take care of a manor. Keiran cannot afford to waste time being with me, not to mention that I don't want either of you around when I go after Jeeve."

"By the fat Bitch, you are one dumb asshole," the killer said. "Do you even know what Tracking magic is?"

Keiran shook his head. Of course he knew—after all, he had witnessed Luca do a lot of tricks and experiments and knew more than the average man about magic due to her influence—but he thought it better not to admit it.

The killer grinned generously. "I've been on the bastard's trail a long time now, dumbass. Because of the coins. I even approached him and offered him a job. When he declined—he walked out on me, just like that—it angered me enough to send someone after him. How could I have known he's got a thing for little girls?"

Keiran could only assume the man was talking about Luca. Folding his hands and tilting his head in what he hoped showed interest, he stood and listened.

"He killed my second man, and the third. Then I hired a witch and a wizard. Useless, just like the rest of them."

The man spat on the floor. Then with a furious gesture, he wiped Keiran's few possessions off the table. They clattered to the floor, the piece of string landing between Sammy's paws.

"Lousy job, they did. Said they were the best, and they couldn't even kill one of you. But I was there. I was always there because the coins in his pouch showed me the way."

Keiran could smell the man's foul breath even though he stood a few feet away.

"I lost him in Coldwell. I thought I could track him down, but I was weak, and the magic in the coins not strong enough after so long. Did I hate searching for him!"

With small shuffles of his feet, Keiran got closer to the rambling man, hoping he'd be able to overpower him—until the killer suddenly focused on him. A flick of the knife, and Keiran's cheek had a long, bleeding gash.

The man was fast, mad or not.

"No stupid tricks," he hissed.

He dug his free hand into Keiran's hair and pulled his head back. The knife's tip found the vulnerable spot above the main vein.

"I've come too far to allow an imbecile like you to stop me now. I killed the damn thief back in Coldwell because Rage paid him with my coins. Their pull was strong. Even I could sense them although I was nearly drained of magic. My coins, with my Tracking magic on them. And for what? Medicine! He was healing while I suffered in that fucking town! I was so fucking pissed off, I strangled that thief once I realized I'd wasted my last bit of strength only to find him and not the bastard assassin. I set his hut on fire for good measure. Hoped the whole damn town would burn down, but it didn't."

Keiran swallowed, not daring to move.

Rage had paid Teddy, and he'd paid Lindsay with the coins from his pouch. She must have spent them the moment she'd got them, not only the five pennies she'd given him. Otherwise, the killer would have tracked them down while they were recovering from the magicians' attack.

"I even went to the city guards. Hoped they'd find him. I waited at the prison, not daring to go back to the Shadows, but they came back empty-handed."

Unexpectedly, the killer rammed the knife deep into the kitchen table, right next to Keiran's hand. "Do you understand, I couldn't accompany them? Too much fucking tension in the whole town. They would have noticed me. They would have accused me of having set the fire."

He inhaled deeply, like a drowning man. "I hate him," he hissed. "He always escapes. Took me ages to figure out his identity—he was always gone by the time I tracked him down. Then when I finally find him, he refuses the job I wanted to give him. Bastard! I lurk at the outskirts of the Shadows, hoping to find him with the coins and using my last bit of magic to not be seen. I sense the coin, think it is him—and find you! You! With my last coin in your pocket! Can you blame me for clubbing you? Every trap I set, he manages to get out of. He always wins, he always bests me, and I *hate* him!"

Spittle flew from the man's lips. Involuntarily, Keiran took a step back only to have the killer grab the front of his shirt and pull him close enough to smell his foul breath. "Only when he rode out of Coldwell did I manage to get on his trail again."

The look on the man's face was awful.

"I'm afraid I was by then a little obsessed with him. I followed him all the way back to Babylon Manor. I couldn't shoot him, see? Too easy. The hunt would have been over. So I decided to wait. And to watch. Him and Lucius…. Hmmm. What a sight."

Admiration showed in his gray eyes. The tip of the knife drilled into Keiran's skin.

"I bet you want to know how I managed to lose him again once he'd left Babylon Manor."

Very carefully, Keiran nodded once.

The killer pushed him away with a sudden move, and Keiran staggered, crashing into a shelf lined with half-filled bottles behind him. The broken glass cut through the fabric of his clothes, some cutting his skin.

"It's obvious," the killer said, wiping his hands on his trousers. "I lost the bastard because of the fucking dogs. Can you imagine? I got caught on the way out. The beasts nearly ripped me apart. Don't know how he managed to get past them. Normally—well, before he destroyed my life and my magic—I would have killed them or become invisible or whatever. As it was, I'm glad I got past them more or less unharmed. See here, where they bit me? Once my issues with him are sorted, I will go back and break their necks, each and every fucking dog I can get hold of." The last words were spoken through gritted teeth. The killer had the left leg of his trousers rolled up, revealing a sickeningly white leg with deep bite marks.

Good boys, Keiran thought and bit back a grin just in time.

The blow to his head came too fast for him to duck it. He slammed hard to the floor, glass shards drilling like sharp needles into his knees. Trying to stop his fall with both hands didn't work—more glass, more pain—and he wondered what he had done to deserve this.

"When I walked in here and found just you—again!—I wanted to kill you," the man whispered in his ear. "But you are interesting, did you know that? I bet you didn't. I bet you don't have a clue why I hit you and why I will take you with me."

Tell me, then, Keiran thought dizzily. *Tell me everything.*

Once more, the killer touched him. This time, it hurt, and it made him feel disoriented, weak, and feeble. It made him feel as if he were drunk or poisoned. Thinking was difficult, making decisions impossible.

He was dragged outside where the sky was gray and cold and last night's rain had frozen in milky puddles on the muddy ground.

A horse neighed nearby. The killer let go of him and put a foot across his throat instead, pressing him to the ground. Keiran felt like a beetle about to be crushed under a careless boot.

As if he had all the time in the world—as if there wasn't a landlord around somewhere, the possibility of guests arriving, or a maid stumbling upon them on her way to the cowshed—the killer checked his horse's harness and unfastened a large bag that hung from the saddle. With a thump, it landed in a puddle right next to Keiran's head. Too close to see it clearly. The bag was rough cotton and tied closed with a rope. Wet—with blood?—on the bottom.

Maybe it was just the melting ice seeping into the fabric.

"Don't need it anymore, do I?" the man said with a chuckle as he threw Keiran over the horse's back as if he didn't weigh more than a bag of beans. "Thought it would come in handy. I planned to shock the damn assassin or at least get him into trouble. Once I realized I had lost his trail, I figured I may as well finish what he'd started. But just when I was done with dear Lucius, I sensed the pull of one of my coins. Boy, was I excited. Of course, it was only you. The imbecilic little brat who'd stolen the coin. You should be glad you have potential, or you would be dead by now, rotting, disemboweled, lying in there next to the corpse of the fucking cat."

Giving the bag on the ground one last smile, the killer swung up behind Keiran. "Giddyup," he cooed, taking the reins with his left hand and placing his right on Keiran's exposed neck.

The horse broke into a gentle trot. From the sky, small snowflakes drifted to the frozen ground.

Keiran's stomach heaved at the touch. Retching, he received another blow to his temple. This time, it was hard enough to render him unconscious.

"LET'S GO," Rage said, shouldering his bag. "The weather looks bad. I want to be on my way as soon as possible."

"Finding Jeeve."

"Finding Jeeve and killing him with you and Keiran safely on the way back home." He opened the door. Outside the room, it was quiet. No voices, no footsteps, no one clattering about with dishes and glasses. Obviously, no customers had yet found their way to the roadhouse, and the landlord seemed to be still asleep.

Too quiet.

Rage didn't halt his step at the sudden warning his senses gave him—sudden warnings weren't new to him and bore no threat, as he knew how to deal with danger.

Keiran was nowhere to be seen. No rummaging from the kitchen. No meows from the cat.

A cold breeze blew upstairs. The front door must be open.

Automatically, Rage held out his hand and stopped Luca from following him. Surprisingly enough, she didn't push past him as he'd half expected, but stayed where she was.

"You don't think Jeeve has found us here, do you?" she whispered, and finally something clicked in his mind, and he knew what had been bothering him ever since he'd interrogated Lucius of Babylon.

Lucius had said Jeeve didn't live at the manor anymore. *Vanished some weeks back. Thought he'd finally managed to get his neck broken by an outraged husband.*

Rage clearly remembered Lucius's stammering words.

"Luca," Rage said, beckoning her closer. "Tell me, when did Jeeve leave the manor?"

Shoulder to shoulder, they stood on the staircase, waiting, watching.

"About two weeks before you kidnapped me," Luca answered. "My fath—Lucius thought he'd been killed. I reckoned he ran away with a woman who was willing to leave her husband for him."

Rage took another step. He was halfway down the staircase now, and still, the house was too quiet. "It doesn't make sense. The whole plan, Jeeve being there once it was time for taking over, wouldn't work with him gone."

"Yes, but…. No, he…." Luca frowned. "You're right. Jeeve would have needed to be at the manor, assuming control once his plan had worked out. If he came back now, people would become suspicious, probably believing him to be part of the plan."

Rage pulled his knife and crossed the distance to the bar. He saw the broken bottles right away and the cat's motionless body on the floor.

Damn.

Keiran was nowhere to be seen. The wind banged the door against the wall, causing a hollow sound that resembled the one Rage's heart drummed out

"If Jeeve really is behind this, his plan obviously isn't to take over the manor."

Luca came up next to him. Her hand found a way into his, and he felt more than saw the tears building up in her eyes.

She'd seen the dead cat.

Rage replaced the knife in his belt. The room was empty. Whoever had been here had gone. No use for a knife no matter how much Rage wanted to cut the throat of the person responsible for this mess.

"Then what is his fucking plan?" Luca gripped his hand hard. Rage couldn't bring himself to shake her off.

He turned to her. "We know this wasn't Lucius's plan. And if Jeeve isn't after the manor, the only logical conclusion is that this isn't about you, either."

She was staring at the cat's body lying motionless under the table. "I was just the bait."

"Yes. And if you were just the bait, this is all about me. I'm his target, always was, from the moment Jeeve bought me a drink."

CHAPTER
Fifteen

METHODICALLY, RAGE searched the house for Keiran. All he found were dozens of broken bottles, an insignificant amount of blood, and the small, broken body of Sammy.

Carefully, Rage placed the cat onto one of the tables. When he touched him, expecting the cold stiffness of a corpse, he felt a heartbeat under the fur, feeble but definitely there. At least for now, Sammy was alive.

"Jeeve always liked cats," Luca managed to say. "Killing one like that…. He must have changed a lot since I last saw him." Hesitantly, she stroked Sammy's nose, touching his white whiskers. The cat's paws twitched, and she pulled her hand back, obviously fearing her touch would push him closer to death.

"Easy, little one," Rage soothed, his voice a low, reassuring rumble. The cat relaxed under his touch. Without looking up, Rage asked, "If I keep him still, can you heal him?"

Constantly, the door banged its hollow beat against the wall; insistently, the wind blew its icy breath inside. He gently stroked the cat, calmed it, and took its pain and fear away so Luca could do her magic. Her hands were shaking, and her eyes were suspiciously shiny though not a single tear appeared on her cheeks.

Luckily he was as good with cats as he was with dogs.

"Do you think Jeeve was here?" she asked, concentrating on the cat. Her lips moved as she wove the magic needed to mend Sammy's broken hind leg.

Rage continued to brush the cat's fur. "I think so. Someone was here, and someone shed blood and hurt the cat. And Keiran is gone."

"You think…. Do you think Keiran's dead?"

After a moment of consideration, Rage shook his head. "He's alive. I would know if he were dead."

Sammy meowed, a pitiful sound that clearly said he'd rather be chasing mice than being healed with magic.

"Just another minute," Rage told him.

Luca managed a shaky smile. "I would have expected you to break Sammy's neck given how badly he is injured." One last spell and only a bit of dried blood around the cat's fangs bore witness to the broken bones she had just healed.

"I like cats."

Sammy stretched his legs, arched his back, and hopped off the table as Rage went outside. The wind hit him fully, the temperature having dropped below the freezing point.

Snowflakes danced around him, quickly building a thin, white cover over the frozen ground. Their breath formed clouds in the cold air.

"Go find me a coat," he called to Luca over his shoulder. "I've got a feeling I'll be needing it."

Luca was back quickly, wrapped up in a large, warm jacket. "Here," she said, handing him a cloak, its hem braided with sheep fleece. "It should fit you. It's even black. I guess it belongs to the landlord. He won't be happy, us stealing his things."

With large steps, Rage crossed the distance to the stables. "Stolen coats are the least of his problems. Don't you think he would have been downstairs by now were he able to move at all?"

The stables were warm, being shelter not only for the horses but for the cows and pigs as well. At least the cows had been milked and the pigs and horses fed. The maid must have taken care of them.

She wasn't here anymore, though. And one of the two saddles that hung on the wall was missing.

"Seems the maid might have gone to the village," Luca concluded. "Maybe the landlord went with her. Maybe—"

"The second saddle is still here."

They saw the legs at the same time. Male legs, stretched out as if the man attached to them had decided to take a little nap. The upper part of him, however, was hidden in an empty box.

"Tell me it's not Keiran," Luca said hoarsely.

"Can't be. His legs are longer, and he was wearing different trousers when he left to look for breakfast." He crossed the distance and removed the box to reveal the man's face.

It was the landlord. The killer had smashed his head in, and the horse in the next stall was pacing nervously because of the smell of pooling blood. For a big man, the landlord looked surprisingly small in death, and there was a puzzled look on his face, as if he couldn't understand how his life could have ended with the back of his head being split open. Rage took a saddle blanket and threw it over the dead man. Then he moved the nervous horse to another stall.

"Jeeve must be losing it," he said. "He found us, but didn't come upstairs. Instead, he killed the landlord. Looks like he took Keiran with him, given we haven't found his corpse yet. Which doesn't make sense either. The boy would only slow him down."

Luca didn't comment, her eyes fixed on the dead man beneath the blanket. Only when Rage took her by the shoulders and pulled her outside did she look up at him.

"He's dead," she said weakly. "The man who owned this place—I didn't even know him, and now he's dead. And Jeeve, he hates my cat, and Keiran is gone, and I don't know what to do!"

Her long hair waved in the wind, her eyes wide and pale, her skin cold. She looked like a child overwhelmed by a cruel, unbearable reality. Her lower lip trembled as if she'd cry at any moment, and she bit it, nearly drawing blood.

"Luca," Rage said, taking her face between his hands. "Luca, listen to me. Are you listening?"

Her eyes were filled with tears, yet not a single one fell. "I'm listening," she whispered.

"Keiran isn't dead, or this would be his corpse, not the landlord's. Jeeve took him for whatever reason, but you having a fit won't help him. Jeeve has been playing cat and mouse with me ever since we met. I'll go after him. I'll find him and bring Keiran back to you. Understand?"

"No."

"Which part is unclear?"

"The part where you say *you* will go after him. You, as in not us. If you think I'll let you go after them on your own, if you think I'm going to go back home and wait for you to bring back my friend, you're totally nuts!"

Rage pulled her face close enough for him to see his reflection in her pupils. "At home, you are safe. In my company, you will most likely die. Do you want to die?"

The sea green of her eyes darkened, flooded with sudden anger. She freed her face with a sudden jerk of her head and stepped back.

"How do you plan on finding them, anyway?" she shouted, furiously kicking a large bag out of her way. Or at least, she tried to kick it out of her way—it was frozen to the ground. "And what are you going to do if you find them? For all we know, Jeeve is really good with magic. After all, he found us wherever we went. You, on the other hand, cannot even do Fire magic. You need me, and you know it."

Rage was next to her before she'd even seen him move. Tiny flakes of snow were landing in his hair and on the black cloak. With a swift flick of his knife, he knelt and cut the rope that bound the bag at Luca's feet.

"Why bother with that?" Luca said impatiently. "Let's go find Keiran!"

"That's blood soaking through the fabric."

"So?"

"So something able to bleed is inside. Could be an animal. Or bloody clothes. Or something worse."

Luca crossed her arms over her chest and grumbled, "Can't be worse than what I've already seen."

"It could be proof that Keiran's dead."

"You said he is alive!" she yelled, and before he could stop her, she knelt down next to him and opened the bag.

A foul stench hit them. Luca retched, but didn't let go of the bag, not even at the sight of the dirty, bloodied mass of hair peeking through the opening.

"Keiran's hair is brown. This… mess… is blond," she managed to choke out.

Rage slapped her hand away as she tried to reach inside the bag. Yanking the opening toward him, he blocked her view with his body. "It's a head, Luca. You don't want to have a severed head in your hands no matter the hair color."

Luca sat back in the snow, silenced by his words. She turned to watch Sammy carefully place a paw outside, eyeing the snowflakes suspiciously, and distracted herself by stroking him until he purred when he came over and hopped onto her knee.

It seemed to calm them both.

Bracing himself against the stench, Rage grabbed a fistful of bloody hair and lifted out the head.

"Fuck," he said wearily as he looked the dead man in the face. "Fucking shit."

Luca looked up. "Is—" she managed to say before a small, strangled sound emerged from her mouth. Pushing the cat away, she jumped up and stumbled a few feet away before slipping and falling to the ground. One hand on her mouth, the other pressed to her stomach, she barely managed not to vomit. Tears streamed down her face, though she didn't seem to notice.

Rage returned the head to the bag, found the rope, and tied it again.

He went over to Luca, knelt beside her, and hugged her tightly. "I'm so sorry," he murmured, not knowing what else to say.

She cried into his cloak and muttered words he didn't understand, her whole body shaking, hands like claws digging bruises into his flesh.

"Why did he kill Lucius?" Luca sobbed. "Why? Tell me why!"

Exactly. Why did Jeeve kill Lucius, and why had he been carrying his head around?

IT TOOK the girl a long time before she could let go of him. They knelt, buffeted by the cold wind, snow melting on their heads and dampening their clothes. She pressed her head against his shoulder, locking out the world, the roadhouse, and the bag containing her father's severed head.

She knew now that he hadn't been her father, but Rage knew that no matter how much one might hate another person, one could still grieve.

Eventually, Rage managed to get her back inside, never letting go of her, steering her as though she were blind. Had he not taken care of her, she would have walked headfirst into the wall, and she was more than glad when he pushed her onto a chair. Rage closed the door, keeping the wind and snow outside and even most of the cold. He made a fire and hung up her jacket and his cloak, never saying a word.

When Luca stopped shivering—Sammy had a part in that, having curled up in her lap, purring gently—he went into the kitchen, washed his hands, and made coffee. Thick, black, and sweetened with three spoons of sugar. He handed her one cup and had one for himself.

She wrapped her fingers around the warm earthenware, took a sip, coughed, and wiped her nose on her sleeve.

"Lousy morning," she whispered. "It started so beautifully. And now… and now…."

She hiccoughed. "And now Keiran is gone and the landlord is dead and…."

She hiccoughed again. "Lucius. He's dead too. And it isn't even midmorning."

Apart from the first sip, she hadn't touched her coffee. Her lips as well as her fingertips were blue from the cold even though she was sitting close to the fire. Her cheekbones cast sharp shadows on her pale skin.

Silently, Rage went to the kitchen, found some oats and a not too dirty pot and made porridge. Placing a plate in front of Luca, he said, "Eat. And drink the coffee. You won't be able to sit in the saddle very long without nourishment."

"I'm going nowhere near a saddle anytime soon." She pushed the plate away.

"You will eat your breakfast, and afterwards we will leave. The maid will be coming back soon. She will find the landlord, she will scream, and eventually, the guards will arrive. We need to be on the road by then." Patiently, he pushed the plate back toward her.

"The guards can put me in prison for all I care. At least Jeeve won't be able to get me there." Hesitantly, she took the spoon, stirred the warm oat grain, and slowly began to eat.

"Jeeve seems to be able to do whatever he likes, given he came here unnoticed, killed the landlord, and kidnapped Keiran."

"You don't even know which direction he went." Then her eyes widened. "*We* need to be on the road? Does that mean you're taking me along?"

"If I keep you with me, at least I'll be sure you won't do anything stupid. And I might be able to protect you should Jeeve decide to come after you next."

Luca took the mug and leaned back in her chair. She was less shaky, and a bit of color had crept back into her cheeks. With a fierce gesture, she pulled her hair out of her face and bound it at the nape of her neck.

"Do you think he's out there watching us?"

"He might. He could be killing the boy right now. He could have had an accident. He could be hiring an army. You wanted to come with me, so move."

Taking his cloak, he swung it around his shoulders and fastened the clasp. He looked like a ghost, the cloak's fur highlighting his pale features and the blackness of his eyes.

"We need to leave," he said. "You are responsible for the cat. Pack as many provisions as you can while I get the horses."

THE HORSES were glad to get out of the stable, away from the stink of blood and death. While Luca packed bread and cheese, Rage got the bag with Lucius's head, added several stones so head and bag would stay submerged, and threw it into the river behind the roadhouse. Hopefully Lucius would vanish and eventually be eaten by the fish. It was what he deserved.

He was watching the bag sink to the bottom when Luca's voice ripped him out of his thoughts. "Food for a day, two at the most." She stepped next to him, a bag in her hand.

"Let's go, then," Rage said.

Luca didn't move. "I remember him shouting at me when I was small, barely able to walk," she said, staring at the bubbles that disturbed the calmness of the river. Although there was no sun, the sky hung low with snow-pregnant clouds, and the river reflected some of the daylight. It danced across Luca's face, making her eyes seem deeper and showing they were filled with tears.

"Why did he shout at you?" Not knowing if the gesture would be welcome, Rage put his arm around her and pulled her close. She didn't resist but leaned her head against his shoulder again.

"I don't know. I never knew. All I was certain of was he didn't love me and didn't want me near him. As soon as he learned I liked something, be it a toy or an animal, he either destroyed it, sold it, or claimed it for himself. When Keiran and I became friends, I made sure he didn't find out, or he would have found a way to end our friendship. That's why I never asked Keiran to marry me. I feared Lucius would be angry enough to kill him."

"Well, he's dead now," Rage said softly. He could feel her shaky smile more than see it.

Wiping the back of her hand across her eyes, she cast him a lopsided grin. "That first night up in the hay barn—when you had threatened to kill Sammy so I would stay put?—after you'd fallen asleep, he curled up on your chest, and he was purring. It was so cute, and it occurred to me you must have saved him. I figured a man who saves cats can't be that bad, no matter what his profession is. In any case, you didn't touch me, so coming with you was the logical choice, especially after that man tried to shoot us."

"Cute. No one has ever called me cute, girl." He brushed a strand of hair behind her ear, wondering how he had managed to get stuck with her.

Luca took a deep breath. She closed her eyes, gulped, then looked up at him and said earnestly, "I'm so glad I'm married to the cutest assassin this side of the empress's city. And I'm glad I can come with you."

"Then let's find Keiran," he said. On impulse, he kissed her lightly on the cheek.

To his surprise, her smile deepened.

Together, they headed back to the horses. The bag of food hung off the saddle horn, and when Rage mounted his mare, Sammy jumped up onto his leg.

"Forget it." Rage picked the cat off his leg and threw him over to Luca. "Keep him warm. It doesn't look as if the snow is going to stop anytime soon."

"Are you planning on looking for tracks? What if there aren't any? What if Jeeve used magic to erase them? What if—"

"Useful ideas would be welcome." Rage wouldn't have admitted it, but he was anxious to find the boy. *My fault he's been kidnapped*, Rage thought. *My responsibility to save him.*

Luca came up alongside him. "You two are connected. I don't know how or why, but as surely as Keiran found you here, you can find him. If you dare. And if you accept my help." She lifted a hand before he could say a word. "Don't deny it. Keiran told me that to him, you are as bright as a flame in complete darkness. I don't believe it's a one-way thing. With my help, you could use the connection to our advantage."

Rage leaned over, their knees touching as he pulled her closer by the collar of her jacket. "There is no link," he said calmly. "Accept it. He's a pastime for me, nothing else. Nothing more."

"Keiran loves you. Love is the strongest link ever, even if you don't love him back. I believe you will be able to find him through this link. He's out there somewhere, Rage. If he is still alive, he will be hoping and praying we find him. Try it, that's all I'm asking. Try to find him. Please."

The snow was falling heavily now. There was nothing but white all around, interrupted only by an occasional bush. Very soon, the horses would have trouble finding a path at all.

Finding any tracks was a fantasy. And it didn't make any sense whatsoever to continue without even knowing where to go.

Letting go of the girl's collar, Rage considered his options.

There were none.

"I'll try," he finally said. "I know it won't work, but I will try just to stop you from nagging me."

"Thank the Lady, there is some intelligence hidden in the man. Fine. Let's do some magic."

CHAPTER
Sixteen

WARM FUR under his nose: a horse moving slowly and steadily.

Needle-sharp coldness in his face. Snow, whipped by wind strong enough to be called a storm.

A hand on his neck, squeezing ever so slightly. Dizziness, worse than when he'd last been awake.

Keiran struggled.

"Hold still, or I will knock you out again," the killer said, his voice muffled by the scarf wrapped around his face.

Keiran's stomach heaved. He retched.

The killer grabbed him by the back of his shirt and threw him off the horse. The snow on the narrow mountain path softened his fall, but it also soaked his already damp clothes.

It didn't matter that more snow filled his shirt; the cold had made him numb. He didn't feel it, or not much, anyway. The cold competed with his hunger and his fear. All in all, it was the least of his problems.

Keiran crawled away on hands and knees until he hit rocks, which seemed to reach miles up into the sky. Throwing up the milk and bread he'd had for breakfast, he eventually managed to get up on wobbly legs and take the long needed piss that had made him struggle in the first place.

He had lost track of time. Was it still the same day, or had he been hanging over the horse's back for longer than he'd thought?

If only he could find a way to get away, everything would be fine. Problem was his head hurt, he was weak with hunger, and it was cruelly cold up here. Running wouldn't get him far, and even if it did, he'd freeze within hours. The killer had a horse; he didn't. The killer had a coat; he wore only trousers and a shirt.

The wind burned his lungs, making him cough. But apart from feeling absolutely horrible, his brain began to work again. The dizziness vanished—maybe because of the cold—and his stomach had calmed down too. All in all, an improvement.

Wiping his mouth clean with a bit of snow, Keiran took some more and ate it. It made his teeth ache, but it quenched his thirst and washed away the bitter taste of bile. More snow cleaned his face and hands. He felt nearly human again and began to wonder why they were here, in the mountains, in the middle of nowhere.

Rage and Luca must have realized he was gone. They would have found the broken bottles and the traces of blood on the floor.

Luca would want to save him. He wasn't so sure about Rage.

"You done, boy?" the killer asked as though they were companions on a journey, thrown together by fate, not brutality.

Keiran looked up at him, forcing a hesitant smile. He wanted the killer to believe he was harmless, too stupid to be watched closely, so should an opportunity arise to flee he could use it.

"Seems you don't like horses too much." The killer nodded at the mess in the snow, not that there was much to be seen as the ever-falling snow had already covered most of it up. "Pity for you we have another hour before we reach our destination. Your choice boy. Wanna continue our journey with your head up, or shall I knock you out again?"

It's a trap, Keiran thought, carefully avoiding showing fear on his face. So instead of simply pointing to the horse, he smiled hopefully and lifted his shoulders. *I don't know which would be better*, his body language said, not entirely sure it was a wise idea to act this stupidly, but not knowing what else to do.

"Goodness, boy, it is no fun messing with you. Come here," the killer ordered, and when Keiran did, he got a rope put around his neck. "You'll walk. And I'll strangle you should you try to run. Get along. I want to reach the monastery before sunset."

A jerk, and the rope tightened. Keiran had to hurry to stay close to the horse and was glad the path was slippery. Had the horse been able to go any faster, he'd have reached their destination as a corpse.

Foot by foot, they made it up the narrow path with Keiran squeezing his eyes shut against the wind and snow. He had placed one hand on the horse's back and dangerously close to the killer's boot—being so near him made him dizzy, but he didn't have a choice if he didn't want to trip and fall.

His lips cracked from the cold, and he could taste blood. His throat ached from lack of water. Not a single part of his body could even remotely be called warm.

At one point, the killer got off his horse and went on by foot, dragging him on. The path had become too steep for the animal. Keiran feared were he to take off his boots, his toes would come off with them.

Wish I had stayed in bed this morning.

Damn Rage for not getting breakfast himself. The killer wouldn't have stood a chance against him.

Damn him for staying upstairs with Luca, talking to her, comforting her.

Rage, Keiran thought desperately, reaching out instinctively for the black flame burning inside him.

Touching it. Cradling it in his mind. Crying for help.

The black flame flared up, as clear and bright as ever and hot in the darkness of his own mind.

Keiran!

Keiran missed a step and struggled. The rope around his neck tightened, and he nearly fell.

"Watch your step, stupid," the killer snapped.

Gasping for air, Keiran managed to stay on his feet. His legs trembled, and stars danced in front of his eyes. They must be high up in the mountains by now, the air having become thin.

Had he heard Rage's voice in his mind? Really? Or was he so desperate for help he'd imagined it?

"We're here," the killer announced after another eternity had passed, a strange mixture of pride and hate in his voice. "Only took us the better part of the day, but it was worth it, don't you think?"

Jerking at Keiran's rope, he pulled him closer, his hand landing on Keiran's neck.

Dizziness instantly exploded into a storm in his head, blowing away all thoughts.

"You can feel it, eh?" The killer pulled him closer. Keiran was pressed against the man's leg and the saddle. "I know you can feel it, and there is nothing you can do about it. But don't worry. I won't kill you yet. Who would have thought you'd become so precious to me?"

THE LAST time Rage had used magic deliberately had been at the age of eleven when he'd tried to light a fire in his father's house. An easy enough magical trick because all one needed to do was concentrate on the smell of burning wood, the sound flames made, and on the beautiful colors of orange, gold, and black.

Back then, he had lit the roof instead. Moments later, his home had been burning, reducing his sister as well as his parents to tears. It had been the last straw—his parents had forbidden him from ever using magic again and threatened to cast him out of their house and the village should he disobey.

Upon seeing the ruins of their house, he had agreed. And after his family's death, he had kept his promise no matter the circumstances. Of course, it was inconvenient not to be able to dry himself in seconds or obscure the eyes of people looking for him. At times, he had been close to death because he couldn't use Healing magic. But he'd learned to live with it. Nowadays, he hardly ever thought about his magic, knowing it was safely locked up deep inside him.

Today was the first time in many years Rage wished he wasn't magically crippled. He wished he could tap into his magical resources and find the boy. It would make searching for tracks unnecessary since they'd be able to ride fast and catch up with Jeeve before nightfall.

Snowflakes kissed his face as he sat on his horse, unmoving, tiny reminders that winter had decided not to wait any longer. His horse was restless; it wanted to get going, out of the wind and the snow.

There was no way he could accomplish this. None whatsoever.

"I will help you find him if you are willing to trust me." Luca took one of his hands into hers. It was an uncomfortable position for both of them. Dismounting, on the other hand, would have meant standing ankle deep in snow.

Rage frowned at the sight of his scarred fingers touching her smooth, cold skin. "You are aware it's very likely that my magic will rip you to pieces?"

"I controlled your magic once. I can do it again. It's not that hard now that I know how it feels." She sighed, then frowned. "I don't know how to put it. It's like trying to keep water in the hollow of your hands. Not easy, but possible. Maybe a few drops will fall to the ground. Maybe a bit of your magic will escape my shield. I can control most, maybe all of your power, but even if a few drops get out, there won't be any harm. You just need to relax and open up to me. I'll make sure we get out of this alive. All you have to do is think of Keiran. Call for him with your mind and your heart." She sniffed, and it somewhat ruined the seriousness of her words. "That's how it should work, anyway."

Rage snorted. "How reassuring."

Her grip on his hand tightened. "Let's do this," she urged. "Before Jeeve kills him."

He nodded. Now that he'd agreed, he could at least try, as promised.

"Think of Keiran," she said quietly. "His face, his eyes, the color of his hair, the fragrance of his skin. You know him. You've made love to him."

The cold ceased to exist the moment he closed his eyes. Almost instantly, he saw the boy's face, his smile, and the sparkle dancing in his eyes.

The fragrance of his skin was in his nose. He could nearly feel soft fingertips brushing over his chin.

Easy now. If he tried too hard, if he scared the image away, this would be over before it had begun. One hasty movement, one harsh memory....

The boy doesn't like hasty, Rage thought, wondering if he was asleep and dreaming. *Slow and tender is more to his liking. I can nearly feel his skin, his lips. If I lean forward just a little, I will be able to kiss him.*

He was there, with him in the darkness of his soul. Rage was aware of his presence—and his fear.

Keiran! he whispered, not aloud, just with his heart. Just like Luca had advised him.

For a brief moment, Rage's mind wanted to protest at the fact he was listening for the boy. For a brief moment, he considered opening his eyes, ending this experiment. He might have done so, even, if his magic had not chosen that moment to fight against his intention.

Rage!

A desperate, hopeless voice in his mind. His magic had found the trail and was following it.

It had found the boy.

And it was about to lash out. It was needed, it was being used, and it felt too good to end so soon. No way he could end this now. No way his magic would allow him to break the contact now that it had been established.

Warmth flooded him, combined with joy—this was good! This was his magic doing a brilliant job. It belonged to him, and he should have never given it up!

Instantly, his fists clenched around the girl's hands. Distantly, he heard her gasp.

"Easy, Rage!" she called, and vaguely, he heard her mumble, "Truly, this name is silly. You need to tell me how your mother named you someday. Anyway, all is well. The magic wants to get out, but I am controlling it. Find Keiran, do you hear me? Find him!"

Rage nodded, eyes still closed. He'd already done that; he'd found the boy, knew he was alive. He might as well think of other things now that this ridiculously easy task was done.

Reality faded away. The day wasn't cold anymore. It was spring, and he was excited because today he would be going to the little lake in the woods with his love. They would take a swim, and maybe, hopefully, they would kiss.

There was his sunshine. Water was pearling on his back, and he was laughing because of something he'd said or done. He'd forgotten how beautiful—

"He's not the one you're looking for," a voice said, and his sunshine was gone, blown away by the winter wind.

"The one you are looking for is still alive. You said so. He kissed you less than a day ago. You fell asleep next to him and woke up with his arms around you. Keiran. He loves you. He needs you to find him."

"Done. Shut up." Was that him, talking in that dreamlike manner?

The grip on his hands tightened. "Is he well?"

There was the boy, a shadow on a snowy background. A moment ago, he hadn't been there.

"Alive, but not well. Cold. Hungry. Frightened and tired. Sick."

He didn't know why he'd said that last word. Sick? He didn't look sick.

His magic, eager at being used, flared up, showing him the boy more clearly.

"He's in the mountains. North, hours ahead of us. He's not alone. Stupid path to choose."

The horses shifted, complaining.

"Who's the one with him? Is it Jeeve? Is Keiran injured?" Luca asked, prompting him.

Stretching his neck and rolling his shoulders, Rage sat up straighter in the saddle. When he finally opened his eyes, he felt drugged by his own magic—he saw something, but nothing that was nearby.

"A horse. A man. White hair barely visible under his scarf. He's dangerous." Rage turned his head and looked straight through Luca; he didn't even know she was there anymore. "I am using Keiran's eyes to see. He's not injured. Scared. Dizzy."

Barely controlled panic in Luca's voice. "I've never met anyone before whose magic is this strong! I want you to stop this, Rage. Do you hear me? End it. We know where they are—"

And then his magic flared up like a bushfire, greedy, deadly. It wanted more than just a brief glimpse into the boy's mind. It wanted more than to be used and then put away. It wanted everything.

With cruel strength, Rage felt Luca tightening both her grip on his hands and her grip on his magic. Her shield crushed him, and he heard her yelling, ordering him to keep his magic in check, ordering him to end the connection with Keiran. He would have obeyed, even though she was so much younger—only he couldn't. He'd never been able to keep his magic in check no matter what he'd tried. No one had ever taught him how it was done. He was a farmer's son, and he'd never seen a school from inside.

His body cramped as Luca redoubled her efforts to control him. Her hands, sweaty but hard in his, threatened to crush his fingers, and he heard himself scream as his magic fought against her barrier.

The image of Keiran became pale and lifeless before vanishing. The white-haired man—gone. The dizziness—gone.

Rage went limp. Somewhat surprised that he couldn't keep himself in the saddle, he tried closing his fingers on the reins, and failed.

Luca let go of his hands and caught him by his shoulders as he slumped forward, stopping him from falling off his horse.

Hateful, dangerous, his magic attacked the shield one last time. Then it recoiled and was gone.

The snow on Rage's cloak melted. The fabric dried. Muttering a few words, Luca took care of him.

Surreal.

Blood dropped from Rage's nose into the snow.

And then it was over, just like that. The horses calmed and stood still. Rage, shaking his head as if he'd just woken from a nightmare, wiped the blood off his nose with the back of his hand. He didn't so much as tremble.

"I know where they are," he croaked.

TEARS FROZE on his cheeks. Keiran tasted bile in his mouth and feared he would throw up again. He could still feel the hand on his neck like an iron harness.

The killer had thrown him backward the moment he'd begun to retch. Now, sitting in the snow, Keiran remained calm only because he knew Rage was out there, looking for him.

A moment ago, their minds had touched. Rage knew where he was and would follow him. All he had to do was stay alive until he arrived.

But given the sight in front of him in combination with the prospect of being touched again, Keiran wasn't so sure he could.

"Isn't it marvelous?" the killer said fondly. "The Forbidden Monastery, they call it. I haven't visited the place in a while. When I was around fifteen, I spent a night inside its walls. Great experience! You should try it one day." Then he chuckled. "Silly me. You *will* be spending the night here. With me. Ah, the pleasure of anticipation!"

Shaking with cold, Keiran looked at the monstrosity on the other side of the abyss. In front of him was a bridge, behind him was a mountain path blocked by snow, and next to him was the killer.

He shuddered, and not simply from the cold. The sight of the place filled his heart with even more fear. It looked evil, as if it could suck out and devour your soul.

"Looks like a dozen eyes are watching you, eh?" Admiration laced the killer's words. "It's the windows. And the ghosts, I guess."

Keiran wiped the snow out of his face with a shaking hand.

The abyss was so deep he couldn't see the bottom but could faintly hear a river roaring. It was spanned by a narrow, rotten-looking bridge, which swayed slightly in the wind. It looked as though it would disintegrate the moment someone stepped upon it, and the sheer thought of doing so made his stomach heave.

Forbidden Monastery. The name implied monks had once lived here, serving the Lady. Because that's what monks did, didn't they? They prayed and looked after the poor and did good wherever possible. Monks were gentle and quiet. They were old and wrinkled, and they forgave sins.

There weren't any windows, though, just holes in the black rock. The broken gate that guarded the entrance looked like a mouth ready to devour anyone who dared to enter. Whoever had built this place had considered it wise to carve its rooms directly out of the mountain rather than carry timber up here.

Had there not been a rope around his neck, Keiran would have tried to run, no matter if it would have meant he'd die from the cold before nightfall.

In the dim, wintry light, it seemed as if the rocks touched the sky. The rough surface was black by nature, and only the snow had managed to lighten it a bit, making the monastery's windows indeed look like eyes—or rather, like empty sockets.

They made him feel small and unimportant; they made him feel like prey.

The rope around his neck tightened, forcing him to his feet. A strong wave of evil emerged from the place on the other side of the abyss, and Keiran thought he could hear screams in the quiet air. For a brief moment, he could have sworn a man tried to climb out of one of the windows, only to be dragged back inside by cruel hands. No more than fifteen windows, all in all. Fifteen eye sockets, staring at him hatefully.

Vigorously, he shook his head, and for once, the killer had no problem understanding his meaning.

"Let's get across," he said, pulling the rope tight enough to make Keiran fear he would be strangled at any moment. "It's a perfect place for us. Here, I learned everything important. Here, I learned how to properly use my magic. We will both cross the bridge, and we will have some fun together." He patted Keiran's head. "We have all the time in the world. No one knows where we are, and no one will find us up here."

He looked down at Keiran, forcing his face up with a hand under his chin. "In the end, you will be dead, of course. It is the sole reason why I brought you here—to kill you. But don't worry. I will do it slowly and with care. Your death will not be in vain."

Great, Keiran thought, drowning in the killer's eyes. He barely realized when he was kicked in the back. He didn't even scream with fear as he stumbled onto the rickety bridge. Because not even the ghosts calling out for him were as awful as the killer's hand on his neck.

THE BLOOD from Rage's nose had painted a colorful pattern in the snow, and he frowned as he looked down at the crimson drops. "I saw Keiran. Or rather, I was him. How did you do that?"

Luca shrugged. "I didn't do anything other than make sure your magic didn't escape. You did the rest. Your magic is a lot stronger than I thought. Much stronger than mine, and that means a lot. I had a hard time keeping it under control."

Rage turned his horse north, toward the mountains. "I know where he is. Let's get him back instead of wasting time talking about magic."

Luca grinned. "How lovely it is to find a subject you don't want to talk about," she mocked and let her horse fall into step with his. "You know, magic isn't all bad. You've just witnessed firsthand how helpful it can be."

"I just witnessed firsthand how badly it hurts."

He chose a steady pace, not too fast, which would allow them to cross miles and miles without needing to rest the horses. Hopefully, the girl would quit talking about magic.

"Can you tell me where they are heading?" Luca asked.

Briefly, Rage considered lying to her. But to what end? Eventually, she would find out and have to deal with it.

"Have you ever heard of the Forbidden Monastery?"

Luca nodded. "Of course I have. It's the place those mad monks built ages ago. They killed a lot of people until the empress finally decided to ambush the place. All the monks died. It's in ruin now, I think. Why would Jeeve want to go up there?"

Hunching his shoulders against the cold as well as the memories welling up inside him, Rage wished he would be more confident they'd get the boy back alive.

"Hello?" she called to him. "Are you going to answer my question?"

Rage sighed. Apparently, she wasn't going to shut up anytime soon. "I don't know why Jeeve would go up there. But I know it means he is mad. It also means that whatever he has in mind for Keiran, he doesn't plan to keep him alive."

Simply crossing the bridge to the Forbidden Monastery was madness in itself.

"You've been up there?"

And she was far too smart for her own good.

"Once. It nearly killed me."

Speeding up his horse a tad, Rage tried to remember how long it had been since he'd even thought about that place, or the job he'd done up there for that matter. It was a memory he preferred to keep hidden. Apart from coming back half-dead, the experience had given his life a new turn, one he still wasn't sure he liked. He'd ended up separating himself from the few people he'd once been close to, choosing to walk a lonely path rather than stay close to the city…. Yes, he hated to even think of the monastery, not to mention going there.

Unfortunately, some memories couldn't stay hidden forever. Voices whispered in his head, calling for him. Howling through broken windows, the wind resembled the cries of the ones he'd killed.

"Are you planning on telling me more about the Forbidden Monastery sometime today?" Luca asked, riding next to him, oblivious to his fear of the place. Just as well. It was more than enough that he knew what awaited them. No use scaring the life out of her before they arrived.

"It was built by magic," he said, choosing his words carefully, "carved directly into the rocks, its windows overlooking an abyss several hundred feet deep. The bridge crossing it was rotten last time I was there. I truly hoped it had fallen to pieces by now, but from what I just saw, it's still intact. I have no idea what awaits us once we catch up with them, but I don't think Jeeve is aware of us following him."

She managed to stay quiet for a mile or three before asking, "Why? Why were you up there in the first place? Come on, Rage, I need you to concentrate when I'm talking to you. I understand the experience of contacting Keiran has shaken you to the core, but it was just a bit of magic. I promise not to ask you to do it again unless it's absolutely necessary. You have been up there. You said it nearly killed you. Tell me more!"

Rage thought of how it had felt to be so strangely close to the boy, about the dizziness he'd sensed, and the deep fear.

Concentration. Yes. Good advice. There was nothing he could do about the boy right now anyway.

"The empress had a problem with the Forbidden Monastery. The men who built it were wizards, not monks. They wanted a place where they could study magic and learn how to gain power. They wanted to control the world, and they wanted to achieve this goal no matter what the cost. Their victims' skulls and bones decorate the riverbed and the big hall in the center of the mountain."

He halted his horse and dismounted—time for a quick break. They had covered several miles by now. They needed to be well on the path into the mountains by sunset, or they wouldn't have a chance of keeping the trail, but they also needed to catch their breath every now and then.

"The empress's guards fought the monks and managed to kill most of them. For the rest, I was hired. I was just over twenty and ridiculously proud of my skills. The wizards taught me more about pain and fear than I'm willing to tell you."

Luca had gotten off her horse too, stretching her legs while Rage fed them. A small brook was nearby, half-frozen but flowing enough to quench their thirst alongside the horses.

Luca cast him a glance. "Did you kill them? The remaining monks, that is. I mean, there won't be any mad old men waiting for us?"

Rage handed Luca a piece of bread, keeping one for himself. "The Forbidden Monastery is soaked with dark magic. It took two days and two nights to kill the remaining wizards, and all the time I was close to screaming. Behind every corner, I saw ghosts from my past, accusing me of having killed them. It was that which made me succeed. I wanted to get out of there as quickly as possible but couldn't do so without fulfilling my task, so I found the wizards and shot them. It was one of the harder jobs in my career. I must have been drunk for a month afterwards. At least. But no, there aren't any mad monks awaiting us. Just mad Jeeve."

CHAPTER
Seventeen

BEING DRAGGED across the bridge and through the low, wide door was one of the worst experiences Keiran had ever suffered through. Each step felt like it would be his last due to his wobbly legs and foggy, snow-filled head. Each breath he took burned his lungs. And whenever he tried to slow down, the rope around his neck tightened.

But even worse were the voices calling for him. Seducing, tantalizing, promising voices that offered him peace if he would only jump.

Come to us, they whispered in his ears and in his soul. *Come to us and be free!*

One of the voices sounded like Rage.

The river roared, a low and dangerous sound. *The river wants me, the ghosts want me—I should jump*, Keiran couldn't help thinking, and then the rope bit into his neck, and he steadied himself by clutching the thin, strangely soft ropes that served as handles.

"The monks used human hair and bones for building the bridge," the killer said in a conversational tone, tenderly stroking the bridge's handrail. "Nice idea, don't you think? When I first saw this, I instantly admired the boldness of the builders. My uncle told me all about this place. Of course, he meant it as a warning. Stupid old fool."

Mercilessly, he pushed Keiran on until they reached the other side of the abyss. Keiran's legs gave way. He could barely feel them anymore, and his toes vanished inside a large cushion of numbness when he tried to move them. Maybe they'd frozen and crumbled into nothingness.

I want this to be over, he thought wearily, trying to get back onto his feet. *If I have to jump to make this end, I'll do it.*

"The moment my uncle told me the story of the monastery, I wanted to visit. Of course, my uncle wouldn't allow it, so I had to wait until I was strong enough to escape his clutches. I crossed the bridge. I went inside, and I could hear the voices of the ones who had built this place. They whispered of wonderful promises if only I would stay the night. So I did. What an extraordinary thing to do! Can you imagine? I even dared to dine in the great hall! In fact, I think I shall show it to you. It would be a great idea to slaughter you on the big table, as a gift to the ones who were brave enough to shed their worries and reach for higher treasures, ignoring morals and laws and other such rubbish."

Keiran sighed. By now, he was too cold and too exhausted to care much about the man's threats. For all he knew, he was stark raving mad, talking nonsense whenever he opened his mouth. He might have never killed anyone in his life; he might never even harm Keiran, fainting at the sight of blood if he tried.

Bullshit. The man was mad, and he was dangerous. He was going to kill him, Keiran was certain of it.

But—there had been a connection. He had heard Rage call his name.

It had been the oddest feeling. Suddenly, he wasn't alone inside his head; suddenly, there was someone else there.

He'd been born mute, a tiny child who hadn't breathed at first. While the midwife tended to him, his mother had died, leaving her husband alone and helpless with a newborn that couldn't even cry. His father, David, had come close to hanging himself when taking care of his son proved too much for him. Neglecting his duties as well as his personal hygiene, he had taken to drinking, eyeing the rope more often than his son—and if he did look at him, hate was barely concealed in his eyes.

Had the widow next door not taken a liking to him, David would have dangled from the beam before Keiran turned a month old. Loretta made sure his father ate regularly. She fed the baby and kept the house clean. It was she who pulled the strings that made Keiran's father an employee at Babylon Manor, and it was she who kept feeding the baby although it soon became clear he would never utter a single word.

Keiran worked hard ever since, trying to compensate for his lack of magic with strength and skill. He'd grown fast, become strong and handsome, and somehow managed to gain Luca's friendship. His family had prospered, and Keiran became accustomed at a very early age to being independent and responsible for everything he did or didn't do. If he made a decision, he had to face the consequences. So far, he'd always held his fate in his own hands.

Until now. He'd been turned into a victim, bound and at the mercy of a madman. Waiting to be rescued was not to his liking at all.

Rage's voice in his head had made him cry out for help.

Like a bloody virgin in a bloody fairy tale, he thought, balling his fists and clenching his teeth in self-disgust.

The man who had captured him so easily wasn't as tall as he, nor did he look all that strong. There was only this rope around his neck, so now that they were out of the cold, he should be able to escape. The monastery was big enough to hide in for weeks. He could drink melted snow so he wouldn't die of thirst, and maybe the previous inhabitants had left some provisions that were still edible.

An escape should be, must be, possible.

Problem was, he didn't feel like escaping. In fact, he was feeling dizzier than ever. The surrounding rocks seemed to crush him and take away his ability to think straight.

It reminded him of a snakebite he had some years back. The woman who'd saved him—Keiran remembered her sharp, piercing eyes and birdlike features—had cut deep into his calf and bled out the poison, leaving him weak as a kitten.

Here, in the great hall of the Forbidden Monastery, Keiran had the same feeling of weakness. It was like he was fading away, his life bleeding out with every heartbeat.

He tried to get outside. No way. The killer pulled at the rope, and Keiran was forced to follow him deeper into the darkness. His legs felt like jelly, leaving him to wonder when exactly they would give way again.

One of the big doors hung loosely on huge, rusted steel hinges. Keiran could see symbols carved into the dark wood, weather-beaten but still recognizable as magical, their meaning a riddle. What he did know was that following his captor wasn't that bad of an idea. It was sort of warm in here and quiet. No voices. No threats.

Not that bad.

To the left and right, large staircases led to the upper floors. Many steps were broken. The left staircase was beyond use, and the right had holes large enough to make one seriously question whether the upper floors were even reachable.

Dust on the ground, dirt on the walls. Some, if not most, of it was blood, old and blackened by the years. The large tiles that once had decorated the floor were broken and split. In a corner, Keiran could see a skeleton, and it was obvious that a fight had taken place here a long time ago, and not a small fight, either.

Join us, the shadows whispered in his ear. *Lie with us, dream with us, be with us.*

So much for the absence of voices.

Goose bumps rose on his back and arms. He gave in to instinct and fought against the rope around his neck, refusing to take another step, not caring that the rope tightened and cut off his breath.

"What? Don't tell me you are scared." The killer turned to him, sounding surprised. "They are just the voices of ghosts. Actually, once I learned how to listen properly, they told me great things. My uncle had described them as the voices of horrible monsters. But to me, the sound was always soothing. They're dead. They cannot harm you. And you are mistaken if you think I'll leave you behind."

Brutally, the killer jerked on the rope, making Keiran's legs give way. He fell to the stone floor. The wounds on his knees where the glass had cut him in the roadhouse tore open, bleeding once more, adding to the blood shed upon the stones once upon a time.

The killer was next to him in a heartbeat. "You're not going to die on me, are you?" he asked, stroking Keiran's tangled, snow-wet hair. "I need you, boy. I'm weak and tired. Without you, I won't survive. I brought you all this way because you can help me survive. You will not die, do you hear me?"

Fuck off, Keiran thought desperately. He had no intention of dying, not now and certainly not in the presence of this madman. He would die as an old man in the arms of his lover, surrounded by friends and children after having lived a long and happy life.

Yep. Good plan.

Too busy trying to shake the dizziness out of his head, Keiran barely noticed that the killer had pulled the rope off over his head.

"Come on, you, off the floor you get. There's a nice table over there. Just a few steps and you can rest." A hand under his elbow supported him as he got up. An arm around his waist steadied him, step by step. Keiran could see the table. It looked more like an altar, huge and forbidding and obviously not used for just meals.

Bad idea, getting closer to this table. Hadn't the killer just taken off the rope? A glance backward confirmed it. There was the rope, rolled up on the floor like a sleeping snake.

I'm free. The thought dropped slowly into his brain. *I can run now. He's slow. If I'm fast enough, I will manage to escape.*

Then why wasn't he moving? Why was he still allowing the killer to lead him toward the table?

A chuckle near his ear. The grip around his waist was tender, caring, intimate even—not unpleasant, being held like this. He was taken care of. Why should he run away at all? No need for this, no need at all. All he needed, all he wanted, was to sit down or, better yet, lay down on the long, polished table. Its surface was smooth, scrubbed clean of blood and dirt and covered only with a layer of dust.

The killer helped him to lie down. How friendly of him. He dried his clothes, gave him warmed wine, and bound his hands almost gently to the rings attached to the wood of the table.

The killer kissed his cheek. "I'll kill you slowly," he said fondly, admiration evident in his voice. "First, I will cut out your tongue, then your eyes. I will break your fingers, sever your hands from your arms and eat them, either raw or fried in your own blood. You will like that, won't you?"

Madness, Keiran thought, the one word hopping around in his brain and causing a headache.

Beyond that, thinking was impossible.

There was the chuckle again. Cold hands opened the buttons of his shirt, brushing the fabric away just like a lover would.

"You're strong, boy. And you don't know how to use your strength, so I will do it for you. Use you. Take what you have to offer. Haven't you realized that by now?"

He was close now, so dangerously close, but all Keiran did was stare at him.

"The voices whispered advice into my heart and soul. They told me not to be stupid and grab the power. They said it was all within my reach, power, money, and freedom."

Another kiss. Keiran felt as if the snake had bitten him once more, but he was bleeding to death this time.

"And so I did. I listened and I learned. My business prospered, my competitors shriveled to dust whenever they became too rich, and even my private life improved. All of a sudden, I could persuade anyone I wanted to follow me home. They surrendered to me, they begged me for more if I wanted them to beg, and they never even complained afterwards."

The killer's cold hands stopped just before they reached the top of Keiran's trousers, and he stepped away from the table.

After a minute or two, Keiran realized he could use his brain again. The dizziness hadn't vanished but had subsided, reduced to an annoying hum in the back of his head.

He opened his eyes, which had fallen shut of their own volition the moment he had been laid on the table. Although the daylight was dim, it pierced right through his pupils into his skull, and he had to turn his head away from the window.

He found the killer standing a few feet away, staring at him as though seeing him for the first time. The man breathed in shallow gulps, his face covered with an oily film of sweat.

Keiran struggled, trying to free himself, and was surprised to find his hands bound.

He gave up after only a few seconds of struggling; the ropes cut deeply into his wrists the more he tried to wriggle out of them. When he lifted his head and looked down his body, wondering why the killer had stepped away from him, all he saw were his booted feet, his snow-wet trousers, and his half-naked chest.

His eyes darted to the killer, and the greedy look on the man's face scared him deeply. He hadn't expected to see lust and longing in the killer's face—not now, anyway. He'd been in the man's possession for hours. Something must have changed. Just what it was, however, he had no idea.

The killer's breathing became even shallower, and he took another step back. "I didn't expect you to taste so sweet," he said hoarsely. "Your essence, your soul. This changes things. This changes things completely."

The farther away he is from me, the better I can think. If I can get him to leave me alone for ten minutes, I'll be able to make it out of here. Keiran closed his eyes, but only for a split second. He feared the man would come closer again if he took his eyes off him.

"Sweet. And gorgeous." The words were but a hoarse whisper. The killer's eyes wandered down Keiran's body, lingering on his chest and abdomen, his fabric-clad thighs, and his crotch.

Fuck.

"So far, I have always used women for my games. Soft flesh and tender skin, big breasts and even bigger asses. They've always been perfect. But now I have you on my table." The killer tilted his head thoughtfully and licked his lips.

Double fuck. If Rage didn't hurry, Keiran was sure only his corpse would be left to find, given the look on the killer's face. Maybe he had liked women in his bedroom and at his mercy, but right now, the killer wanted him and him alone.

Languidly, the killer reached between his legs and slowly began stroking himself.

With as much effort as he could muster without making the other man suspicious, Keiran twisted his wrists within the bindings. The magic ropes tightened and his fingers became numb, but he didn't care. He needed to get off this table, or he would be dead by nightfall and raped long before that.

The killer wiped a hand across his mouth. "Women are so loud," he mused. "Even before I inflict pain, they yell and shout. It takes all the fun away." He leaned forward. "You won't scream, will you? Of course not. You're mute. Gorgeous and sweet and silent. Perfect!"

He took a step toward the table. Then another. The closer he came, the less Keiran was able to think. Just like before.

What was the man doing to him that turned his brain into a wet sponge whenever he was near? What was he doing that made him feel so damn weak?

Bleeding. His soul was bleeding out onto the smooth surface of the huge, old table that had been witness to many tortures throughout the centuries. From out of nowhere, he knew the monks who'd built the monastery had been fond of torture and that they'd used the table for their experiments during mealtime. He knew it was dark not from age but from the blood that had been shed upon it, and he thought he could hear the table laugh, treasuring the moment when it was sharing its knowledge. The closer the killer came, the clearer Keiran could hear the voices of the dead calling for him, persuading him to give up all hope as well as his fear.

"I like it when my toys are afraid of me." Once more, the killer licked his lips. "Fear is such a strong emotion, so pure, so clean—don't you think? I can see you are afraid of me, horrified even. You were the girl's lover before Rage took her for himself, weren't you? I bet you are the gentle type. Not used to the pain love creates, not used to being hurt in order to find release. Of course, we're talking of my release, not yours. You are going to wish you could scream, boy. In the end, you will die, but before that—by the Lady, I promise you have never experienced anything like it!"

Gently and without touching him, he put his mouth to Keiran's ear. "I'll cut you and I'll bite you. I'll bleed you and I'll fuck you. You will give me everything I need, and you will do it willingly. And when I am done with you, I will be more powerful than ever before!"

He sighed. "Not yet, though. I like to prolong the pleasure, postpone the actual act. I thought you'd like to know what I have in mind for you. You still have time to think your petty little thoughts."

One of Keiran's hands slipped out of the rope. He had continued turning his wrists as the killer stood over him, and somehow, the rope had responded to the careful twists of his hands.

Desperately, he searched in his mind for Rage, his voice, his presence. He'd been there before. There had been a connection and right now, he needed it to happen again.

"Are you looking forward to our encounter?" the killer asked, genuine curiosity in his voice. He brought his face close to Keiran's, breath smelling of cold ash. "Will you welcome me willingly? Will you welcome the pain? When I cut off your cock and place it next to your heart, when I mount you and enter you, when I come as you are bleeding to death, will you smile for me?"

The killer put a hand on Keiran's bare chest.

Suddenly, Keiran's mind went blank. It was wiped clean, unmarked like freshly fallen snow. There was only the hand on his naked skin, slowing his heartbeat, and the voice in his ear, muttering unintelligible syllables. The words had no meaning, but the man smiled when he said them, so Keiran smiled back.

"I knew it," the killer said. "You are my toy now, and we will have such a wonderful time together!"

And there was a black flame, a presence vaguely familiar. It burned and flickered and prompted Keiran to struggle wildly as the hand on his chest clamped, cold fingers digging holes into his skin. The flame was more important than the hand, more important than anything.

Rage, Keiran thought. His vision was blurred, and there was blood and bile on his tongue, but he still managed to slam his free hand into the killer's chest in an attempt to push him away. Rage was inside his head, and in front of him was the killer, talking to him, perhaps getting ready to kill him, so pushing him away was what needed to be done.

He couldn't do it. The killer was too strong, and Keiran was too dizzy. He even forgot what he was about to do. Like a rag doll, he fell back to the table.

"Bastard!" A murderous hiss in his ear, annoyed, disbelieving. "How can this be? How...? He's following you? The bastard assassin knows where we are! Damn... double shit!"

The killer jumped backward, staggered, and fell, scurrying away from the table until he reached an outer wall. Pale-faced and wide-eyed, he stared at his victim.

Keiran managed to turn to his side, his free hand supporting himself on the table's blackened surface. He coughed violently and feared he would be sick again. His throat ached, he longed for water, his wrist was nothing but raw flesh—if he didn't act right now, this very moment, his chance to get away would be lost.

With painful slowness, Keiran reached for his other, still bound wrist. Fumbling with the rope wasn't easy given how numb his fingers were.

Had he imagined Rage's presence?

Get me out of here! he screamed in his head, not caring how much he hated being dependent on others. *Find me and help me, or I am dead!*

Keiran didn't know whether or not Rage got the message. A fist connected with his chin, slamming him back to the table. His head connected with the wood, but it didn't really matter. All thoughts of Rage were ripped out of his mind the moment the killer touched him. All that remained was his fear, unnamed and enormous.

"He's coming after you." The killer's fist drove into Keiran's stomach.

"He's near. He knows where we are." Another blow broke his ribs.

Keiran spat blood, this time not from cracked lips.

"I wanted to find him and kill him. I didn't want *him* to find *me*! And then I touch you and find you thinking of *him*? He's like a fire burning inside you. How much does he know?"

Rage!

Just that name, familiar and safe. Keiran tried to catch the dwindling flame behind his closed eyes as the killer broke his bones with every punch.

"I can't play with you now, can I?" the killer spat. Blood dripped from his knuckles. "There's no time. I need to set a trap for the bastard. And I had so been looking forward to a bit of fun!"

One last blow to his temple sent Keiran reeling into unconsciousness. Had he been able to think at all, he would have considered this one of the better things that had happened to him today.

CATCHING HIS breath, the killer wiped the sweat off his brow, smearing blood all over his face. Dismayed, he looked at the boy's motionless body. His fists twitched, wanting to continue beating him. Fine, so maybe he'd lost control a little bit. Maybe he'd gone a tad too far. But the boy was special. His magic tasted sweet. He needed him, but that there was a connection to the assassin was a shock.

Rage knew where the boy was, and for some unknown reason, he was coming after him.

Subconsciously, the killer hid his hands behind his back to keep them under control. Sometimes they did what they wanted. Sometimes he lost control.

Muttering to himself, he paced the big hall, stepping over fallen rocks, skulls, and bones long since turned to dust. More nervous than he would have wanted to appear if anyone other than dead bones had been there watching, he raked his hands through his nearly white hair until it stood up on all sides.

His knuckles hurt. Checking for the boy's pulse, he was relieved to find it beating strong enough that he need not worry. All he needed was a plan. A way to trap Rage alive so he would be able to first take the boy and then take care of the assassin.

His uncle would have been able to think of a plan in a matter of seconds. The old man had been smart, and he'd always got what he wanted. He'd even managed to escape despite the killer's efforts to keep him alive.

Thinking about the old man made him even more nervous than he already was. His downfall had begun with the death of his uncle. He'd lost most of his power, and he'd lost a lot of money due to his lack of power. He would end up in the gutter sooner rather than later.

Furious, he kicked a rock out of the way. It hurt and he yelled, hopping around on one foot before finally realizing how stupid he must look.

He spared a glance at the unconscious body bound to the table. "Hit him a bit too hard," he mused, wiping his dirty hands on his trousers. He had felt the boy's ribs crack under his fist, heard him gasp with pain. His knuckles were still covered with the boy's blood.

"I wish I hadn't dumped Lucius's head," he said to the unconscious body on the table. "It would be good to have him here now. At least he would listen to me. I'd place him on the table so we could look at each other in the eye. Well, sort of. At least he wouldn't have shuddered in fear at my idea of fun. He knew about fun himself, that man. No, I shouldn't have left him behind."

But he'd had to take care of the boy, and the head hadn't seemed so important at the time.

The darkness of the monastery embraced him, but he barely noticed. It seeped into his mind just like the last time he was here. It twisted what was left of his soul, ground his mind until it was flat and thin.

"I could do with a friend right now." A tear slid down the killer's face, and he didn't think it odd. "Didn't I put Lucius out of his misery? He was screaming so badly when I found him, with his eyes burned out, naked, and hurt. I couldn't let him suffer, could I?"

Why was he talking to an unconscious body?

He stepped over to the table and looked into the boy's still face. Maybe talking to an unconscious listener was better than talking to the walls and the air?

"I choked Lucius to death. It was easy. He didn't struggle much. I don't understand why his servants didn't help him. Probably as useless as my own lot back at home."

The boy's skin was clammy, and there was blood on his lips. One hand dangled over the side of the table; almost gently, the killer placed it back on the table.

"Cutting off his head was the logical thing to do. We were alike, Lucius and I."

He grinned.

"Such a lovely head he had too. That mouth, so full, those lips, and those neat little teeth! He might even have sucked me off had I asked nicely." He laughed at the thought, remembering dead Lucius's half-open mouth and the swollen tongue. Too bad he hadn't thought of having some fun with the head before.

The boy was here, though.

Touching the boy was good. The slow heartbeat, strong despite his injuries, was proof his victim would live through the more complicated pleasures he had in mind. The body was muscular, the hands large and calloused—clearly, the boy worked in the fields, swung a scythe and ax on a regular basis and could handle cattle as well as bale hay. The skin was golden, clearly from sweating under the hot summer sun. For a heartbeat, the killer thought he could smell freshly mowed grass.

He swallowed with sudden greed at the thoughts rushing through his mind. His hand slid lower on the boy's body and this time didn't halt when it reached the waist of his trousers.

He didn't want his toy to wake up, not now, because if he woke, if he began to struggle, to fight, he wouldn't be able to restrain himself and would begin to play even though he didn't have time.

Still, a bit of looking and touching couldn't do any harm, could it?

He pushed the boy's trousers down his legs and absently licked his dry, cracked lips.

There was blood on the boy's knees from falling, but it had dried. Same with the rest of his body—the blood wasn't fresh enough. He liked fresh blood. The coppery smell and the texture of the skin underneath blood was unlike anything else in the world.

He bent over and bit deep into the boy's inner leg, close to the balls, until he drew fresh blood. It spilled into his mouth, warm and sweet. It heightened his senses. A marvelous taste, nearly as good as tears. He could have sucked and drunk forever, but then, this wasn't why he had bitten the boy, so he drew back and watched the blood run down the boy's skin in thin tendrils. He wouldn't bleed to death from the wound, but it was more than enough to dip his fingers in and paint them red up to the knuckles.

One last lick. He had half a guilty thought that he shouldn't be doing this right now, not with the bastard assassin out there, alive and waiting for him to make a wrong move.

But the temptation in combination with the dark magic radiating off the walls was too much for him. The boy, though still unconscious, had somehow managed to wantonly spread his legs, inviting him, begging him for action. The blood on his fingers was still slick—what a shame to waste the opportunity—and he was so hard, so lonely, his cock throbbing with the need for release, that he had to do something about it.

"I can do this and still think of a way to kill the assassin," the killer murmured, ignoring the warning voice in the back of his head that was asking him what he was doing.

His left hand found the boy's nipples, twisting them brutally. His right, fingers slippery with blood, reached lower, between the boy's buttocks.

"Wish I could fuck you, but can't. Too dangerous. Just a bit of foreplay. Enough time to place the trap."

The killer dribbled saliva onto Keiran's chest—he barely noticed, being too busy rubbing his cock and fingering the hole between the boy's legs. He couldn't wait any longer. No one possessed that much self-control. This was it, the moment he'd been looking forward to—and the boy wasn't objecting, was he?—and so the killer pushed his fingers into the boy's ass, hard and deep.

Destroy him, the voices murmured in his head. *Kill him. He belongs to the bastard assassin. He doesn't follow you. He's following the boy. Kill him, destroy him!*

"You look so cute when you're at my mercy!" He bit the boy again, drawing blood as he humped the table and wishing he could hump his toy instead. It wasn't perfect—there was so much more he wanted to do!—but it would have to do for now. If only he could close his mouth around the boy's cock, licking and nibbling and drawing more blood, biting and chewing and finally finding his sweet release.

But he wouldn't; he couldn't! Losing control right now was a bad idea. He thought he was being watched; he imagined he could hear someone breathe, someone other than the boy, someone standing right behind him with a knife in his hand.

The bastard assassin was still inside the boy's head!

His still pumping hand cramped, and his cock became limp. The blood in his mouth suddenly tasted of ash, and he choked. Cursing, he jumped away from the table.

"You dumb fuck!" he screamed at himself. "There's no time to play, with him so close!"

Frantically, he pulled the boy's trousers up and turned his back to the table resolutely. He needed a plan to trap Rage. A good plan that would allow him to take all of the boy's strength without allowing the bastard assassin to interrupt or stop him. And there was so much strength to take. He could feel it. He wanted it.

Licking the fingers of the hand that had been inside the boy, he briefly closed his eyes with longing. So sweet was the taste, a mix of blood and shit. So sweet was the thought of shedding his clothes and fucking the boy properly—now, here—and not caring about the consequences, not caring about the assassin, not caring about anything but his pleasure.

No. Pleasure would have to wait.

His eyes fell upon a half-buried skull under some fallen rocks. He pulled it out, brushed off most of the dirt, and stared into empty eye sockets. It had once belonged to a seventeen-year-old girl, slightly dim-witted, but sweet and beautiful. She had been used by the wizards, partly to provide them with whatever magic they could draw from her, partly to still their more earthly desires. When she had died, she had screamed for her dad, and the wizard who had killed her had laughed at her pleas for mercy. He knew it upon touching the skull just as if the girl herself had told him.

Now, the skull was simply a rotten piece of bone, the jaw lost somewhere in time, the sockets uneven from where rats had nibbled on them. Just the companion he needed. Not as good as Lucius's head, but the skull would listen, it wouldn't object to his plans, and most importantly, it would in no way be a temptation.

"Now listen to me, my dear," the killer said with a cruel grin. "This is what I have in mind for a trap."

CHAPTER
Eighteen

RAGE AND Luca sat huddled together beneath an outcropping of rock. The horses were blocking them from the wind, and Luca, once more, had dried their clothes with a bit of magic. They were very much in need of a break.

"We're both exhausted," Rage had argued, pulling Luca off the horse. "We won't be any use to Keiran if we drop dead the moment we find him."

"Let's walk on for a little while longer," she'd pleaded, apparently unaware of the constant shivering of her body. "It can't be too far, can it?"

"We will reach the bridge by nightfall, but we won't cross it before morning. It's too dangerous. So it doesn't really matter if we have a break now."

"But—"

"No buts, Luca. If you aren't happy about it, you are free to walk on without me."

That had shut her up. She didn't want to do this on her own, so she bit her tongue and held back the words that wanted to rush out of her mouth. Lucius had had to live with her rude bluntness from the moment she had learned to speak.

Lucius, who was not her father. Lucius, whom she had hated with a passion.

Dead Lucius.

She should be devastated, shouldn't she? After all, he had raised her. True, he'd done a lousy job, but still, she had believed him to be her father until a few hours ago.

"Eat some bread," Rage said, interrupting her thoughts. "Swallow it down with some snow if you have to, but don't take too much, or you won't be able to fight the cold and the wind once we are higher up in the mountains."

He sat beside her and pulled her close, sharing his body heat with her as well as the long, warm cloak he was wearing. She moved closer, leaning against him, glad he was there and alive. There had been too many deaths recently for her taste. She wouldn't mind going the rest of her life without seeing anyone else die.

"Do you think we will find Keiran?" she asked when the bread was gone. "Before… you know, before Jeeve harms him?"

Taking a handful of snow, Rage watched as it melted in his palm, then licked the small puddle. "I don't know. I hoped we would reach the monastery earlier, cross the bridge today, get it over with. I don't know what Jeeve will do with the boy during the night."

She sighed. "Stupid question. How about a plan, then? You must have something in mind. After all, you've been there before. You know how to find your way around the place…." Her voice faltered at Rage's continued silence. "No plan?"

"None so far."

"Great."

Rage smiled humorlessly. "What did you expect? I barely made it out of there alive last time. I know nothing about Jeeve. Any plan is bound to fail."

Luca's breath hitched. "But—you'd know if Keiran died, wouldn't you? I mean you've been in contact with him, there's a connection between the two of you, so… well, wouldn't you?"

Rage was quiet for a long time. Finally, he said, "I believe I'd know if he were dead. I have no idea whether or not I'd feel it if he were being tortured."

She moved a bit closer to him, seeking warmth as well as simple physical contact. "You could—that is, I could help you make contact again. Just to make sure and all."

Rage tensed. Luca thought it was because of what she'd said, but then he groaned and clutched his head. Eyes rolling up in their sockets, he slumped against her, and it took all her strength to not be crushed between him and the rocks.

"Rage? What's wrong with you?"

He groaned again, and his arm tightened sharply around her waist.

"Rage, can you hear me?" she called out, slightly panicked. Instinctively, she searched for his magic, fearing he was about to lose control. But there was none.

"Listen to me, you need to open your eyes. Talk to me, Rage!"

"Rage!" she shouted when he didn't react. Shaking him didn't work, nor did shouting—it was all she could do to keep him upright, lest he land facedown on the rocks.

She'd never been more scared in her life. If he died up here, she would have to go after Jeeve without him. If he died up here, she'd be sitting in this tiny little alcove with a corpse at her side.

If he died....

She didn't dare to think what would happen if he died. So she slung her arms around him and held him, felt him shiver and shake, heard him mutter and moan.

Outside, the sun went down. Darkness crept into the little cave.

Suddenly, his head jerked up. His eyes flew open, and he retched. Doubling over, he caught himself on his palms and threw up the few bits he'd eaten. After several long moments of just kneeling, he took several handfuls of snow to wipe his mouth and face clean.

Luca kept her hand on his shoulder the whole time out of fear he would lose consciousness.

"You back with me?" she asked, unable to keep the tremble out of her voice. "Don't do that again, do you hear me? It's creepy."

"Tell me about it," he croaked. He got up and stalked out into the wind where he leaned his head against the snow-covered fur of his horse. "Didn't know something like that could happen."

Luca was behind him instantly. "Was it Keiran? Or Jeeve? Who did what to you? Rage!"

"Keiran. I was with him again. He tried to escape, but the killer overwhelmed him. He's unconscious, but alive." He took a deep breath.

Luca snorted, unsure if she should cry with frustration at Rage's refusal to give any more information or with joy that Keiran wasn't dead.

"You just slumped as if you had a stroke. I shouted at you and shook you, but you wouldn't wake up. Look, it's dark. You've been gone for at least half an hour. For the record, you are surprisingly heavy for such a bony man." She handed him the last bite of bread she had originally saved for later. "Here, eat this. It will help with the nausea, and have some more snow too. And what did you mean, alive but unconscious? What did Jeeve do to him?"

Rage looked at her with a frown. He was paler than usual, the lines on his forehead standing out like deep cuts. "You don't want to know," he said flatly. "He's injured. He won't survive for much longer."

"Anything useful you can tell me?" She knew she was being unfair, but she couldn't help it. Her fear for Keiran threatened to strangle her, and if snapping at Rage helped, she would snap at him until the end of the world. "I mean, injured in what way? Beaten? Broken bones? Blood? I can deal with that."

HOLDING ON to the horse, Rage closed his eyes. His throat ached from screams he hadn't screamed, his body ached from blows he hadn't received, and his mind burned.

It had been the boy who'd cried for his help. And it had been the boy who'd been tortured. Yet he'd been there.

Rage felt soiled. The need to shed his clothes and wash Jeeve's fingerprints off his skin was becoming more overwhelming with every passing second.

Luca didn't need to know what he'd witnessed. It wouldn't help her to know how mad Jeeve really was, no matter how urgently she demanded answers. And so, with an effort, he swallowed his hate lest he tell her in detail about the table, the bites and the blows Keiran had received, the pain he was suffering from, and those clammy, greedy hands all over his body.

Keiran's body. Right now, it was hard to tell the difference.

There had been blood in Keiran's mouth, bittersweet and dry. Breathing hurt, and thinking was impossible. Somehow, Jeeve's presence was tampering with Keiran's mind.

Get me out of here!

He could hear the boy's soundless voice in his head. He could feel his panic thundering through his veins.

Find me and help me, or I am dead!

But it was dark now, and crossing the bridge in the darkness was impossible.

IN THE morning light, the bridge looked harmless. The mountains were blocking most of the light cast by the sun, which was weak and barely able to chase away the clouds.

"You're sure this bridge will carry the both of us?" Luca blew into the hollow of her hands, trying to warm her fingers. "It doesn't really look all that stable, and besides, it would be the perfect place for a trap." Glancing over her shoulder, she confirmed that Sammy was still with the horses—she had told him sternly to stay behind and not to dare follow her. As he had eaten the small piece of meat she'd saved for him and curled up for a nap after breakfast, she hoped he had actually been listening to her.

It had been strange to find another horse in the cave Rage had singled out for their animals. Looking only mildly surprised at the new visitors, it had continued munching hay. There had even been a trough filled with water, only thinly covered with ice.

"Jeeve's horse," Rage had said. "He must believe he will be walking away once this is over."

"He's wrong, of course."

Rage hadn't even bothered looking at her. "Of course he's wrong."

And now they stood at the bridge, and Luca wondered if there was another way across the abyss. "We could climb down and go up the other side." The mere sight of the rotten ropes made her skin crawl. "Or I could find some branches and transform them into a new bridge. It would be makeshift, but at least we wouldn't have to cross this one."

"It is not the bridge you need to be scared of," Rage said. "It is the river below and the magic this place radiates. No other bridge can be built. It has been tried, and it didn't work. There are ghosts living in the river, too. They call for you and tamper with your mind. I wouldn't dare go anywhere near the river, never mind wade through it."

"But—"

"Luca." Rage turned to her. Underneath his eyes were deep, dark rings telling of the sleepless night he'd spent in the small cave. "There is the bridge and nothing else."

"Still no plan?"

"That's it. I get across, I find Jeeve, I kill him. Simple. Easy to see through." Rage put a foot onto the bridge.

"Yeah, but he knows you want to kill him. I mean, why else would you be here? Don't you think he will have taken precautions? And I'm not staying behind!"

Rage didn't turn back to her. "I never said you should. There is a bigger chance of getting to him with you and your magic by my side." Another step. He was standing on the bridge now, both hands on the ropes running on either side.

The crease between his eyes deepened; in the harsh light of the early morning, he looked more like one of the weathered, ancient rocks behind him than a human being. Luca felt a hysteric laugh building up in her throat—this was madness, and she didn't know why Rage didn't see it.

"He will kill you just like that if what you say is true—that he is watching us. That's the whole point of this, isn't it, him wanting to kill you? We could have crossed the bridge during the night had you not insisted on staying in the cave. Damn you, Rage, you're an assassin! You must know a million tricks to outwit Jeeve!" Desperately, Luca tried to keep her voice down but had a hard time maintaining it. She wanted to save Keiran so badly she considered pushing Rage aside and running across the bridge before him, but her brain insisted that a better plan than the one Rage had was necessary if they wanted to actually do some saving at all.

She saw his hands tighten on the ropes. She also saw a bead of sweat sliding down the side of his face although it was a cold morning.

Why was he sweating? And why did he look as though he'd begin screaming at any moment?

"You don't get it," he said flatly. "Jeeve holds the strings, and we are the puppets dancing to the tune he whistles. He has Keiran. It is either cross the bridge and face whatever he has in store for us, or turn around and leave the boy in his clutches."

"Why didn't we cross the bridge at night? He wouldn't have seen us, you could have killed him, and we would be already on our way back home."

"Because it is impossible. Don't you ever listen to what I say?" He held out his hand. The cloak fell back from his arm, and she could see the muscles standing out in his wrists, their wiry look betraying the calmness of his voice.

He was scared. That was not good.

"Put your foot onto the bridge," he said. "Careful. It is not a pleasant experience."

Frowning, Luca took his hand. "It is just a brid—" she began. Then her foot touched the wood, and she screamed.

Voices, whispering in her mind, called to her. Shrill, quiet, angry, persuasive voices. Her mother, pleading for her to help. Lucius, begging her to give his head a proper burial. Unknown voices, laughing and crying at the same time.

Hands on her face—cold, dead hands. Pulling at her, pushing her—

She jumped back, ripping her hand free from Rage's grip. Stumbled. Fell. Her scream echoed back from the mountains, hanging crystal clear in the air.

Wide-eyed, she stared at the bridge, then at Rage. "By the good Lady, what the hell was that?" she gasped. "How can you stand there so calmly? Don't you hear the voices?"

With a smooth motion, Rage stepped off the bridge and knelt next to her. "I hear the voices, Luca. During daytime, it takes a lot of courage to cross the bridge. At night, it is impossible. The first time I came here, I tried to get across after sunset although I had been warned not to try. I put one foot on the bridge. Hands gripped me, trying to rip off my head. Fingernails sharp as knifes slashed my flesh. I lost my footing and fell and would have died hadn't I secured myself with a rope. I can only beg you to wait for me this side of the bridge until I am done with Jeeve. I will come back with the boy, or what's left of him. If that proves to be impossible, I will not come back at all. In that case, you being here might give you just the time you need to get away alive."

Each answer made it clearer than ever that they couldn't win. "Why hasn't he killed us? Why are we able to stand here and argue while Jeeve does nothing?" Damn, but she was nearly crying.

Angry with herself, Luca pushed Rage away and got up. The Forbidden Monastery was waiting, the bridge was waiting, Keiran was waiting. There was no time to argue and certainly no time to cry. To hell with those voices. To hell with reason or logic or plans. If Rage could do it, so could she.

"Even if Keiran is dead, I want him back," she said. "Even if there is nothing but a corpse to rescue, I will not turn my back on him."

"Then come along." Once more, Rage held out his hand. When she put her foot onto the bridge this time, she didn't scream, and she didn't jump back.

CHAPTER
Nineteen

THE KILLER was watching them. Since long before dawn, he'd taken up position at one of the windows. His back pressed against the monastery's cold stones, he welcomed the heat that the prospect of killing the bastard assassin sent through his body.

Soon. Very soon.

Languidly, he rubbed himself, never reaching his climax and wishing he never would. The front of his trousers was damp with precum as well as piss—he'd become a bit sloppy with his personal hygiene since he started his quest. Well, he could take a long, hot bath once this was over, with both the boy's and the assassin's heads watching from the windowsill in his bathroom, and dwell upon all the memories.

When the morning light finished chasing the night away, he became more alert, expecting the assassin to come around the corner at any moment. Sweaty palms bore witness that he was, in fact, a bit nervous—he had never killed a professional before, and he was very much looking forward to the experience.

It had been a long night. On his hands was blood, some old, some fresh. He'd been careful not to kill the boy, but he had indeed played with him a bit.

A look over his shoulder confirmed his precious was still securely tied to the table. He was breathing, albeit unevenly. He was bleeding too, though not too badly.

The boy had given him the strength he needed to see this through.

Perfect.

Walking onto the bridge in the middle of the night had been an extraordinary experience. The voices had called to him, had tried to seduce him, and he had welcomed the madness they offered. They'd taught him once how to strengthen his own feeble magic. They'd driven him insane back then already. He knew that. It had been a small price compared to the knowledge he'd gained.

Movement on the other side of the bridge. Horses. A man.

The bastard assassin. Finally!

And a girl. Now that was surprising. The killer would have sworn Rage would have disposed of her by now. She was just a little brat and kind of ugly with her loose hair. Decent girls didn't wear their hair loose. Decent girls stayed at home and mended their husbands' socks.

Well, she didn't have a husband. Jeeve had told Rage all about her, and at the center of it all was that she refused to marry.

"Doesn't matter," the killer murmured. "The trap is in place. Once inside, he won't manage to get out again."

He glanced over his shoulder, trying to make out the table in the dim light. The boy was strong. He could use him until the bastard assassin was dead.

Watching, waiting, the killer sat on the windowsill and longed for them to fall into his trap. He'd placed it at the center, and there was no way Rage would find a way around it. He'd created it carefully, using the boy's blood and hair and a bit of his shirt.

"Here they come," he whispered. The skull sat on the windowsill with him, looking at him through empty sockets. "Are they talking, or are they arguing? I really don't understand why he brought her along. He would have been faster without her."

He slipped off the windowsill, stretching his legs and back. "I'll go get him now," he said to the boy although he was pretty sure he was still unconscious. "The bastard assassin is here. He's followed you, although I really don't know why. Maybe, he fucked you too? How sweet. I bet he won't be happy to learn I've already had my fun with you."

The air was cool as he stepped into the shadows beneath the broken gates. From outside, he wouldn't be seen. Not yet, anyway.

The bridge swayed gently in the breeze, or maybe it was swaying because the assassin and the girl had finally decided to come across.

"Come to me, little Rage," the killer whispered. "Come into my arms so I can play with you."

THE FIRST step was the worst. Immediately, the voices were back, the invisible hands, the faces hiding just outside her vision.

Determined not to do something stupid, she tightened her grip on Rage's hand, and surprisingly enough, the voices dimmed to a whisper. It seemed as if the ghosts were backing off.

She concentrated on her feet. The gaps between the planks were considerable, and if she wasn't careful, she'd miss a step and fall right through into the ghosts' realm.

The bridge swayed in the winter wind. Luca could see the monastery at the other end of the abyss with its huge, old gate and the door hanging off its hinges. Broken windows stared at her like blind eyes.

"And you had come here to kill someone?" she whispered. "In that place? You must have been mad."

"At the time, I needed the money. I'd hoped I would never see this place again." Rage, walking half a step in front of her, went on steadily, as if he weren't balancing over an abyss full of ghosts. Only because she was so close could she feel the tension in him.

When Jeeve stepped out of the gates of the Forbidden Monastery, Rage stopped so suddenly she bumped into him. They hadn't yet crossed more than a third of the bridge. Still, she could see Jeeve smiling broadly, his white hair flowing in the wind.

Luca narrowed her eyes. The light, reflecting off the snow that had fallen overnight, was harsh, and she had trouble making out details.

Something was odd.

"Hi!" the killer called. "I didn't expect you would follow me, but once I figured you'd want the boy back, I just had to wait. Took you long enough to get here. Are you coming over so we can have a nice little chat?"

Luca stared at him. His voice was strange, and he sounded crazy.

Maybe that was it. Maybe spending the night in that place had driven him crazy, and that was the reason he didn't sound like the Jeeve she knew.

"Would you *please* come over?" he said when Rage didn't move an inch. "The ghosts' voices must be bothering you. I know how persuasive they can be. Come over, you fucking bastard! Let's talk. Let's play!"

Before Luca realized Rage had moved, he'd pulled out one of his knives in a smooth, well-practiced movement. His whole body hummed with tension, and when his arm snapped back, she knew he was about to throw it and kill the man at the end of the bridge. Just like that. No arguing. No complicated planning.

She saw the knife leave his hand, saw it rotate once, and knew it would pick up speed. She heard the soft swish and imagined the sound it would make when it sank into the killer's heart.

Only it didn't. Jeeve—was it really Jeeve?—screamed a word she didn't understand, and the knife was blocked by an invisible barrier.

In the middle of the bridge, the knife fell and clattered to the planks where it slid toward the gaps, tumbled, and lay still. The hilt had gotten caught between two planks, the tip pointing down into the abyss.

Unimpressed and seemingly not all that disappointed, Rage crossed the distance to the barrier, knelt, and picked up his knife. He checked for damage, then stored it back in its sheath before holding out his hand.

Luca followed quickly behind. The moment she'd lost contact with him, the voices had come back with a vengeance. For some reason, Rage had a protective air around him, and she would be damned if she got left behind.

"A barrier?" Rage asked, his voice easily crossing the abyss. "Now what?"

Luca slipped her hand into his. With her other, she reached out and touched the barrier Jeeve had created.

"It's strong," she whispered. "I don't think—"

Jeeve said another word, again one she didn't understand.

"He could make the bridge crumble underneath us," she breathed, hating the quiver in her voice. "He could make the mountain drop onto our heads. He—"

"He wants to play." Reassuringly, Rage squeezed her hand. "He won't kill us, not now, not this easily."

With a dry mouth, and hoping with all her might Rage was right, Luca watched light erupt in the middle of the bridge, shades of purple and gray. With the light came sound, a harsh, ear-splitting tone. It was gone before she could so much as blink.

On the other side of the barrier lay a body where a moment ago there had been nothing. Now, half-conscious and bleeding, there was Keiran.

Keiran's body cramped. His hands searched for something to hold on to but found nothing. Coughing, he spat blood onto the bridge and tried to sit up.

Magic pressed him onto the planks. Luca thought she could hear bones breaking.

But not a sound could be heard.

Her legs moved of their own accord, and she would have run straight into the barrier had Rage not held her back.

"It's an illusion," he said into her ear. "I can see right through him. I can see the bridge planks through his body, Luca, and so can you if you take a closer look."

"You asked 'Now what,' Rage? Here's your answer. You watch the boy suffer. You watch me torture him. You watch him die. Then you will watch me kill the girl. And then"—the killer took a step forward—"then I will kill *you.*"

The killer laughed, raising his arms high above his head as if daring Rage to throw another knife or try to break through the barrier. He laughed like a madman, his whole body shaking with joy at defeating an assassin.

In his right hand, he held… something. It was small; it had arms, legs, and a head.

"It's not just an illusion!" A tear slid down Luca's cheek. "He's made a puppet, Rage, a Keiran puppet. It's in his hand, and whatever he does to it, Keiran feels it. He must have used his blood, hair, and clothing to maintain the connection. He could kill him just by squeezing too hard. Do something!"

"How long do you think you can watch him suffer before trying to break the barrier?" the killer called out. "I've learned a lot about you in the past few months, assassin. I know you can't do any magic. And the girl—well, she's strong, but she's also tired. And young. Try to break through the barrier, and you will die."

He frowned and took a step toward the abyss. "You will die anyway, of course. What I meant to say was break the barrier, and you will die sooner rather than later. And if you try anything stupid, I'll just tickle my little doll a bit more until you budge." He grinned. "Be a good doggie, Rage. Sit and watch your master do some tricks."

The sun, having climbed higher into the sky, had lost some of its brightness due to some thin, long clouds. Or maybe Luca's eyes had adjusted to the snow and the thin air—in any case, she was now able for the first time to get a clearer picture of the man who stood just a few feet away.

His hair was white, just like Jeeve's, and he did have a large nose. But that was about all the resemblance she could see.

"That is not Jeeve," she said, too surprised to lower her voice. "I have no idea who it is, but it is not Jeeve."

INSIDE THE monastery, Keiran was lying on the huge wooden table that had once been used for meals as well as for the monk's experiments. He'd woken up to a voice. A man had said a few words, but now he was gone. The big room around him was quiet, and when he shifted, he realized his hand was still free. The blood around his wrist, now dry, reminded him of how he'd twisted it until it had slipped out of the rope.

He'd tried to escape, and failed.

What had happened?

Keiran was in pain. Every part of his body hurt, and when he fumbled his other hand free, his shoulders groaned in agony.

Sitting up wasn't easy. Breathing hurt, and when he touched his ribs, he nearly threw up from the fresh bout of pain that shot through him.

Broken ribs. Great.

And bite wounds. Bruises from where fists had hit him.

His shirt was gone. When he looked around, he saw it lying on the ground, ripped to pieces.

Something told him that was not good.

His trousers were filthy. Soaked with blood, for one. But there was more.

Carefully, he slipped off the table and pushed the fabric down only to see more blood and many more bite marks.

Someone had touched him. Someone had bitten him.

Keiran swayed, the sudden shock of realization hitting him hard.

He whirled around, all of a sudden absolutely sure the killer was standing behind him, watching him, his arms outstretched for another round of torture. But there was no one. He was alone in the big hall.

He couldn't get his trembling under control. Moments passed where he just stood, one hand clutched at the waist of his trousers, the other pressed to the table so he wouldn't sink to the ground.

He'd spent the night on that table, unconscious, whilst the killer had used his body to amuse himself.

But he wasn't yet dead.

Pressing one hand on his ribs, he took a careful step. It hurt worse than he had expected.

He needed to get out of here before the killer came back. He couldn't think when the man was close. Once he escaped, he would find a nice quiet place to lie down and rest.

Outside, then, and across the bridge. Down the mountains and into the plains. Rage was on his way. He might even meet him halfway down.

Voices. Someone was outside.

Hope surged through him, and that was all he needed to keep going. Steadying himself against a pillar, Keiran tried to catch his breath and focus on the big gate. Inside the hall, the light was dim; outside, the sun was shining. It was so bright Keiran could barely see more than a foot beyond the entrance.

Rage's voice.

Outside he would be safe.

Slowly, with his hand pressed securely to his ribcage, Keiran stepped out into the light.

RAGE TURNED to Luca. Fear showed clearly on her face, along with her uneasiness about the bridge and the voices and her surprise.

"That is not Jeeve," she said again.

Rage looked at the man. "Middle-aged. White hair, crooked nose. That's the man who tried to hire me. He said his name is Jeeve."

Luca shook her head. "I thought it was him, too. The hair, the nose—but now that I can see him better, Jeeve is at least ten years younger than this man. He's taller, his eyes are blue, not yellow. Really, although there is a resemblance, that is not Jeeve."

Taking another step toward the barrier, Rage felt its power. It made his head ache and his skin crawl.

"Who are you?" he asked, sick of playing games, sick of hunting down someone he didn't even know, and admittedly, worried about the boy's well-being. A night in the killer's company—only the Lady knew how badly Keiran was wounded.

But he was alive. Rage knew it.

The killer laughed. "What—you still haven't figured out my name? You believe I am that man, what's his name—Jeeve? You're kidding me!"

Only a few feet separated them. Rage could see the man clearly now. He was aware of Luca standing right behind him on the narrow bridge, her arm lightly wrapped around his waist. It was she who was keeping him grounded, or he would have tried to break through the barrier, no matter that doing so would probably kill him.

"I don't give a fuck who you are. Jeeve, Lucius, the man next door—I don't care. Let's end this."

"Jeeve." The killer stared at him and lowered his arms, the doll forgotten in his hand. "What a jerk. Whiny and drunk. I met him in a bar, and he immediately began to talk my ear off. I guess he thought since we looked a little alike, we also must *be* alike." Still grinning, the killer shook his head. "He told me everything. About his master, the household, the little bitch here." He nodded at Luca. "And how much he'd like to be elsewhere."

"You killed him."

Very carefully, Rage moved another bit closer to the barrier. It felt strange, but not unpleasant. Touching it didn't hurt, as much as it was possible to touch it at all. The barrier was like a soft layer of nothing right in front of him, but when he tried to push his hand through, it was impossible, and his hand turned cold. Colder than it was already, for the wind had picked up, the clouds had obscured the sun, and it would snow again soon.

"I was looking for *you*, Rage. After I'd found out what you'd done, I was furious and tried to locate you, but without my constant source of strength, I couldn't. By sheer luck, I found Jeeve instead. I listened to what he had to tell me, I took his strength, and then I killed him. I also figured, hey, why not play with you for a while. Why not offer you a job and watch you do it. How could I have known you have morals?" He spat out the last word as if it tasted foul.

The doll hung in his fingers. Rage could see a strand of brown hair and a bit of fabric that could have been taken from Keiran's shirt. The doll wasn't much larger than a man's hand.

The image of Keiran had grown still, frozen midmotion—a picture, no more alive than the planks underneath him.

"Keep him talking," Luca whispered. "As long as he's concentrating on you, he might forget about using the doll."

Rage spat over the side of the bridge and crossed his arms over his chest like a man who was thinking about leaving rather than listening to the annoying tales of a drunkard.

The killer took another step toward him. "Don't you want to know why I didn't kill you when we were in that bar together? I could have killed you back then. I could have killed you many times since then. I could have shot you when I followed you from Coldwell back to Babylon Manor. I was on your trail. Killing the thief gave me strength. I was finally able to locate the last coin with my Tracking magic, but of course, it was only the boy."

"Why didn't you kill me?"

The doll dropped to the ground as the killer raked both his hands through his hair. It rolled toward the bridge and, just like Rage's knife, got caught between two planks. He didn't seem to notice. The moment the doll fell from his hand, the image on the bridge vanished.

The barrier didn't, though.

"Because I'm not stupid!" the man yelled. "Look at me! I'm fifty-eight. No match for you. Do you think I would try to kill an assassin of your reputation face-to-face?"

One last step, and he was at the bridge. He put his hands on the ropes and shook the fragile construction until the bridge swayed heavily. Rage clutched at the ropes and held on as Luca wrapped her arms around him and pressed her face against his back.

Rage could feel Luca tapping into his magic. Her body was radiating heat, and she was sweating despite the cold. Her hair waved in the wind, strands of it blowing around their bodies. A few blew in front of his face, and he wiped them away.

She was trying to break through the barrier using his magic.

"Hurry," he murmured. "Do what you have to do, but try not to kill us."

"Right," she murmured back and tightened her grip. Her arms were like steel ropes around his waist, her magic like a knife in his temple.

The killer couldn't have been aware of what she was doing, or he would have tried to stop it. Maybe the barrier was preventing him from sensing Luca's magic. Maybe he simply wasn't strong enough.

Rage leaned forward, just a little. The barrier was still there, and it was still cold. But—was it a bit softer than before?

"You sent those assholes after me and the girl? Pietar and that other man, the one I killed right underneath Luca's window? You sent the one with the crossbow and the witch and the wizard?"

The killer shrugged. "Had you taken the raping job, I would have been there, watching you do it. Whilst you were busy, I would have shot you. But you declined. So I thought, let's push him. Let's tire him out. It worked, didn't it? You look like shit."

Rage didn't just look like shit, he felt like shit too. Spending days drinking after several weeks of travel, still suffering from an arrow wound in his leg and burns on the rest of his body, neglecting his health, and night after night of not enough sleep had taken its toll. And now the girl was drawing on his strength. He had to steady himself by leaning hard against the barrier or he would have fallen to his knees.

The barrier was much softer now than it had been a minute ago. Like wet cotton, the barrier's magic pressed against him. Whatever Luca was doing, it was working. Now the only question was whether or not he would survive it.

"I could have killed you on the way back to Babylon Manor." Repeating himself, the killer sounded prideful. "But I didn't. I followed you instead, only because I was curious. Watching you torture Lucius was worth it. If those fucking dogs hadn't delayed me...." He absentmindedly wiped sweat off his forehead.

The killer might have been sweating, but Rage couldn't feel his feet anymore due to the cold and Luca's magic. His lips were numb as he said, "You don't really believe you'll be walking away from here, do you? This place is already killing you. All I have to do is wait for the dark magic to bring you to your knees. You've spent the night here. It won't be much longer, and you'll be jumping into the abyss without my help."

Keep him talking, he thought, jaw set, hands half-frozen on the ropes.

"Why did you come here at all? This place is driving you mad, I can see it in your eyes. You could have taken the boy anywhere but here."

Shit. He shouldn't have mentioned the boy. If the killer noticed he'd dropped the doll, if he picked it up....

But he didn't. His eyes were wide and shiny, as if he were about to cry. Spittle ran down his chin and mixed with the sweat on his face that had already plastered his white hair to his skull.

"I killed Jeeve," he said. He grinned, revealing the blood on his teeth. "Left him in the butcher's cauldrons, chopped to pieces. A few people had a nice big piece of meat on their table that night."

The killer swayed.

"You really haven't figured out yet who I am? After what you've done to me, what you've taken from me, you don't... you don't even know my *name*?"

"I don't give a fuck about your name."

Luca's arms loosened a bit, and he heard her sigh. "I'm hurting you, aren't I?" she whispered. "I've never taken anyone else's strength before. It only works because you let me do it willingly, but I know I'm doing a crude job here. It is working. Hold on, Rage. I'm nearly done with the barrier."

The wind whipped her words away, and for a moment, Rage wasn't sure she'd said anything at all.

Then he felt his hand slip deeper into the barrier. It was not a wall anymore, but more like a curtain, soft and yielding. It nearly made him forget the splitting pain drilling into his head.

"I'm Ethan. *Ethan*. Ethan of Sweetchild Hall!"

"Ethan," Rage said, frowning.

"You know who I am, you—"

"The only thing I know is that I will kill you. Taking the boy was a bad idea, Jeeve. He's a good enough fuck and a reasonable cook, but both skills would be wasted on you. You aren't even able to wipe your cock clean after a piss, judging by the state of your trousers."

The killer spat at him. What was left of the barrier, though, prevented it from reaching Rage.

"Don't call me by that name! I'm Ethan. *Ethan*, you damn bastard!"

He was losing it.

Her body still pressing against his back, Luca reached out to the left and right of him, spreading her hands. Like a constant wave, her magic, powered by his strength, pushed against the barrier.

Soon.

"Jeeve," Rage said softly. "I think you came here because this place called for you. In your dreams, you could hear the ghosts whispering your name. In your dreams, you thought it was a good idea to come back. You have been here before, haven't you?"

A shot in the dark. But as he saw the killer pale, he knew he'd been right.

"This place… this place is sacred."

One more step, and Ethan would tread upon the doll wedged between the planks.

"This place was built by a bunch of madmen." Rage had trouble breathing now. Keeping calm, pretending this was nothing but a friendly chat, became harder with every beat of his heart. "I killed the last three remaining monks twenty years ago, Jeeve. The ghosts have no power over me. Nor have you. Stop playing around, Jeeve. Vanish the barrier. Be brave at least once in your life."

Rage's throat was dry with thirst. Talking hurt, but then, every movement hurt. Luca draining his magic felt worse than bleeding to death, and he feared he wouldn't last much longer.

He pushed. His hand went into the barrier, went most of the way through, then stopped. Another inch, no more. Another minute.

"I'm Ethan of Sweetchild Hall," the killer bit out. "Not *Jeeve*! George of Sweetchild Hall was my uncle. You killed him. He even *paid* you to kill him! And you did it without even thinking once what my uncle's death would mean to his only nephew!"

With each word, the killer's voice grew louder until he was shouting, spittle flying from his lips. "You ruined my life, you bastard! I was living on his magic. He was too old to stop me, too weak, but his magic was strong. I was like a tick in his pelt. It made my life so easy. And you killed him!"

"George of Sweetchild Hall. Yes, I remember him." Lazily, Rage leaned against the barrier. In reality, he had to seek support, but if Ethan thought he was bored, even better. Provoking him was working. If he was distracted the moment Luca broke through the barrier, it would be easier to overcome him.

George—the name brought back memories of a foggy morning some months back, in early summer. He'd waited for sunrise on a big oak tree, sneaked into the old house unseen, and talked to the man who'd been waiting for him.

"George," Rage mused. "An old man way beyond the pleasures of life. He hired me, and he paid me. Asked me to kill him at sunrise, and so I did. He died peacefully."

"But he *died*!" Ethan screamed. "I had him locked up in his rooms, he couldn't escape, and he was healthy for a man of his age!"

He shook the bridge again, cursing and spitting. "My fucking ancient, dumb uncle dared to bribe his fucking ancient, useless butler into helping him die. Took me ages to figure out who did it, and without the charmed coins, I would have never found you. Now who's stupid, assassin? I've got your fucktoy. I created the barrier. You are here at my mercy. I *win!*"

"You're about to keel over by the looks of you."

Ethan leaned forward.

"I've got more power than you know," Ethan hissed, grinning. "I learned from the ghosts how to drain others, if their magic is strong enough. And don't think you can have the boy back. I've marked him as mine. I've bitten him, drank his blood. It tastes fresh, like summer wine. Oh, and I had my fingers up his lovely, tight little ass. I could barely keep myself from fucking him properly, having him on my table all naked and bleeding. If I'd done it, though, there wouldn't have been enough time to prepare a trap for you."

The barrier gave way, and Rage took a step just as Ethan painted a complicated pattern onto one of the bridge's ropes, tongue stuck out in concentration. Blood began dripping from Ethan's eyes, mingling with the sweat running down his cheeks. Whatever he was doing, it was costing him more strength than he had.

Desperate to get through, Rage pushed ahead, but it was too late. The barrier grew stronger in a matter of seconds, and Rage was thrown backward. He staggered and fell against Luca, his whole body burning with fresh, hot pain.

"You won't survive a night on the bridge, assassin. The ghosts are hungry at night," Ethan said, stretching. He smoothed his hair back and took a look over his shoulder toward the monastery's gates.

"Fuck," Rage hissed under his breath. "So damn close!"

Then he followed Ethan's gaze and saw Keiran.

The boy looked like a living corpse. His labored breathing was loud enough to be heard over the wind howling through the broken windows. His eyes were unfocused, and he was limping with arms clutched around his middle, obviously having a hard time keeping himself upright.

"Fucking shit!" Rage's heartbeat sped up at the sight of Keiran. His eyes snapped back to Ethan, fearing he was going to attack the boy, but Ethan just staggered backward, visibly shaken at this sudden and unexpected change of events.

"How did you get free?" Ethan screamed. "You're supposed to be unconscious! I made the doll so I could leave you safely inside, but now you're out here anyway?"

Rage pushed against the barrier with new determination. His nose began to bleed, and there was ringing in his ears as Ethan's trap closed around him, but he didn't give up even when Luca tried to pull him back. At first, her arms were around his waist, but when he wouldn't budge, she grabbed his shoulders and finally closed her hands around his throat, strangling him, trying to make him stop.

"Don't! You won't survive this, Rage! The barrier is too strong, and you are too weak. I took too much of your magic. What am I supposed to do when you're dead? Stop it!"

He gave up only when dark specks began to dance in front of his eyes. Gasping for air, he staggered backward into Luca and away from the barrier.

That was the moment a dark shadow jumped on Ethan, digging its claws deeply into his back.

"Sammy!" Luca screamed, and a moment later, "Keiran!"

Ethan screamed too, trying to get a hold of the attacker. Frantically, he turned around and around until he caught the furry little body and with both hands threw the cat away.

Sammy landed on his feet, hissed, and then backed off indignantly, tail high in the air.

Ethan's foot slipped. Fighting to remove the cat had brought him too close to the abyss. Not that he'd been far from it to begin with, but now he was about to fall. With flailing arms, he tried to keep his balance, his foot hanging in midair.

"Push him!" Luca yelled. "Keiran, push him into the abyss!"

But Rage knew that Keiran was in no condition to move quickly. He probably hadn't even heard her. Keiran took a step toward the abyss and toward Ethan, then another one before he stopped, head tilted, as if listening to something only he could hear.

Then suddenly, it was as if he'd been forced forward—someone, or something, seemed to have pushed him. Keiran ran and caught Ethan a second before he lost his balance.

All color had left Keiran's face. His lips were blue. His eyes had rolled up in their sockets.

"Pull me back!" Ethan yelled, frantically trying to get his knees underneath his body.

Keiran, bereft of his own will, did as ordered. Nothing more than a gentle poke would have been needed to get rid of the killer, but Keiran pulled Ethan back to safety instead.

Panting, Ethan sunk to the ground, his arms slung around Keiran, who did nothing to stop him. "I knew you wouldn't let me down," Ethan gasped. "Good thing my grip on you is as strong as ever!"

Luca and Rage stared at the scene, disbelieving, shocked.

Rage stepped away from the barrier. It was, once more, as solid as a rock. No chance of getting through even if Luca took all his strength, tapping into his magic and managing to keep it under control despite the fact that she was shaking with exhaustion.

Luca, her face gray and her eyes filled with tears, shook her head. Her feet gave way, and she sat down hard on the planks. Exhausted, Rage wasn't able to hold her upright. At least he managed to stay on his feet. For now.

Like lovers, Ethan and Keiran slung their arms around each other. Ethan had his face pressed against Keiran's neck, and Keiran held him tight.

Rage might have believed Ethan had somehow turned him, promising him whatever treasure would bring the boy over to his side had Keiran not looked so deeply terrorized.

"He's drawing on Keiran's strength."

Luca's words dropped slowly into Rage's tired brain. At first, they didn't make sense. Only when he turned them around in his head and examined them did they have any meaning.

"His strength? You mean—his *magic*? Keiran doesn't have magic. We both know that."

But it made sense. It was impossible, but it made sense.

Luca closed her eyes, hair falling over her face. Arms wrapped around her body, she was crying as she said, "It's said that everyone has magic, even the ones who are disabled. They just cannot access it. If this is true, we cannot win."

"You cannot win against me!" Ethan called as if he had read her mind. He placed a wet kiss on Keiran's mouth. Keiran didn't try to turn his face away.

Ethan touched Keiran's sweaty, dirty cheek. "So much strength," he said admiringly. "Ah, well. Back to business, shall we? I've got enough fresh magic, and I'm bursting with strength. I can keep up the barrier forever, no matter what you do."

"Coward," Rage said, knowing full well no provocation in the world would make the killer angry enough to attack him directly.

Behind him, Luca lowered her head onto her knees, wrapped her arms around her legs, and cried.

"Take your bitch and leave," Ethan said, brushing dust and dirt off his sleeves as if he were standing in the entrance hall of his manor instead of at the brink of an abyss. "Go back down to the plains. I'll be spending another night up here, draining the boy—it is nowhere easier than here, and nowhere so much fun than with the monks' ghosts giving advice on how to do it best. When I'm finished, I'll come down and take care of you. At least the girl will survive." He grinned, then laughed—he was lying and was enjoying every moment of it.

Carelessly, he pushed Keiran out of his way, not even turning when the boy hit against the bridge's wooden support. The impact was hard—Keiran had hit the pillar headfirst. Blood spurted from a gash above his eye as he slung his arms around the beam.

Ethan laughed when Luca screamed. Stepping forward, he grasped the other pillar and yanked as if trying to pull it out of the ground. His eyes were on Rage as he shouted, "You took what was mine, bastard. Now you'll die, and I'll take my time with what's yours. I'll throw the boy into the abyss when I'm done with him. That's a promise!"

The bridge was swaying badly now, several feet to each side, and the wind helped it along. Rage had to get down on his knees for fear the ropes would break.

A plank right in front of him cracked, then another one, closer to the end.

Rage's eyes fell on the crudely made doll that was locked between the planks. He'd forgotten about it until now.

One of the two planks holding it was about to break.

"Luca," Rage said quietly, reaching out and finding the girl's shoulder, grabbing it. "The doll. What happens if it falls?"

Ethan continued to shake the beam. Keiran clung to his like a drowning man clinging to a piece of wood. He looked sick.

"What?" Wiping the tears out of her eyes, Luca crawled next to him and wrapped her arms around him like a child, then looked to where he was pointing.

The doll had dropped an inch. Its legs were dangling above the abyss, one arm and the head had slipped through the gap, and only the fabric, which had caught on a splinter, connected it to the plank.

"No." Just a whisper.

Rage's stomach clenched. He'd feared hearing that exact word, in that exact terrified whisper. And there was nothing he could do because of that damn barrier.

The plank broke with a dry crack. It was surprisingly loud given all the other noise around, and it was loud enough to make Ethan stop laughing. He had dug his heels into the ground in order to dislocate the pole holding the bridge.

"What?" he called. "Afraid of dying?" His face was red, his eyes wide with madness.

"It's going to fall." Luca, still on her knees, pressed her hands pleadingly against the barrier. "The doll is going to fall, Rage!"

Ethan followed her gaze. All color left his face.

Eyes wide, mouth agape, he shouted, "No! Fuck! I forgot about the damn doll, I—"

Ethan took a step onto the bridge toward the doll, but the vibration caused by his feet shook the flimsy bit of fabric free of the plank. As if in slow motion, the doll turned over in midair as Ethan lunged, both hands outstretched, reaching for it.

Trying to catch it.

His hands closed around nothing.

And it was gone.

CHAPTER
Twenty

For several heartbeats, Ethan stared into the abyss, flat on his belly. His legs lay on the rocky ground, his torso on the bridge, and his hands and forearms were wedged into the gap left by the broken plank. His shirtsleeves had been pushed up to his elbows, showing where the plank's splinters had left thin scratches on his skin.

"No," he said in shock. "No, no, no, that didn't just happen. How could I have forgotten about the doll?"

He looked up, right into Rage's eyes. "I forgot about the doll." He blinked. "That's not good."

With one hand on the rope for support and the other on Luca's shoulder, Rage got as close to the barrier as possible. It hummed, as if the cracking of the plank had stirred it. Like vibrating glass, close to its breaking point.

"He'll jump."

Luca got up, her fingers digging into Rage's cloak. "He'll jump. Keiran. If the doll was bound to him, he'll jump! Cut the magic. Ethan, cut it off or he'll die!"

A surge of cold hate bubbled up inside Rage, drowning his fatigue and the pain and most of his disgust at the man who'd forced them up here.

"Keiran," he said, focusing on the boy. "Keiran, step back from the abyss."

Ethan tried to get up. His sleeve got caught on the edge of the plank, and when he tried to get his feet beneath him, he slipped on the wet ground.

"Keiran," Rage said again, completely oblivious of the killer's predicament. His only concern was the boy, who was still clinging to the bridge's support, eyes still wide and incomprehensive of his surroundings.

Then, very slowly, Keiran blinked.

He looked down into the abyss, frowning, and let go of the beam. On tiptoes, he stood, balancing at the brink.

At the same time, Ethan, who was trying frantically not to fall, ripped his sleeve free only to lose what was left of his footing. He managed to grab one of the bridge's unbroken planks just as his legs swung out from underneath him. Screaming, he dangled above the abyss, trying to find purchase in the rocks with his heels, trying to get a better hold on the planks, trying not to die.

Rage watched Keiran. He was only dimly aware of the girl standing next to him. She was saying something, but he wasn't in the least bit interested in what she had to say right now. All that counted at the moment was that Keiran didn't do anything stupid. The doll had fallen—but so what? It was just a doll. The girl had said Keiran would jump, but so far, he hadn't moved much. He just stood at the brink, arms hanging limply at his side.

Slowly, Keiran turned his head toward Ethan, who was screaming his lungs out.

He didn't reach out to help him like he had before.

Keiran blinked, like a man waking from a dream. He squinted and looked up at the sky, where the sun was hiding behind the clouds.

"Keiran, step back." Rage's voice was warm, seductive even.

Inside, cold fear accompanied the hate that still burned in his soul. The faraway look in the boy's eyes was still there, and he was still way too close to the abyss.

With sudden force, Luca tapped into his magic and began banging against the barrier with her fists. She might as well have hit him over the head with a hammer.

"Boy!" Ethan screamed. "Help me, you worthless little shit!"

Keiran's gaze flickered back to Rage. Once more, he blinked. He shook his head as if to clear it, dazed.

Help me.

Rage heard the words as clearly as if Keiran had spoken them aloud.

Time seemed to slow down.

A lone crow flew over their heads. Strands of Luca's hair blew across his face. Ethan's screaming became long and low and hollow, as if he were miles away.

Insignificant.

Only Keiran's eyes, wide and scared.

The pain of Luca draining his magic seemed to split his head in half.

Rage!

Ethan swung his legs upward, wrapping them around the supporting beam. He cursed and scrambled, frantically trying to reach safety.

Rage didn't push against the barrier. He knew there was no chance of getting through it in time. He just stood and watched as the boy tipped forward, horror painted on his bruised and bloodied face.

The horror of falling. The horror of dying.

Please! Help—

A tear slid down Rage's dirty cheek as Keiran lost his balance.

"No! Nonono, you stupid ass, don't jump. Don't do it!"

Ethan, still screaming. Luca, still trying to break the barrier.

Slowly Keiran tipped over the brink, arms stretched out wide as though he were trying to fly. Only a few feet away and still not solidly back on his feet, Ethan reached out to catch him just as he'd reached out to catch the doll.

For a heartbeat, Keiran hung in midair, a picture frozen in time—his mouth open in a silent scream, his hands stretching toward Rage.

Rage threw himself against the barrier, and it shattered under the onslaught of their magic in combination with the physical impact. In a shower of glass-like shards, the barrier fell down around them.

From below, the river roared, singing out its satisfaction at having devoured yet another victim.

Keiran was gone.

RAGE LEANED over the bridge's rail, staring into the abyss, the rope digging under his arms. He had both hands outstretched.

He'd tried to catch the boy. In vain.

He thought he could see the place where Keiran's body had landed, his bones and skull shattered to pieces.

His heart broke. It hurt. Everything hurt.

Most of all, it hurt that he hadn't been able to save the boy.

Ethan staggered to his feet, looking down as well. His face was pallid. "No," he murmured. "Stupid. Stupid asshole!"

Turning, he pointed a shaky hand at Rage. "It was an accident," he stammered. "I *had* to bind him to the doll. Without the doll, I couldn't have drawn on his strength! Without his strength, I wouldn't have been able to keep up the barrier!"

Rage turned away from the abyss. Nothing to be done about the boy. He might just as well finish what he'd come up here to do.

Within a few steps, he'd crossed the bridge, not thinking about what he would do next, not hearing Luca's sobs behind him, and abandoning any acknowledgement of how much the boy's death pained him.

The killer stumbled, shock written on his face. His eyes flickered from the abyss, to the place where Keiran had fallen, to the bridge's beam, and back to Rage.

"It was an accident! I didn't want him to fall! It was an accident, you hear me?"

Rage reached out and took Ethan by the collar. Pulling him close, he lingered, just for a heartbeat, taking in the man's fear, the stench of his clothes, and the blood on his teeth.

Rage! Help me!

The boy's blood. Ethan had bitten him; he'd said as much.

"I didn't want him to die like that," Ethan whispered.

Rage broke his jaw with a single knock of his fist. Blood splattered and Ethan screamed.

Another blow. Rage heard bones crack.

A wonderful sound.

Ethan's legs gave way as Rage continued slamming his fist into his face. At first, Ethan screamed and begged and cried out for help. Then a few teeth came loose, ended up in his throat, and screaming became impossible.

He choked.

When Ethan's face was nothing but a bloodied mass, eyes blind and broken, nose flattened, jaw nothing but splinters, Rage landed a fist into Ethan's ribcage right above his heart so it would stop beating.

He could hear the boy calling for him.

Ethan's gaze broke as he fell unconscious. His tongue, bitten half through, hung out of his mouth. But he was still breathing, and his legs were still twitching. The boy was dead, and Rage continued to beat his killer to death, steadily, rhythmically, without missing a single blow.

There was blood on his face and blood on his clothes. His knuckles were in pure agony, his arm and shoulder burning from overexertion, but he didn't stop.

He'd never stop. Not as long as there was life in the man. Not as long as he was recognizable as a human being.

Rage had never beaten anyone to death.

He had never known how good it felt.

Help me!

Blinded by tears, Rage felt Ethan's bones break under his hands, one after the other. He heard him gurgle and choke, gasp for breath, and fight for life.

Dropping the body, Rage fell to his knees, breaking what was left of Ethan's ribcage as he came down hard. One hand kept the man's head in place; the other punched holes into his flesh the size of fists.

He didn't stop beating. He couldn't. No matter the body underneath was dead. No matter all that was left was a slippery, stinking mess.

When Luca put a hand on his shoulder, he jerked his head around and nearly knocked her out.

"Rage."

His fist was raised for the next blow.

"Rage, it's me. Luca."

His body began to tremble, and moments later, he was violently shaking from head to toe. He tasted blood and spat, trying to get it out. Then he wrapped his arms around his body to stop them from trembling and aching.

It didn't work.

"Get away from me," he rasped.

"He's dead," Luca whispered.

Looking at his bloodied hands, at the corpse next to him, and then at the abyss, Rage pondered on that for a moment. "I know," he said, frowning. "I saw him jump."

Darkness spread inside him, laced with a strange, bitter feeling he couldn't name.

Luca, sitting next to him, shook her head. "He didn't jump. He was pulled. The doll—if the doll hadn't fallen, he wouldn't have followed it. If Ethan had cut the magic in time, he wouldn't have jumped."

She looked at the corpse. Had they been in the plains, flies would have already been feasting on the blood and flesh, but as they were so high up in the mountains, only dust and a single snowflake fell upon it.

"I hate him." A strangled sob, nothing more. Kicking her foot, she connected with the corpse's hip. A wet, sickening sound.

The ground was covered with snow. It was cold, and the rocks were icy from last night's frost. Ethan's slippery corpse, set into motion by Luca's kick, slithered toward the edge and fell.

Nothing was left but a large patch of blood on the ground, mingled with dirt, a few bits of fabric, and some unidentifiable matter that might have been brain tissue.

For many long minutes, neither of them said a word. Then Luca gently touched Rage's face and said, "I didn't believe you loved him."

"What?"

"I didn't believe you loved Keiran. That you liked him, yes. Even that you liked him more than you would admit. But not that you loved him. I thought you'd gone after him because you wanted to kill Jeeve—Ethan—whoever he was."

"What?" Rage asked again because her words weren't making sense. Nothing made sense anymore.

"You're crying," she whispered. Her fingers were warm on his cheek. "You wouldn't be crying if you hadn't loved him."

Rage touched his face; it was wet. Surely, it was blood. He never cried. Not since he'd killed his village, his family, his lover.

His heart, which had broken without him noticing it, twisted painfully in his chest. It shouldn't hurt. *He* shouldn't hurt, not this much. True, it had been a hard few weeks, but he'd suffered from worse. He'd been drinking before, he'd been smoking before, he'd been pushed to his limits more often than he cared to recall.

"Must be blood because…."

The boy was dead.

The strange pain in his heart was tearing him apart.

"I never cry," Rage managed to say. "I don't… I haven't cried since the day…."

His voice trailed off, and he stared at his fingertips and the small, silver drop he'd caught on it. Not blood. A tear.

He was crying.

And the boy was dead.

Love. It always beat him. It always brought him to his knees. Why didn't he think better than to fall in love again?

Rage! Help me!

He turned to the brink, staring into the abyss. Maybe, in a little while, he would manage to gather what was left of his strength and jump.

EPILOGUE

THE MAN in black walked slowly. He was tired—he hadn't slept properly in days, if not weeks, and he couldn't even tell since he'd lost all track of time. A few hours of dozing whenever his body screamed loudly enough for it was all he got every now and then. Perhaps a nap on the still frozen ground when his feet refused to take another step. But never a full night of sleep and never in a bed. Not since he'd left the mountains. Not even when he'd returned to the attic room in Lindsay's tavern. There, he'd just sat on the bed and had fled the place before sunrise because even there, he hadn't found peace.

Winter was about over, but spring took its time to chase the frost away for good. For more than three months now, he'd been on the road. Occasionally, he thought about killing a hare, but as he knew he couldn't be bothered to start a fire, skin and cook the animal, he never even pulled the slingshot out of his bag. Instead, he stole bread and wrinkly apples, which was all most farmers had left this time of year. The winter had been hard. Half a sunny day every couple of weeks was all they got, quickly followed by icy winds, rain mixed with snow, and low-hanging clouds.

The man in black didn't mind the winter. His mood was dark and fit the weather perfectly. He loathed seeing people, so the fact that the farmers were all indoors—the ground was frozen and unsuitable for plowing and sowing—suited him. His thieving skills were enough to get the sparse provisions he needed.

He'd lost weight in the past few months, and he'd lost the spring in his step. The sparkle in his black eyes was gone as well as his will to speak. The man in black wasn't the same man he'd been before he'd taken the steep path to the Forbidden Monastery. For the second time in his life, he'd experienced firsthand how dreadful the place was. And once again, he'd come back to the plains changed and slightly mad.

Of course, the madness was also a result of the voice he still heard, the boy's voice calling for help, but which he chose to ignore as much as possible. The voice was nothing but a creation of his exhausted brain. If he began listening to it seriously, the madness would get much worse.

The man in black walked slowly, with his head hung low. Around his mouth, one could have seen the lines of bitterness his self-accusation had carved, if there had been someone there to see him and to get close enough. But there was no one he'd have allowed near him, and so no one was there to soothe his pain.

He was walking, looking for something—or someone?—he couldn't remember. Mile after mile melted away under his feet, heartbeat after heartbeat he felt his life shrinking. But not his sorrow and not his shock. They remained as fresh as they had been when the boy died, and he had no reason to believe they would mellow anytime soon.

After sunset, the soft rain that had dampened his clothes for the better part of the week turned into snow, making a crunching noise under his boots.

He might freeze tonight. Fatigue washed through him and drowned his burning mind in a dizzying fog.

Not for the first time, he considered just lying on the frozen ground, closing his eyes, and falling asleep. It would be an easy way out.

The man in black shook his head in self-disgust. The easy way out was not an option.

Snow dyed his black hair gray; together with the crow's feet in the corners of his eyes and the hard lines around his mouth, he looked older than he really was. Not that he was a young man anymore—he'd stopped being young the day he'd killed his friends and family—but he wasn't old, either. He just felt like it.

As always when the temperature dropped below freezing point, his leg began to hurt. The arrow that had hit him some months back had been poisoned, and it had been hours before the head had been removed. Usually the limp was inconsequential. Tonight, the man in black wished he had a stick to lean on, as with every step, pain shot up to his hips.

Every now and then, he stumbled; every now and then, he fell on the uneven ground obscured by slush. Hidden branches, hollows filled with last year's leaves—there were traps everywhere, and in a matter of half an hour, the man in black was as wet as he could possibly be without taking a bath fully clothed. His hands and face were covered with scratches. They just added to the scars already on his body and palms. He never bothered to check if he was badly injured.

Around midnight, he realized if he didn't find shelter, he would die.

He hadn't chosen a particular path, hadn't even set off in a particular direction, but his feet possessed more sense than his head at the moment and took him to a place they'd been to before. His feet wanted to rest, though his mind told them rest wasn't an option.

In the darkness, the man in black bumped into a wall, not even managing to raise his hands in time to prevent his nose from breaking. Blood spurted down his face, soiling his jacket and shirt. Pain shot through his head. His hands flew to his face and covered his nose, touching the bridge in order to determine the damage. There was a bulge—he'd need to fix it now, as he knew doing it later would most likely be impossible. The nose would swell, and the pain would increase.

Vaguely, he wondered if he should bother. A broken nose—so what? One more injury simply didn't matter.

When blood ran down his throat, he retched, spitting it out and leaving red patterns in the snow. He hated the taste of blood. Better fix the nose to stop the bleeding.

His fingers found the place where they needed to grip. He'd set broken noses before; he knew what to do. A quick jerk of his head as his fingers tightened their grip, and the bridge was straight again.

Had he broken his neck by bumping into the damn wall, it would have suited him better.

Faintly, the voice in his head told him to turn and go back to the mountains.

He ignored it, as always.

Wiping his hands clean on some snow, he didn't even think of cleaning his face. He just put his hands flat against the wall blocking his way and wondered where it had come from. Solid stone, not wood. Tall enough to prevent him from scaling it. And a long wall to boot—whatever was behind it was either a rich man's mansion or a nunnery.

The sisters of the Lady would offer him shelter. If he knocked, they'd save him from tonight's death.

He searched his way along the wall until he found a door. Thick and solid and without ornament of any kind.

Rich men tended to decorate their gates. The sisters serving the Lady tended to spend the money they earned on the people who needed their help.

He nearly knocked. He had his hand already raised, fingers balled into a fist, but then he hesitated. The sisters would ask questions. They would want to know his name, and they would try to tend to his wounds as well as his soul. He didn't want that. Freezing to death was a lot better than answering questions.

But maybe the voice would be quiet in the warmth and light and company.

A thought worth pondering. He'd do nearly anything to escape the one calling for him for even a small amount of time.

He could climb over the wall and find shelter in the stables without bothering the sisters. Despite his failing leg, he was still able to get into any house he wanted without being noticed. Knocking was unnecessary and so was facing the sisters' curiosity.

Slowly, his hand dropped to his side. The wind tugged at his clothes, and had there been light, he would have given the impression of having escaped hell itself with his face covered in blood, his hair dirty and wet and standing up in spikes all over his head, and his body nothing but bones and sunken flesh. The hands would have reminded an observer of a skeleton, and an observer would have shied away from the darkness in those black eyes.

No, better not knock. Better climb the wall and sneak into an empty stall. He might even find a half-eaten carrot in one of the troughs. It would be enough food for another few days.

Just as he was about to turn and find a convenient place to break in, he heard the call, faintly, from a long distance away. His head jerked up, eyes widening in sudden hope, and he was just about to turn and run toward the voice when his brain caught up and told him it had been nothing but the howling wind and the madness in his heart.

Again.

Disgust flared up in his eyes, along with hate and bitterness.

He couldn't climb the wall. He was too weak. But neither could he spend another night alone. It had been weeks since he'd seen another human face. It had been longer since he'd spoken so much as a single word. Without the help of the sisters, he'd take his knife and cut his wrists, no matter that he didn't deserve an easy death. It was the sole reason why he hadn't jumped into the abyss: it would have been too easy.

He did not deserve easy.

So he raised his fist and knocked on the door, ignoring the call of the wind and the voice, ignoring the hope that ate up his heart.

He was now hoping with all his might his knock would be heard through the oncoming storm's wrath.

"SISTER LAURE?"

Sleepily, she opened one eye. It had been late when she'd gone to bed, and she guessed she hadn't had more than half an hour of sleep. Something bad must have happened for one of the young sisters to wake her up.

"Hmm?" Laure mumbled as she tried to figure out where her hands and feet were—they seemed to still be in dreamland.

A shadow moved into her small bedroom, holding a single candle. In the flickering light, the abbess could make out a face, or rather, a pair of eyes behind the blue veil they all wore when on duty. Only at nighttime were their faces open and unguarded.

"Helena? What is it?" she asked, clumsily swinging her feet out of bed. "Did someone die?"

Helena shook her head. "No, everyone is safe and sound. But there is a man at the door, seeking shelter. He's bloody all over, he's wet and shaking with cold, and he is far too thin for a man his height. But he refuses to come into the kitchen. I fear he won't survive the night if he doesn't allow us to tend to him, so I thought I'd get you."

"I see." Getting up, Laure stretched and yawned. "Did he tell you his name?"

The young sister shook her head once more. "No. He didn't say anything, actually."

"Why do these men have to arrive in the middle of the night and not during daylight?" Laure muttered to herself, already looking around for her clothes.

Keeping her personal belongings in order wasn't something she was fond of. Her clothes were in a heap on the small table, her shoes kicked carelessly underneath the bed.

"Shame on me," she said and saw Helena hide a smile. Her sisters knew her as well as she knew them. They all had flaws of their own, so Laure smiled back and added, "Let me get dressed, my dear. I'll be downstairs in a minute."

Helena sighed. "You need to put on your boots, Laure. The man insisted on heading for the stables. He's found an empty stall and seems determined to spend the night there. It's snowing outside. Don't just put slippers on."

"Thanks for the warning," Laure replied. "The stables, yes? What a curious choice."

It took her five minutes to get dressed and put the veil over her face, but she needed three more minutes to find her boots, which for some reason were hidden on the windowsill. Helena was waiting for her by the time she got downstairs, wringing her hands impatiently.

"He refused bread and cheese," Helena said. "He just sits there, head bent, knees drawn up to his chest. I can see he is in pain. It seems he takes comfort from my voice, but he neither responds nor asks questions. Please talk some sense into him!"

The wind nearly ripped the door out of her hands. Outside, Laure could hear the howling wind and feared, as always, that it would be strong enough this time to take the tiles off the infirmary roof. Winter had come early. She hadn't been able to have it repaired although she had had the money to do so. That was unusual in itself. Money was always sparse no matter what they did. But last year, a man had brought them a patient and left more money on her table than she'd seen in the past two years. Had the weather been better, the roof would have already been repaired.

Laure took a lamp from the hook next to the door and stepped out into the night, facing the most horrible weather they'd had in weeks. The wind had become stronger in the last few hours—at dinner, it hadn't been as bad as it was now. This was a storm. No wonder the newcomer had chosen to knock on her door.

Clutching the lamp tightly in one hand and keeping her coat from being blown away with her other, the abbess made her way to the stables, glad she had ordered Helena to stay behind. If the newcomer was as disheveled as Helena had described him, it was more likely she would get some information from him if they were alone. She had a gift when it came to speaking. It was always she who interrogated the men who brought in patients, young girls or freshly wed women most of the time. It was always she who managed to get the stories behind the cracked lips, bruises, and broken bones simply because she knew what to ask, how to ask it, and where to apply pressure in order to get the truth. A single man, malnourished and injured, posed no threat to her.

Laure shuddered in the winter wind and was glad when she finally reached the stables. The nunnery kept cows and pigs, some horses, and a small flock of sheep. This time of year, they all lived in the stables, together with the chickens. The animals didn't like it too much, but the alternative was staying outside in inclement weather, so they managed somehow.

Of course, the sisters never put any guests in there. They could be loud, or dirty, they could be drunk, it didn't matter—guests were fed in the kitchen and housed in the small guesthouse attached to the infirmary.

"Well, apart from this guest," Laure sighed. The short time it had taken to cross the yard had wet her coat as well as the cap she'd put on her head. Gratefully, she welcomed the warmth that greeted her when she entered the stables. One of the horses neighed sleepily. Other than that, it was quiet.

The door creaked as she opened it, so Laure assumed the newcomer knew someone had come to see him. However, in case he'd fallen asleep, she didn't want to scare him by showing up like a ghost, so she muttered under her breath as she made her way to the one empty stall left in the stables, even knocking over an empty bucket. The noise scared the cows awake, but better scared cows than a scared, injured man.

There it was, the empty stall, right next to the outer wall. Laure held up her lamp so she could get a glimpse of its inhabitant. There was only a bit of leftover straw in there, nothing anyone could hide behind.

The first thing she saw was a worn-out leather rucksack, blackened from many seasons outside. Calling it old would have been an understatement—it seemed held together by dirt and hope alone. The leather was crumpled, and no lumps were visible, indicating it was empty.

Sitting with his back to the outer wall—the coldest place in the barn—sat the owner of the bag. As Helena had told her, he had his legs pulled up to his chest. Both arms were wrapped around his bony shins, his head resting on his knees. Laure could see the sharp angle of his wrist bones, visible evidence that this man hadn't eaten properly in a long time.

"Good evening," she said softly, holding up the lamp so he could see her face once he looked up. "Or good night, if you prefer. It is a little late to be calling this evening, wouldn't you agree?"

The man on the floor didn't look up. In fact, he didn't move at all. Despite his wet clothes, he wasn't even shivering. Laure even had trouble seeing him breathe. If it hadn't been for the pulse beating noticeably in his throat, he would have looked dead.

"Don't you want to come into the kitchen and have a cup of tea with me?" she asked as if talking to a frightened child.

There was something about the man that made her cautious, and in a way, he seemed vaguely familiar. *Ridiculous*, she thought. *I can't see anything but the back of his head, his shoulders, and his drawn up legs. He cannot look familiar.*

She carefully hung the lamp on the wall that separated the stalls; then lowering herself on her knees, she spoke again. "I'm Sister Laure, stranger. I'm the abbess here, and I don't like guests staying in the stables. So please come to the kitchen with me. I promise not to bother you with any more questions as long as you let me offer you a cup of tea."

She held out her hand invitingly. Instinct told her that gentleness would bring this one down quicker than anything else.

She was right. The stranger lifted his head, checked the barn with a quick glance, then focused on her. His expression suggested he didn't even know where he was. The flame of her lamp, flickering as it was, cast more shadows than it brought light, and for a moment, she could only see the pale oval of his face, unable to make out any details. There was blood, just as Helena had said, mostly around the lower part of his face and even on his throat.

"Did someone beat you up? We can do something about the pain if you come to the infirmary."

"Abbess Laure," the man said, his voice as dark and hollow as if it came directly out of a grave. "Just my luck to end up here of all places. Just my luck to bump into your wall instead of freezing into a nice, clean death outside in the woods."

Laure frowned. The voice was as familiar as the man himself but also different enough for her not to make an immediate connection. "You know me?"

It didn't happen often that she was confused, but this man had managed to throw her without any effort. "If you'd be kind enough to tell me—"

"I bet you haven't had a chance to get the roof repaired yet," the man in black said. His laugh was harsh and bitter and laced with madness.

Laure's eyes widened as she took in the short, spiky black hair, the black clothes, and most of all, those charcoal black eyes. "It's you!" she breathed. "Oh, by the dear Lady, what has happened to you?"

Rage didn't answer. He lowered his head to his knees and when Laure dropped next to him, placing a soothing hand onto his shoulder, she felt the sobs racking his haggard body.

Stay tuned for an exclusive excerpt from

Empress and Child

Rage: Book Two

By Sam C. Leonhard

Broken by the death of Keiran, Rage is lingering on the brink of suicide, but Lucinda refuses to accept that her best friend is gone. Stubborn as ever, she won't allow Rage to sneak out of her life before he has solved a few critical issues. Together, they get back to the Forbidden Monastery, face the past, and find out Keiran is not as dead as he is supposed to be.

Their hope for peace and rest is not to be fulfilled. Keiran has to deal with the burden of unwanted magic his would-be killer has put on his shoulders. Lucinda has to face a murder trial, and Rage needs to seek out old allies in order to sort out the mess they are in.

They have to tread carefully in the empress's city, a place humming with political obstacles and filled with plotting lords, grieving mothers, and one very crazy monk. The threesome stumbles upon a scheme to start a large-scale war and somehow must find a way to foil the plans. Slowly Rage comes to the realization that sometimes even the most important rules must be broken to save an entire kingdom.

Coming Soon to
http://www.dsppublications.com

PROLOGUE

IT WAS late at night when Luca woke up. *Stomach cramps again,* she thought wearily. *Don't I just love them.*

Nausea washed through her body, and she retched, pressing one hand to her mouth and fumbling with the other for the bowl that stood next to her bed just for those occasions. It wasn't the first time she was sick although usually it happened closer to morning.

Slightly shaky, she put the bowl on her bedside table. She was sweaty, her nightshirt was sticking to her clammy body, and she pondered if she should get up and get changed. Most likely she would be sick again; most likely, she wouldn't stop sweating, either. And her warm bed was much more comfortable than the idea of freezing night air sending a chill down her spine whilst hunting down a clean garment.

Sighing, Luca fell back onto her pillows. Once awake, she hardly ever managed to find her way back into dreamland, and staring at the ceiling was what she usually did in such a case. One out of three nights, she didn't sleep through. Tonight, apparently, was one of them.

Besides, being awake wasn't that bad at all. When awake, she couldn't dream, and if she didn't dream, no nightmares could bother her. "Damn them," she muttered, not for the first time cursing her overactive brain, which insisted on plaguing her with dark images of blood and loss. Even worse were the dreams of Keiran. Keiran's voice, pleading for help. Keiran's hand, reaching out for her. In those dreams, she always tried to reach him before he was lost in the abyss.

Of course, she always failed to save him, just as she had failed to save him three months ago.

Luca thought of Rage as well. During the day, he hardly ever crossed her mind. He'd abandoned her, hadn't he? He'd sunk to his knees at the spot where Keiran had fallen, not responding to her plea to come back with her. So she'd had to leave without him, and at first, when she'd turned her back on the cursed monastery, she had believed he would follow her. At first, she'd been sure he'd get up at any moment, getting across the bridge and away from this horrible place.

But he hadn't. She'd left him behind, unable to persuade him to follow her. For all she knew, he might still be kneeling at the edge of the abyss.

He might have even jumped.

He surely is dead, Luca thought, sleep tiptoeing closer. *He either jumped to join Keiran, or he stayed in the monastery and went mad. No one can survive up there.*

Only she was quite sure he was alive.

Stupid thoughts. She had a manor to run and there was simply no time for useless daydreams.

So why do I think I should go and find him?

The branches of the tree outside her window rattled against the glass, causing the small hairs on her neck to stand up. It sounded like bone fingers begging to be let in.

Luca shuddered and pulled the blanket a bit higher. *This is my room*, she told herself. *I grew up here. It is safe. No one is outside. No one wants to get in. Keiran is definitely dead. Rage is probably dead. Get used to it.*

Not that it was an easy task to accomplish.

Right, sleep wasn't as close as she had hoped. Even trying to keep her eyes closed was a lost fight. So instead of continuing to try, she lit a candle and found the book she'd been reading earlier. If she read for an hour or two, she might be able to take a nap shortly before sunrise, and if not, she would at least be so tired by lunchtime that she could doze off at the table.

But instead of opening the book, she pulled her knees up under the cover. Wrapping her arms around her shins, she thought of how she had managed to get away from the Forbidden Monastery. She had found the horses; she had packed Sammy into one of the saddlebags and had headed home, seeing no sense in leaving one horse for Rage should he decide not to stay up in the mountains. The assassin was used to walking, and the horse wouldn't have stayed behind alone anyway.

Not once had she looked back. She'd been terrified of seeing Keiran's ghost, accusing her of abandoning him. Had she looked back, she might have climbed down into the abyss to at least get his corpse back.

An impossible task. She'd stood on that bridge for less than half an hour, and it had driven her nearly mad. Getting closer to the river—no. Impossible. Keiran would have to stay down there, alone.

She didn't know how she'd made it back to the plains, and she had next to no recollection of her journey home. One day, she had just ridden through the gates of Babylon Manor, haggard, pale, and dirty. A servant had seen her, and he had nearly chased her off, thinking she was a beggar. The servant lowered his ax only when he recognized Gus, a horse who had been born on the manor. Then he had recognized her as well, and he'd dropped his tool just in time to catch her.

She'd spent two weeks in bed.

Four weeks later, the nausea had begun.

"Damn you, Rage. I wish you were here so I could shout at you," Luca said to the flickering shadows dancing across the ceiling. "I'm so tired of doing this on my own. Running the manor isn't as easy as I had thought, but that's not the point. You left me alone! You are out there somewhere—if you aren't dead, that is—and I bet you don't waste a single thought on me. I bet you even forgot we are legally married. I could do with your help, you know? I could—"

No. She wouldn't walk down that path. Only grief waited there, and truly, she'd had her share of grief recently.

Maybe she should get up. There were some of last year's apples down in the kitchen, old and wrinkly and meant to go into an apple pie tomorrow, but suddenly those apples made her mouth water. She wanted them. Now.

Her dressing gown was on the floor where she had dropped it, but when she couldn't find her slippers, she put on some thick, warm socks instead and sneaked out of her room.

As expected, the corridor was cold. Only a few candles were burning. They barely cast enough light to see where to put her feet. The carpets were always somewhat ruffled up and more than once, she nearly stumbled over one of the folds. Saving money, though, was her most important goal. She'd use as few candles as possible until she had found a way to secure her status as Lady of Babylon and her right to rule her manor the way she thought fit.

When she reached the kitchen, she heard someone move and groaned inwardly. She didn't want company, but when she entered the kitchen ready to throw out anyone who dared to be in there at that time of night, she saw it was only Sammy. Busy chasing a slender, ginger-colored cat, he didn't even stop to acknowledge her. He swooshed past her and followed his playmate out into the corridor.

All that was left was silence and some pots gently dangling from where the cats had brushed past them.

Fine. She went to bed alone, she woke up alone, and there was no reason why she couldn't eat an apple alone too.

Her feet were cold despite the socks, so she went to get her apple, sat on one of the chairs, and took a bite. It tasted just as good as she had imagined—sweet and juicy despite its looks. But now that she was fully awake, the problems came back as well. Usually she managed not to think about them during the night, but then, usually she stayed in bed, pretending to be asleep after her stupid stomach had woken her up. "I hope this stops soon," she sternly told her body but knew all too well it wouldn't.

Placing the hand that didn't hold the apple on her flat belly, she continued, "I am sick of being sick, do you hear me? It is bad enough I am facing a trial concerning my somewhat dubious status as a married woman without a husband. I am still only sixteen, you know. In theory, I need a legal guardian until I am eighteen. But I *am* married, which changes things. Or would change things if I could present an actual husband." She crunched the last bite of the apple, looked at the core, and ate it too. The dark seeds were bitter, the stem hard, but what the hell.

Now a glass of milk laced with powdered chocolate seemed a good idea.

"Imagine that only a few months ago, my biggest concern was to prevent Lucius from hitting my best horse. And now he is dead, my best friend is dead, Rage is the Lady knows where—or dead—and I am pregnant." Sternly she looked at her belly as if staring could change the facts. "And I don't know who your father is. My dead friend, or a most likely dead assassin. If the court finds out you might have been conceived outside of marriage, they will put me in with the sisters until you are born, and then they will take you away from me. You will grow up in an orphanage. Babylon Manor will be sold. Luckily, Lucius didn't have any relatives. It would kill me, knowing I have to pray all day for forgiveness of my sins whilst someone related to that bastard lives here and takes what is legally mine."

It would kill me to give up my baby, she thought.

Luca flattened her nightgown over her belly. Apart from her, no one knew she was pregnant. She would be able to conceal it for another two, maybe three months at the most, but afterward, she'd need—

Help me!

Luca jumped up from her chair; it fell and clattered loudly to the floor. Bewildered, she looked around, searching for the voice's source. Someone had called, someone in pain, someone scared. From outside, a cold breeze sneaked into the dark, silent kitchen. The cats must have pushed the window open, and she hadn't noticed until now.

Help! Me!

"Who are you?" Luca barked out, cold shivers running down her back. She wasn't used to bodiless voices in her own kitchen. She had left all those voices behind in the abyss belonging to the Forbidden Monastery.

Then the truth dawned. There was no one in or near the manor pleading for help. She'd fallen asleep, and she was dreaming of Keiran calling for her.

Wearily she wiped a tear off her cheek. "Stop it, Keiran," she murmured, knowing he couldn't hear her and hoping she would wake up soon. Once her eyes were open, the voice would vanish. "You are dead. You cannot call me, and anyway, even if you could, I cannot help you. Stay in your grave, however wet it might be, will you? I've got enough problems without you disturbing my sleep."

By the Lady, her feet were cold. Even the socks couldn't warm them up, so Luca pulled her legs up and began rubbing her numb toes. The rest of her body was warm enough, the tiny spark of life growing inside her miraculously serving as a very special oven, but her feet were a different matter. Hopefully spring wasn't that far away anymore.

Rubbing her feet heated up her hands, but her toes stayed immune to their treatment. She even banged her elbow to the table in front of her—it hurt worse than she'd expected, and she cursed.

Then she froze in midmotion, left foot tucked in the hollow of her hands, her hair half escaped from the braid she'd woven it into.

Help me, please! the voice whispered into her mind.

She wasn't dreaming. In a dream, one couldn't feel pain that clearly. In a dream, one couldn't reason one was only dreaming.

She was awake.

But then—where did the voice come from?

"Keiran?" she whispered, horrified as well as wildly ecstatic at the implications of that voice, which wasn't a dream voice anymore. "Are you… don't tell me you are still alive!"

SAM C. LEONHARD lives in southern Germany and is a journalist by profession. Writing has been part of her life since age twenty, but somehow it was never enough to report the latest news about small-town politics. She wrote short stories for friends and family until a few years back she discovered the world of fandom. The Petulant Poetess is where she feels at home; slash became an addiction as soon as she stumbled over the first story.

If not writing—which isn't half as often as she'd like—Sam takes care of her son, her dog, a few cats, the madness at work, and life in general. She likes to believe she's got some humor left after years of dealing with people who usually don't understand what she's talking about when she says she's writing fantasy with gay porn on top of it.

E-mail: sc.leonhard@googlemail.com.

http://www.dsppublications.com

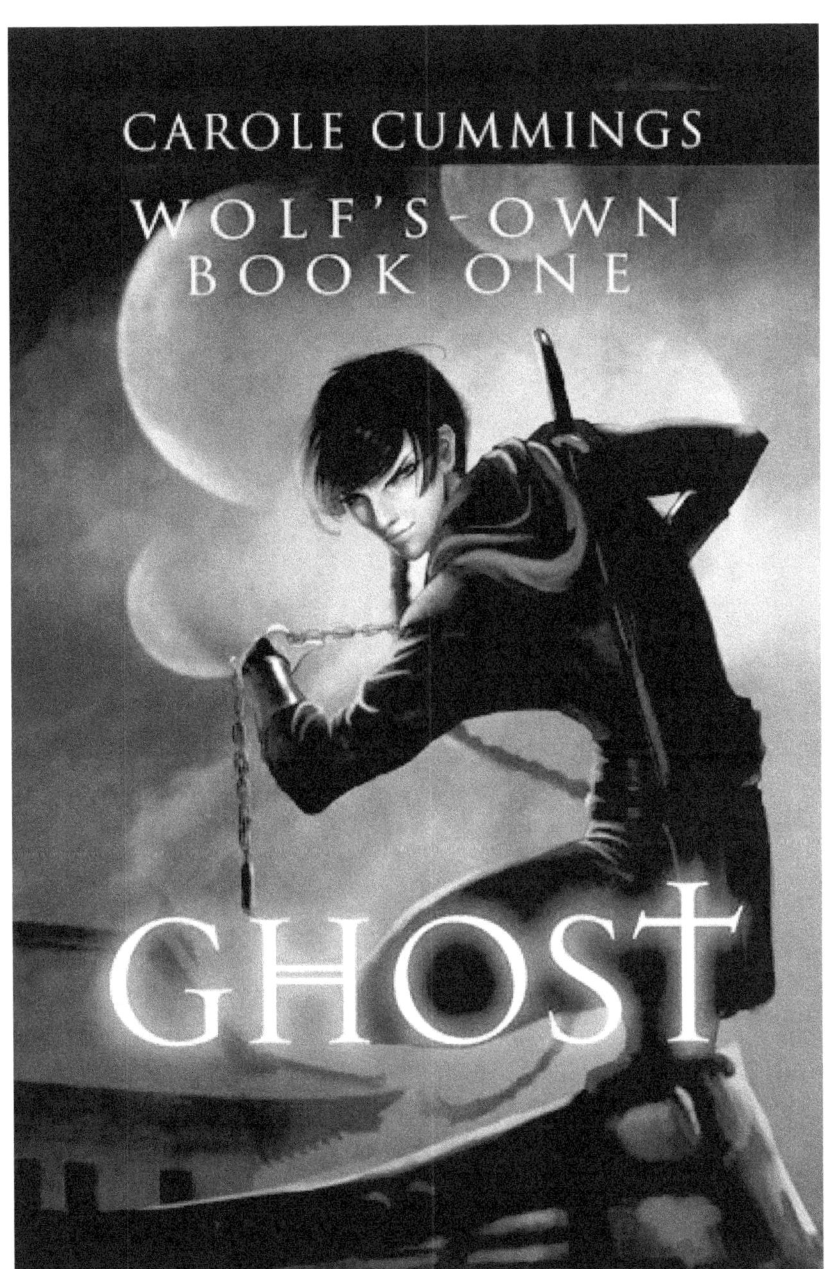

http://www.dsppublications.com

DSP PUBLICATIONS

visit us online.

WWW.DSPPUBLICATIONS.COM